Praise for *A Ricoch*

"This is a wonderful coming of age piece, a worthy successor to Salinger's *Catcher in the Rye* and Knowles's *A Separate Piece.*"

Morton Randall, *Wonalancet Literary Review*

"It is a comic and moving coming-of-age tale in the great tradition of the bildungsroman. The main character is very appealing and we're rooting for him to triumph."

-- Ruth Doan MacDougall, author of *The Cheerleader*

"A great story, a great read. We've all been there and it's fun to revisit our growing up. Schuck creates deeply etched scenes and brings believable characters to life with gentle humor. His language is unique and compelling, his imagery sublime. Don't miss this journey."

--von Tolkacz Review

A RICOCHET
FROM CIRCUMSTANCE

A Novel

Philip Schuck

ANTLERS PUBLISHING

PORTLAND WONALANCET

ANTLERS
Portland, Maine

This is a work of fiction. Names, characters, places, and incidents either
are the product of the author's imagination or are used fictitiously.
Any resemblance to actual persons, living or dead, is entirely coincidental.

Library of Congress Cataloging-in-Publication Data
Schuck, Philip.
A Ricochet From Circumstance : a novel / Philip Schuck.
ISBN 0-9764670-0-3 (acid-free paper)
1. Teenage boys—Fiction. 2. Preparatory school students—Fiction. 3.
Coming of age—Fiction.
4. Connecticut—Fiction. 5. Oklahoma—Fiction. I. Title.

Library of Congress Catalogue Number
2005902834

Printed in the United States of America on acid-free paper

Antlers Publishing
antlerspublishing.com

ISBN 0-9764670-0-3

This Book is for Abby and Sarah

CONTENTS

ACKNOWLEDGEMENTS

There are many today, and there will be those to whom I will be grateful tomorrow. Abby for asking "Why are you the way you are?" Sarah for her watchful eye. Helen for being there, wherever necessary and whenever needed and having the good ideas and the right words and no limit to her time or patience. Susie and her friend 'Wayne D'. Janet because she's good at whatever she does. And to:

Denney
Ann
Fred
Tom
Don
Sally
Ruth
Amy
Chele
Barbara
Diana
&
Henry

with hope
theirs has been as much fun.

A RICOCHET FROM CIRCUMSTANCE

1

CROSSING THE RIVER

On the second Monday of September in 1956, Arthur May sat in the passenger seat of his father's 1954 green and white Ford Ranch Wagon looking out the side window as he and his father drove past three black cows tearing grass from a pasture in northwestern Connecticut. Arthur and his father, Carl, were on a trip; they were driving Arthur from his home in Grape, Oklahoma, to his new school in Connecticut. Arthur wasn't driving, he wasn't old enough, and the school was only new to Arthur; it had been educating boys for several generations and would last past Arthur. They crossed the Housatonic River, and when they were on the other side, the school came into view at the end of the rumpled, blacktop road. It was about a quarter of a mile outside the town it was named after, The Bridge School, Bridge Connecticut.

"We're almost there, but not yet," Carl said, looking to his right, at Arthur, who sat in the passenger's seat.

They'd rehearsed this line since Arthur was little. Arthur would ask, "Are we there yet?" and Carl would respond, "We're almost there, but not yet." They'd been through it a hundred times so it was ritual; it reminded them of earlier times and brought with it the warmth of small tradition.

The view out the car window didn't look much like Oklahoma. There were Maple trees and stone walls along the side of the road, making it feel more crowded than Oklahoma; the stone walls and trees pushed right up against the tarmac. And the roads weren't straight like Oklahoma's; they were narrow and crooked, avoiding lumps and rocks and streams. The fields in Connecticut were too small and the rocks in the fields were too big. People in Oklahoma didn't leave boulders on their front lawns.

1

A RICOCHET FROM CIRCUMSTANCE

There were lots of hills in Connecticut; Oklahoma had some roll but not little hills close-packed. And the sky in Connecticut was crowded out by the hills and trees so the clouds didn't appear till they were right on top of you. In Oklahoma you could see the clouds coming at you for miles.

Arthur noticed the sweet smell of rotting apples and pears, leaves going to mold, goldenrod drying up in the late summer, and wilting grass fallen along the side of the road. Oklahoma smelled of pig lagoons and corn silage; it smelled of the dust from harvesting soy beans and hot asphalt melting in the seams of the road. Oklahoma smelled like things were happening, like a car smells in the summer just after it's been shut off. Connecticut smelled like his grandmothers sewing kit, of Almond Joy, of Milky Way and fresh broke bales of hay. Connecticut was not much like Oklahoma.

They turned off the road onto the school driveway. Neither Carl nor Arthur had seen the school before. It didn't seem strange to them that this was their first visit; neither of them had any experience with New England prep schools, where normally you at least looked the place over before jumping in. Carl thought it was like the Army before he joined up in 1941, he didn't have to look it over; there wasn't much choice. His view was you just went ahead and did it, got it over with. At least that's the approach he took with his children where not a lot of time was wasted getting expectations synchronized with reality.

Carl thought children were little adults with the same emotional handicaps and only slightly less intellectual ability, and he treated them like that. If you wanted to figure the expectations before the event, that would have been great with him; have at it. He believed in letting children figure things out for themselves. Carl had no idea Arthur's cellophane expectations would probably bump into reality, not survive the collision and cause hurt feelings. He wasn't inclined to waste time on other people's feelings.

Carl and Arthur had started the trip three days earlier in Grape, Oklahoma where Carl was a physician, chief of staff at the county hospital. Carl and Arthur lived together in Grape. Carl and Roz, Arthur's mother, were divorced and when they divorced Arthur and Carl moved to a new house across town from where Arthur had grown up. Arthur's two sisters, Susan and Gretta, stayed in the old house with their mother. Carl moved to the new house because he had taken up with another woman, Liz, who had grown up in Grape and was supposed, by rumor's judgment, to have been the cause of the divorce. The rumor was wrong. The cause was Carl and his inability to stay focused on anyone, other than himself, for any significant period. While he was in the Army there was enough variety to keep him awake nights, but when he moved to a small town and small hospital his cup seemed a little empty, so he decided to top it off.

Carl was handsome. Striking. He looked like a model for a Greek sculpture; he could have been a Nazi poster boy, the Aryan genotype. His features were cleanly developed, in the right proportions, sharp, and maybe a little large for the size of his head. His hair was brown and wavy and he had blue eyes under a straight brow. His posture was beyond military, watching him walk you got the impression he might tip over backwards. He was lean and angular, long limbed and held postures which made the angles fluid. He was a sculpture from the temple of Athena, and he liked it.

Beyond beautiful, he was smart; for Grape he was brilliant. He had gone to the Harvard Medical School and then had done his residency at Mass General with Paul White who was the who's who of heart medicine. He joined the Army in 1941, and after two years, at age 31, was made full colonel. He was a flight surgeon and pilot. He spoke three languages, not including Grape's. He was a Golden Gloves boxer, a Mid-West squash champion, and a competitive rower while at Harvard. He enjoyed his perfection and spent a fair amount of time considering it.

Arthur was not Carl, and Arthur could not reconcile the differences between himself and his father. He saw himself not in a pantheon but in a shadow of uncertainty. When he looked he saw himself as stocky, round, and fuzzy-headed, inside and out. Burr hair cut, mousy brown without distinction, a nose like potato bud and small blue eyes pushed between doughy lumps of cheek and forehead. His skin resembled a garden where things had gone wrong, patches of color where there shouldn't have been, and none where there should. Unaccounted splotches of pink grew on his neck and cheeks and rough red gouges oozed clear yellow where Arthur had attempted, with his fingernails, to remove things that had grown in the night.

Where Carl was brilliant, Arthur saw himself as dull. He had neither interest nor ability; he didn't know which he discovered first. His attempts at sports were painful for him and whoever watched. He was obtuse. None of his limbs appeared to be connected to his torso; each had a mind of its own, so when he walked he looked like a Halloween mask balanced on top of a sack of puppies. His clothes looked like they belonged on someone else. They either looked too new and unwashed stiff, or too old and small at the thigh and rump, coats too narrow, bunched at the shoulder. Shoes scuffed to courthouse brindle.

He could read but moved his lips silently pronouncing each word with difficulty, so speed was a problem, and occasionally he had to stop his silent oration to mop up small leaks at the corners of his mouth. He unconsciously used his tongue, his sleeve or whatever was handy for this cleanup operation, oblivious that anyone might watch and find it repulsive.

He was a fatalist without searching. How else could he explain the differences between himself and Carl, if he were of a mind to explain those differences, which he wasn't. And how would he explain his horizon, which mostly covered yesterday, the time before he learned to appreciate the tortures of comparative analysis and the differences between himself and Carl. He was doomed to the dimness of his shadowland by fate.

But he was alone in his analysis. His friends and family and his teachers found him an average fourteen year old boy groping in an adult world.

They had started the trip three days ago and Arthur could not imagine what was ahead of him, so he didn't bother trying to figure it out. He was neither curious nor afraid; he was naked of expectation. He was not used to looking forward; he went through his life in a rowboat going downstream with the current, looking backwards at what he had already passed, learning occasionally from his experience and almost as frequently forgetting the lesson. He had no idea he might turn around and use the oars to direct his course. He drifted with the flow. He had never been to Connecticut, never been to a boarding school, never been without either his mother or father present, every day, managing the where and when and what and how of his existence. His capacity for projection was beneath the task of anticipating what boarding school would be like, and attempts at imagining it hurt.

On the first day of the trip they left Grape in mid-afternoon having planned to leave before noon. They got off late because Arthur was not packed. He had no idea what to take and no one had told him. Carl was too busy; he was going to meet his new friend, Liz, in New York City after dropping Arthur at school. Liz was going to fly to New York separately, spend a few days there by herself and then meet Carl when Carl came to the City from Connecticut. After their weekend in New York, they planned to drive back to Grape together. So Carl had some serious packing to do for himself. New York held special appeal for Carl; in his musings he thought he belonged there, people there would appreciate him: his talents, looks, intellect, humor. They made a good martini in New York. You couldn't get a martini in Oklahoma, no one knew about Vermouth in Grape nor how little was enough.

In the middle of the summer the School had sent the "new boy" parents a list of all the things a new student would need: shirts, pants, underwear, socks, ... Everything had to have a name tag sewn in so it wouldn't get lost in the laundry. When Carl received the pamphlet, he didn't do anything; he put it aside since it didn't concern him directly. However, when Liz was visiting Carl one day she saw the list on a table in the hall and read it and wondered what Carl was doing about Arthur's clothes. When nothing was done, Liz, realizing Arthur needed school clothes, told Carl to take Arthur to the store to get the items on the list. So Carl took Arthur to Sears one Saturday morning and they bought all the necessaries. Suits, two; sport jackets, two; ties, three; socks, winter hats, gloves ......everything but boots. Liz had planned ahead and sent away to someplace in Saint Louis that returned a long, white, cotton cloth ribbon, sort of like a narrow piece of adhesive tape, about as wide as a pencil with *Arthur May* printed in red script, one hundred and fifty times in a continuous row. Arthur was impressed with the tape; he'd never seen his name in print and felt he was making up for lost time and he was happy with Liz for thinking ahead.

Liz spent an afternoon at Carl and Arthur's house sitting on the edge of Arthur's bed, legs crossed at the ankles with a sewing basket on the floor beside her. Arthur watched her pile the school clothes on the bed to her left. She leaned over and rummaged around in the basket for a while and came out with a thimble. She put it on a finger; then she took out a little paper packet about the size of a matchbook, but it wasn't matches, it was needles, about ten of them neatly arranged on a little black cloth patch inside the package; you could see the needles on their black cloth bed behind an even smaller cellophane window in the cover of the package. She took one out and then hunted for some red thread, explaining since the lettering on the tags was red they should use red thread, and then she threaded up the needle by peering at it in a squint and pointing the end of the thread at the needle and she willed it through the little hole in the top. It almost made it the first time except it crumpled as it hit the side, so she took it back and put the thread between her lips and got it wet and tried it again.

Arthur was mesmerized. Liz concentrated, her eyes fixed on the needle, she parted her lips, heavy, moist with dark red lipstick; she wet the thread, pulled it from between her lips and it stayed straight enough to go through the eye of the needle.

"Arthur, do you know what subjects you'll be taking this year? Have you thought about classes?" she asked as she pinched the thread on the other side, pulled it through about 14 inches, doubled it back, bit off the end and tied a knot in it. She said the knot would keep the thread from coming all the way through the other side of the material.

Arthur responded, thinking about the classes he'd gone to last year. "No, not really. I guess it's like the stuff here at Wilson," He didn't have a view of the new school but assumed a school was a school and you showed up and they told you what to do.

She didn't respond right away. After threading the needle she looked down to her basket and took out the white ribbon tape with the names on it. She stretched out a piece of tape and holding the end between thumb and the index finger of her left hand, she held the remainder of the roll in her palm. With her right hand she got a pair of scissors and cut one name off the tape, placed the name on the bed next to her, the scissors and ribbon in the basket, and picked up the shirt which was about to get christened. She laid the shirt on her knee, picked up the name tag, folded the ends under and placed it on the neck of the shirt just above the label. She studied its lie and orientation by cocking her head and squinting and with a little nod took a pin from the material lining at the top of the basket where a lot of little pins were stuck in waiting to be called on, and pinned the name tag to the shirt.

"I saw the pictures in the catalog they sent. It looks like you're going to play sports. Is there anything you want to play, football or tennis?"

"I don't know; I took some tennis lessons last year but I'm not very good. Do you think everyone plays sports, I mean do I have to or is it like school here where you only play if you want?"

She lifted her head. She had read the pamphlet and the catalog and they said every boy played at least one sport each semester. "I think everyone plays sports. They said it builds character. Maybe you should read the catalog before you leave. It might answer some of your questions."

She began the stitching at a corner where she took the first stitch from under the tag, between the tag and the shirt, so the fall end of thread wouldn't show. She stitched around the edge of the tag till she met the stitching at the beginning. Each stitch was exactly like the one next to it. There were the same number of stitches on one side as on the other and when she was finished you couldn't see where she had started or she had stopped. It was a miracle. She did every piece of clothing, and when she was finished, she had a neat, folded pile of new clothes on the bed to her right.

Arthur sat in a chair beside the bed watching. She looked up, "It looks like you have enough clothes if the laundry is regular. Have we forgotten anything?"

"I don't know," he said.

Carl borrowed a trunk from an old fellow who lived next door, Mr. Rush. He was a retired pharmacist and had lived on the street all his life except when he had been in France in the First World War. Carl said he had been gassed and that's why he couldn't talk He had something wrong with his voice; it sounded like he talked in coughs. He was thin, with knobs showing through everywhere. His skin was so thin you could see the bones and purple veins where they pushed against his wrists and temples. He leaned over almost in a crouch from arthritis and walked with a cane barely sturdy enough to get the job done.

His hair was white and thin, not like some old people who have yellow hair, his was white like cream of wheat. Little thin wisps here and there that Arthur didn't think he bothered to have cut anymore.

Mr. Rush walked every day, managing to crab his way down the seven steps from his front porch to the front walk with the aid of the porch railing and his cane. He walked up and down the street in the afternoons but didn't cross. His daughter, who visited about once a week, told Arthur not to let him cross the street. Arthur wasn't sure how he was supposed to stop Mr. Rush but he said OK.

Mr. Rush seemed lonely to Arthur; he was by himself most of the time. His wife had died of heart disease long before Arthur knew him and his children were away except his daughter who kept an eye on him but seemed preoccupied and anxious to leave just about the time she arrived at his house. She didn't seem comfortable around Mr. Rush or in his house. Occasionally Mr. Rush invited Arthur into the house for some water or a chat or to show him pictures from the war. When Arthur visited the house it was neat, tidy, clean; it looked like no one lived in it. None of the stuff in the house looked like it was used and when Mr. Rush went to get Arthur a drink of water he'd open the fridge and there would be a glass pitcher of water, a desiccated orange, celery, a pint of skimmed milk, butter unopened, catsup, and that's about it . The contents of the fridge made Arthur think Mr. Rush was planning to move out. When Arthur went over to pick up the trunk, Mr. Rush said he didn't think he'd be using it anymore so Arthur could have it. Arthur and Liz carried it next door to Carl's. Liz packed the trunk and put a present in the bottom; she told Arthur he couldn't open it until he got to school. Arthur watched the packing and wondered where he was going to wear all the clothes.

The next day, after Liz had packed the trunk, Carl took Arthur and the trunk to the rail station. It was a rectangular red brick building with a waiting room on one end and a ticket and baggage room on the other. It had a long wood platform on the railroad side with carts and boxes packed up against the brick. Passenger trains didn't stop at Grape anymore so the station was only used as freight office. They went inside. The place was worn down pretty hard; the wood floors were dirty with sand and grit and paint that had peeled from pipes and left white chips on the floor and window sills. There were four tall windows, four panes each, two up two down with black painted frames against crumbling cream colored walls. The windows were dirty with handprints and bug remains. It was a dusty, bright place that made you squint with your eyes and your nose; it smelled of urine and diesel fuel.

The ticket window had a little grille in it to keep people from jumping into or out of the office, Arthur wasn't sure. But it didn't make any difference now since the trains didn't stop and there wasn't much cause for jumping one way or the other. There was a fellow in the ticket office so Carl walked to the window in his military stride, gabardine, Brooks Brother's suit, blue and silver silk tie and polished shoes. He leaned over, not toward the window but parallel to it, turned his head to the right and regarded the agent who sat at a desk behind the grille.

The fellow at the desk looked like the skin on his face was going to slide off the bones and leave his skull perched upon his neck. It seemed to be attached in only a few places, like a hairless bloodhound. The skin was grayish yellow and sagged like a spoiled pumpkin after a hard frost; it had cracks and crevices like ruined cement. His eyes were black dots barely visible under drooping hairless brows. Great, yawning, brown bags that looked like something a cowboy might have strapped to the side of a saddle hung beneath his eyes.

He had a cigarette dangling from his lower lip, which itself was drooping so far down that Arthur could see all of the man's gums and his missing and soon to be missing teeth and the inside of the man's lower lip, a great fleshy wet half liver with purple veins and light yellow scars. He wore a dark blue, hard top conductor's hat with a metal band and a round, greasy, dull badge commemorating a

8

forgotten accomplishment pinned to the side. The hat was tipped back at a reckless angle, his few hairs were plastered to the irregular contour of his head, and a dirty undershirt completed the ensemble.

Carl regarded the place and then the man with disinterest, as if he, Carl, had just walked off the *Queen Mary* and were surveying the New York waterfront.

"Whaddya want?"

It was the ticket man from behind the grilled window, not looking up, coughing the inquiry through phlegm mixed with cigarette smoke.

The door to the ticket office was open wide enough so you could see the little man clearly from the doorway or you could see his head and shoulders from the window with the grille. It would have been easier to walk into the office and conduct the transaction, but it appeared the man liked the status of the grille and proximity of lines forming at his pleasure.

"I have a trunk in the car outside. I wonder if we could send a trunk to Connecticut?" Carl asked.

"Where in Connedicut? Depends on if they got a rail station," the ticket man said, partially answering his own question.

Carl continued, "Bridge, Connecticut, I believe they have a train station; I have the address here." He stuck his hand in the left side suit coat pocket and pulled out a postcard which he surveyed for a moment. He gently pushed the card over the worn, stained, maple counter and under the grille to the ticket man.

Carl leaned over, bent at the waist, still not leaning toward the window but at right angles to it with his head turned to the right toward the man so he could see him. His necktie hung straight down toward the floor outside his buttoned suit jacket. He was perfectly still, perfectly at ease, as if he had written a play and this was a rehearsal gone a little wrong and he was coaching the ticket master, and the ticket master was confused about his lines.

The ticket master took the card and looked at it; then he reached somewhere under the window and brought up a pair of glasses so full of dandruff and scratches it was doubtful they would improve anyone's sight. He studied the card a moment and then reached down again and retrieved a book that looked like a worn phone book, thumbed ,stained with use, torn cover, tattered leaves, and he added to the thumbing and tatters with hands and fingers that were the victims of years of service to diesel and coal fired engines. The little finger of his left hand was missing. Not even a stump, just a gap in expectation and a scar that looked like it was made from crushing rather than cutting. The scar was spread over half his hand, red and purple and white, nothing like normal skin. His fingernails were as dirty as were the creases in the skin on his hands. The nails looked as if they had been torn off rather than cut. He had a purple sore on the side of his face

"Yea. We cun git it thar for yu. When yu wan' it delivered?"

"Next week. Can you do that?" Carl asked.

Neither man looked at the other; the gulf between them was beyond three dimensions.

"War's the trunk?"

"Outside in the car."

"OK. You brang it on round the buildin here, to the other side, whar the train platform is. We got to weigh it and fill out the papers? They's carts, baggage cars, on the side a' the buildin if you care to use one."

Carl straightened up, looked at Arthur, and they went outside and found a baggage cart with iron wheels, one broken, three operable, and took it to the car. Carl opened the back deck of the station wagon, pulled the leather handle of the trunk, and the handle broke from dry rot.

Carl looked at the leather strap in his hand and dropped it to the pavement. "Arthur, would you get in and push it from the other end. I'll try to get a hold on it out here."

Arthur went around to the left rear passenger door, opened it and crawled in on the decking between the back of the front seat and the trunk. He put his back against the seat, his feet against the trunk and pushed; it slid out far enough so Carl could grab it. They loaded it on the broken trolley and Arthur pushed the trolley up a ramp and onto the creosoted wood platform where the ticket man waited next to a balance beam scale mounted on another broken baggage cart. The trolley made a sound like Arthur imagined a derailed locomotive would make tearing up the roadbed before it stopped. If he tipped the trolley too far forward, the broken wheel snagged the platform and it stopped altogether. So he pushed the teetering load, tipped away from the broken wheel, to the ticket master, and stopped next to the scale.

"OK then. Put it on thar so we can see what she weighs." Ticket master said to no one in particular, except it was clear he was not doin the puttin.

Arthur slid the trunk on the scale and watched the balance beam as the agent pushed the cylindrical weights along the brass rail till the thing leveled out and the beam floated between up and down.

"Eighty-four pounds." Looking down at a paper on a clipboard, the agent noted the weight. "Just leave it cheer. The freight man will move it after the tickets been put on." He turned and went back into his office. "I got the address on there while you was gett'n the trunk. You fill this here form out with yer name and address, and I'll figger out what you owe." He handed Carl the clip board and a pencil and he went back to his phone book of rates and time tables and lists of stations and added more greasy thumbing to his book.

Carl reached in his suit coat pocket and pulled out a gold pen. He uncapped it, laid it on the counter, took his glasses out of his shirt pocket, unfolded them, put them on, tilted his head, and read the form. Then he leaned forward and printed in elegant hand, in broad black strokes the information required. He capped the pen, returned it, and stood waiting for the ticket agent to rehearse his lines one more time.

"OK," looking at the book. "That'll be twenty-seven dollars and thirty five cents. That's cause you wan it there next week. If you done care when it gits there, then it's lots cheaper."

Carl pulled out his pen and checkbook, placed the checkbook on the maple counter, avoiding putting his hands on the wood, and made out a check in bold, black strokes, filling each line with his art. His signature was suitable for the Constitution. He folded the check back on itself, tore it from the book and with precise dexterity, slid it under the grill.

"You got any i-dentification. We ain't sposed to take checks without i-dentification or knowing the person."

"Yes. Will a driver's license do?" Steady, quiet, poised as if ordering lunch at the Oak Room, The Plaza , New York, which he hoped to be doing soon. Without looking down Carl lifted the rear hem of his coat, reached in and pulled his wallet out of his right hip pocket, opened it, lifted some cards, and came up with his license which he slid across the maple counter and under the metal grille.

The agent picked up the license and looked it over then picked up the check and seemed to take quite a while trying to decide what to do. He put the license down and slid it back to Carl. "That's it then. It'll be thar next week. Here's a copy of the ticket, it's insured for two hunerd dollars. You need more in-surance?"

"No. Two hundred is fine," said Carl.

Carl didn't leave; he stood for a moment looking at the man behind the cage, "That sore on your cheek, you need to see someone about that."

"You a doctor? "

11

"Yes. I'm a doctor."

"Yea, that thang won't quit botherin me. I had it about a year now. What d'you think it is."

"I'm not a skin doctor so I really can't tell without a better look and maybe some tests. But from here it looks like it needs tending."

"I don't have money for no doctor. I ain't got a doctor. Can you maybe take a look an tell me what you think?"

Carl turned to the door, walked in and introduced himself: "I'm Carl May; I'm a heart doctor. I don't think I've seen you before." He had his hand out offering to shake the agent's.

The agent looked away from Carl, shy or ashamed, he seemed to wither. He didn't offer his hand as if it were an unfamiliar gesture, as if getting close or touching a stranger was difficult.

"Jed Buehl," he mumbled. "I'd shake your han but I been working on this coal stove in here and my hans is all tore up." He stood silent looking at the floor.

Carl moved to a window, put on his glasses, took off his jacket, and laid it on a chair nearby.

"Mr. Buehl, this is my son Arthur; we're sending his trunk off to his school. He'll just sit in the chair while we chat. Why don't you come over here where we have some light so I can take a look at your scar."

Arthur sat in the chair not far away, closer than he wanted to be.

Carl stood patient as Jed considered what to do. He moved closer not walking straight to the window, sort of coming at it sideways, like a dog that was unsure if you're going to pet it or hit it. Carl reached out to Jed as he got close and took Jed's left hand in both of his and raised it to the light from the window. He looked Jed in the eye, not as confrontation but as if in invitation, and he then looked down at the hand in his. Jed seemed confused that Carl was looking at his hand rather than his face.

Jed's hand was not as large as Carl's; it was round where Carl's was long and slim. It was knotty and bunched where Carl's had manicured nails on tapered fingers. His was rough with dark lines, creases filled with soot where Carl's was soft skin from watching and caring. The back of Jed's hand looked like a scar in three phases. One phase was pale white and looked like an old accident that had crushed the left edge and taken the little finger with it, and appeared to have healed without surgical assistance as the scar was indented and the edges ragged without clear lines of sewing and repair. Next to that scar was a patch of purple brown skin that looked brittle and dead and outlining the purple was dark red inflamed border invading the healthy.

"Does this bother you?" Carl asked looking at the back of Jed's hand and then looking up at Jed, objective in manner which precluded any feeling of challenge or embarrassment on Jed's part, as if they had both been looking at a wing nut that had fallen off the chair.

"No. It don't hurt. In the dark part I cain't feel nothin a'tall; it's numb?" Not looking at Carl; looking at Carl's hand holding his.

"How long has it been like this?"

"Couple a years it's been growin. It started out as a blotch and then spread and changed color then got numb. I thought it would go away."

"Do you have any more spots like this?"

"Yea. I got some that's started on my feet and lags and you seen the one here on my face that won't heal up." He said reaching up to the sore on his face.

"Let me take a look at that." Carl kept Jed's left hand in his right, and slowly Carl raised his left hand and took Jed's chin in the cup of his palm and let it sit there for a moment as if waiting for Jed to get use to the idea. Jed didn't move; he kept his eyes on where Carl was holding his hand. Carl moved Jed's head so they were looking at one another for an instant then Jed looked away as Carl turned the left side of Jed's face to the light. Jed was forced to look out the window at the light reflecting off the building next door.

"I think you need to see a dermatologist about this. I understand about not having a doctor and not wanting one. It's up to you, but my recommendation is you see one."

"Who you think I otta see, you know somebody here in town?"

"Yes; I know someone. He's a friend of mine; I have coffee with him every morning at about seven in the emergency room at Mercy Hospital. If you wanted, you could meet us there about seven tomorrow morning. Maybe he'd take a look."

"I guess I could. I don't have to be to work till eight, my wife, she drives me, she could drop me down'air. How long'll it take?" Still looking out the window, his chin in Carl's hand, not knowing where to go next. He had been captured by the part of Carl that Arthur had seen people respond to before. Carl captured them; he wrapped himself around them without any sign of effort at all and then he swallowed them as if it were the most natural thing in the world.

"I don't know, not too long, not till eight. So I'll see you at Mercy emergency tomorrow morning?" Carl turned and got his coat off the chair, put his glasses in his pocket and started for the door.

"Yeah, OK. Thanks Doc." he turned to his desk.

Carl started for the door and Arthur followed him out to the waiting room and then to the car where they got in without comment. Carl started it, backed out of the parking lot onto Liberty Street and headed for home.

"What's wrong with that guy? His skin looks bad, like it's dead." Arthur wondered aloud hoping Carl would answer.

"You're right. His skin is dying; so are some of his organs, probably his liver and kidneys are seriously involved. It's a strange disease, rare, and I suspect it's from long term exposure to chemicals or fungi or toxins of some kind. Some people are more sensitive than others; allergic reactions take different forms. I don't expect he'll live more than a few months. I'm surprised he can still get around; he must be sick and in pain all the time."

"Why did you ask him to meet you at the hospital tomorrow?"

"This man is from Appalachia, maybe eastern Kentucky, West Virginia, East Tennessee somewhere in there. He lives here now because a lot of the folks in Appalachia moved to Oklahoma for indoor jobs when heavy industry moved here during the two world wars. His people are from Appalachia and they are, as a rule, suspicious of professional people, doctors and lawyers, tax and accounting folks, for good reason. They haven't been well treated by the professional community where they came from, and they don't expect things to be better here, and they aren't.

"So my guess is he would not have gone to see another doctor tomorrow or anytime. He was just curious enough to let me see him in his territory. He probably would not have called a doctor's office and dealt with a receptionist and a nurse and sat around till next month waiting to get an appointment. He is suspicious and he is poor and uneducated. He is uncomfortable working outside his family and friends."

"Can you do anything for him?"

"I don't know, I don't think so. I'll ask Jim Barr to meet us at the hospital tomorrow and take a look. If it's what I think it is we can get him some medication to make things easier, but there's no cure and the end gets ugly. We'll probably have to tell him what's going on tomorrow so then he'll have to call his wife but she probably works, so we'll have to call the place where she works to get her off her shift so she can come down to the hospital. We can tell them what's the best thing to do, how to treat the sores, how much medicine. Then we'll send them home, and the odds are they'll probably go back to Kentucky or wherever they're from and we won't see them again.

"This will involve their whole family in fear and hurt. He probably has the best job in the clan, and he probably sends money back to wherever they came from, to others in the family, his mother and brothers and sisters. Not much by our view, but a lot to the folks back in is home town. So what we start tomorrow is going to cascade to lots of other people in different places and it's going to change their lives.

"Tomorrow morning will not be kind to the Buehl clan," Carl continued as if thinking out loud.

Arthur thought he knew Jed's son. There was a Frankie Buehl in Arthur's class for several years. They didn't talk much but Arthur had played games with him on the playground when they were younger. He was shy, his hair matted and his coat always looked too small. The zipper was broken, so he had to hold it shut with his hand when it was cold. He wasn't dirty, that wasn't it. He just looked used up, defeated, no joy in the game and he always went right home after school; he didn't hang around to talk or play basketball in the school yard.

2

AMEN

Carl drove the car around a corner and the road became one-way, up a small hill where the trees opened to grass lawns, and Arthur saw the first of the school buildings. The largest was white frame, four stories high with a black fire escape dangling like Virginia creeper from its west end. There were too many windows to count, each framed by black shutters. Arthur was looking at the back of the building, and as they rounded a corner they came into a courtyard surrounded by other buildings, some white wood and others red brick. The courtyard was made of flagstone. Other cars were parked there and students walked to destinations certain, the sun was out, the sky was blue, clouds moved, dogs barked, everything was as it had been for the past hundred years, except for Arthur and Carl it was new.

Since Arthur had started the trip numb, he continued there. He looked out the window at the buildings, cars, other boys as if they were a movie set, still distant and he was not a part. This could have been Pakistan or Rio or on the TV. The set was not real; he was with his father and they were in their car.

Carl got out of the car. "I'll find out where you go."

No comment necessary as Carl drifted off toward the front double doors of the main building. He gave no indication that he was under any strain; tweed coat, tie, polished shoes, manicured nails, erect, he disappeared inside.

Carl and Arthur had spent the previous night in a motel in Utica, New York. It smelled of industrial chemicals, the blankets were thin, the sheets too small for the beds, the water tasted like roofing nails in paper cups. In the morning, when they were getting dressed, Carl told Arthur to put on a jacket and tie because that's what they wore at the Bridge School. Jacket and tie on weekdays, suit and vest on the weekend. The little book had said so, and they had bought a suit with a vest at Sears in the summer. Liz had packed his suits in the trunk so it would already have made the trip and would be waiting for Arthur when he arrived.

Arthur got a clean shirt and tie out of his suitcase. It was B4 bag Carl had kept from his days in the Army Air Corps. It was khaki green, folded in half and zippered closed; it had big pockets on the sides, lots of pockets and zippers. Arthur liked it because it was his father's; it was exotic and looked military, commanding, like it had been places. He put on gray flannel pants that itched, put the tie around his neck under his collar and asked his father to tie it.

"Don't you know how to tie a tie?" Carl assumed everyone was born having been genetically encoded with whatever was necessary, like tying ties. He approached Arthur. "Here."

Standing in front of Arthur with his feet spread wide so he was about Arthur's height, he looked at Arthur's chest, took both ends of the tie, one in each hand, and evened them up. Then he made the fat end a little longer than the thin, wrapped the big end around the little one a couple of times, slid the big end under one of the wraps, pulled the knot tight, slid the knot up the tail end and there it was, the perfect knot. Arthur couldn't see a thing; Carl had done the whole exercise under Arthur's chin in three seconds. Arthur supposed he had been shown and would figure it out next time. They finished dressing and went to the car and drove out of the lot. They stopped at a diner for breakfast, toast and eggs for Arthur, cigarettes and coffee for Carl. They got back in the car and the next thing Arthur remembered was the three cows on the other side of the stone wall.

Arthur sat in the car; time had stopped. There was movement but Arthur was not a physicist so time had stopped for him. The vague uneasiness which had surrounded the trip became more defined and appeared to take focus in his stomach; his hands were clammy; he couldn't hear himself breathe. The air in the car was hot and Arthur was sweating.

Carl came out of the main building headed for the car, came to Arthur's side, and opened the door: "OK, We're all set. We'll go in and meet the headmaster; then I'll take you to your room."

Arthur wanted to hide but he couldn't so he got out and followed Carl into the main building. His legs were rubbery but they seemed to work without his having to tell them what to do. They went up a set of stairs, turned right, Carl knocked on a door, and they went into a dark study lined with books and pictures. Everything looked old, worn out, like it should smell musty; instead it smelled of pipe smoke and wet dog. There was a large desk at one end of the room, a worn oriental carpet on the floor.

Arthur focused on the patterns the sun made as it came in through window panes, patterns of light and dark wine colors on the rug, the patterns moved and changed as the clouds obscured the sun and light bounced as the leaves danced in the breeze outside.

Arthur didn't hear the conversation; he willed it out of his horizon. Carl said something, the man behind the desk said something, he came from behind the desk and shook Arthur's hand then said something else. Carl shook his hand; said goodbye; the patterns on the carpet changed, and they left the office and the building and went to the car. It was a dream and all Arthur had to do was wait, and then he would wake up at home.

They got in the car and Carl started it. Arthur had the impression Carl was disappointed in him, maybe for not saying anything to the headmaster. Arthur didn't know. Carl turned the car around in the courtyard, went down the drive a short way then turned left on another drive and headed farther up the hill to a group of buildings. At the top of the hill there was a large white brick building, newer than the buildings in the courtyard, but not real new. Carl pulled up at the back. "This is your dormitory. You're on the third floor. I'm a little late getting to New York so I need to be on my way. Go on up to the third floor and find your bunk, then someone will be around to show you what to do."

Arthur sat frozen; he had no idea what came next. "Where do I go?" came out of his mouth, but he really wanted to yell for help.

"There's a door around front. There are other boys there; they'll show you where to go."

"OK. Are you leaving?" asked Arthur, not registering yet that this was good bye.

Carl looked at Arthur, sitting in a car in a strange place on a hillside in Connecticut "Yes, I need to get to New York by five tonight, so I need to get going."

He paused. "Arthur, do you know what 'amen' means?" Carl asked as if this were a perfectly natural question.

"No"

"It means 'so be it'. This is your hunt, do the best you can."

"OK."

Arthur walked like a stick man; he opened his door, got out, shut it, went around to the back of the car, got the B4 bag, walked around to the driver's side, and said, "Bye."

Carl smiled, stuck his right hand out the window, shook Arthur's hand, waved and drove off, headed for New York City.

3

IN A STRANGE LAND

Arthur watched the back of the car slide down the hill and disappear in the green of the maples at the curve in the drive. He stood in the gravel watching the clouds move noiselessly, he watched other students walk with purpose to places he did not know, he heard voices of boys laughing, shouting hellos, heard windows open, doors slam, smelled ruined fruit from the orchard behind him, watched a dog lift its leg on the corner of the building then shamble off across the grass around another corner and out of sight. The clouds continued to move; there was a breeze.

He stood for a moment registering his new surroundings.

He did not remember taking his bag up the two flights of stairs or who he saw on the way. He got to the top landing and opened the only door to a hallway leading to a cavernous room filled on either side with single iron beds and wood bureaus pushed against the walls; there were picnic tables end to end down the center of the room. The picnic tables were cluttered with newspapers, packing boxes, clothes and hangers. The floor was littered with junk. The walls were stark white, painted brick with windows along the sides spaced eight feet apart. There were two bunks and two bureaus between each window. It smelled of the same disinfectant the motel had smelled of the night before.

The room was dark except where the sun played in trapezoids on the hardwood floor. A boy stood over a bed looking at a suitcase while his mother unpacked into a bureau next to the bed. They talked but Arthur couldn't make out what they were saying. He walked down the hall to the main bay of the room and saw the beds closer up. They were tubular metal frames with wire mesh in the middle. Each bed had a mattress folded at one end and on it a pile of linens white against the gray mattress. A piece of adhesive tape was stuck to the foot rail

21

of each bed and it advertised the name of the boy who would occupy it for the next school year. He walked down the right hand side past where the mother helped her son unpack. They said: "Hi." He nodded and continued the search. Halfway up the left side he found his name on a bunk; the window was to the left. Sunlight caught the corner of the folded, striped mattress studded with little metal buttons that kept it from falling apart.

There was a bureau next to the window with five drawers which got smaller as they went up. It was finished in brown varnish; the drawers were deserted, half open and bare. The top was marred with bottle rings without cigarette burns. Arthur picked up the towels and sheets and put them on the bureau, unfolded the mattress and sat on the edge of the bed facing the bureau. The room smelled of warm dust from being closed all summer, the window was open; there were no curtains. He didn't know what to do next.

Another boy walked around the room as he had; he walked along the other side looking at Magic Markered names on adhesive tape. He came to the bed next to Arthur, looked at the name, turned around and just short of a shout said "Here it is!" to a woman who had just entered the room. He put his suitcase on the floor and turned to watch his mother catch up to him.

Arthur didn't say anything; he watched. The boy was tall, taller than Arthur, angular, with shiny, blond, wavy hair, longer than they wore in Oklahoma. He had a tweed jacket, blue button down shirt, khaki pants, and new brown shoes. His face was clean lined with each feature distinct and well developed, his eyebrows were thick and blond and nearly met over a prominent nose. His lips were full and curved around sparkling teeth. His blue eyes were kind, and he had no spots on his face.

His mother arrived. She looked like she had just stepped out of a Breck commercial. Her hair was perfect, light brown, almost blond, and it was shiny and exactly in place as if held there by the will of the photograph she just came out of. She wore a blue suit with a cream silk blouse and pearls. She was nearly as tall as her son and her eyes had the same kindness.

She came toward Arthur. "Hello." she said as she put out her hand. "I'm Clara Clement and this is my son Dan." Taking Arthur's hand and then indicating her son who stood next to her smiling.

Dan stuck out his hand and Arthur took it. Not feeling comfortable looking them in the eye, he looked down in shyness.

Mrs. Clement looked Arthur in the eye. "I'm sorry, I didn't hear your name, can you tell me again.?" she said with a smile

"I'm Arthur May." Still shy, still unable to look her in the eye.

"Arthur, what a nice name. Are you waiting for your parents, Arthur?"

"No ma'am. My father dropped me off a while ago; he's on his way to New York."

"Are you from New York?"

"No. I'm from Oklahoma, Grape, Oklahoma. My father and I drove up here yesterday and then he dropped me off this morning."

"So you're starting off by yourself?" she asked, seeming concerned.

"Yes, I guess so."

"Do you have a trunk?"

"Yes, but I don't know where it is."

Dan interrupted, "They're in the basement. They get delivered to the basement, then we have to bring them up here."

"Arthur, why don't you and Dan go to the basement and bring up your trunks."

Dan led the way down three flights of steps to the basement which was dank, poured concrete. There were two bare lights in the ceiling and in a room next to the boiler they found about seven trunks on the floor in no apparent order just dropped where they came off a dolly. Arthur and Dan identified theirs and decided to take Dan's up first. It weighed about two hundred pounds. It took all their strength to get it up the first set of stairs out of the basement; Arthur couldn't imagine why it was so heavy. When they got to the first floor they rested a minute and another boy came down the stairs and Dan asked if he would give them a hand. He agreed and the three of them wrestled the thing up to the third floor. They went down for Arthur's trunk which was light by comparison and got it up. They slid them across the floor for the last part of the trip, to their beds, making skid marks on the floor, fresh skid marks next to old ones.

When they got the trunks situated, Arthur sat on his bed and watched them unpack Dan's trunk. He had four suits, six jackets, fifteen shirts, four pairs of shoes and twenty ties. Wool and silk and leather in muted tones, tweed and oxford cloth, new without looking like the store. They found a closet at the end of the room and put Dan's suits away. His hangers were made of wood, thick at the shoulders so the hanger wouldn't ruin the cut of the jacket. The rod for the pants was wood with a metal bar to keep the pants from sliding off. His shoes had shoe trees in them, and all of them were shined, not like glass, like silk. Arthur could not imagine why a boy in eighth grade needed so many clothes

Mrs. Clement got the sheets off the dresser and made Dan's bed. He had two Hudson Bay blankets and two pillows from home.

When she finished his bed she looked at Arthur who was still on his bed watching. "Aren't you going to unpack, Arthur?" she asked in so soft a voice; Arthur could hardly hear her.

"Yes, ma'am." Arthur sat on his bed.

Mrs. Clement came around to his side of the bed and said, "Here, let's get you set up."

She reached down and got Arthur's B4 bag and put it on the bed next to Arthur. She unzipped it and took things out and put them in the bureau. Dan sat on his bed with a smile. It only took a minute.

"How about your trunk? Do you have the key?" she asked.

The key, Arthur hadn't given it or anything else any thought. Yes, the trunk was locked and no, he did not have the key. "I guess I forgot the key." He said standing and looking at the securely closed hasp on the front of the trunk.

Mrs. Clement looked at Dan and thought for a moment. "Why don't we try Dan's key; the locks look the same?"

Dan stood up, reached in his pocket and came out with a small flat key. He walked to Arthur's trunk, put the key in the keyhole, turned it, and there was a click as the hasp popped out of its recess.

"There. That worked. Let's get things put away, then we'll get some lunch." Mrs. Clement started unpacking Arthur's trunk. She put things in the bureau and then she gave Arthur things to put in the closet; she put his other pair of shoes under the bed.

When he came back from the closet Mrs. Clement was looking in the bottom of Arthur's trunk. "What's this?" she asked.

Arthur went to the trunk and sitting on the bottom was a box a little larger than a shoe box. It was wrapped in brown paper, the kind used to make paper bags at the grocery. It was sealed with tape and tied with string and on the top, under the string, there was a light blue envelope with Arthur's name.

Arthur remembered Liz had put a present in the bottom of the trunk but he had forgotten until now. He reached and brought out the package which he laid on his bed. He took the envelope from under the string, opened it, and inside was a sheet of light blue stationery with Liz's name and address at the top.

Arthur:

You are probably at school and unpacked by now. I put a little something in the box to help you stay dry and warm.

Please write to me when you can. I will miss you.

Love,

Liz

Time stood still again. It seemed to Arthur he couldn't get going in any kind of way that allowed him to be smooth. Things happened as if he were in a movie and the film broke every now and then, leaving him stranded in a scene waiting for someone to fix the film.

"Well, Arthur," Mrs. Clement realized the film needed fixing. "What's in the box; aren't you going to open it?"

Arthur stood over the box, untied the string and took off the paper. The box had a logo L. L. BEAN   Freeport, Maine, in green lettering on a tan background. Arthur opened it, and inside he discovered a pair of Maine Hunting shoes, 14 inches tall with molded, two tone, rubber soles and high, dark brown leather shanks and laces made of rawhide strips. When he opened it he the noticed the box smelled of leather, waterproofing and rubber.

Arthur didn't know what to do; he'd never seen boots like these, and then he remembered the list sent by the school which recommended he bring a pair of high boots for hiking in snow, and they recommended Bean hunting shoes. He hadn't heard of L.L. Bean before, and he didn't think any more about it when he and his father hadn't got any boots at Sears. Here they were. They were almost too outrageous to believe, especially in the late summer. They were huge, new, perfect. Perfect for what he did not know; he couldn't imagine wearing them but they were perfect for now, right here.

"They're beautiful," said Mrs. Clement. "You will certainly be able to use those this winter. How nice."

Arthur nodded and put the lid back and put the box under his bed.

When they had stored Arthur's kit she made his bed as he watched embarrassed, not knowing whether to help or stand by, so he stood by and watched until Dan suggested they return the trunks to the basement storeroom. When they came back one of the Hudson Bay blankets was on Arthur's bed. Arthur had forgotten to pack a blanket and Mrs. Clement noticed. Dan noticed too but didn't seem to mind.

Mrs. Clement came to the rescue again. "OK. Let's get some lunch. Arthur have you had lunch?"

"No, ma'am."

"When I talked to Mr. Webster he said they would have lunch for boys and parents at noon in the dining room,   sandwiches and drinks, so let's go down there and get something before I go back home."

A RICOCHET FROM CIRCUMSTANCE

Mrs. Clement led the way down the stairs and out the main door. She went straight ahead like she knew where she was going, down a path toward the main courtyard and into the main building through a set of double doors into the dining room. There were lots of boys and parents milling around, picking tables, chatting, introducing. Mrs. Clement went to a table with two parents and a boy about Dan's age and asked to join them. Yes, sure, happy to have you. Introductions, where are you from, Philadelphia, Greenwich, and Grape. The lunch, a sandwich and Kool Aid buffet, was a blur. New people, names, new building, lost, time was not moving in a smooth motion, it came at Arthur, over him, waves engulfing him and carrying him along.

After lunch they walked back up the hill to the dormitory, Mrs. Clement came up to the third floor with Dan and Arthur, she looked around, smiled and said goodbye to Arthur, shaking his hand and giving him a hug. She smelled of coconut and honeysuckle. She was warm and soft. The sun's pattern through the window had moved across his bed.

Dan went downstairs with her to say goodbye.

Arthur sat on his bed and looked out the window at the hill behind the dorm. There were derelict apple trees with fruit still hanging to some of the ragged branches. Some of their limbs had broken, fallen down but remained attached at the stem while others lay bare on the ground in the grass. There were sounds of cars on the gravel drive and of boys shouting, car doors closing and dogs barking in the distance. More people came into the dormitory and unpacked and made beds and hugged and said goodbye.

4

YOU WILL KNOW THEM BY THEIR CLOTHES

Dan came back to the dormitory and sat on the end of his bed. Arthur thought he would look sad but he didn't. He smiled and looked at Arthur. "You're from Oklahoma, right?"

"Grape, Oklahoma. Its north of Oklahoma City if you know where that is."

"No, I don't. That's right. I was in Cleveland one time to visit my cousins; is that near Grape?

"No. It's pretty far away. Where are you from?"

"Greenwich."

"Where is that?"

"It's here in Connecticut. Down by the Long Island Sound, not too far from New York City."

Arthur had no picture of the geography of Oklahoma much less New England so he had no idea where he was, or where Greenwich was, or New York, what direction, how far or how big. The only thing he knew about New York was his father was on his way there.

"What form are you in?" Dan asked.

Arthur didn't understand the question. "What?"

"What form are you in?"

Arthur still didn't get it. "What form? What's a form?"

"Form, like what grade are you in? They call it a form here. I'm going in eighth grade so that's the second form. Ninth grade would be third form. New boys are either second or third form."

"I guess second form; I'm going in the eighth grade," Arthur was confused.

"All the kids in this dorm will be new boys, second and third formers. The second formers from last year don't have to stay in this

27

dorm, they get regular rooms. Did you get your class schedule? If we're in the same classes then you're in the second form."

Arthur didn't have his class schedule, he had no schedule, he had no idea what he was supposed to do or where he was supposed to go next or after next. He sat on his bed and that's as far as he had got. "No. I don't have a schedule. Where'd you get yours?"

"They mailed it to my house; I got it last week; my mother got it. It's here." Dan handed it to Arthur along with an orientation schedule of things that were going to happen that day.

Arthur looked. He saw there was a school assembly in the schoolhouse at 4:45 that afternoon. After the assembly, chapel, and after chapel, supper in the dining room. "Do you know where the schoolhouse is?"

"Yeah, it's in the first floor of this building, right downstairs."

"How do you know about these things, about the forms and where things are, trunks and stuff?"

"My brother went here; he graduated last year; he told me about it. He's in college now."

An older boy came through the dorm looking for someone. He stopped by Dan's bed. "Are you Dan Clement?"

"Yes," said Dan getting up. Dan was pretty tall and almost as tall as the older boy.

"I'm Rod Butler; I'm a friend of your brother, Tom, I told him I'd keep an eye on you this year. Did you get all your stuff put away, anything you need?"

"I'm all set, thanks." Then Dan looked at Arthur. "Maybe you could tell us where Arthur could get a copy of his orientation schedule and his class schedule; he left them in his father's car, and they're on their way to New York?"

"Sure," Rod said to Dan. He looked at Arthur. "Arthur, why don't you meet me after dinner outside the common room? I'll get a class schedule for you and give it to you then."

He turned back to Dan, "OK. If everything's all set I'll see you after dinner." Rod left.

Dan sat back down on his bed. "That's Rod Butler, he's our prefect. He has the room just inside the door as you come off the landing,"

"What is a prefect?"

"A prefect is a sixth former, a senior. There are three prefects, one head prefect and two regulars; I guess they're regular prefects. Anyway, they set the rules and make sure everything happens as it should. They are the head of the senior class; the seniors, sixth formers, run the school. They make sure people get where they're supposed to be on time, make sure things are clean; they run the dorms. The faculty really only deals with the class room stuff and coaching. The rest of the time the seniors look after the school. My brother was a prefect." said Dan.

"Who's the headmaster?" Arthur asked, "I met him this morning; what does he do.?"

"The headmaster runs the whole school. The faculty, prefects, coaches, cooks, everybody reports to him." Dan got up and went down the hall and out the door.

Arthur sat on his bed wondering about nothing in particular. Other boys milled around, chatted, put things away, sat on their beds reading. Arthur got the L.L.Bean box out from under his bed and looked at the boots again. They were perfect. The leather was smooth and clean, the laces were stiff from being new, the bottoms had an embossed chain design for a tread and on each heal was a little sign L.L.BEAN, in white printing on a brown background. He liked the details of the sign and tread and how they were neat and tidy and the right thing in the right place. He put them away.

A bell that sounded like a train's bell rang outside. The other boys looked around and someone said it was time for assembly so Arthur followed the group down the stairs to the main floor, which was one large room like a basketball court. It was painted soft yellow and had tall windows along each side with none at either end. Pictures of people Arthur didn't know hung between the windows; they looked old and important. There were about forty desks in the middle, four columns of ten each, two on either side of a central aisle with benches around the outside under the windows, and in the front there was a desk with benches behind it. People were already sitting on benches and some at the desks. At the front of the room there was a large wood paneled area with names and classes posted on it in raised brass letters. Arthur couldn't read the names, and he wondered for a moment why they were there.

Someone said in a loud voice, "If you're a new boy, your seating assignment is on the wall. Take a look at the diagram on the wall, then find your seat."

Arthur went to where others gathered around a bulletin board at the entrance, there was a diagram of the study hall with pictures of benches and desks and he found his name about midway up on the right hand side. He went to the desk and it had his name on it in Magic Marker on adhesive tape. He sat.

A RICOCHET FROM CIRCUMSTANCE

Rod Butler sat with two other prefects at the head of the room behind a large desk; the rest of the older boys sat on benches on either side and around the outside of the room. The bell rang again and everyone stopped fidgeting, stopped talking and became quiet as the headmaster walked up the center aisle; stopped in front of the desk, turned and was silent for a minute. He was tall and angular, in his mid fifties. He had black hair with some gray, about as thick and black and long as an old Labrador retriever, cut short over a creased forehead. His eyebrows were thick and appeared to be one. He had a narrow face with hawk like nose and thin lips; his blue eyes came direct, out from under a crag. He stood for a moment. He was impressive.

"I want to welcome all of you back to school; especially I want to welcome the new boys who are here for the first time. New Boys, would you stand please so we can welcome you."

They stood, the room clapped, they sat.

"This year will be the…"

Arthur noticed the sun was shining right through the room in one window and almost out the other leaving patterns of light and dark on the floor and desktops. The boy in front of Arthur had thick curly blond hair and a long neck. It was Dan. The windows in the room were so high that as Arthur sat at his desk he could not see the ground outside, only the upper part of the trees and sky which was softening. There was no breeze through the open windows.

"…the start of a great year."

The headmaster walked out of the room and no one moved until he left the building. Then the boys at the front of the room, the prefects and the sixth form, rose to leave and when they were out the rest of the school rose in a sudden chatter of conversation like a flock of birds surprised at a water hole.

Arthur fell into the middle of the crowd. It seemed everyone was talking to his neighbor as they left the schoolhouse and went down the path toward the main building. Rather than going to the main building they turned a corner and went toward the chapel, a large red brick building with a white steeple perched on a steep slate roof. It had many paned windows framed in white against the red brick. He looked inside and saw wood floor, wood panel walls, wood posts, wood beams, wood rafters, wood perlins, wood roof, all clean, all hand cut. The front, the backdrop for the altar, was cream colored, rough plaster over brick. The lamps on the sides and hanging from chains in the ceiling were made of black iron.

As the boys entered they knelt on one knee for a second before taking a pew. Arthur had no idea what they were doing so he copied the boy in front of him and entered a pew and knelt as was the boy who was already there. Arthur didn't know whether this was the right place to sit and if it wasn't what would happen if the person whose seat this was demanded it; there were no Magic Markered adhesive taped directions. He looked left and right, boys streamed in and took pews and the commotion stopped and then there was silence. Every one had found a place; no one demanded Arthur's.

The sun came through the windows catching some boys direct, leaving others in shadow. The place smelled of bees wax and incense and wool. A boy dressed in a white smock over a black cassock came in from the left side up front, went to the center aisle, genuflected, took the three steps to the platform before the altar and lit the candles. The organ started and the boys on either side of Arthur stood; they took hymnals out of the rack in front of them and opened to a page. Arthur did the same but didn't know which page so he peeked at his neighbors and the boy on his left said, "315. It's on the board up front." Arthur turned to 315 and looked up and found a board posted at the front of the chapel which listed 315 and another number.

The singing began. It was huge; it filled the chapel and the campus and could probably have been heard in the town nearby. It seemed to Arthur that the school was trying to lift the roof off the building, the organ was nearly overcome by the sound of two hundred voices, most of them good, all of them save Arthur knowing the hymn. Boys sang in harmony and they filled the different parts. Arthur had never heard anything like it. He did not sing, he listened, he had no choice. It was more than listening, Arthur felt the music through his feet, through the book he held. He was surrounded by it but not a part; he swam in it but was not a fish. This sight and sound of voluntary harmony, the words of joy were new.

The head master lead the prayers, then the sixth former on the altar read the lesson, more prayers, some communal, The Lord's Prayer, The Nicene Creed, others were offered by the headmaster. Then another hymn that loosed the roof beams. It seemed everyone knew the routine, everyone knew the words to the communal prayers, everyone said "Amen" at the right time. Arthur sat and watched and listened to evening prayer.

The younger boy on the altar rose and snuffed the candles with a long brass rod with a little bell the size of a strawberry on the end. The head and the sixth former rose, met the younger one in the middle, the three of them faced the crucifix, genuflected together and left. Silence. Arthur rose and left with the others and followed them down the stone path to the dining room.

Each step in this ritual was familiar to the older boys but it was new and dangerous for Arthur. The danger was not fitting in. He knew the danger for a minnow was to be on the outside of the school where it would be a target for larger fish, and Arthur felt this instinctively. He watched where each step took him, and he followed, but he did not want to be at the end of the line: he did not want to be exposed.

The dining room had a foyer with double doors; and a seating chart was posted on the foyer wall. Two hundred boys, forty of them new, milled about waiting in turn to look at the seating chart. Arthur stood in line next to older boys who talked about summer vacation, where they had been, what they had done, someone had wrecked a car, someone else had been to Europe, "...did you hear about ...". As Arthur entered the foyer it was packed with noise and bodies and motion. He looked at the wall but he was too far away and all he saw was the Harris tweed jacket of the fellow in front of him. He waited and was pushed through in the current into the dining room. He waited just inside the door until the crowd thinned and there was room to see the chart.

He found his name and the number 12, then he looked at the chart for number twelve. It was against the far wall. He walked in and went in the direction of the far wall but all the tables were full when he got there so he turned around and started back out to the seating chart. By this time everyone was standing behind his chair waiting for Arthur to find a spot. He continued to the foyer and then heard the headmaster start grace, "Bless this food..." Arthur stopped and waited and there was a collective "Amen." Followed by two hundred chairs scraping the floor, two hundred voices saying hello, two hundred tweed jackets unbuttoned, and silk ties tucked into shirts, flannel pants sliding into oak chairs.

Arthur looked at the chart again and thought he was right about where to sit but didn't know what to do. He was caught as if outside after the doors had closed. The doors were open but he was not going to walk through the dining room again to find a full table, then what? If the table was full where would he go, stand there, return to the foyer? He stood frozen not knowing what to do, letting time solve his problem.

"Hey. What are you doing?" An older boy came around the corner.

"I'm looking for my table."

"What's your name?"

"Arthur."

"What's your last name?"

"May."

Looking at the chart he said, "Here it is. You're at Mr. Humphry's table over there," pointing to the side of the room. Arthur looked and saw a table with an empty seat. "Thank you." The boy had already left. He still didn't know what to do, should he go over to the table or wait where he was?

"Lost?" came the voice of an older man behind him.

Arthur turned and there was a man about fifty coming through the foyer. He had short cropped red hair, a round face with red cheeks, watery blue eyes and an encouraging smile. He looked rumpled as if he had just gotten up from a nap; his jacket and pants looked like they hadn't been pressed in a while nor had they seen a hanger; his shoes were brown, scuffed, broken in places with mended shoe strings of unequal and inadequate length. His shirt was not exactly white nor was it gray. His smile was what stood out.

"I'm supposed to be at Mr. Humphry's table; should I just go on over there?" not able to look the master in the eye.

"Sure, I'm going in that direction; come on along."

He put his hand on Arthur's shoulder as if to jump start a dead battery. They walked to the table and the master pointed to the empty seat at the end. Arthur looked around; no one seemed interested in his late arrival. He pulled out the chair and sat. He didn't say anything; the conversations around him continued.

The table held eight boys, three on each side, one at the head, one at the foot. Arthur was at the foot. It seemed that the older boys sat toward the head and the younger toward the foot. There were napkins, glasses, and silver on the table with a stack of plates at the head, water pitchers and salt and pepper in the middle. Conversations continued. A boy in the middle got up and returned shortly with a tray of platters and bowls, meatloaf, potatoes, beans, which he set in the middle of the table. The boy at the head took a piece of meat from the platter, placed it on a plate, and passed it down. It reached Arthur and then another plate passed till everyone had a plate. Beans went around the table, then potatoes and the conversations continued around the serving.

"You, at the end of the table, what's your name?" It was the older boy, a senior, at the head looking at Arthur.

Arthur looked up and saw that the question was directed at him. "Arthur," barely audible.

"Arthur what?"

"Arthur May"

"May, what kind of name is that?"

"I think it's English."

"Are you from England?"

"No."

The other boys at the table stopped talking; they were paying attention.

"Where are you from?"

"Grape, Oklahoma." Arthur looked around to see if anyone was watching; everyone was watching. When he said Grape, Oklahoma, he saw two of the boys on the right smile at each other.

"Oklahoma. Do they still have Indians in Oklahoma?" the boy at the head looked at the boy on his left as if to ask "Isn't this fun?"

"I don't know."

"OK. Arthur from Grape, Oklahoma, you don't know about Indians. How about that tie, where did you get that tie?" More sniggering at the head of the table. The boys closer to Arthur were not smiling; they looked at him waiting to see what he would say.

Arthur had a flash of memory. He recalled going to Sears with his father where they walked around the store and picked out his clothes. Sears was the best store in Grape. He remembered picking out the tie; they bought two of them just alike, one for Arthur and one for Carl because they both liked it so much. It was rayon, blue and red striped with little yellow spear points in the red stripes. It was Arthur's turn to say something, his turn to join the conversation.

"I got this tie at Sears in Grape. I got it with my father." Looking down at his tie, the end of which he held up so they could see it above the table.

The fellow at the head of the table had adopted a very serious expression. "At Sears? Don't they sell farm implements?"

Arthur couldn't believe the fellow had heard of Sears in Grape. It wasn't that big a store, not so big that people from the East would have heard of it. Arthur looked around; the rest of the boys at the table looked at him waiting for an answer, some reply. Arthur thought they did sell farm equipment at Sears but he didn't know what to say. No one smiled. He looked at the head of the table.

"Did you get your zits there too?" from the boy at the head. Some of the boys laughed, the rest studied their plates, continued eating and talking. Arthur was on the outside watching from a distance. He didn't get it; what was funny? It was the end of the conversation, but he didn't understand why the boy at the head had made fun of his tie and his zits.

After dinner Arthur rose with the rest of the boys, said grace and went out of the foyer door and found Rod Butler talking to a group of older boys. Arthur stood for a moment, then Rod looked his way.

"Hey, Arthur, here's your class schedule and orientation package. Everything working out OK?" Rod handed him a manila envelope.

Arthur said thanks and turned toward the steps to the dormitory. He went about halfway up the hill and stopped by a flagpole; the sun was down, there were no clouds, there was still a glow in the west. He looked at the valley below, the school buildings changed from red brick to maroon, beyond the buildings the pine and maple green had turned black. The flag pole stood white in the evening sky. He thought if he stayed here for five years, he had one thousand and forty nine days left.

Later, Arthur sat on his bed looking at his boots. Dan came in and asked if Arthur had seen Rod and did he get his schedule. Yes to both. Arthur told Dan about his experience at dinner, about not being able to find his place and about the Sears incident. Dan listened not smiling. He looked concerned; he sat on the edge of his bed, feet on the floor; elbows on his knees, chin in his hands, looking out the window while Arthur told the story about the tie and the zits.

"Some of the guys here are assholes," Dan said looking at Arthur. "My brother said some of the older guys will pick on the new boys, bully them. It doesn't mean anything except they're assholes. The prefects try to stop it and most of the sixth form doesn't do it."

"What's wrong with my tie?" Arthur asked.

"Your tie's fine. Some of the boys here are snobby about clothes. If you don't get your clothes at Brooks Brothers or J. Press or places like that then they'll make fun of you. If you wear the same clothes every day they make a point of it. My brother told me. Some of them will laugh at you, some will snigger behind your back. Don't worry about it." Dan took his jacket and tie off, put them on a hanger and went to the closet.

Arthur already had his jacket and tie off; they were in a pile on the end of his bed. He picked them up and took them to the closet. When he returned to his bed he opened the manila folder with his class schedule in it: Latin, English, Math, Religion, History. Classes every day, eight to three except Wednesday afternoon. Saturday morning classes eight to noon. Sports three-thirty to five, jobs, assembly, chapel and then supper. Study hall seven to nine, lights out at nine thirty.

The other boys in the room fiddled with their bureaus, read schedules or chatted with neighbors. Voices were subdued; it was the beginning of friendships when politeness plays the biggest part, polite until status can be discerned. It was dark outside. The only lights in the dorm were overhead, big glass globes with bulbs inside that gave off a creamy light that filled the center of the room.

Rod Butler came down the middle corridor. "Lights out at nine thirty, that's in twenty minutes. I want you guys to pick up all the trash on the tables and around your bunks before going to bed. Bring it up here and we'll put it in the trash can by the bathroom. Tomorrow morning we'll get up at six thirty, get dressed and head down to breakfast. Everyone has to go to breakfast. If you're late then you'll have to run to the monument in town before you can eat."

Dan and Arthur picked up boxes and papers around their beds and from the tables in the middle of the room and carried the trash to the cans by the bathroom. They didn't say much; when they returned they got in bed and the lights went out; no one talked. Arthur lay awake; he heard bedsprings complain as people turned trying to get comfortable, sneezing, someone got something from his bureau. Slowly the noises drifted away and the only thing left was the sound of someone crying across the room.

5

JOB

The next morning the schoolhouse bell rang at six thirty. The sun was up shining in the dorm windows. Arthur got up and went into the bathroom to find forty boys trying to use eight sinks and eight toilets at the same time. He waited, got his turn and couldn't go because boys were watching, waiting for him to finish. He stood there for a minute then gave up and went to the sinks and waited again. While he waited someone yelled "Let's go, we're going to be late." He hurried, ran through the dorm, grabbed his clothes from the closet, put on the same shirt and tie from the day before. He hadn't untied it, simply loosened it and slid it over his head, took his jacket and ran unwashed with other boys down the hill to breakfast.

He went to the board in the vestibule to see where he was supposed to sit. It hadn't changed; he was at the same place. He went to the table, waited, said grace, sat, the conversations started around him, over him, behind him. Scrambled eggs appeared; they were light green slabs on a tray, bacon thin as paper and greasy, hot chocolate, milk and oatmeal. Cold toast hid on a platter. The eggs didn't taste like eggs, they tasted like a penny that's been dropped in your mouth; they were grainy. The bacon tasted like wet brown paper packaging smelled. The hot chocolate was OK. Arthur ate oatmeal and hot chocolate. After breakfast he thought he would go back to the dorm and get cleaned up, at least wash his face.

No one said anything about his tie or shirt; no one talked to him. About the time everyone was finished, the head prefect stood at the head table and made some announcements. One of the announcements was about jobs. Everyone had a job; new boys should check the roster in the common room to find out what their assignments were. Arthur wondered what kind of job.

After breakfast Arthur went to the common room with Dan; Rod Butler was there waiting for all the new boys to assemble. When the new boys had gathered around, Rod said, "Everyone in the school has a job; the jobs help keep the place clean. Your job assignments are posted on this bulletin board." He pointed behind himself to a glassed case with papers hanging in it. "Each day after breakfast, before morning assembly, you will have to report to your jobs, finish them, get them inspected, then clean your area in the dorm and make your bed. I'll read off the names and the jobs and tell you where to go. These assignments will last for a week and then next week they will change."

"OK, Dan Clement, you're working in the library. Go up to the library next to the schoolhouse, you know where it is, don't you?"

Dan nodded.

"Go up there and tell Mike Peterson you're working there; he'll show you what to do."

Dan left.

"Peter Echman, you're...

Arthur looked out the window as he heard the announcements in the background, he watched the boys leave for their jobs in the reflection of the glass windows. He thought about Oklahoma; he should have been on the bus to Wilson Junior High School with Fred and Peter, sitting in the back talking about Mrs. Carr, their math teacher, or about the Bundy twins who had set off firecrackers in geography class during a movie. The geography teacher, Mr. Cotes, who was about eighty, showed a lot of semi-educational movies and he always dozed off about ten minutes into them. One day during a movie, that had been shown about ten times before, while the lights were out and blackout shades were down and Mr. Cotes had his head on his desk in recline, one of the Bundy boys went to the front of the room and put a string of firecrackers in a book on Mr. Cote's desk. The Bundy boy lit the string with a match which he struck on the crack between his two front teeth. He walked back to his seat and waited, not very long, before the firecrackers went off Bang bangbabangbang, one on top of the other for about twenty seconds.

Mr. Cotes jumped out of his chair and ran to the windows. He must have been temporarily lost, thinking the big black shades were the doors as he charged them and knocked himself down. He crawled to his desk while the last of the crackers cooked off and when he got up off the floor, he leaned on his desk, head down and he was crying. All the girls in the room screamed and ran out the door. Someone set off the fire alarm, which was a good thing, because the room had filled with smoke and bits of paper from the book and the remains of the firecracker wrapping.

Fred and Arthur had gone out with the rest of the kids to the school's front lawn and waited while the fire engines showed up. It wasn't long before the assistant principal came around asking if Arthur knew what had happened. He said someone lit some firecrackers off in the room but it was dark because of the movie and he couldn't see who it was. Fred told him it was the Bundy boys. Arthur didn't think Fred was too smart as the Bundy boys wouldn't like it if they knew who told on them.

While they waited on the lawn, Tiny Morgan came over and asked Arthur if he wanted to take a ride in Tiny's car. Tiny wasn't tiny; he was huge. He was nineteen in ninth grade. He had a beat-up maroon Hudson parked in front of the school; it was dented, the paint was dull and bleached through in spots, the seats were torn, and there was acned chrome on the dashboard. The front seat was broken; it had come off the tracks that held it to the floor. A normal seat would slide front and back as the driver adjusted the position depending on how close he wanted to be to the steering wheel. Tiny's seat sat on the floor, loose, not attached to anything, and as a result, every once in a while when Tiny tried to take off too quick from a stop sign, the seat would flop over into the back of the car. He'd hold onto the steering wheel so he'd end up sitting on the floor of the car as the seat squirted out from under him. There he'd be, sitting on the floor of the car holding the steering wheel unable to see out the windows or touch the pedals. Sometimes he did it on purpose, he'd let the seat flip over backwards so whoever was riding with him in the front ended up on their backs, looking up at the tatters of the ceiling and the ruined head liner. He thought it was funny and when he did it on purpose everybody in the car cracked up laughing. So if you were riding with him you had to ride in the back to keep the seat from falling over. Arthur wasn't big enough to keep the seat up by itself.

Tiny liked Arthur because one time Arthur had lent Tiny his BB gun to hunt pigeons. Arthur didn't start hanging out with Tiny on purpose; it just happened. Arthur had a BB gun just like all the other kids and occasionally he went down the hill behind his house to the Co-Op feed store, down on "B" street, to shoot pigeons. The Co-Op was a Victorian, red brick monstrosity of a building which was originally a brewery and remained so until Prohibition when it was turned into a farm co-op. The most fun thing to do was get on the roof and shoot the birds from there.

To get on the roof he had to climb a tree, go out about ten feet on a limb over the roof and drop down. If the folks who ran the co-op, mostly tired old men, knew Arthur was up there they'd come after him through a door that opened from the inside stairwell onto the roof.

One day Arthur was on the roof and just about to start shooting when the door opened and three fellows charged toward him. They got him cornered at the edge and he had a choice, give up or jump off. As one of them lunged, he jumped. It was a good thing he didn't look or he wouldn't have done it since it was close to a 12 foot drop. When he hit the ground his legs collapsed into his chest and he folded up like a little drink umbrella; he had knocked the wind out of himself and couldn't breathe.

Meanwhile all the fierce accountants and feed salesmen and weigh masters were on the roof looking down and hollering, "Are you OK?"

Arthur thought: No, I'm not OK; I'm all curled up in a ball gasping for breath looking like I am done for. But he didn't say anything; he just lay there looking close to dead.

Pretty soon he began to feel better and he heard them squabbling on the roof as to whose fault it was going to be that this little kid had fallen off the roof and killed himself while three grown men were up there chasing him. One was saying "What are we going to do?", another said "It was your idea." Another, "I wasn't even a part of this. You were the first out of the door. Why did you have to scare him?" and on and on. You would think they would come down to see if they could help save his life, but they thought he was going to die and they were going to jail and so helping wasn't the issue right then, blame was.

Finally after deciding the other guy was to blame, they came down to see if Arthur was OK and on their way they called the police or an ambulance because Arthur heard the life squad warming up its siren a few blocks away. It was time to leave. The three Co-OP guys came like a posse running around the corner, concern on their faces, fear in their eyes, fingers ready to point at their friend and coworkers. Arthur popped up in front of them, laughing and ran back up the hill to his neighborhood; he knew they couldn't catch him because they were just a little too slow, too fat, too smoked out. They knew it too, and didn't bother.

The next day at school the most fearsome of the "B" street gang, "Tiny", wandered over to Arthur on the playground and asked if he had a BB gun. He said he did, and Tiny said he had seen Arthur jump off the roof of the co-op and give those guys the "bird", which he hadn't done. Arthur allowed as how he had nearly got caught in a trap and his only way out was to jump. Tiny laughed and thought it was pretty funny. Tiny asked if he could borrow the BB gun sometime and Arthur said, "sure." From then on Arthur was welcome in the "B" street neighborhood.

They were hanging around in a group while the principal and assistant principal tried to figure out who had lit the fire crackers when Tiny said school was about over and Arthur wouldn't be missed if they took a little ride. So Arthur went to Tiny's car not intending to get in, just talk a while. There were other kids there, waiting, standing around, leaning on the hood and fenders. One of them was Martha Schummaker. She was in ninth grade and was the hottest thing the Wilson Junior High had to offer. She had long shiny brown hair that she parted in the middle and let fall down over her shoulders just to the top of her breasts. Her face was soft, her features smoothed, she had huge brown eyes, lips that looked big and curved and as pink as a dog's tongue. She wore lots of makeup and she wore tight sweaters every day. Under the sweater she had two mounds that could not have had more effect on the boys at Wilson if they had been atomic bombs or balloons of heavy water. They were warm, fuzzy, sweater covered mounds that stuck out from her front and jiggled when she laughed and they took every boy's breath away. She didn't know who Arthur was, but Arthur knew who she was. Arthur had never been this close.

Arthur walked to the group following Tiny. Some of the boys and girls were lounging around the Hudson, leaning on the fenders and hood, disinterested, as if fireworks were an everyday event in geography. They were mostly ninth graders, some of them for the second time, so they were older than Arthur, and while he had seen them around school, they didn't know him more than he didn't know them. One of the guys in the group, undistinguished except for the amount of grease it took to keep his hair in constant spasm of waves and curls, asked Tiny what Arthur was doing there. Tiny told him Arthur was a friend.

The group got in the car one by one, each interested in knowing where Martha was going to sit. When the car was nearly full Tiny told Arthur to get in the back with two others, a boy and a girl Arthur didn't know. Arthur, who hadn't thought about going went along with the flow of things and squeezed in back with the two who were already there. Martha made no effort to join; she watched, undecided if she was going for the ride or going home.

41

A RICOCHET FROM CIRCUMSTANCE

Tiny stood by the open driver's door and called to Martha over the roof of the car; he told her to get in if she wanted to go. She said there wasn't room, so Tiny leaned over and peered in looking at the back seat and then reappeared over the top and told her to sit on Arthur's lap. She slid in over Arthur's legs, turned sideways facing the center of the car and lowered herself onto Arthur's lap. He was in shock. Technical shock, medical shock, his heart stopped, his breathing was cut off, he could not swallow. He didn't know what to do with his hands, there was only one place for them and if they were going to stay attached to his shoulders then they were going to have to go around her because that's the only place there was room. He put his right arm over her shoulder and his left hand on her thigh. She leaned against him and he smelled her hair, small wisps tickled his face, it smelled like Ivory soap, her breath of cinnamon. Her eyes were large and brown and wet like stones you could see in a clear stream. He was so close he saw her lashes beat against each other, he saw where the whites of her eyes disappeared beneath her eyelids. He saw the little fuzzy hairs on her cheek and at the nape of her neck, saw where her red lipstick was wet, with little cracks showing the true color of her lips as she talked. Her sweater was soft and he felt her warmth on his legs.

They drove around for a while, then Tiny stopped at a grocery where he bought four quart bottles of beer which they passed around as they rode. Arthur put the bottle to his lips once but he didn't drink any; it didn't smell too good. Martha didn't drink any but watched as Arthur faked it.

Then they stopped at a gas station and took up a collection amongst themselves to get money for gas. Arthur had some but it was in a pocket he couldn't reach. Martha pushed herself up and Arthur arched his back and straightened his legs so he could to get into the pocket. He had two dollars and change which was most of what they had. He handed it up front. When he sat back down, Martha relaxed on him again, only this time her left arm was around his neck on top of his shoulder and her left breast pressed warm against his chest. Her face wasn't three inches from his.

He wanted to kiss her. He didn't know why, he simply had an urge to put his mouth on hers and have hers on his, to taste her and her lipstick, to steal some of her heat. They rode around and he thought about kissing her and then he couldn't, till he thought about it again, and again chickened out for a thousand times till...

"Arthur, hey Arthur, are you here?" It was Rod in the common room looking at Arthur waiting for a response. Arthur was startled at the transition Rod's question provoked.

42

Arthur turned, "Yes ."

"Arthur, you're assigned to the second floor hallway of the administration building. The building is the next one on the right as you walk out the door here. You can see it ." He pointed out the window at an angle stretching his neck around so he could see along the side of the building. "See the door there, the green door, go on in there and up the stairs. Steve Black will be there to show you what to do."

Arthur nodded and walked to the door, out, down the steps, turned right, went across the courtyard, up the steps to the porch and through the green door. These were the steps he had gone up to meet the headmaster yesterday. He climbed the steps to a poorly lit hallway about fifty feet long with one window in a door at the end that featured a view of the fire escape. There were six recessed doors, three on either side, all closed. The floor was hardwood, refinished too many times so there were serous gaps between the planks; the last refinish didn't include stain so the wood was dirty blond. The walls were a combination of dark wood paneling about half way up with yellow painted plaster to the ceiling. The brass light fixtures about every twenty feet were just enough to push the place from dark to dim.

Someone came down the hall toward Arthur; he couldn't make out who it was till the person was about ten feet away. It was Steve Black, the sixth former from his table in the dining room, the one who had asked about his tie.

"It's you," Steve said. "How're you doing, Grape?"

Steve was about six feet tall and rounded, smoothed off like a sculpture half done. He had shiny black hair he let droop over his forehead in front and pushed back on both sides. His face was round and white with the shadow of heavy beard on cheeks and chin; his nose was straight, well formed but looked too small for his face, as did his mouth which was round and his eyes which looked like small holes drilled into his cheeks and filled with black marbles. His eyebrows were thin, black and arched in perpetual question. He had on a tweed jacket, blue shirt and yellow tie; his gray flannel pants were perfectly creased and his shirt looked like cardboard from too much starch. Approaching dapper, he looked like somebody who was just stopping off at adolescence for a short visit on his way to becoming a serious alcoholic.

Arthur hadn't noticed it before but Steve had a slight southern accent, a laconic drip to the pace of his words, an oily unhurried smooth.

"I'm here for the job. Rod sent me."

"Yeah. I know why you're here. Your job is to sweep the hallway and then clean the can." He bent his head sideways to indicate a closed door to his right. "There's a broom and dustpan in the closet." He pointed to another door. "The cleaning stuff for the bathroom is under the sink in there." Steve stood looking at Arthur waiting for something. "Well, go get the broom."

Arthur opened the closet door. The closet was only about a foot and a half deep and was crammed with boxes and office supplies. There were dirty rags on the upper shelf that smelled of furniture polish. The broom was pushed flat against the back wall behind a box. The dust pan was on the box, it was one piece of stamped metal painted black; the handle was just an extension of the pan with the sides rolled over into a tube and it was dirty as if the last person who used it had tried to shovel mud.

Arthur wrestled the broom, a long wood handled industrial sized thing with a wide wood head, maybe fourteen inches wide with two inch whiskers, out of the closet. He stood holding the broom, head on the floor, handle upright before him, looking at Steve who was looking at him.

"Just start down there, by the door, and sweep up here; then pick it up in the dust pan and put it in the waste basket in the can."

Arthur went to the end of the hall and pushed the broom about ten feet down the hall then he turned around to repeat the maneuver.

Steve stopped him, "Don't you know how to sweep?" Steve came down the hall to Arthur and grabbed the broom. He put the head on the floor and pushed it about an arm's length and then he snatched it back so it came in the air back to the starting point. He moved it about ten inches sideways and did the same movement again except at the end of the stroke he jerked the broom handle back and forth real quick so the broom head danced up and down in the same spot. He moved it another ten inches to the side and repeated the push, pull, jerk, jerk, jerk routine. An amazing amount of dirt came up where Arthur had already swept.

"You make it dance there for a bit so the dirt falls off the bristles before you bring it back to you or the dirt will stay on it and you're just pushing the dirt back and forth in the same spot. Now you try."

He handed the broom handle to Arthur and stepped down the hall watching. Arthur pushed and jerked and shuffled and bounced but couldn't make the broom dance. He yearned for the Sorcerer's Apprentice. He pushed again and jerked and fiddled and pushed.

"Helpless, I guess." Steve said as he turned to leave. "I'll be back in a bit to check how you're doin."

Arthur danced the broom to the end of the hall, picked up the pile of dirt with the dustpan and went in the door to the bathroom which he guessed Steve had called the "can". He went in. There was a commode and a sink with a mirror over it and three lights, one on either side of the mirror and another one on the ceiling. It was well lit, painted yellow, sort of cheery. The sink was near used up. It had rust stains under the faucets which ran like dirty tears down the sides to the drain. The drain was black, dirty brass where the nickel had worn off from rubbing. There was a desiccated, curled sponge, which at one time had been yellow but looked more like the color of wet corrugated cardboard, sitting on top of a round fiberboard can of Sexton cleaning powder.

Arthur leaned over, picked up the can and the sponge, stood, turned on the hot water which dribbled from the faucet and shook the can over the sink. Nothing came out. The can made a clatter as if someone had hidden rocks in it but nothing came out. He shook harder and all he did was make more noise like he was a spastic percussionist in a Caribbean band. He looked around, no more cleaning powder. He put the sponge under the water and got it soft and wiped the bowl of the sink leaving a dirty trail in his wake.

Steve came in. "The hall's not right; did you sweep it?"

"I tried."

"Yeah, OK, we'll do it again tonight; what are you doing to the sink?"

"There's no soap."

"What's in that can?" Pointing to the percussion piece.

"It's globbed up; won't come out." said Arthur.

Steve went around Arthur to the sink and tucked his tie in his shirt. He took the can, shook it, looked at it, then took an end in each hand and twisted it so the seams broke open in a spiral. He reached in one half and took out a golf ball sized clump of congealed powder and threw it straight down at the sink. When it hit, it splattered into sand and dust. First he cleaned the sponge then he scrubbed the bowl and the drain till the stains were gone and the brass ring around the drain glowed yellow. He did it in about twenty seconds.

"OK, Grape, we don't have time to finish up in here. This isn't going to cut it; you can't stand around waiting for things to fix themselves; you got to git after it. We better go or we'll be late for assembly." Steve took the broom and put in the closet and headed for the landing. Arthur followed. They went down the stairs, out and

45

then up the hill to the schoolhouse and got there just as the bell rang. Arthur went to his desk.

The head prefect stood and made some announcements about sports for the afternoon. New boys were supposed to show up at the field house to get football uniforms, old boys were to go to the basement of the schoolhouse. When he finished, the headmaster, who had been sitting behind the desk, rose and walked around to the front and looked back at the clock on the wood paneled wall.

He turned and faced the assembly. "What we are about, gentlemen, is preparing you to make choices. Each step in your life is like a step of a journey. The difference in this journey is you can't go back, you can't retrace your steps. In your life's journey each step is indelible. You can take each step unprepared; you can take each step without contemplation if you choose, but be sure, it is a choice to be blind. And if you are blind, you will end up somewhere. That is certain. But it is highly unlikely by going blindly through your life, by taking each step without thought, without consideration, that you will end up anywhere that you will want to be and importantly where others want you to be. As a friend once said, 'It is highly unlikely that a hungry man standing on a mountaintop with his mouth wide open crying about his condition will have a roast duck fly in.' We are about preparing for choice using three tools: Knowledge, Principle and Faith. These tools require investigation, practice and discipline because they are constantly eroded, challenged by Fear, Superstition, and Greed. Tomorrow I'll have more to say on this topic, for today you have the theme."

The Head walked straight down the center aisle of the schoolroom and out the door. The head prefect got up with the sixth form and left; the rest of the school stood prepared for first period class.

Dan came to Arthur's desk. "Hey, where were you? I waited in the dorm room till the bell rang"

"Was I supposed to be there?"

"Yeah. We had to clean the room and make our beds. I made yours. Rod didn't say anything but I think he noticed you didn't show."

"I was in the administration building sweeping and cleaning the bathroom. Steve Black was there, he's the sixth former from my table who asked about my tie."

"Did he make you stay?"

"No. I was slow getting there and then I couldn't get it right, then it took too long and I forgot about the beds and dorm room."

"I think it's all right. I brought your folder with the class schedule in it. All of us have the same schedule, all the second formers. We start off with English on the second floor." Dan turned to go. His hair was combed, teeth brushed, face scrubbed, pants creased, he was the immaculate perception. He looked like he just stepped out of a barber shop. Arthur felt as if he had slept in a dust bin. His pants itched and they were too short; he felt a breeze on his ankles.

6

READ MARK LEARN AND INWARDLY DIGEST

Arthur went up the stairs in the stream of boys following Dan. They went to a classroom and took seats in the back. They were eight boys, two sat in the front row, the rest were spread with the weight of distribution toward the back of the room. A master came in. He was about forty-five, medium tall. He had an ungainly gait, as if he were trying to take steps that were too long for his legs. He wasn't stooped so much as bent over, in a hurry and wanted his head and shoulders to arrive before the rest of his body. His jacket was worn and had chalk dust on the sleeves and the hem. His tie, on which Arthur was becoming an expert, was loose woven wool. It looked homespun with horizontal stripes of rust and medium blue. It was square on the end, one end much longer than the other, going nearly to the master's crotch while the short end was at his throat struggling to hold onto the knot. His pants were gray flannel, worn, the knees looked like blown out sails. His shoes, which had been black once, were gray and scuffed. One lace was untied; it was broken, and one of the broken ends still had the knot and loops hanging onto it as it tried to keep up with the shoe, but dragged in defeat on the floor. He had a great, lopsided, incongruous grin, large nose, huge bushy eyebrows that made a straight, uninterrupted line across his brow above twinkling black eyes. His hair was cut short, black, bristly, wild with gray at the sides.

He dropped a stack of books on the desk at the front of the room with a boom, backed up, put his hands on the chalk tray at the bottom of the blackboard behind him, brought his left foot up, backwards, against the wall, leaned against the blackboard and said, "Well."

That was it, "Well."

Arthur and the rest of the class sat waiting for whatever was to follow.

Nothing.

The master stood leaning against the blackboard and looked at each of the new boys as if he were picking out puppies at a pet store. It went on for some time, long enough that Arthur began to feel guilty, as if he might have forgotten an assignment and the master was waiting for him to say something. Arthur looked at his hands.

The master looked down at the desk and picked up a little book. It was black, thin and long; he opened it. He looked some more at one of the boys in the corner then down at his book then raised his head looking directly at a boy in the right corner and said, "Dan Clement?" as a question.

"Yes sir," Dan replied from the other corner. Dan was not the boy the master had been staring at.

"Good," said the master of the one syllable, four letter words. He turned to look at Dan who was still in the other corner of the room. They were making progress.

More delay, more looking at students, "Jon Small?" another question, looking at one then another boy.

"Yes sir." Following Dan's lead. He was not the boy Mr. Smith was looking at.

The master looked to the back row surprised. Arthur figured he was trying to guess which boy had which name by looking at them and making a guess before calling out the name, like a game of phrenology.

He was losing.

"Arthur May?" looking at someone else.

Arthur said, "Yes sir."

Surprise.

Five more names. Apparently phrenology wasn't foolproof.

"All right, gentlemen. This is second form English, I am Allen Smith. I will be your teacher this year." All of it leaning back against the blackboard, hands on the chalk tray, the mystery of chalk dust on sleeves and elbows answered.

"First let's pass out some of the texts we will use this year. The first is *The Elements of Style*." He leaned over the table and took a small gray paperback book from a pile and held it up, waved it at no one in particular then put it back down. "The second is ..."

Arthur looked out the window, the sky had clouded, the trees were green, their leaves hung still, a dog barked, in the just perceptible distance children called for Muffy, the room smelled of chalk dust. Arthur looked at Dan who was equally lost. The rest of the class fidgeted, looked about, regarded names carved in the desk tops, picked at themselves, yawned. The two fellows in the front row were the scouts for the class, paying close attention they kept their heads and nodded simultaneously. They would run interference. Should the master have a question or need a confirmation, they would raise their hands first, saving the rest of the class from sneak attack, surprise question, unanticipated interrogatory.

Mr. Smith passed out the books: The *Elements of Style, English Grammar* and a book of short stories.

"For tomorrow I would like you to look at the first chapter in the grammar book. Everyone should know what a noun is and what a verb is."

The bell rang. They went next door to math class and more books, more first chapter, more yawning. Then to Latin and History and finally lunch. Arthur found he could hide, nearly make himself invisible if he sat to the side of the room near the back next to the door. If he looked down at his desk with his eyes just high enough to see where the masters were looking, he could act as if he were picking something off the floor or opening his book to the right page if someone looked at him.

Arthur went to the dorm and washed his face and hands and brushed his teeth. He felt better. He ran to lunch. He was late. Steve Black let him sit before he asked Arthur where he had been. Arthur told him he had to wash his hands and face since he was late this morning. Steve nodded and let it go. Tomato soup, fried eggplant, bread and lima beans with Kubota figs for dessert.

7

THE ROAD TO DAMASCUS

There were more classes after lunch on the second floor of the schoolhouse. The second form moved as a group and the two boys who had sat in the front row for English, John and Scratch, stayed in the front for the rest of the day.

John was tall and lean and he had long straight blond hair which hung over his forehead. His face was long and his eyes were pond green. He was neat and tidy, easygoing, but competitive in a quiet way.

Scratch was the opposite. He was short, dark, compact, a compressed spring, unsmiling. He had a shock of black hair hanging in his face, his shirt was un-tucked, his shoes un-shined, his jacket thrown on; he was put together at the last minute.

The others found equilibrium in the middle with a few choosing the rim of the bell shaped curve. It was hard to think after lunch in the over-warm classroom. The master and his students were drugged with food and heat and the vacuum of low expectation.

After last class the new boys were instructed to go to the basement of the field house to get fitted for football uniforms. They trudged along as a loose formation, down the hill past the administration building through an abandoned apple orchard to a medium sized, two story building. The beginnings of associations were forming; Dan and Arthur followed along toward the end of the gang, chatting about class; Scratch and John led the way nearly racing each other to see who would be first.

The building was wood frame; the first floor was a locker room and shower; upstairs was a small dormitory for upper class boys. They went into the locker room where the walls were lined with small open closets, three walls with hooks on them. There were benches in the middle of the room; the floor was raw cement and the place smelled of dirty underwear and mildew. The shower was simply four or five sets of hot and cold water pipes run up the wall at one end of the room with a sloping concrete floor to the drain. Spartan you might call it, while someone else might call it cheap or maybe efficient.

The math teacher stood at one end of the room with his left foot up on one of the benches; he rested his left elbow on his raised left knee, his chin on his hand, bent over in thought, consideration, looking like the *Thinker* at the great pile of equipment at his feet. He still had his coat and tie on. His head was large, tanned and shiny bald except for a small fringe of hair around his ears and the back of his neck. Even his ears were tanned and shiny. He was large, muscular, rounded, sloped shouldered like a bear, powerful looking. His eyes were walnut brown and sad but his mouth was large, loose, and had a smile.

He straightened up. "All right, gents, gather round here so you can hear me."

He looked around counting heads. "What we're going to do today is try to get you mutton heads suited up to play football. Some of you have already played football and that's good, some of you haven't, and that's OK too. Doesn't make any difference. Like the Prince over there," pointing to Dan, "The Prince has played before at Greenwich Country Day so it's going to be easy to get him suited up and Tim-Tim here, he played at Indian Mountain, so he knows what we're going to do."

"First I want Tim-Tim and the Prince to start sorting this stuff on the floor. Put the helmets in one pile, shoulder pads in another, pants in another: got it. You there what's your name?"

"Arthur."

"Arthur. Let's see,…. you're going to be, let's see ….Arturo, Arturo, you help the Prince and Tim-Tim sort." Pointing to the pile on the floor.   "You three by the door, yeah, you, Winkin, Blinkin and Nod, you three mutton heads go out to the truck in the driveway and bring in all the shoe boxes in the back." He pointed to the door. "The rest of you come on over here and find a shirt that fits, you look like a large, take a large, that's it, now write your name on the clipboard, put your size next to your name, and then put your number next to the size. The number is the big red thing printed on the front and back of the shirt. You can spell your name? Got it?"

The boys nodded.

"When you've got your shirt, then pick up an undershirt, same size, right here in this pile." Pointing to a bench with three piles of t-shirts stacked up. "Then, when you have your shirts, come on over here to the next bench and get two pairs of socks." Indicating piles of socks on yet another bench. "When you girls got all your underwear figured out, come over to the pile of helmets and I'll fit you for a helmet then the Prince over there will fit you for a pair of shoulder pads and Tim-Tim will fit you with pants and Arturo there who looks like he has to take a pee will fit you for thigh pads."

Arthur went to the pile of uniform parts and joined Dan and Tim throwing different parts in their respective piles. Boys started through the line and Dan showed Arthur which thigh pads went with each size pant.

When they were finished the master called "Arturo, come on over here and get your helmet."

Arthur went to the master and stood.

"OK, Arturo, my name is Pa Brunt. You can call me 'Pa', everyone calls me 'Pa'. Got it?"

"OK."

"Arturo, what size hat do you wear?"

"I don't know."

"Well then we'll just have to try one on." He leaned over and took a helmet off the pile at his feet. It was orange leather and shaped like half a watermelon rind, hollowed out in the middle with a chin strap dangling from one side. He clapped it on Arthur's head and it did not fit, it was too small and sat on top like a derby.

"You got a big noggin, Arturo."

He bent down for another. It too was red orange leather and looked like a football cut in half, pointy, with penny size holes where the ears might have been and in the top for ventilation. It was loose like it had been washed and then left in the dryer too long, it was floppy. Pa took the two flaps which were the ear sections in his hands and pulled the helmet over Arthur's head like he was putting on a sock. It went on with no trouble, more than that with too little trouble, it was stretched out loose and three sizes too big; Arthur could spin it around on his head without it touching anything but the crown of his skull. The front came down so low it nearly covered his eyes, the earflaps rested on his shoulders.

"There. That's great." said Pa, tilting his head and looking in admiration. "You got a pointy head, fits all sizes of hats." He turned to the pile of shoulder pads, grabbed one at random, it looked like a bunch of coconut shells tied together with shoe laces. "Here. Try that on."

Arthur couldn't figure out how to put it on, there didn't seem to be a front or back a top or bottom; it should have been a wind chime or a mobile. Pa grabbed it, loosened a couple of the shoestrings and dropped it over Arthur's head right over his shirt and tie.

"Great" says Pa. "You're not playing for the Giants so you don't have to look like Frank K. Gifford. Now the pants." Pa grabbed a pair of pants off the pile. They had been white once, they weren't any more, they were gray and yellow with grass stains at the knees. They had a woven cloth belt with a broken buckle and buttons in the front. "Try those on."

Arthur took off his trousers and pulled on the pants. He had no idea how they were supposed to look until he saw Dan who had on a pair of new pants that were white, tight at the hip and crotch, swelled for his thigh pads, pieces of armor on long legs, then they were tight stopping just below the knee. He looked like Frank Gifford.

Arthur's pants were baggy and stopped just above his ankles, the thigh pads covered his knees and his knee pads looked like grotesque bulges, strange growths on his tibia. The crotch was so low he couldn't take a full stride, the belt didn't work so Pa took the ends and tied a knot in them so the pants were gathered just above his hips, ballooning out toward his knees.

"Great, you're gonna kill em Arturo. OK boys, shoes. Look at the boxes there and pick out a pair that's about half a size bigger than the size you normally wear, then get a pair of socks and try them on. They shouldn't be tight or you'll lose your toe nails and that's no good, parents don't like us sending their sons home without all the parts they came with."

Arthur went to the shoe table and the only size left was a size and a half too big. Arthur stood wondering what to do. He got a pair of socks. Pa came over.

"What's the problem, Arturo?"

"None the right size."

"Just take the next best size, you're not playing in the pros."

Arthur took the box of too big shoes off the bench, sat, took off his school shoes and tried the new ones. It was like putting his foot into the shoe box itself rather than putting on the shoes, lots of room to move around. He tightened the laces but all that did was hurt the top of his foot, his feet were still swimming around inside. The end of his toes came to just about the point where the shoes folded when he bent them taking a step.

"Wear two pairs of socks, you'll grow into them." Pa looking at his handiwork. "OK gang, get suited up and we'll head down to the practice field."

Arthur claimed one of the lockers or stalls by putting his coat and tie on a hook. He took off his socks and started building his uniform. T-shirt, shoulder pads, pants, socks, shoes, shirt. His number was 89; he wondered if there was any significance to the number. He put on his shoes. They had spikes on the bottom. Hard, black rubber pins screwed into the bottom of the shoes that made noise on the floor, clack, clack, clack . They were slippery on the concrete, and they felt as if he were skating inside them. He looked at Dan whose uniform fit; his shoulder pads stuck out and made his shoulders seem immense and his waist like a wasp's. His pants were white, and he had brought his own shoes from home. His helmet was red plastic with a black stripe down the middle, Riddell, round, fitting his head with a face guard and white plastic chin strap. He looked even more like Frank Gifford than before.

Dan was the best looking of the bunch. The rest of the group looked respectable, you could tell they had dressed for football. Arthur and Scratch looked like caricatures of ill dress. They looked like sacks of melons on swim fins, their helmets like World War One leather flight hats gone crazy on steroids. It would have been difficult looking at them to determine what they were dressed for or escaping from.

When they got to the practice field they were separated into two groups. Dan and Tim went into a group which had boys who had played football before. The second group of about twenty with Arthur and Scratch included boys who were new to the sport. Arthur went where he was told. Pa was their coach and he had an assistant, Mr. Grand, who was the shortest man at the school by six inches. What Mr. Grand lacked in size he made up for in sarcassm.

"Gather around," said Pa. "First off we're going to try to figure out how fast you are so we'll try some forty yard sprints. Five of you, any five, line up there on that line and then get down on all fours like this." He demonstrated a sprinter's stance. "When I blow the whistle you take off as fast as you can down to Mr. Grand there. When you get there the fastest two split off to the right the slower three split to the left. If you can't figure it out then Mr. Grand will let you know who's fast and who's slow."

Pa picked out five boys, lined them up and blew the whistle. They took off down the field, then Pa picked out the next five including Scratch and Arthur. They lined up and Arthur and Scratch struggled to see who was going to be second to last. Arthur won but they were both put in the slow lane. Next time around it was five slow boys struggling to keep from being last, and Arthur was successful.

Pa took the fast boys and Mr. Grand took the slows, about twelve in all. Mr. Grand then set about teaching the boys how to block. He had a blocking sled, a contraption that looked like a giant dog sled or a big step ladder tipped on its face. Mr. Grand stood in the middle of the thing with his hands on two four-by-four padded wood uprights about five feet tall, he looked out the back of the sled from between the uprights. Beneath him, connected to the uprights, was the sled part with runners which he stood on. The idea was to get two boys to put their shoulders against the uprights and push Mr. Grand and the sled down the field as he yelled instructions from inside the contraption.

He picked two boys and showed them where to put their shoulders and then gave the command, "Mush." The boys pushed and grunted and heaved and sighed, heads down, looking at their feet.

"That isn't going to work boys," he said. "First you have to take little, choppy, quick steps and second you have to keep your heads up and watch me. OK, you two, line up and try it again."

The unlucky lined up.

"Mush!"

The sled moved about three feet; their heads were down and their feet were glued to the ground, no quick, little, choppy steps.

"OK, who's next, you two." He lined them up. "Remember, quick steps, heads up. Mush."

The sled moved about five feet. Heads were halfway up and steps were shorter.

"One more time, Mush!" with the enthusiasm of Sgt. Preston of the Royal Mounted Police

There was some small movement accompanied by lots of panting and huffing and puffing.

"Who's next, you two." Indicating Scratch and Arthur.

Arthur had his helmet on with the chin strap buttoned, but the strap was so loose it hung down to his shirt. The helmet came nearly over his eyes so he had to tilt his head back to look out from under the rim. He walked forward; Scratch was already there, ready to go, lined up on the sled and anxious. Arthur took a three point stance as he had been told about two feet from the sled and waited for the command.

Scratch couldn't wait. He jumped the gun and hit the sled a glancing blow; he tried to correct and fell down before Arthur had a chance to do anything.

Mr. Grand was irritated by this lack of discipline. "Hold your horses. Wait till I give the command; can't be jumping out of the starting gate without a signal. OK. Line up."

Arthur and Scratch lined up.

"Mush!"

Arthur charged, he couldn't see a thing, his helmet had slipped down over his eyes. Scratch had jumped the gun again, this time just enough so he hit the sled first and turned it slightly sideways. When Arthur hit it, he hit it more sideways and knocked it over and raked the skin off his shins as he fell into it on top of Mr. Grand. Mr. Grand and Arthur lay tangled in the wreckage.

Arthur crawled out and Mr. Grand found his way with some help. The other boys stopped laughing when Mr. Grand stood.

"OK you two," indicating Arthur and Scratch, "for being totally incompetent and failing to follow the directions you are going to have to run the 'reverse gauntlet.'" Mr. Grand got the other boys lined up in two rows, one facing the other about an arms width apart. He told Scratch and Arthur to put their helmets on backward, no big problem for Arthur. Next he told Arthur and Scratch to get on all fours and to crawl between the two lines of boys, backwards. Scratch got on all fours with his helmet on backwards and when he was at the head of the column Mr. Grand told the other boys to kick Scratch in the seat of the pants as he went by. Scratch crawled and some of the boys kicked but no one kicked hard. Then it was Arthur's turn and he crawled and got kicked a little; nothing hurt.

When practice was over, they walked back up the hill to the field house. Arthur didn't care about the gauntlet, the other boys thought knocking the sled over was funny, everyone seemed to be happy football was finished for the day.

As they walked up the path to the field house they passed through the ruined orchard were a few of the trees still had fruit. One of them, a pear, had little green nodes hanging from nearly leafless branches. Scratch stopped and took one of the pears off the tree and tested it. He ate it while some boys watched, but most were uninterested and went on to the field house. Scratch told Arthur they didn't taste too bad as he was into this third. Arthur picked one but the one he got was hard as a rock and only had a slight smell and no taste, so he didn't eat it. He tried another with the same result. He left Scratch to the pear eating and went alone to the field house where he and the rest of the boys took off their uniforms and went to the showers, four shower heads for fourteen boys. They took turns under the thin spray then dried with towels that could have been cheap motel pillow slips. They laughed, kidded Arthur about the sled, dressed and went to their jobs. Arthur went to his and Steve wasn't there so Arthur practiced sweeping and cleaning without supervision and he thought he was getting the knack of it.

That evening after study hall and before lights out, Arthur, Dan, Tim, Scratch and Jon sat at the picnic table in the middle of their dormitory in pajamas. Since Dan had played football the year before and because he was fast in the sprints, he was not on their football team, he was picked for a more senior squad so he had missed Arthur's and Scratch's "reverse gauntlet". He overheard Jon kidding Scratch and he asked what had happened. Jon told the story while Dan listened. Arthur and Scratch smiled and laughed.

"I don't think that's fair," Dan said when Jon was finished.

Scratch didn't mind. "It didn't hurt. Nobody kicked very hard," he said.

"I don't care; I don't think its right for a master to make fun of you guys," Dan turned to Scratch. "Didn't you feel stupid?"

"Yeah."

"Well, that's dumb. Masters are here to teach us the right way to do things. Making fun of people is bullying. It makes me mad. My older brother went here; he graduated last year. The first year he was here he came home for vacations and told stories about how people had picked on him and the other new boys, and how it made him mad. He told me not to let it happen to me."

"It doesn't seem like anyone is picking on you," said Tim.

"No, that's right, they know my brother was a prefect and still has friends in the sixth form." Dan told the group about the incident in the dining room with Arthur's tie and later on the job with Steve Black.

"OK. So how do we stop it?" asked Arthur.

Scratch jumped in as he was used to doing, everything a cascade of noise and flurry of words. "I guess we could tell the prefects, but I don't think we should because then the prefects will tell the sixth formers and then they will think we are tattletales, babies and make it worse for us. Same for Mr. Grand."

"Why don't we get them back?" This was the first thing Jon said.

Scratch asked, "What do you mean get them back; what could we do?"

"I don't know. Maybe sabotage or kidnap," suggested Jon.

Dan broke in, "I'll call my brother and ask him."

Rod came to the head of the hallway, "Lights out." He flipped the switch and darkness surrounded them as the boys jumped on their beds; springs groaned and night noises from outside, bugs in the grass, dogs across campus and cars on the gravel drive below joined the breeze and slid through the windows.

Later that evening Arthur heard someone thrashing around then getting sick. Whoever it was groaned and coughed then went to the bathroom. The lights came on and there was a green vomit puddle by Scratch's bed. Scratch wasn't there. Rod came down the row of beds with a dustpan and a wad of brown paper towels. He pushed the mess in the dustpan, wiped the floor and returned to the bathroom. The lights went out but Scratch did not return.

Scratch was on his way to the infirmary, too many green pears. One of life's maxims was confirmed, not for the last time: "There is no free lunch."

8

ON THE THIRD DAY

The next morning Arthur had a better idea of what he needed to do to be on time. He got up before the bell rang, went to the bathroom where a few other boys were already washing, brushing, peeing, staring in the mirror. He washed, brushed, went back to his place in the dorm, made his bed and got dressed. It was much easier getting ahead of the crowd.

At breakfast Steve Black didn't say anything. Arthur didn't know any of the other boys at the table; he was the only new boy so he ate and observed. It appeared the other boys knew each other. When breakfast was finished, he went to the hallway for his job. Steve wasn't there so Arthur started sweeping the hallway attempting to make the broom dance as Steve had, without much success. He finished the hallway and went into the bathroom ready to start there when the door opened and Steve came in, his shirt pressed to plywood perfection, shoes shined glass-like, pants without a wrinkle, hair shiny black hanging over his forehead, his nose still too small for his face.

Steve's face was red; his questions were blurted between closed teeth. "Grape, did you sweep the hallway?"

"Yes."

"Where's the broom?"

Arthur went to the closet and got the broom; Steve followed him from the bathroom into the hall and grabbed the broom handle. He went to the end of the hall and started sweeping, making the broom dance and shuffle, bob and weave in Arthur's direction. Arthur didn't know what to do, should he go back to the bathroom and start cleaning in there or should he stand and watch Steve sweep. Arthur was prone to standing and watching and that's what he did.

"OK Grape. I'm going to sweep this hall, where you just swept." Steve interrupted himself in a pant "Get the dustpan. All the dirt I get up from where you just swept is going in your jacket pocket, and I want you to carry it around for the rest of the day and think about what you're supposed to be doing. You're supposed to sweep the floor, not brush the dirt into the cracks. Look at this." Steve regarded the pile of dirt in front of the broom which had grown pretty impressive by the time he got to Arthur. The pile was the size of one of Pa's gray athletic socks coiled in front of the dancing broom.

Arthur continued his standing and watching.

"Don't just stand there with your thumb up your ass. Get the dust pan." Steve in a huff not looking at Arthur but looking at the pile on the floor.

Arthur retrieved the dustpan and brought it back to the pile. He stood not knowing whether to put it on the floor in front of the broom or hand it to Steve.

"Christ. Don't you know how a dustpan works? Put it on the floor in front of the broom."

Arthur put the pan on the floor and held it while Steve swept the offending pile over the lip. Arthur moved it back a bit, Steve swept, the pile rolled into the pan.

"OK," Steve said. "Give me the pan."

Arthur handed him the pan. Steve took it, tilted it to the left so all the dirt was on one side, reached to Arthur's left coat pocket, held it open, deposited the dirt in the pocket, let the pocket flap close, patted it and said, "There, now to the bathroom."

They went in the bathroom where Steve produced a new can of cleanser. He put it on the sink and coached Arthur in the refined art of scrubbing a sink. Arthur didn't know there was so much to learn. Steve wanted the brass fixtures to shine, the porcelain streak proof, the pipes under the sink wiped clean, no residue of cleanser on metal or porcelain surfaces. New toilet paper, trash can emptied, mirror spotless. Finally he wanted the sponge cleaned and soap free and put on the shelf under the sink.

"You better get going or you're going to be late for assembly." Steve turned off the light and they went down the hall to the stairs.

Arthur made it to assembly on time and slid into his desk, a gang had entered the schoolroom with him and they found their seats. Bright sun created carpets of light and dark across the assembly. When everyone was seated and quiet the head prefect made some announcements. Then the headmaster stood, looked over the group as if looking beyond the back of the room and said nothing for a minute. It seemed a dramatic pause received in obedience rather than anticipation of the message.

The headmaster started, "If you will recall, yesterday we talked a bit about choice, about preparing to make choices, about the criteria we use to make choices, Faith, Knowledge and Principle, about the sharpening stones we use to keep Faith, Knowledge and Principle fresh, Inquiry, Discipline and Practice, and we noted the challenges we face in our traverse: Fear, Superstition and Greed, which will be our constant companions."

"Today I want to talk about choice. Everything you do is a choice. Some choices are trivial as in the choice to put one foot in front of the other; some choices are more cognitive, but not important, as in how much salt to put on our food or which tie to wear today. These choices require some thought, but they will not, as a rule, determine the endpoints of our lives."

He paused, "There are other choices, however, which will indeed determine the endpoints. The most important of these are choices we make about how we treat our neighbors, our friends, our families, our classmates and all those people who will become attached to us, even by the finest of threads, over the course of our lives."

"This is not a new concern. For all of our cumulative history we have wrestled with this issue, and for all of that history we have consistently identified it as the single most important question we have faced for thousands of years. The evidence for this is its inclusion as one of Christianity's two great commandments. 'Love thy neighbor as thy self.', and its being subject of six of the Ten Commandments which have survived for more than five thousand years without improvement."

"You, as the latest members in this unbroken stream of humanity, now face the same questions. How are you going to treat your neighbor, what choices will be presented to you and how will you proceed?"

"The point today is this, how you treat your neighbor is a choice, it is a continuing choice and it is the most important choice you will make. On this issue hang all the laws and all the prophesy and the remainder of your lives."

The headmaster said no more, he walked straight ahead, out of the room in silence as if he were alone. When he had gone a cacophony of moral release erupted as boys rose in chatter to the sound of chairs scraping hardwood floors and folding desktops clattering shut.

Arthur caught up with Dan as they left the schoolroom, they walked up the stairs to their class together. Jon was beside them on the landing.

"That guy's pretty serious, isn't he?" Jon said to both of them. Arthur nodded. He hadn't listened too hard, he was thinking about the dirt in his pocket; it was gritty and smelled like the hallway. He wondered if the other boys knew about his pocket full of sand and dust balls. They went into class together and took the same seats they had taken the day before where Tim and Scratch took the front scout positions, Dan in the rear, Arthur to the right side along the wall.

Mr. Smith entered wearing the same jacket and pants he had on the day before. The shirt could have been the same or not, there was no way to tell from Arthur's position. He slapped a stack of books on the desk, the little skinny, long one on top. He backed up to the chalk board, put his heel against the wall and, the same as yesterday, he surveyed the room. He took his little book and looked at each student then at his book as if taking attendance without calling the names. His smile grew as he went down the list.

"Hasty Davies," he said looking at Tim. Bad guess. His smile vanished, he became serious as if losing what he thought was a winning hand of cards. More looking at names and faces.

Hasty Davies said, "Here sir," from the other side of the room.

Mr. Smith put the book down and said. "Well, I suppose you're all here. Where else would you be? In the future I'll ask one of you to take attendance and inform me if someone is missing. Would anyone like to volunteer to take attendance?"

Scratch's and Tim's hands flew into the air simultaneously, before the question was finished.

"OK, you there, you can take attendance each morning, you will tell me if anyone is absent," pointing to Scratch. Scratch one, Tim zero.

"What if Scratch is absent?" asked Hasty.

"Well, then, I guess you," Mr. Smith pointing to Tim, "will have to do the attendance."

Scratch one, Tim one-half.

"How will they know who is supposed to be in the class?" Hasty asked without raising his hand.

"I suppose I will have to give them a list, I'll make a list and pass it out tomorrow" Mr. Smith said, considering this logistic difficulty seriously.

"What do we do if you don't come to class?" Hasty again.

Mr. Smith looked over their heads, as if the question had occurred to him for the first time. "One of you will have to go to the head master's office and tell the secretary that I haven't shown up and they will get someone to fill in for me."

"What if no one comes?" Hasty again.

"Enough on that, I suppose you will carry on in that instance." Mr. Smith turned to the blackboard and looked for a piece of chalk. Only stubs, hardly large enough to hold onto, little white trapezoids; stubs to confound the fingers. He surveyed the chalk tray from one end to the other.

Hasty blurted, "Do you want me to go get some chalk?" It was clear that Hasty was ready for anything but verbs and nouns.

Mr. Smith looked perplexed still staring at the chalk tray. "Yes, would you check in the next classroom?" Mr. Smith took the largest of the stubs and wrote on the board Verbs .. big dividing line .. Nouns. He had to switch stubs as one ran out before he was finished with nouns. At the end of nouns he was reduced to pushing the stub along on the end of a finger. He carefully removed the sliver of chalk from his finger and placed it in the tray.

"All right then. I asked you to take a look at verbs and nouns in your grammar books. Would someone like to volunteer to define a verb?"

Before Tim or Scratch could get his hand up, Hasty returned with two pieces of chalk. He walked to Mr. Smith and reported that he had had to go to all the classrooms on the floor to beg chalk as there appeared to be a general shortage in the school, so perhaps Mr. Smith would like to take one with him so he would have something for tomorrow. Mr. Smith considered the question then placed one piece in his pocket and the other in the tray behind him.

The bell rang. They had approached English and they had nearly got verbs and nouns in their sights when the process was interrupted. Maybe next class. Hasty hoped not. He went to Tim and pulled ten pieces of chalk out of his pocket.

"Look at this."

"Where did you get those?" Tim asked.

"From Mr. Smith's classroom. My job is to sweep the classrooms on this floor, so this morning I took all the chalk from this room so I could volunteer to go get some more, which I had in my pocket all along. I stood outside the class till he asked the question about verbs, then I came back in. Pretty funny. Yeah?"

There were four other boys who heard Hasty's story. Some thought it funny, some found it troubling because it was deceitful that Hasty had taken advantage of Mr. Smith's good nature. Dan didn't like it and thought it was the same kind of thing some of the seniors like Steve did to the new boys. Arthur thought it was funny and felt Dan was too serious, bordering pious, although it was clear Dan was sincere.

They went to math where Pa told stories about the Second World War in Europe, not much math going on there, but fun, as Pa told great stories and called everyone by their nicknames which stuck only in Pa's class and on the football field.

After math they went to Latin where Mr. Grand was serious. Hasty tried some delay tactics which angered Mr. Grand and failed in their objective. Mr. Grand knew their names and didn't have to take attendance; he knew who was there and who wasn't and he seemed to have Hasty's number. He gave a short quiz on yesterday's assignment. Arthur hadn't done any of the assignments, he had never done any homework nor cared about the results of tests or quizzes. At his junior high school in Grape no one cared about tests and everyone seemed to move from one grade to the next unless there was a serious problem. Arthur figured you'd have to be illiterate not to make it to the next grade and a few of his classmates qualified each year.

Because he hadn't done any of the work, he couldn't answer any of the questions on the quiz; his paper was empty except for his name primitively scratched at the top. Arthur had a strange reaction, he felt as if he had been bushwhacked, cheated and embarrassed at the same time. He was angry but couldn't place the source of his anger; it was a combination of anger at Mr. Grand for the quiz and embarrassment and disappointment in himself for having failed to do what was necessary. He had never felt that way before. It was a lodestone in his gut that weighed him down in confusion and fear of being left behind, in self pity at being tricked, in hate at being embarrassed, it was a confusion of darkness that swept over him. He was judged and found wanting. He was blinded by rage and at his failure to foresee this eventuality. One minute he had been sliding along, comfortable, all the world known, he was safe watching others, safe as a minnow who seeks the anonymity of the middle of the school, turning, darting, diving, avoiding the exposed flank, seeking the safety of universal proximity, and the next moment he was exposed, vulnerable, empty without resource, without recourse without an answer, an empty page.

The feeling was new and Arthur had no idea where it had come from, what to do with it or how long it would last. He sat in class, his mind reeling in tumult, in confusion, an emotional maelstrom to which he was captive and sole audience. He felt as if his emotions and body were in huge conflict, that he would explode into pieces, as if his head were going to fly off, held only by loose threads, his arms were bloated sausages, and colors, orange and violet mixed at the top of his head. He was enraged at his stupidity, a condition he had never before considered.

The rest of Latin passed in a blur as if seen through a Coke bottle and the rest of the day without memory until he got to the dorm after study hall and remembered the dirt in his pocket. Arthur took his jacket to the waste bucket by the bathroom and emptied it by pulling the pocket inside out while holding the jacket upside down. Dirt and fuzz fell out; Arthur scraped and slapped at it till most was gone, then turned the pocket back right side in and hung the coat on a hanger. In study hall Arthur had thought about the Latin quiz and the heat of confusion and anger returned, not so immediate but there. It subsided and he did his assignments grudgingly as if under threat without any concern for the quality of the result. His cooperation was reluctant; he was at odds with himself, finding new territory.

9

SHEEP MAY SAFELY GRAZE

The next weeks passed without event. Arthur got the drift of jobs; he learned to dance with the broom, a foxtrot; the tango remained elusive in reserve for the future. In football, he learned to block and to tackle and he came within one standard of dismal, leaving a few boys behind his talent and the many in front. He got a hint of homework's importance; a random, distant light that showed him a way beyond humiliation. He got its azimuth right without yet understanding its weight and elevation, being able to scribble a few answers on quizzes without getting them entirely right, without yet receiving joy from achievement. In his major struggles he returned to the middle of the minnows; notoriety's glittering exterior was outside his talent, finding safety in the bowels of his class.

His anonymity had unfortunately extended to Grape. He had not heard from his father despite his three letters home. The school had a policy, one of many designed either to maintain its hold on antiquity or to increase its general fund, which required each boy to write home once a week. The deadline was Monday morning, so, on Sunday evenings each boy, old or new, spent time writing short notes with messages weighed heavily on the side of requests for clothing, food or funds. Arthur did his share of writing but received no response. He sent his last letter to Liz remembering how, in her note on the boot box, she had indicated her wish to hear from him.

The school had a mail room in the basement of the administration building. The workings of the facility appeared to have come secondhand from a defunct Post Office. There was a wall of letter boxes which had small brass doors with smaller windows and two brass dials for combination. One brass dial had numbers the other letters. Arthur had bad dreams about forgetting his combination and not being able to get the mail that filled the box. Reality was

71

opposite; he remembered his combination but had nothing to retrieve. Each day after lunch when the mail was posted to the boxes the boys went to the mail room to check for letters. Older boys cared more for letters from girls than from parents while the younger boys survived on letters from home. Arthur was on a mighty lean diet, neither girlfriend nor family teased his combination. It was a continuous cycle of hoping, expecting, imagining followed each day by emptiness. He'd rather have been stung by a wasp. The mail was only one step in the day's routine; it was an unpleasant interruption which Arthur couldn't avoid because the hope factor got larger with each empty view.

There was rhythm in the school's life. Each proceeding was linked to its antecedent and tied to its postscript and then repeated the next day or week, each building on the last. Jobs followed breakfast which preceded assembly which were in turn followed by classes. Each day's progress was no more distinguishable from the previous than the weather from yesterday's; as time passed the seasons appeared in retrospect, leaves dropped from the trees, not all in any day but they were, on noticing, gone; jobs changed, it was dark outside during study hall; these were the graduals.

The specifics changed too. The headmaster's continuing homily teased Arthur's attention. Arthur's interest was drawn more to the nature of the man than to the message. The man was a mystery. Arthur had never known anyone like him and was both attracted to and afraid of him. He appeared each day at the head of important settings, he spoke at morning assembly, he said grace at meals, he led evening prayer. He was serious and powerful and threatening in some ways, but he was not personal. He left you no scent by which you could track him or tell by which route he had come. His figure was so large he could accommodate any stereotypical attribute you might want to attach to him: wise, serious, Yankee, intelligent, thoughtful, stern, but those attributes told you only how you perceived him and nothing about his person. How did he get to this point, what path did he take to come to the position he held for the community; also what gears and connections made him work? It was clear the man was sufficient in what Arthur could see. There was more in his limited view than in most people Arthur had known, yet the view was superficial; there was obviously more.

The headmaster's homily continued along the lines set out in the first two days of school. He said, repeating himself, that choice was present in all action. He said that man could not hope to make the right decision about bombing Germany, which targets, cities versus military installations versus industrial centers, unless he had prepared for that decision ahead of time.

Arthur had tried, during one of the talks in which the headmaster made references to fire bombing Germany and Japan, to recall an example of an important choice he had made which had a serious effect on other people. He couldn't think of one right away and he wasn't really trying, so his thoughts wandered. He thought about fire and bombs, and as he daydreamed, he slid from the headmaster's talk to a recollection of his father's experience with fire and bombs.

In the summer before Arthur had come to school, Carl had talked about building a barbecue grill. He wanted to build it himself because the grills for sale at Sears were small and flimsy and were inadequate to Carl's vision of the Oklahoma barbecue macho mystique. Carl wanted a magic machine with a life of its own. Carl wasn't alone in his pursuit of the perfect grill; he had a neighbor, Mr. Stuart, who was an engineer who liked martinis as much as Carl, he liked fires and grills, and he liked the backyard Oklahoma mystique.

Building the grill was Mr. Stuart's idea but he didn't have to do much selling to get Carl involved. They spent a weekend sitting at Carl's kitchen table drinking martinis and drawing plans for their construction project. The more they drank, the bigger the project got until finally they were satisfied either with the drink or the enormity of their plan. The next weekend they disappeared to Mr. Stuart's garage which was a major machine shop. They had collected huge sheets of one quarter inch thick stainless steel, military, scrap atomic reactor parts. They scored it and ground it and cut and welded and drank martinis. Arthur was allowed to visit but he was not allowed to touch anything; he didn't want to touch anything because most of the machinery in Mr. Stuart's garage either created a fire or cut your hand off or both. It was a frightening place, and appealing at the same time. Something the law and the neighbors might appreciate as an attractive nuisance; grinders that could take skin to bone in a wrong wink, saws that would cut as if you were no more than a hot dog, hammers Arthur could not lift, riveting machines with pneumatic hoses, overhead neon light, the racket of hell, the smell of ozone and grease.

They worked in the shop all weekend. When Arthur saw them next, they were wheeling a gargantuan, stainless steel, public utility sized blast furnace down Mr. Stuart's driveway on giant wheels. The thing resembled no grill Arthur had seen in Grape. It was made with sheet metal, one quarter inch stainless steel, a thing to behold. In the sunlight it was so bright and angular Arthur could not look directly at it without hurting his eyes. It was supported by four posts, legs the diameter of baseball bats, cross-membered for lateral stability, mounted to caster wheels they had taken from a broken safe dolly (Carl had told Arthur the wheels were the only ones they could find that were strong enough to support the grill). On the four posts rested a giant, glittering pan. One end of the pan was open, and if you looked in, which was about eye level for Arthur at the time, he could see flanges welded along the sides. The rack was three feet by four feet and had two handles welded on the front so Carl or whoever was operating the grill could adjust the height, and it weighed about forty pounds. Arthur couldn't conceive who was going to move it once it was in place and hot. Certainly neither of the Martini Engineers.

At the backside of the pan was a vertical chimney about three feet high with an adjustable flue for draft control. The chimney was held in place by welds and riveted to the back of the pan by pieces of triangular sheet. The grill was not coming apart, and it wasn't going to be stolen. It was great, it was grand, it shined and had wheels and was huge by an army's standards. When he first saw it, Arthur couldn't believe it was a grill at all; he thought it was a machine from an automobile manufacturing plant.

About the time they got the grill to the end of Mr. Stuart's driveway, the Martini in Chief, Carl, decided they should roll it down the hill to Arthur's house, and they decided to roll it in the middle of the street. The hill was not steep, barely enough to get a bicycle going good and the distance short, maybe 50 yards. Carl and Mr. Stuart pushed the grill out of the Stuart's driveway and headed for the middle of the street but the thing started to get away from them, the wheels were free to rotate for better maneuverability so there was no way they could keep it pointed across the street. Casters or not, these two fellows, martinis in hand, could not stop its progress once it got up a head of steam and mind of its own.

What had started as a maiden voyage with smiles and proud ownership turned into a bad dream in slow motion. First they realized they had a problem and they talked real civilized, then their faces transitioned to red as they tugged to restrain it, then they involuntarily were nudged up against minor panic when they saw indeed the thing might get away, then real panic when their first fear was fulfilled and replaced in quarter time by the thought it might run over them, then horror as they realized it was on its own and headed for a neighbor's car which was parked at the curb and in the trajectory far enough down the hill to allow for some good speed. There they were, the magnificent engineers, standing in the middle of the street as they watched this battleship on wheels sail down on a neighbor's car. And they were, as they say, sore afraid.

It looked to Arthur like the thing had a mind of its own. It bore down on the neighbor's Buick Roadmaster and hit it dead center in the front, caving in the car's bumper and radiator back about six inches into the engine block with a thunderous crash as if the car had been hit by a truck, but with no screeching of tires or cloud of smoke that usually accompanies a head on collision. It nearly parted the Buick down the middle. Then it stopped, silent, waiting for the two engineers who were by that time running down the hill as if they wanted to be near the impact but helpless to supervise it.

After the crash Carl was not pleased to have Arthur a witness to the idiocy which wasn't quite finished. So Carl told Arthur to go in the house and take a nap. Arthur went to his room and watched out the window which faced the scene as the police and a fire truck showed up and the old lady who owned the Buick stood looking in amazement from her front porch. She'd survived the two world wars and the Depression and just about the time things are looking up the Martini Gang lets loose on her car with a runaway grill. It looked as if the car was a total loss.

The fire truck left without much ado, but the police stayed around for a while and stopped traffic when a tow truck arrived. The tow truck got up the hill and put a cable on the grill and pulled it out of the front of the car. It came right out; it wasn't even stuck in there and once it was free it looked menacing as if it was ready for round two. Some fellows got blocks of wood and put them under the grill's now famous caster wheels. The tow truck hitched up the mangled Buick and left. But the grill was still in the middle of the street and presented a reasonable threat to all those who lived below, including its owner. In a little while another truck, it belonged to Mr. Stuart, came with a real big forklift, which they got off the truck by means of a hydraulic lift. The forklift picked up the grill and brought it down to Carl's driveway where all the neighbors gathered around to take a look.

Carl didn't look happy, but he was not about to be undone by circumstance. He contemplated outdoing circumstance but he had no idea the seriousness of the battle he had joined. After taking a good look at the grill, he and Mr. Stuart decided it was in perfect shape and ready to go for next week's debut. The barbecue of the ages. Arthur took a good look at the grill the next morning after his father had gone to work, and he couldn't find a scratch except where the forklift had picked it up.

A RICOCHET FROM CIRCUMSTANCE

The next Saturday Carl started early, drinking martinis, cooking huge bowls of pasta, ordering kegs of beer and slabs of ribs and hind quarters of great beasts, corn on the cob, bread, burgers, dogs and every imaginable barbecue ingredient. He started early and Arthur's mother helped but you could tell Carl was way ahead and bound to stay there, this was his show. He was going to make up for the last weekend's circumstance.

About two o'clock the help showed up, two Negroes, one man and one woman. The woman was supposed to help in the kitchen and the man with the barbecue. Carl made the man get dressed up in a white apron and a tall white hat and together they stacked all the barbecue stuff on a picnic table beside the grill

Around five in the afternoon neighbors and friends and some folks who were simply curious showed up. The beer started to flow and folks were talking, but when Arthur looked closely and counted them, everyone of the guests eventually sidled over to the grill, examined it, some more obvious than the others, then walked away. There was something of a sideshow atmosphere about the goings on, but Carl was too wound up in the martinis and next extravaganza to realize it.

He had bought about a hundred pounds of charcoal for the grill and just to make sure it started right he had mixed half of a gallon of gasoline and half a gallon of wood alcohol in a plastic Clorox bottle as the primer. That's what he called it, .. primer, as he put 50 pounds of coal on the pan and splashed on half the jug.

With a flourish, Carl took his trusty World War Two Zippo out of his pocket, put his hand up close to the pile he had built and it exploded. Arthur didn't see Carl's thumb hit the lighter, and didn't think he had; the grill was just ready for the second round with Carl, and, as if to get a jump on the program, started by itself. Sort of spontaneous circumstance.

Carl and everyone else jumped back as sheets of flame leapt from the pan and great clouds of smoke boiled from the chimney. The chimney was spectacular, it was a working model of a primitive jet engine; it gathered vapor and oxygen and mixed them to saturation, spit the concoction from the top where it roared with gargantuan lust, spitting flames fifteen feet in the air. The initial sonic boom subsided, flames roared from the flue and from the pan and from just about everywhere within ten feet of the thing. The black fellow, on seeing Carl saturate the place with primer, had wisely backed up as everyone else moved forward to see the great event. And when it commenced they were, as they say, sore afraid.

The fire spilled over onto the table where the barbecue ingredients, burgers, ribs, dogs, buns, great shanks of beasts were stacked up. The table caught fire, and pretty soon the jug of primer, still half full and sitting patiently in silent accord with the grill, cooked off with another minor atomic blast. By this time everyone was well back or heading for home. Carl, realizing that circumstance had dealt him another losing hand, decided he could rescue part of his show, so he hustled around the side of the house and reappeared with a garden hose. He was a sight, his white apron reduced to ashes, his eyebrows singed away, and what little hair he had on the top of his head had been blown away as if by a dirty tornado. Quite the dapper chef, which effect he was about to take under control, when the fire trucks came rumbling up the hill for the second time in a week. All thanks to Carl's imagination mixed liberally with gin and circumstance.

So Arthur thought about circumstance and how maybe it could be a topic for one of the headmaster's talks on getting prepared for things that don't go like you expect they might.

10

CANA

Football practice continued, six days a week with boring three hour sessions on Wednesday and Saturday afternoons. Mr. Grand assigned Arthur guard duties on the single wing offense and guard duties on the defense. The team spent more time rehearsing the five offensive plays they knew than they spent on defense. They spent so much time on these five plays they could duplicate their inept blocking and molasses running against imaginary foes with amazing accuracy. They did not get better, or faster, or smarter, they simply got more practiced at mediocrity. They had no other team to work against so everything for the first few weeks was run dry, without opposition, and that's the way they expected the game was played, with holes opening in the opponent's lines and the opposition falling to the ground with no more effort than calling the play in the huddle.

With their increasing ability to reproduce stumbling inaccuracy and halting assault, and without criticism or competitive context, their initial modesty fell victim to their limited horizon, so that on the fourth Monday at the beginning of practice when Mr. Grand announced they would travel to another school, the Cutlery, for a Wednesday scrimmage, the boys became excited and cheered the opportunity as the British Light Cavalry may have cheered when finding they would face the Turks in Crimea or, early on, the residents of Hiroshima may have wished a more substantive role in Japan's war with America.

Monday's practice was savage mediocrity. There was lots of shouting, name calling, bravado and imitated pro-football antics, holding the ball on high after an imagined touchdown, patting each other on the rump after a particularly good assault on the hobgoblins of their imagination, who nearly always allowed the offense ten yards except when the ball carrier stumbled and fell down. They would play as they practiced, against imaginary opponents who vaporized in their attack. Tuesday was artful in its abstraction, a Stravinsky ballet for the blind, a dance, with a club foot.

The astonishing myopia of youth held them high through Tuesday's practice and walked with them on their retreat from the practice field. They mounted the path through the Scratch's orchard in brave triumph, each practicing his part in the hero's welcome that awaited him on his return from the Cutlery, on Wednesday afternoon, tomorrow.

Tuesday evening was heady and jittery for Arthur. He could not study; he could not pay attention to the figures in his books, and had no idea if he were doing maths or Latin. His breath came in short sips, he had a slight fever, and couldn't sleep for the uneasiness of vague anticipation.

Wednesday morning was cloudy; it had rained in the night, leaves had fallen on the sidewalk, they were slick and woody smelling. Breakfast was quiet and Arthur felt removed as if watching from a distance; classes were opaque like the day and each boy had, over the night of waiting, receded into himself in contemplation where nagging doubts lurked around the corner from hope's door. At Wednesday's lunch the headmaster stood behind his chair after grace. He paused, then announced that the fourth team was going to the Cutlery for a game; he wished them well and the school cheered. Arthur felt as if his lunch were not settled, he was sick and he was nervous.

The plan was to go to the Cutlery dressed to play, in uniform, on one of the school's buses. So, after lunch, Arthur's team gathered in the field house and changed into uniforms which no longer felt strange or looked unusual; they'd gotten used to their appearance and saw no one who looked much different. Arthur no longer thought his uniform bizarre. He changed and went to the bus and he and Scratch sat together without talking. Mr. Grand was not on the bus with them; he went early in his own car to make arrangements.

They drove for thirty minutes through the country and came to a village with a sign The Cutlery School. The sign included an arrow pointing to a two-lane wide paved highway between forty foot high stone pillars. This was the school's entrance and driveway. Arthur tasted vomit creeping up his throat; it was nearly to the back of his teeth. They went for a few hundred yards between manicured playing fields and approached stone buildings, some of them bigger than the whole Bridge School. They took a right turn and went down a slight incline to a parking lot which could have accommodated half the New York Giants' Sunday crowd. The only car in the lot was Mr. Grand's black VW. The cleats on their shoes made a light clickity-click background staccato as Arthur and his team descended the bus steps and walked across the blacktop in the direction of the field. Mr. Grand said they would play on the field next to the parking lot. It had bleachers, end zone uprights, and white paint on the grass marking the ten yard lines. It was a real football field, not the pasture they were used to practicing in.

They followed Mr. Grand to the side of the field without the stands. It had two benches on the sidelines. Mr. Grand told Arthur and team to "have a seat." When they were seated, he started his talk.

"All right gentlemen, this is not a game, this is going to be a scrimmage. All we want to do here is get a feel for what a game will be like when we finally play. We won't keep score; we'll switch possession every six plays. The idea is to try out our plays and try out our defense, see what works and what doesn't. The other team will be down in a minute so why don't you go out on the field and warm up."

"Tim, why don't you lead the team in some jumping jacks, then the line can get in formation and do some sprints while the backfield throws the ball around. Loosen up."

Tim got up from the bench; Arthur followed with the rest of the linemen. They lined up and on Mr. Grand's command sprinted about ten yards and then lined up again. The backfield formed a circle throwing the ball around. No one said a word. Arthur was lined up looking at the ground waiting for the next command. Nothing happened, everyone had frozen in place; the ball the backfield was throwing dropped to the ground and stayed there.

Arthur looked up and saw thirty boys trotting down the blacktop drive toward the parking lot. The noise of their cleats on the pavement was not the racket of random amble, it was the rhythm of disciplined cadence, shoes hitting blacktop in unison as if one huge pair of feet were clattering toward the field. Each of the opposition looked exactly the same. Their pants were brilliant white; they had never been worn before today. Their shirts were light blue, almost electric, clean and tucked under belts that worked. Their helmets were brand new Riddells, one design, light gray with numbers stenciled on the back that matched the numbers on their shirts, and they were painted with "clear coat" so they sparkled in the sun. Their shoes were polished and hit the pavement in unison, their shoulder pads made them look like pros. They came to the field chanting a theme, animal and guttural, it wasn't friendly "hello, how are you" song; it was a war chant.

Two coaches trotted at the side of the formation wearing gray, school monogrammed, sweatshirts and sweatpants. The team with coaches at its side came onto the field in formation and then they split into two squads, one offense, one defense, line and backfield with choreographed drills and warm up procedures. Their coaches, neither over thirty, trotted to Arthur's side of the field.

Mr. Grand was not impressed by the spectacle; he'd been here before. The two young coaches who took their clothes seriously crossed the field toward Mr. Grand who watched in amusement. They introduced themselves and shook hands. The coaches stood with Mr. Grand and talked for a few minutes; Arthur couldn't hear what they said, he was fixed on the team across the field. When they finished the younger coaches headed for their side of the field and Mr. Grand came back to Bridge's sideline. He called to the boys as much to break the trance as to get their attention. He called them to him.

"They certainly dress well don't they?" he said not looking at anyone in particular. "And they have a nice approach. It almost looks military."

He got the team a little closer by signaling with his hands that they should gather around for a little chat. "Don't let the clothes fool you, boys. They are new boys just like you; they aren't any bigger, they aren't any older and I doubt they're any better; they simply look good, if you are inclined to be impressed with clothes. Here's the plan. They'll take offense first. They will run six plays, then we will take the offense and we'll run six plays. We will start at the fifty yard line, right out there," pointing to the middle of the field for those who may have had a doubt since their practice field at Bridge had no yard markers; it had a few large rocks poking through the pasture and piles left by the cows who shared it with the boys, but no paint or end zone architecture.

He was interrupted by a huge cheer as the opposition broke into teams, one squad advancing to the fifty yard line. They had enough boys for separate offense and defense. Bridge had barely enough to field one squad which would go in both directions, offense and defense. Their offense stood on their side of the fifty yard line looking at Arthur and the Bridge team waiting for them to line up.

Mr. Grand pointed to the field and said, "All right, let's get out there and show them how this is done."

Arthur had lost any confidence he might have brought with him, and he and his fellow teammates tried to sneak onto the field in the hopes the Cutlery wouldn't notice their trespass. They lined up opposite the adversary and a referee dressed in black and white

Grettaically striped shirt, white pants, and shined black shoes came to the side of the formation and blew a whistle. The Cutlery boys went into a quick huddle and returned to the fifty yard line where they lined up again, took a three point stance, and their quarterback shouted numbers.

Arthur was confused; was he supposed to stand there or get down in a three point stance? He couldn't remember so he leaned forward in compromise and looked to the sidelines for Mr. Grand who was looking at a clipboard. The next thing he knew someone ran into him, knocked him into the air and onto the ground. When he opened his eyes he was lying on his back looking at the geometry made by the bottoms of passing gray clouds. He didn't know where he was. His breath was knocked out and he saw stars. He lay still for a minute; everything was quiet. He felt a little panicky about not being able to breathe, but pretty soon the referee came and stood over him. Arthur continued looking up; the sky was blotted out by a man in a striped shirt whose face was upside down.

The referee said, "Are you OK?"

Arthur couldn't breathe, so he didn't reply. He lay still.

The ref reached down and lifted Arthur by his belt so Arthur nearly folded in half backwards with his feet and head still on the ground and his middle held in the air by his belt. The belt broke and he slumped back flat on the ground with a small thump; he could breathe.

"Get the wind knocked out, did ya?" the ref asked.

Arthur remained flat then moved his head and looked around and remembered being hit. He rolled over onto his side, came to his knees, and then pushed himself to standing. He was dizzy.

The ref backed up and blew his whistle. "Second down."

Arthur walked to the huddle.

It was the wrong huddle; Arthur tried to join the other team; they seemed inhospitable.

Mr. Grand came onto the field and took Arthur's arm, turned him in the right direction, led him to the sidelines and sat him on the bench. "What happened out there? Didn't you see that boy coming? He nearly knocked you back to Bridge."

Arthur didn't respond; he could hardly hear Mr. Grand. He felt as if he were a third person watching from a familiar distance a conversation between Mr. Grand and a boy named Arthur.

Arthur sat on the bench for a while not thinking about the game but looking at the clouds and feeling a little better. After a while

Mr. Grand came back and asked if he was ready to play again. Arthur nodded. He trotted back onto the field.

Cutlery was on offense again; Arthur had missed Bridge's first offensive series. The ref blew the whistle; Cutlery went to a huddle, cheered, and came back to the line. They got down in three point stance and so did Arthur, this time watching out for anyone who might want to hit him. Cutlery's quarterback yelled some numbers and then the Cutlery line charged. Arthur was too quick for them. He sidestepped a boy who looked as if he was trying to knock Arthur down, and as the opposing lineman ran by Arthur, Arthur looked up to see a boy carrying the ball running straight at him. Arthur knew what to do; tackle him. Arthur stood tall, spread his arms, and waited for the boy to fall into them.

The boy with the ball had other ideas. He put his head down, ran faster, planted his gray Riddell helmet in Arthur's sternum and continued to run so that as Arthur fell backward the ball carrier ran right up Arthur's legs, then his abdomen, his chest and finally over his helmet and was gone. Arthur was on the ground again looking at the bottom of a different set of clouds. He rolled over, pushed himself up, and regarded the damage. The opposing ball carrier had run all the way to the goal line, not for the first time, and most of both teams were about forty yards downfield from where Arthur stood. Arthur looked at the ground and found that one of his shoes was still on, the other had escaped and was some distance away looking like it needed a shine. His pants were down around his knees. His shoulder pads had come out of his shirt and hung around his neck like a cheap tropical necklace of coconut husks tied with shoelace. His helmet had come off and lay a few yards downfield, he supposed the offending team had taken it with them in their charge. Arthur thought he understood why his uniform was dirty and theirs were clean.

When it was Bridge's turn to take the offense Arthur was supposed to block the opposing line so the Bridge ball carrier could advance down the path Arthur had cleared for him. On the first of these plays Arthur tried to block the opposing lineman, but instead of allowing Arthur to block him, he grabbed Arthur by the shirt and threw him aside. Rather than tackling the Bridge ball carrier, the Cutlery boy had pushed the Bridge halfback up straight, snatched the ball out of his hands and run to the opposing goal line.

It went on like this for nearly an hour and at the end Arthur had hardly any uniform left at all. His shoes refused to join the battle, escaping at any opportunity. His socks were uniformly black, caked in mud as they did most of the pushing. His pants, the belt broken and not enough of it left to tie, he held up with one hand till it was time to get knocked down, at which point he let go of the pants and covered his face with his hands because his helmet was not much good save for blocking his view. His shirt held up pretty well to the grabbing and wrestling from the opposing linemen.

When it was over the two teams cheered each other with complimentary shouts: "Hooray for Cutlery."…. "Hooray for Bridge." Then the boys lined up and walked past one another and shook hands. Sometime between the scrimmage and the hand shaking the Cutlery had managed to get their uniforms cleaned and pressed and their shoes shined. They trotted, heels clicking in unison, back to their locker room while the Bridge boys shambled and scuffed their way onto the bus, leaving clods of mud in their wake the only evidence they had been there that day.

The bus ride back to Bridge wasn't much fun and Arthur thought he understood why Mr. Grant had driven himself. Scratch looked to be in as bad a shape as Arthur, forlorn, downtrodden, filthy. Arthur recalled someone talking about a day which would live in infamy. He couldn't remember who that was but he doubted the author of the expression had a better handle on the idea than he did.

When they got back to Bridge, Arthur found the school had not burned down, the electricity had not gone out, the faculty had not been raped, no children murdered. Everything was normal.

For a short time Arthur was possessed by guilt from the great disgrace. It wasn't long before he was back in the swim of things mundane, the Cutlery becoming a bad memory easily dismissed with teammate post-game analysis which consisted mostly of , "If only I woulda…"

11

FROM WHOM NO SECRETS ARE HID

Football practice continued, and in a few weeks there were real games against teams that were nearly as bad or as good as Bridge. Arthur didn't get knocked down much more often than he knocked his opponent down. He learned how to tackle, having figured out from his experience at Cutlery that contact with the ball carrier was only the first of several problems: how to avoid being run over, how to wrestle the opponent to the ground, how not to let the opponent get under his center of gravity, these things he took into consideration from experience. He learned them for himself, as Mr. Grand had no idea, never having worn a football jersey nor taken a coaching class.

He repaired his pants and asked Pa for a new helmet which Pa, after hearing from Mr. Grand about Arthur's troubles at the Cutlery, handed him with a great smile and an encouragement, "Go get 'em, Arturo. I hear you're making great strides for the team." It wasn't a new helmet but it was better; he could see out from under it and its paint and padding helped shield the lumps on his ego cultivated by Mr. Grand and his scrimmage. The football season progressed; Arthur and the team realized they could make five yards simply by having the running back run behind Arthur's blocking. They used this strategy for third downs and were able to make a touchdown on most possessions. They won the games remaining in the second half of the season, but if asked, they would not have wanted to get back in the box with the Cutlery again.

Arthur's jobs and table assignments changed and so he escaped Steve Black who had taught him to dance with a broom and to polish a sink. He got the drift of the chapel and had nearly memorized the common prayers of evening service but was not yet able to swim comfortably in Sunday communion. He liked the language and rhythms, which were to him more substantial both in the weight of their message and the beauty of their song than the mumblings of radio announcers. Each line an idea worth the time of considering, each verse a song of notes and rhythm.

> Almighty God,
> unto whom all hearts are open,
> all desires known,
> and from whom no secrets are hid;

Arthur was more comfortable with the routine and more confident in his abilities and his social horizon widened. In the beginning he followed Dan as much as he could. They were good friends. But because their athletic, academic, and social skills were different, Dan was not always available. Arthur and Scratch had similar football experience so they became close by sharing the first months' humiliations at Mr. Grand's supervision. Scratch always did his homework, always tried to do more than was asked, and was competitive in class as if he owned first chair. He defended his position and sometimes became angry or pouted when another boy answered a question before Scratch or got a higher mark on a test or got an approval from a master for a job well done. Scratch wanted all these firsts and thought he deserved them and fought for them. And Scratch dressed like Arthur. His clothes were nondescript, they were cover rather than adornment; he hunched inside them and closed them around him in a defensive posture so that they were tools and necessities but they were never decoration.

While they were sitting at a table in the dorm one evening, Scratch asked why Arthur had not done his homework; why he'd gotten mad at Mr. Grand for the quiz. "How come you didn't know any of the answers."

"I didn't do the assignment."

"Why not?"

"I don't know. I never did it at home so I didn't do it here."

"Why did you get so mad after the quiz?"

"I wasn't mad."

"Yeah, you were. You got all red in the face and slid down in your seat and wouldn't look up."

"I was surprised. I didn't know there was going to be a test on the second day of class."

"How come you didn't' have to do homework at your old school?"

"Nobody did."

"How did you study?"

"Everybody just picked up what they could in class, if they wanted, and if they didn't, they didn't; nobody cared."

"What about your parents; didn't they care?"

"I don't know; we never talked about it."

"Didn't you have final exams?"

"No. The year ended and that was it."

"You know, if you don't do your work here they'll ask you to leave or won't invite you back."

"What do you mean, won't invite you back?"

"They won't invite you to come back. In the summer they send out letters, some of the letters say what your classes will be, what the schedule for vacations is, that kind of stuff. Other letters go to the parents, one page, saying that you're not invited back to the school in the coming year and the parents should make other plans. They don't say why; they just say goodbye."

"How do you know about the letters?"

"My father went here. He stays in touch with the school; he was on the board of trustees for while. He isn't anymore."

"Do you care if you're not invited back?" Arthur asked.

"Sure," Scratch responded as if surprised by the question.

"Why?" Arthur wanted to know.

"Are you kidding? Cause it's where I want to be. I didn't like junior high with all the crap and stupidity."

"What about Mr. Grand, don't you think he's a bunch of crap and stupid."

"Yeah. But that's not all the school."

"Do you like it here?" asked Arthur.

"No."

Arthur surprised. "Then why do you want to be here?"

"My dad went here. We talk about it all the time. He said I might not like it in the beginning, but it would change after a while and to give it a chance."

"What does your dad do?" Arthur asked, interested in Scratch's opinion.

"He teaches French at Yale," Scratch said, seeming to drift to some other place as if the questions inspired a memory.

"Is that where you live?"

"Yeah, we don't live right at the school but fairly close. My father's been talking about Bridge since I can remember. When he was on the board of trustees he brought me with him to meetings and football games. The boys were always nice to me and I liked going to the games and watching the older boys and having my father explain everything to me."

"Why do you sit in the front row in class?" Arthur asked.

"Cause I like to. That's where I thought I'd be when I thought about coming here. My dad told me to try to be the best in the class, do my homework, and if I didn't understand anything to ask questions till I was sure I understood. I like the front." Scratch changed the subject, "You know sometimes if a boy is doing badly in class or has a discipline problem the head master will call the parents and tell them not to bring the kid back after vacation. My dad said boys just disappear. They're in the dorm before you go home for Christmas and you come back and there's an empty space where the kid's bed was. It scares me when I think about going home and then my father getting a phone call that I'm not invited back, that the school will pack my stuff and mail it home in a trunk."

Arthur didn't respond.

Scratch continued, "My dad says there's a couple of ways you can get kicked out. One is to get mad at or threaten a master. That's the easiest way. The headmaster calls your parents and asks them to pick you up that day, and that's it. The second way is to violate the honor code, you know lie or cheat. That's pretty quick too. Smoking and drinking are serious. Those will get you out right away. Bad grades or bad attitude and they wait till vacation and tell you then."

Scratch asked Arthur, "Do you like it here?"

Arthur thought about it. "I don't know."

"What do you mean you don't know?"

"I like some of the boys, Dan and Tim, and some of the masters, Pa and Mr. Smith and Mr. Wattsmore, but I don't like Mr. Grand and I don't like Steve Smith. I don't like jobs but I like chapel. I don't know. I think I'd rather be home." Arthur thought in the background of the question, he really didn't know if he liked it or not. It wasn't as if it was one whole thing, but different parts glued together by time, it was different people in different places who he visited throughout the day, some he liked, some he didn't. And the grass was greener at home.

"What's the honor code?" Arthur asked.

"Didn't you read about it in the little red book they sent home this summer?"

"No, I don't think we got one. What is it?"

"It's a set of rules, what you can't do. Mostly it's about telling the truth and not cheating. If they catch you cheating or lying, they ask you to leave, I don't know how much ask there is in it; probably it's more like tell you to leave. Back when my father was here, every once in a while at morning assembly when the headmaster usually gave his talk, he would stand and remain quiet for a while, like he was thinking seriously about something. Then he'd say: 'I would like to see Slim Jim in my office after assembly.' And he'd walk out and go to his office without another word. After assembly everyone in the school would watch as Slim Jim walked down the hill to the administration building, and he'd go in the green door to the headmaster's office, and that would be it. Jim wouldn't show up at class or at lunch or sports and at the end of the day his bed was gone, his clothes were gone, his athletic gear gone and no one ever saw him again.

"My dad told the story of a boy he knew when he was here. This boy and some other boys had gone into town and into someone's house in town and taken some liquor. They thought the house was empty, but just as they were leaving the family who owned the house came up the driveway in their car and saw the three boys leaving and recognized one of them. The boys didn't know they had been seen.

"The guy who owned the house called the headmaster and told him what happened. Then the headmaster asked around the school, who was where, who had gone into town and he found out who the three boys were. So on the following Monday morning he stood in assembly and asked one of the boys, the one who had been recognized, to come to his office. When the boy was in the office, the head asked the boy if he had gone to town and gone into anyone's house. The boy said no, and that was it. His parents came and picked him up that morning.

"The next morning the headmaster did the same thing; he stood for a minute, then asked the second boy to come to his office. He asked the second boy if he had gone to town and taken anything from a house. The boy said no, and he was gone. On the third day the headmaster stood and asked for the third boy to come to his office. Everyone in assembly looked for the third boy but he wasn't there, and he didn't appear in class or at lunch or at the headmasters office so everyone thought he had left on his own early that morning because he had been at the school the night before. Sometime in the morning the head called the parents and told them the boy had run away and why, so they should come get his stuff.

"No one thought much more about it until that evening when several masters asked the boys in the missing kid's class when they saw him last, did he say where he was going, did they know his plans. No one knew anything.

"The next morning was strange; the headmaster didn't give his talk or show up at assembly. One of my dad's classmates recognized the missing boy's parents in the courtyard talking to the headmaster. They went with the headmaster to his office and stayed there for an hour as different masters came and went, then the parents left. A rumor started around the school that the missing boy had run away because he had not gone home or called his parents. They came to the school that morning to get his stuff, to see what he had taken and what he had left. That afternoon and evening things returned to normal except there was some talk and guessing about where the missing boy had gone, maybe to the City (New York) or to their summer place in Wonalancet, New Hampshire, he had a girlfriend up there. By lights out, school had returned to normal.

"The next day started normal. The headmaster talked, classes classed, jobs jobbed, lunch and athletics. My dad was at practice on the lower field when one of the sixth formers came running to the coach there. The sixth former nearly knocked the coach down, then they both, the sixth former and the coach, one of the masters, ran off the field toward the school. My dad and the others on the team continued what they were doing. The master didn't return, so when it was time to quit, the team went to their locker room in the field house, changed and went upstairs for evening assembly. It was then they heard.

"The boy who had come running across the field to the coach had hurt his ankle earlier in the year, so he couldn't play football for a few weeks. Instead of practicing, he was responsible for taking care of the field maintenance equipment which was kept in a shed between two of the practice fields. When he went in the shed to get something he found the missing boy hanging by his necktie from the beam in the shed. He had been there since the night he went missing."

"Are you kidding?"

"No. That's the story. I heard it from my dad; no one here talks about it much I guess."

"Jesus. I can't believe it. Was he dead?"

"Sure he was, he'd been hanging there for two days," Said Scratch.

"What did they do, I mean the school, what happened?" asked Arthur.

"I don't know. That's all I can remember."

Scratch started picking at his arm. Arthur sat in amazement, it didn't seem possible, how could that happen.

"Why don't you do your homework?" Scratch asked again as if he forgot Arthur's first answer.

"I don't know. I don't like Mr. Grand, I don't like his quizzes I don't like him telling me what to do."

"All he does is try to piss you off, you know. It's obvious he doesn't like you because of the way you acted that first day of the quiz and how you said 'bullshit' after he ran us through his little torture routine at football." They were sitting at a dorm picnic table, no one else was in the dorm on a Sunday afternoon, there was nothing to do and nowhere they had to be.

"It was bullshit," Arthur said, trying to justify what he knew was the dumbness of his reaction to the quiz and to the reverse guillotine or whatever Mr. Grand had called it.

"Why don't we try something different; it's what I did last year with my older sister, she's in college but she lives at home. I wasn't doing very well in school and my dad said I couldn't come to Bridge this year if I didn't get better grades. So she said she would help if I did my work. Every night before I went to bed she checked my homework. I had to write down my assignments in a little calendar book kind of thing, I still use one here. Each day was divided into seven periods and each period was either a class or a study hall. First, I had to write down the assignment on the block in the calendar, then, I'd have to complete and check it off before my sister looked at it. She'd first go through the assignments in the calendar, then look at the work I did to check it against the book. Mostly, it was doing questions at the end of chapters or reading something. She read it too and then asked questions or looked at the answers I wrote in my notebook. It worked great."

"How are we going to do that?" asked Arthur, not sure what Scratch was getting at since neither of his sisters was around to check homework.

"I can take a look at your homework and see if it's what I got. We're in the same classes."

"Is that cheating?" asked Arthur, more to put Scratch off than worried about cheating.

"It's not cheating; homework's not a test. I don't think so."

Arthur didn't like the idea, he didn't want someone looking at his work, one more person telling him what was wrong.

Scratch went to his bureau and came back with a spiral bound notebook. He handed it to Arthur. "This is what I use. It helps a lot."

Arthur took it, the cover said something about a weekly planner. He opened it; it had five columns … Monday to Friday written across the top of the columns; each column was divided into seven boxes. There were no times or dates on the columns or boxes so it could be used for any week. "Is this for me?" he asked.

"Yeah."

"Thanks." Arthur put it aside.

12

THE SIGN OF THE CROSS

Arthur's dorm had both second and third form boys. Third formers avoided second formers because of age and status. The higher the form the more exalted. Since second was the lowest form, it commanded little that made it attractive to older boys and as a result, if the second formers were quiet and stayed out of everyone else's way, they could disappear into the woodwork and do pretty much whatever they wanted. They were below the school radar.

Arthur had no interest in the third form in general; there was plenty to keep him occupied in second. However, he had made friends with a few of the third form boys who reminded him of his friends in Grape. They were not the most highly thought of boys in their class and formed a small subculture that intrigued Arthur because of its trademark attitude. They were skeptical of sixth form authority and of the faculty. They didn't like the school and made it clear privately in making fun of the headmaster and the other masters. They swore a lot; everything was "fucked up" or they were "pissed off". This guy was a "dick head" and that guy an "asshole". They talked about being with girls and "making-out" and about first and second base and who had "scored." In public they made their views clear by chronic tardiness, or slouching disinterest in chapel, or being the last in line or failing to volunteer at all. They had to be explicitly instructed. Arthur didn't share classes with these boys but he saw them in the dorm and at meals and chapel and they let him hang around their sessions of disgust and bad attitude. Although Arthur didn't feel the same way toward the school that they did, he was intrigued by their apparent independence, their revolutionary attitude.

At the core of the group were Mike Cordovan and Doug Strawford. They were shadowy; they were on the periphery of everything, attached only well enough to criticize. They didn't play football because of injuries, didn't sing in chapel because of Constitutional Guarantees, didn't get to class on time because of sensitive stomachs, they were the most frequent visitors to the infirmary and the last to take seats on the chapel. They did things that Arthur sometimes felt like doing because of frustration with Mr. Grand or Steve Smith but things Arthur stopped short of doing because they were at odds with Arthur's feelings for the school and his friends. His had mixed feelings but sometimes it was fun to hang around with this group who called themselves "The Holy Five." They had given themselves a name because they thought they were important; no one cared. They gave themselves a name for their solidarity in the face of school persecution. The school did not notice them. They pouted that they were not more highly regarded and they disliked any authority they found more powerful than their own which was impotent.

Arthur spent time with them on the weekends listening to their boastful recollection of driving cars or sexual fantasies offered as history. One of the boys in the group was from Germany. He wasn't German, he was American but he lived in Germany because his father worked for a US bank in Hamburg. One Sunday afternoon the group plus Arthur was in the dorm sitting at a picnic table when the German fellow, Charlie, said he knew how to give tattoos. There was the expected, obligatory, "Oh bullshit" and "No you don't." Charlie stuck to his story.

Charlie was blond and round and soft. He had the ability to blend into the crowd so if he robbed a bank no one would be able to describe him afterwards. He smiled enough to disarm without charming, he spoke enough to be unnoticed in the chatter, but nothing he said was memorable, he was neither tall nor short. He was usually observing and taking mental notes, assessing what was going on around him without getting involved. He hung out on the periphery of the Holy Five, neither member nor spy.

Someone said, "Let's see you do it."

Charlie looked at Arthur, "You want a tattoo?"

Arthur didn't want a tattoo but he didn't say anything.

Mike spoke up, "Go ahead, Arthur, let him try on you."

Doug chimed in, "You're not a little chicken shit like the other second formers are you?"

Arthur was uncomfortable. He didn't think it was friendly, what they were doing, pushing him into something he didn't want but he was in doubt; they were older, exciting, tough, maybe he should try it. Arthur said, "OK."

"Good man, Arturo, neat."

Charlie went to his bureau and came back with a sewing needle, thread and a ballpoint pen.

"What should we give him?" Charlie asked.

"How about a roman numeral five," said Mike. "That'll make him an honorary member of the Holy Five."

"Great."

"Yeah."

Charlie told Arthur to take off his shirt, which Arthur did. Charlie came around to Arthur's right shoulder and with the ballpoint pen drew a Roman numeral five on Arthur's right shoulder. It was about an inch and a half high. Then he broke the ball point pen in half and put it on a piece of paper on the table next to Arthur. Next he took the needle and thread and wrapped the thread around the needle about twenty times, real tight, about one quarter of an inch from the tip.

"What's the thread for?" asked Mike.

"It makes it so the needle doesn't go too far in. When you push the needle against the skin there is initial resistance on the top layer of skin which you have to push against, then once you're past that, then it goes in real easy, so without the thread the needle would go in too far, about an inch or more before you could stop it. The thread keeps it from going too far." Charlie made sure the thread was tight around the needle.

Arthur began to sweat.

Charlie looked at the needle to make sure it was set up right. Then he dunked the tip of the needle and the thread wrapping in the ink which had spilled out of the broken pen on the table. He wiped a little of the ink off on the paper and moved so he was standing over Arthur's right shoulder looking at the number on Arthur's skin. With his left hand he pinched the skin where the number was, then he put the needle against where he had drawn and pushed it into Arthur. It hurt just like poking a needle in does. Arthur winced but Charlie had him by the skin so his jumping didn't pull the needle out. Charlie pulled the needle out but didn't let go of the skin. He dipped the needle in the ink and wiped, this time there was too much ink and blood on the needle. He asked someone to get him a Kleenex. He put the needle up against Arthur's skin again and pushed and it went in. Arthur felt the initial resistance Charlie had talked about.

After the second puncture Charlie wiped the skin around his art work with a Kleenex, it was bloody when he put it down and then dunked the needle and wiped it and pushed for the third time. Charlie did about fifty or sixty pokes. Arthur's shoulder ached and it still hurt each time Charlie poked. Finally Charlie said he was finished. Arthur looked at it. It looked like a fifty cent piece that had been puffed up, dipped in black ink, then left to ooze blood. It didn't look like a Roman numeral five or a tattoo; it looked like a huge swollen sore. Something like the thing that was on Mr. Buehl's face back in Grape.

OK, Arturo, there it is," said Charlie.

They other boys looked but didn't say much that Arthur could remember.

Charlie started in again, "Remember you can't wash it for two days or the ink will come out. Let it scab-over good and leave the scab on for at least seven days. When it comes off you'll have a great tattoo."

The other boys went away, embarrassed. Arthur put his shirt on and went to his place in the dorm. He didn't have a Bandaid but found some adhesive tape. He put a piece of Kleenex on the sore and then taped it in place. His shoulder felt as if it had been punched real hard right down to the bone.

The next morning when he got up his shoulder ached and was hot. The Kleenex had soaked through so his sheets were marked with blood and yellow ooze. He went to class and jobs and lunch then football. When he was changing for football Scratch asked him what was on his shoulder. He told Scratch he'd tell him later and went to the field by himself; he would normally have walked with Scratch or Dan. During practice he made sure not to irritate or touch the sore, but it was there and he felt it the whole time. On the way back Scratch and Arthur passed Mike.

Mike looked at Arthur and said, "How's it goin', Arturo?" then he slapped Arthur on the shoulder on the sore.

Arthur nearly fainted, it felt like Mike had stabbed him. Mike thought it was funny.

In the shower the sore was running with clear stuff and bleeding where Mike had opened it up.

Scratch said, "What is it, how'd you get that?"

Arthur told him the story of Charlie and the tattoo.

"Why'd you do that?" Scratch asked. "Don't hang around with those guys; they'll get you in trouble."

That night after "lights out" Arthur couldn't go to sleep, his shoulder hurt too much. About eleven o'clock he didn't know what to do so he went to Rod's room, knocked on the door and told him he felt sick and wanted to go to the infirmary. Rod asked what the problem was. Arthur said he had cut himself on a nail sticking out from the wall in the locker room and he thought it had gotten infected. Rod took a look and walked Arthur to the infirmary where they woke the nurse.

The infirmary was one of the nicer buildings on campus. It was built of fieldstone and white wood trim with a slate roof, more central Pennsylvania architecture than New England. It had two floors; the clinic was on the first floor and a few hospital like rooms, the nurse lived on the second in one wing and in the other there were a few more rooms.

Rod and Arthur went in the door and Rod rang a little push-button hotel-clerk type bell on a desk in the entry to the clinic. The nurse appeared at the door in PJ's and robe, her hair was tied in some kind of wrap over curlers. She asked, Arthur lied, she let them in, turned on the light, the only place in the school with more than two twenty watt bulbs so it was bright as sun. She told Arthur to take off his pajama top, which he did and she peeled the adhesive tape and Kleenex off.

"Ouch," she squeaked. "You're right; it's infected. Rod, you go on back to the dorm. Arthur's going to spend the night here; I have to clean it and the doctor will want to look at it in the morning."

Rod said "good night" and added that he would check on Arthur in the morning.

The nurse, Miss Gray was not particularly nice looking. She was about forty-five, small and thin. Her skin was blotchy pink and red, she had thin red hair you could see her scalp through and little yellowish teeth, all of them about the same size, lined up with too much space in between so you could get real good look at the fronts and the backs and the sides at the same time. Some of the boys made fun of her. Arthur didn't know her, and he was surprised she knew his name when he came in.

She was nice to him.

"Arthur, I'm going to have to scrub the ink out of this thing with soap water and a small brush. Then I'm going to clean it with alcohol, put antiseptic and a bandage on it. It's going to hurt. I'm sorry but it has to be done or you are going to be in serious trouble, maybe have to go to the hospital with blood poisoning. I ought to make you do it yourself since you made the sore yourself."

She told Arthur to sit on an examining table. She set pans of soap and water and purple-brown iodine looking liquid on the table along with long wooden sticks, cotton, and a syringe.

"I'll try not to hurt you, and you can try to sit still while I work. If you have to, tell me and we'll take a little break. If you feel faint then tell me, I don't want you falling off the table. Better yet, come here and lie down on the table on your left side with your right shoulder up so I can get at it."

Arthur got on the table and lay down as he was told. The table had a cold clean white sheet on it, no pillow so he supported his head with his arm. The place smelled like the hospital at home; it smelled of clean sheets, alcohol, and iodine. Miss Gray didn't have a smell.

First she sprayed water on the sore with a squeeze bottle. The water ran down his arm onto the sheet. She wiped it up, then got a little brush like a nail brush from one of the stainless steel dishes and scrubbed in a circle around the sore. This was a ruse; as she knew and Arthur didn't, she was going to eventually have to scrub the wound itself. She started on the periphery to see how close she could come without Arthur pulling back. She didn't get very far into the heart of the matter before Arthur protested.

"Eye-yi-yi ," Arthur screeched as he pulled away from the brush involuntarily.

"Does it hurt?"

"Yeah, a lot."

"OK, I know, but try to hold still. I have to do this; the longer it takes the more it will hurt."

She started again and got a little closer before Arthur pulled away. He cried, not because he wanted to, it simply overcame him. They tried again and Arthur got sick to his stomach; he thought he was going to vomit. He told her and she stopped for a minute and asked if he wanted a sip of water. He took a sip; she offered it to take his mind off the pain for a second or two and it did. And again they went after the sore, Arthur pulling back involuntarily and Miss Gray chasing him around on the table as his shoulder moved out from under the scrub brush.

She finished with the brush, then squirted more water and mopped up the mess with cotton swabs on forceps. Next came the purple stuff which didn't hurt that much and the bandage that looked way too big for the wound.

"How are you doing? Still sick?"

"No, not now," his voice stuck high and thin in his throat.

"You just lie there for a minute while I put things away." She busied around and put things in a sink and in cabinets.

"Can you go to the bathroom or do you want to lie there for a few more minutes?"

"I can get up," Arthur pushed himself to sitting; he felt lightheaded. He slid off the table and held onto the side with his left hand for a second while he checked his feet to make sure they cooperated. He didn't know if his right hand worked anymore; it was lost in the hurt in his arm. He thought maybe his school experience revolved around being knocked down and beat up and hurting and pushing himself back up again.

He stood still for a minute drenched in shock.

Miss Gray came to him and took his left arm; he didn't resist so she led him to a room with three empty hospital beds. She told him to get undressed and to put on a little nightshirt which was laid on the foot of the closest bed. She watched as he pushed off his shoes, then his socks, and then let his pants down left handed which he found harder than he would have imagined. He looked up.

"Under pants too, everything off,'" she said watching as a mother would. He didn't care. He took off his underpants and slid the nightshirt over his head one handed; it didn't come down over his shoulders so she helped him into it. He got in the bed as crisp and bright as white wrapping paper, lay down, and she went back to the clinic. She returned a minute later with a glass and some pills in a little paper cup that was about big enough for a good spit. He took the pills, the water was warm. He lay on his back, put his head on a too-fat pillow; she turned out the light and said "Good night, I'll see you in the morning. If you need something ring the bell on the desk."

"Good night." He didn't feel like saying thanks right then, but after she had gone upstairs to her apartment he thought that he should have said, "Thank you."

The next morning he woke up when he heard Miss Gray bustling around in the clinic. The sun was up, the doors and windows were open, so his room was bright white. He went to the bathroom and then Miss Gray came in.

"Sleep OK?" she said, checking his water glass on the table. "There's a toothbrush, toothpaste, towel, and washcloth in the bathroom. The doctor will be here about nine so I'll get you some breakfast from the kitchen in a minute." She wore her white, starched nurse outfit which was not so attractive as commanding with the little hat that looked like folded plastic with black band and a nurse pin on it. She came to the bed and asked Arthur to turn on his side so she could take a look at the bandage. She lifted the sleeve of his PJ and looked, left the room and came back with a new bandage and cleaning tools. Arthur didn't think he could take another round under the brush but she didn't brush, just took off the old bandage and put on a new one and then she left.

The doctor came. He took a look and said Arthur had to come to the infirmary twice a day to have the bandage changed, no football and no showers for at least a week. After he left, Miss Gray told Arthur he could get dressed and go to class.

When Arthur was dressed and ready to leave, she sat behind the desk in the clinic. "Arthur, did you do this tattoo yourself or did someone do it for you?"

Arthur didn't know what to do. He didn't want to squeal on Charlie so he said he did it himself. Miss Gray didn't look convinced; she nodded and told him to report to the clinic after class.

Arthur went to class; he tried to slip into Mr. Grand's Latin unnoticed but failed. Mr. Grand stopped what he was doing and waited till Arthur had taken his seat. Arthur thought maybe Mr. Grand would make a comment about Arthur being late but he didn't; he looked curiously, satisfied himself that it was Arthur who had joined them, and continued. After class Scratch waited for Arthur in the hall.

"What happened to you?"

"You know that sore on my arm?"

"Yeah."

"It got infected so I went to the infirmary and Miss Gray kept me over night."

"Mike Cordovan told Dan it wasn't a sore but a tattoo. He said Charlie gave you a tattoo on Sunday. Did you get a tattoo?"

"Yeah, I guess it's a tattoo. More like a big sore. It really hurt last night."

"Charlie's worried you told the prefects or the nurse he gave it to you."

"I didn't tell; I said I did it myself."

"Why'd you get a tattoo?"

"I guess I thought it would be neat. Charlie said he could do it and the other guys in the Holy Five liked the idea."

"Why didn't they get a tattoo, why you?"

"I don't know."

"That's pretty stupid. You hang around with those guys and you'll get in trouble more than a stupid tattoo."

Dan was in the hall with them. "It's no secret. Rod told me about it; he knows who gave it to you and how it happened. The headmaster is pissed at you and the guys in the Holy Five, what a bunch of jerks. Why do you hang around with them?"

"I don't know," Arthur said getting defensive, "Sometimes they seem kind of neat, like they're giving the school the bird."

"Well, they'll get you and them on a bird right out of this place. The prefects and the Head are pissed." Dan was pissed and walked away. Arthur didn't understand Dan's attitude, what was the difference to Dan?

After their meeting in the hall, Dan was obviously cool toward Arthur for several days until Arthur asked him what was wrong. Dan said the whole thing was stupid. He didn't like the guys in the Holy Five; they just made the school harder than it already was, they didn't join the school, they fought it because they thought they were tough or neat or whatever. Mostly he didn't like the whole thing, the Holy Five, the tattoo or Arthur's getting mixed up in it. It was stupid and bad for the school. Either Arthur played by the rules or Dan didn't have time for him. Dan turned and left.

Dan's attitude stung. Arthur was defensive; he knew the whole thing was stupid but he thought Dan would stick with him on his course through the silliness rather than being judgmental. Dan's reaction encouraged another bout of confusion like the one in Latin after he turned in his blank sheet of paper. He felt bushwhacked, hit from behind, betrayed; he thought he was secure in Dan's friendship. Arthur had failed in Dan's eyes and the recognition hurt in a blind kind of way that on the periphery encouraged a stupid reaction. Arthur blamed Dan for the bad feelings rather than admitting to himself he was wrong.

Scratch on the other hand appeared to take a more understanding view. He didn't like what had happened or Arthur's hanging around with the Holy Five, but he didn't let it terminate his friendship with Arthur. They were still close and palled around together.

A week later the scab on his shoulder came off and he had a light blue tattoo which looked like a crippled spider with no relation to a Roman numeral five. Two days later he had forgotten the tattoo, his trip to the infirmary and the trouble it had caused.

Dan maintained his distance. Arthur felt the separation but was reluctant to try to mend.

About two weeks later, on Saturday evening after dinner, Doug Cordovan came to Arthur's place in the dorm and asked Arthur if he wanted to go to Doug's aunt's for lunch on Sunday after chapel. School policy allowed the boys to leave on Sunday afternoon with family if they were back by Sunday assembly. Boys who lived a good distance from the school were often invited to join families of students whose parents lived closer and came to take them out for Sunday lunch. Arthur hadn't been off school property except for football games since he arrived in September so he said he'd like to go.

Sunday after chapel Doug came to Arthur's place to tell him to meet Mike Strawford in the central courtyard at eleven where his aunt would pick them up. Arthur didn't know Mike was going with them and he didn't want to go if Mike were there. He remembered what Dan and Scratch had said about the Holy Five being bad news and trouble for Arthur, and the tattoo incident was good evidence. He went anyway.

Doug's aunt picked them up at eleven. Arthur rode in the backseat with Mike. Mike didn't have much to say to Arthur so it was a quiet ride with Arthur listening to Doug and his aunt. They got to the aunt's house, sat around with her in her living room for a while and listened to old stories; then they ate lunch. Arthur felt on the outside of the proceedings, witness to a dull afternoon.

After lunch Doug suggested that Mike and Arthur take a walk with him. They went behind the house to a barn which they entered. When they were inside, Mike pulled a pack of cigarettes from his pants, took one out, popped it his mouth as if it were the most natural thing in the world. He passed the pack to Doug who took one and passed it to Arthur. Arthur's conundrum, take one or pass. Arthur's background told him to take one but his instincts remained ambivalent; his gut told him to pass. He could not make the connection between what Dan and Scratch had said and the here and now. He operated on two planes; on one plane there were the warnings and desire to follow the rules Dan was so adamant about. The other plane was a self-destructive impulse to tempt fate, to do the risky thing. He took one. He had smoked before, if puffing on a burning rope counted. He tried to inhale once when he was in Tiny's car, but couldn't get it down without coughing.

Mike brought out a lighter, stroked it casually as he might have seen it done in the movies and lit his; then he passed the lighter to Doug who stroked and offered the flame to Arthur. Arthur puffed the cigarette, it caught, then Doug lit his. The cigarette tasted like burning garbage, paper bags and old celery. He puffed, watched and waited. Mike and Doug inhaled then exhaled slowly letting the smoke linger around their faces and acted as if they did it every day.

It wasn't long before guilt replaced the bad taste of the cigarettes. He was overcome by a feeling of rage. He'd been bushwhacked again. This time a glimmer of connection glowed in the background. He didn't blame Mike and Doug for his smoking. He was enraged with himself for following a path to the emptiness of betrayal. The connection wasn't strong or a bright light; it was a glimmer of the relationship between cause and effect. Mike and Doug got a sense that Arthur didn't like what was going on. He put his cigarette out and didn't say much for the rest of the afternoon which crawled along like a taxi ride with two divorced people who are forced by circumstance to use the same taxi.

He got back to school and went to his place in the dorm and then in confusion to the library where he sat undisturbed. His feelings were in turmoil, neither rational nor connected. One instant he was overcome with fear at being found out, the next he hated himself for stupidity, then the hate was pushed out by rage at the failure and then the "*what if's*" found their way to the buffet of discontent. No thought was allowed to rest unmolested by its usurper for more than a moment; no progress was made save a slide into an abyss of emptiness.

After dinner he tried to do his homework but found no focus, turmoil dominated his recline. He went to bed but did not sleep; the recurring emotions took him on a merry-go-round of changing attitudes, changing venue from victim to betrayer to idiot to coward and back again in no order and no end.

13

FALSE WITNESS

The next morning Arthur was alone. He got up with his friends, went to breakfast and jobs, but he felt as if he had cut an important cord between him and them. It was bitter aftertaste, betrayal; it was new and confusing and he was ashamed. It was no longer rage or hate; it was emptiness where there had been warmth, void where there had been purpose, bitterness where there had been comrades. He had no experience with the depth of the darkness he had brought to this place.

At assembly he was seized by fear; he imagined that the headmaster, rather than giving his morning homily, was going to stand quiet for a moment and then, in disappointment, ask to see Arthur May in his office. As he waited for the prefects to complete their morning business, he stared at the headmaster trying to read his expression which was grave. It was always grave and gave guilt no holiday. Finally the headmaster came around the front desk, stood quiet for a moment, and started his homily.

"As you no doubt recall, we have been talking about choice and preparing for choice. We have talked about the things that make us strong and the things which dog our tracks, the things which reinforce us and the things which invite us to wander away from what is right. Recall that all of us, from time to time, will be faced with choices which are not easy, choices to which there seems no easy answer, no right answer. As an example we talked about the decision to fire bomb Tokyo and Dresden during World War Two.

"I am not going to try today to criticize the decisions which were taken then. That task is too complex for this assembly. What I want to do is to make the point that the people who were faced with that decision were no different from you and me save their preparation for the event. Each of them came to that point with differing experience and variable conviction about the rightness of their conclusion. Each of them had seen faith, knowledge and principle

107

from different perspective. Were they prepared? I don't know. I cannot see into their hearts; I cannot see what they will take to their graves. They do, and that is what counts.

"Will you be prepared to make the right choices? We are here in this school not to teach you Latin or math or history. We are here to help build strength in you and your ability to make the right decisions. Math, history and Latin will help you because they will give you better tools than you would have without. But they, those tools, must be applied with faith and with principle.

"The principles are old and come to us from five thousand years ago without improvement. As I said earlier, six of the Ten Commandments concern how we will treat our neighbor, which is and will remain the greatest of our choices, greatest both in complexity and its reward to us and our society. Those six commandments are admonitions, one for and five against. Honor your father and your mother. Do not murder, do not steal, do not bear false witness, do not covet, do not commit adultery. These are the principles upon which we operate, and they were later summarized by Christ in his commandment to 'Love thy neighbor as thy self.'

"These are the principles which form the basis of our understanding of this greatest of choices, and these are the principles which govern our behavior here at school. If you can accept these principles as they are stated, then you have an easier road than those who take issue with them. But you are by their acceptance no surer of success. You will be tempted at every turn and at every opportunity for gain of money or power or gratification to rationalize these principles in order to achieve something which at the time appears to be better than what you have. You will be tempted by the opportunity for advantage. You will be tempted to appear to be who you are not. And, you will see the new appearance as an improvement, until you achieve it. And these temptations will encourage a watering down of the principles.

"Later, I will talk a bit on those things that encourage us to water down our principles. Those things our friend Dr. Heiddeger, the highly educated and religious German philosopher, found while he swam in a river of relativism, the dilution of principle that led to his drowning in absolute water when he accepted appointment as Hitler's court philosopher.

"Today I want to close on a topic that we will come to us now and again for the remainder of your experience at the school. That topic is truth. Each of the principles we have introduced ultimately rests on our appreciation of its underlying truth. Is it true that we should not commit murder? Or is the better question, am I true to this principle?"

"So, to bring it full circle for today, the most important choices you make will be your answer to the continuing question: 'How will you treat your neighbor?' And the most important issue in the choice is truth. Are the operating principles true in your view, and more importantly, are you true to them?"

With that question left hanging as an introduction to his next talk, he stopped, took a peak at his watch, glanced out the window as if none of the boys were there, and left in great long stiff legged strides while and the audience waited to jump from seat or desk or chair to the hallways and to class.

Arthur was a wreck. He had dodged today's bullet; he did not have to report to the headmaster's study to confess his sin. But he was dogged by the nagging thought that he would have to go through at least a hundred more mornings waiting to see if he had been discovered, waiting to see if he would make the final trip down the hill to his dismissal. He was like a man with cancer who goes to his doctor every week to see if the cancer has spread or if it had spared him. On leaving the doctors office he is ecstatic at his good news, but as the week passes and his next visit comes more clearly into view, his reprieve leaks the helium necessary to keep it aloft, fear replaces joy, and hope is lost to anxiety. For he knows at some time, on one of his visits, he is fated to get the word that the cancer has spread and he is doomed.

On the second day of waiting the headmaster rose from his chair, walked around the desk at the front of the assembly, looked out the window, and started.

"As you know, yesterday, we talked a little about truth. We will deal with truth until you graduate and you will deal with it after you are gone from this place and forever after. It is as inescapable as the air around us and harder to conceive. Many people of greater minds, with brighter intellects, more honorable and more dishonorable than we are here have taken their turn at this topic. For now, let us assume that we all share the scent, that we each of has some common understanding of the essence of truth. Let us accept that for now.

"With that assumption let me ask you to take a few minutes to think about what the principles of your life are today as you sit here. I want each of you to think of seven rules by which you want to live and by which you want others to live. The ideal rules or principles upon which you would found the perfect society."

He turned to the head prefect, said something, then returned to focus on the students. "I have asked Stu, the head prefect, to pass out three by five cards, one to each of you. I want you to write on the cards the seven principles you would ask for in a perfect society. You need only to write on the front side and you need only one line per rule. I will pick up the cards after this assembly, and tomorrow I will tell you where we came out, what the consensus was."

He turned and went back to his seat. Stu, Rod and Jim, the other prefects, handed cards to the front row of desks and around the benches on the side. The front row took one and passed the deck back so in a short time everyone had one. There was some low mumbling about borrowing pencils or pens or not enough cards. The head master took his card and sat in thought. He looked up and said. "There is no hurry; we won't do anything more important today, so take your time."

One of the new boys raised his hand, "Should we put our names on the cards?"

"No. That's not necessary"

Someone else asked if he could go to the bathroom, feet scraped the floor, the school settled to the task.

Arthur was again relieved that his smoking had not been discovered. He had become so paranoid he thought the headmaster's request might be a trick, the head might be able to figure out who had smoked from the principles listed on a card. He thought about one rule, no smoking, then another, no drinking, others no lying, no hurting, no killing. He was relieved names weren't necessary. He couldn't think of any more, then he thought about stealing, that was good, no stealing. He gave up and was more interested in when it was going to be over than in the principles. They sat until Arthur wondered if they were waiting for him to make an admission, maybe they were waiting for Arthur to stand voluntarily and admit he had smoked, maybe they were waiting for him to run out of the assembly in disgrace, heading for town and a bus to Oklahoma. A Stalinesque show trial? Maybe every one knew and he didn't know they knew. What should he do? He looked around imagining the worst, then worse than that.

The headmaster and the prefects sat at the front in thought, taking their time. Some boys were long past finished and had got the jitters, they were looking around, putting their heads in their hands, picking at the things that had grown since their last pick, or which hadn't been picked enough, or things that didn't need picking at all. They looked out the windows hoping for revelation or release.

After forty minutes the headmaster stood and put his card on the front desk and then walked out, down the center aisle as if he were leaving an empty room. Stu stood and asked the other two prefects to collect the cards at the back or the room as the boys left for class. Rod and Jim went to the hall, then the rest of the boys filed out handing their cards to one of the prefects on their way out.

When Arthur and team got to their first class, which was nearly over because they were late, Mr. Smith wanted to know what happened, why they were late. Tom and Scratch both blurted out an adequate interpretation of events. Mr. Smith looked puzzled by their account, he was disoriented by the activity and its interruption of the schedule. The rest of the day was normal.

The following morning after the prefects' business the headmaster took his place in front of the desk. His routine was unremarkable. "Yesterday we filled out some cards, the rules by which we would live and by which we would ask others to live. I have taken a look at those cards, each of them, and I appreciate the thoughtfulness of your response.

"After reviewing them twice, I tried to get the general ideas which were present. While the rules were not the same, there were, as you might imagine, similarities, threads, themes. The most common themes were those forbidding: murder, stealing, lying, cheating, injuring another, they dealt with harming another person, they dealt with how you treat your neighbor. Less common were those which prescribe an action: love your neighbor, love your parents, and love god. Someone was kind enough to write on his card that we should write to our parents at least once a week. Not a bad idea."

The assembly laughed.

"There were some other interesting ideas, which I may get to later, such as 'no smoking.'" No laughter.

Arthur felt as if he had been electrocuted. That was his suggestion, how stupid, why bring that up? What did the headmaster mean, "He would get to it later." Was he going to ask about smoking; did he know about Arthur, Mike, and Doug? He knew everything, that had been weeks ago. Arthur hoped it would just go away and the fear of being called out had receded with each day the headmaster didn't ask, the anxiety decreasing each day knowing he only had to make it to Thanksgiving vacation to be out of jeopardy. Arthur had heard from someone, maybe Scratch, that the headmaster only asked about infractions committed in the current semester; he didn't, as a rule, ask about previous periods in his quest for wrongdoers. Now here it was, on the table again, right out front.

The headmaster started again, "Interesting how the important rules govern relationships."

"You may think everyone shares you opinion on these rules. We, those of us here in this room came up with seven, the most popular were those I just mentioned. Moses went to the mountain and returned with about the same prescription as we, only he did it five thousand years ago. You might ask yourself why these haven't changed. Christ in his Sermon on the Mount gave us two: Love God and Love your Neighbor, which in a broad sense cover all of those we have talked about except maybe for smoking. He laid out his rules two thousand years ago.

"Why do you suppose those rules haven't changed? May I suggest they have not changed because we are not very good at following them. If we were, there would be no war, no famine; no prison, no hate, and maybe less need for the rules. We may all sit here and collectively and individually agree that these are the rules we will follow and these are the rules we expect others in this room will follow. And right here and right now we mean it. But when we leave this room other factors enter the equation, greed, lust, envy, hate, fear, and they have the power to move us away from the rules we agree to. They have the power through rationalization or emotional disequilibrium to hide or distort the rules.

"What are these things: greed, lust, fear, hate, envy, where do they come from, and why do they have power over us?

"I will get to those at another time. For now, let us agree that we have collectively identified seven rules: Love your neighbor, love God, do not murder, do not steal, do not lie, do not cheat and do not hurt anyone. Let us agree that these are worthy goals, worthy principles. I do not ask everyone in the room to swear allegiance to these principles. Swearing allegiance has never worked in the past and I have no reason to believe it would this time. Instead, what I ask you to do is think about this proposition: The most important choices you will make in your lives will be how you treat your neighbor. Add to this the idea that we have identified principles which should help guide us in making those choices. And importantly, we have identified influences which act at odds with our principles. If you can accept this proposition, then we can travel the next few months and years in an investigation of the problems before us. Why don't we live by the principles we adopt, and what can we do to get better at it?"

And again he took long strides exiting the room and taking the seriousness of the event with him. And again Arthur was relieved at not having been singled out to go to the headmaster's study. But not totally relieved. Mr. Webster had said he would get to the interesting suggestion about smoking later. What did that mean?

Football season ended abruptly. On Friday they had practice, Saturday they had a game and the following Monday they went back to the field house and undid what Pa had done eleven weeks earlier. They turned in their uniforms, putting each piece of equipment in a pile and when they left the field house there was a vacuum. They had nothing to do in the afternoon, nowhere they had to be.

Arthur was, in a small way, lost. He had not anticipated what he would do nor what it would feel like to have the afternoons between class and evening assembly free, so he went to the dorm with some of the other second formers and they sat at the tables chattering about nothing. He noticed Dan wasn't in the group. When he thought about it, Dan hardly ever joined the group; he had spent most of his free time in the library. He wasn't unfriendly, he wasn't unpleasant, he was aloof in a strange way. He never said anything in class and he never talked about his grades or quizzes or exams. Arthur thought Dan was distant given the strength of their beginning and Scratch had the same impression.

Arthur, Jon, Scratch, and Tim sat at one of the tables in the dorm and talked about Thanksgiving vacation which was two weeks away. They would get out of school on Wednesday morning and return the following Monday evening. Arthur planned to go to his aunt's house in Boston; he would take the train from school to New York, then get a train in New York for Boston. He had been to Boston before but he couldn't remember it; he was too young. Scratch's parents were coming to school to pick him up and Tim lived pretty close so he could walk if he had to.

On the Monday morning before Thanksgiving at the morning assembly the prefects went about their daily routine and the headmaster took his spot in front of his desk. He stood for a moment before talking, then he stood for a few more moments and Arthur had a sinking feeling. This was not going to be a normal talk about choice; this was going to be a request to see Arthur in his study. Arthur broke out in a sweat. He had dreaded this for weeks, each morning waiting for the question and each morning he got a reprieve. Sweat ran from his armpits down the sides of his chest. He stopped breathing and waited, his fingers were numb.

"We have a problem," the headmaster began, "Twelve new crew jerseys, racing shirts, were taken from Mr. Grand's apartment last night. I want the boy or boys who took them to come to my office this morning with the jerseys."

He left the room. The assembly was quiet until the prefects and sixth form had left, then there was general mumble of voices. Boys looked around and waited to see if they could tell who was going to Mr. Webster's office. No one left. The first class bell rang and everyone headed to the classrooms and no one left the building headed down the hill to the headmaster's study.

Classes were normal. Nothing happened.

After lunch and after grace Mr. Webster stood at his place and said, "No one has come to my office to return the jerseys. I would like to see the boys responsible for taking the jerseys in my office after lunch." He left for the faculty lounge.

Everyone looked around waiting to see who would leave. No one did.

That afternoon after class Arthur, Tim and Scratch sat around the table in the dorm.

Scratch said, "This is serious. No one owned up to taking the jerseys."

Tim wondered aloud, "What do you think he'll do?"

"Who?" Arthur said.

"Mr. Webster," said Tim.

Arthur responded, "What do you mean, 'What will he do?' Either someone admits it or they don't. What can he do?"

"Who do you think took them?" asked Tim.

Scratch entered the conversation, "I don't know, but whoever it is won't be here after Thanksgiving. He might have had a chance if he admitted it right away as a prank on Mr. Grand or something, but now it's gone too far. Mr. Webster is pissed. Did you see him at lunch?"

Arthur had seen Mr. Webster at lunch, but he didn't look any crankier than he usually did and Arthur had become an expert at detecting any change in his expression. The conversation about the shirts continued with speculation about who and their punishment with no resolution but an increase in the anxiety level which normally increased just before vacation without a school crisis.

Tuesday morning at assembly the headmaster stood and without preamble stated, "Gentlemen we have a serious problem. Someone took the jerseys from Mr. Grand's apartment. That is a difficulty we can manage. However, we have a larger problem which we can not manage until it is resolved. The persons responsible for taking the jerseys will not accept their responsibility. That we must fix. I ask the boy or boys who took the jerseys to stand up, here, now."

No one stood.

"We will sit here until someone takes responsibility."

Arthur was confused again. He felt guilty. He didn't take the jerseys, he didn't know who took them, but he felt guilty. He had a faint urge to stand up and take responsibility just to take the pressure off his head. He didn't look around at anyone, he looked straight ahead at the headmaster who stood for a minute, then sat behind the desk. He didn't look him in the eye just in his direction; in the eye would have been a confrontation beyond Arthur's strength.

No one stood. The assembly was silent. The headmaster looked straight ahead out the door; he did not try to read expressions or body language as Mr. Smith had on the first day of class. He waited for someone to stand.

No one stood.

Arthur looked down at his desk at his hands which became numb when he was frightened. On the face of it he didn't see what the big deal was, someone took some stuff, so what. On a gut level he sensed this was bigger than taking shirts; it had escalated into an emotional crisis for the school body, someone in the community had betrayed the place and therefore there was a threat to the school's health. It felt as if it was a personal threat to Arthur's health. He was directly personally involved, thinking about taking responsibility for something he hadn't done just to get the problem behind them. His motivation to take the blame wasn't strong enough to propel him into a crazy admission but it was strong enough to make him think about it.

Each of the boys sat in his closed cocoon. No one talked, the folks on benches looked at their feet, the boys at desks looked at their hands on the desks, the headmaster looked past the boys out the door. They sat for three hours.

Mr. Webster stood and said the boys could have a ten minute break, everyone back in ten minutes. The boys rose silently and went to the bathrooms or walked out the front doors to stand in fresh air. No one talked, little whispers but no conversation. The boys were back in their seats before the ten minutes was up.

Mr. Webster stood again at noon and said they should go to lunch and return to the study hall by 12:45. The noise in the dining room was subdued, conspiratorial, confused, scared. Again everyone was back in study hall before 12:45, sitting, waiting. Mr. Webster entered, took his seat and waited.

At 4 o'clock Mr. Webster rose and said, "We will take a break for chapel and dinner; after dinner we will return here until someone stands up and takes responsibility for this."

They went to chapel and dinner and returned to the study hall. At nine o'clock Mr. Webster rose again, "Gentlemen, we will sit here until someone takes responsibility. If we have to, we will sit through Thanksgiving and the weekend and the rest of the school year but we will close this chapter with dignity."

There was an audible intake of breath. What did this mean? No vacation? Impossible; yet no one in the room doubted Mr. Webster. He said, "We will adjourn for the evening and meet again here after breakfast. Tomorrow morning if no one has taken responsibility for this, the other masters and I will call your parents and tell them vacation is cancelled."

He left the room. The prefects left and there was subdued mayhem. No one understood how he could cancel vacation. It wasn't his to cancel! "This isn't a prison camp." "He's barking up a bigger tree than he thinks if he thinks my parents won't just drive up here and take me home." "He can't do that, can he?" "My whole family has plans for vacation."

And from older boys who had seen Mr. Webster in previous occasions: "Yes, he can." "Just watch, he'll say anyone who wants to leave go ahead and don't bother coming back." "This is serious stuff, he'll do it." "He's tougher than you think."

Arthur didn't know what to think, he was confused as usual, he didn't understand the issues and had never thought through the pros and cons of collective punishment. There were no phones in the school for the students so there was no way to call home to explain or ask for help. He probably wouldn't have called home anyway. This, like many things before, surprised him; he didn't understand but he was getting used to not understanding and being surprised if that was possible. He was more aware now of the size and complexity of the life of the school, the different personalities, different responsibilities, and his small role in the place. His horizon was now large enough to see that he was not the only person in it. Although he saw other people in it, he wasn't sure how to treat them.

When he got to the dorm Scratch and Tim were there before him and they were upset. They were afraid they wouldn't be able to go home for vacation. Dan was distant; he didn't share his thoughts but he wasn't smiling.

Scratch said to himself like a man trying to build his confidence in a sinking boat, "They can't do that; just cancel vacation over some shirts. My dad will come up and straighten it out. I'll walk home, this isn't reform school, we don't have to stay here. Wouldn't it be like kidnapping if he kept us here?"

Arthur went to bed and went to sleep immediately. He slept to escape the confusion. He slept because his own difficulties, worrying about being caught for smoking, wore him out. The next morning everyone went to breakfast and jobs and assembly waiting for news. When they got to assembly the sixth form and prefects were missing. There was no news. The headmaster sat quiet, patient, collected, resolved. Arthur sat confused. Where was this going, why the big deal? He spent only a few moments thinking about who had stolen the shirts because he couldn't imagine, maybe Mike or Doug, he didn't know many of the boys. He didn't care. He wasn't as anxious to go to his aunt's for vacation as he was to see the school back to normal.

Usually on the morning vacation started, the headmaster released the school from morning assembly. The younger boys would run out of the study hall and head for cars parked in the drive or run to the train station in town; their bags would have been taken from the central courtyard during breakfast. The train station was a little one-track job with a platform and wood building and a little gray man who sold tickets and answered questions. The train stopped twice a day and hardly anyone used it during the regular week but on vacation day it was busy. There were about five boarding schools on the line and each school had a car with its name posted in the window. All the schools had the same vacation schedule so there were five extra cars of loud boys on their way home after fall term.

That was the normal vacation day. This day was the Wednesday before Thanksgiving, and the Bridge boys were not on the train. They sat in assembly in the schoolhouse waiting for news that no one seemed capable of producing. Parents had been called early in the morning and told not to come to school to pick up their sons, or not to expect them on the train. The sitting continued after lunch and no one moved much. Some boys put their heads on their desks in defeat and no one was happy.

About two in the afternoon the head prefect came into assembly and approached the headmaster. They whispered for a moment then the headmaster left. About ten minutes later he returned.

"Gentlemen. We have found the shirts. Those responsible for taking them will be dealt with. The masters will call your parents this afternoon to make plans to pick you up and you will be told who and how. Go to your rooms or dorm and pack. You are free to leave when a parent arrives or we have made transportation arrangements." He left.

117

The mood in the room was turned upside down. Boys jumped up and down slamming desktops, yelling, celebrating. They were on vacation.

As usual Arthur was confused. He didn't know where he was supposed to go since he had already missed his train for Boston and wasn't sure if there was another. He didn't know if anyone had gotten in touch with his aunt or father so he went to the dorm and packed enough clothes for the weekend. Scratch packed and ran out as if his father were already there. Tim packed and knew his family would be there soon. Dan sat on his bed, the dorm cleared, and   Arthur sat across from Dan.

Dan asked Arthur, "What are you going to do?".

"I don't know, wait till they tell me where to go.   I was supposed to go to my aunt's in Boston but I missed the train. Maybe there's another."

"My mom isn't going to like this. She doesn't always get along with Mr. Webster, and she isn't afraid of him either. If she planned to drive up this morning, then they cancelled and now changed again, she's probably going to stop in his office when she gets here for a little chat, and he'll get a taste of what its like to go to the headmaster's study, from the other side of the desk." Dan was throwing things in his suitcase. He usually did things, like packing, carefully; normally he was fastidious about his clothes but his temper had obviously got the better of him.

Rod came through the dorm toward Dan. He stopped to chat with a few of the other stranded boys, then got to Dan. "Your mother's on her way; she'll be here about three. She wants to meet you in the main courtyard."

"OK. Thanks, Rod. When are you leaving?"

"The prefects aren't leaving till everyone is taken care of. A lot of plans got changed and now its tough getting things put back together again. The masters are using their home phones to call parents; there aren't enough phones in the office. It'll be a while."

"What about Arthur?" asked Dan.

"Arthur?" Rod looked at Arthur. "I don't know what the plan is. I'll go down to the administration building and check; when I have news I'll come back up and tell you. Don't worry; we'll get something going here in a little while so stick around the dorm till you hear from me." Rod turned to leave.

"OK. I'll be here," said Arthur.

Dan put more stuff in his suitcase, he put his shoes and hockey skates in his laundry bag and put it and a hockey stick on his bed next to his suitcase. He sat on his bed across from Arthur, and asked "Why do you hang around with those guys, Mike and Doug?"

"I don't know; I don't like them much."

"They're trouble, you know. They probably won't come back after Christmas vacation. One of the sixth formers saw them smoking down by the football shack. Mr. Webster hasn't talked to them yet and was probably going to ask them to come to his office yesterday morning but this shirt thing came up. I think they know they've been caught. They've been lying low for the past couple of weeks. Did they make you get that tattoo?"

"No, they didn't make me; I was sitting with them and Charlie and they thought it would be funny, kinda fun, and they sort of talked me into it."

"If they thought it was so fun why didn't they get one; why'd they pick on you?"

"Cause I was there?"

"No. Because you are younger and smaller and they thought they could talk you into it. They won't get one cause it hurts too much for them to do it. But they're real tough with little kids. They know you want to be liked so they took advantage of you. Can't you see that."

"I guess I can now."

"Well, think about it," Dan said in a dismissive attitude. He got up from his bed and picked up his stick and bags ready to go to the courtyard although it was still too early to meet his mother.

"Are you mad at me?" asked Arthur.

Dan looked at Arthur from the foot of his bed. "If you hang around with those assholes, I don't have time for you. You'll end up in trouble and maybe I will too."

"I am in trouble," said Arthur.

"What kind of trouble?"

"I went with Mike and Doug to Doug's aunt's house for lunch about two weeks ago on Sunday. They went to her barn and smoked. They asked me if I wanted to so I said OK, and I took some puffs." Arthur related the rest of the story.

Dan stood listening, still angry with Arthur. "Arthur, you're screwed. I'm sorry you told me. Now if you're asked you have to tell the truth because I know. And if you tell the truth, you're out. So you're screwed." He stood for a minute, "Was it worth it? Good friends are they? They tattoo you and get you kicked out. You know, I liked you in the beginning when Mr. Grand and Steve Smith were picking on you and you took it. But when you started hanging around with Mike and Doug, I didn't like it because I could see they would get you mixed up in their stuff, get you in trouble, then you'd have to act like them because you'd be afraid of being kicked out so you'd have to act like you didn't like it here anyway, you'd have to act like you wanted to be kicked out, like you were above the school to be cool. Now look."

"I'm sorry. I don't like Mike or Doug; I like the school and I like you and Scratch and Tim. Those guys reminded me of some of the guys I used to know in Grape, they were funny sometimes, and cool. I didn't think they'd get me in trouble but I guess they helped."

"If Mr. Webster asks, are you going to stand up in assembly?"

"Yes. I've already thought about it. I'm going to stand up. I've been scared to death in assembly every morning thinking about being asked. I keep thinking maybe he'll forget till next term and then I'll be out of trouble."

"Next term isn't till Christmas vacation, so you have a few more weeks to look forward to and he's going to ask because most of the school knows about Mike and Doug, so he has to ask." Dan put his bags on the floor and fiddled with his hockey stick.

"Should I just go to Mr. Webster now and tell him? I don't want to stand up with those other guys."

"I think you're screwed. I don't know. I'll ask my brother when I get home." Dan picked up his stuff and walked out of the dorm.

Arthur sat on his bed waiting for Rod to come back with some news about where he was supposed to go. He was empty again. He simply swam in the deep water, not in any direction, more like treading water, letting events take him to the next stop. He didn't know how to look forward to the next logical step. Numbness swallowed him as it had at each of his misadventures. He was mad and upset that things had worked out this way, mad that Dan had been so abrupt. That was Dan.

It seemed to Arthur he went from tranquility and anonymity to fear and rage in cycles; things would be going fine, then he'd do something and the whole scene would change. One minute he's having lunch, the next he's smoking a cigarette with guys he didn't like, and then he's hiding out, bobbing and weaving, ducking, scared of the inevitable rejection. He'd gone through the woulda-coulda routine so many times the path was worn and led back to the same position, Arthur sitting somewhere in despair. Woulda, coulda were no release, and they were so well rehearsed by then they were no longer temporary diversion.

He was mostly disappointed in himself. Why didn't he make the right decision before he turned right or left? Why did he have to figure it out in failure, always looking backwards at the wrong turn? Despair, emptiness, loneliness, some dark soup he put on the fire, a mighty lean diet.

"Hey, Arthur?" Dan came through the dorm toward him, "Come on; let's go. You're coming home with us for Thanksgiving. My mother just called your aunt everything is set up. Get your stuff, my mom's in the courtyard waiting for us."

14

MIRACLES

Dan's voice jerked Arthur from his reverie and pushed him into a new situation. Circumstance again determined the path; the future was a cloud he could not see into. Going to the Clements would be like going to a foreign country, a new language. They were different from his family; they were different from anyone he knew in Grape. Mrs. Clement was statuesque, accomplished, confident; Arthur's mother was not. Dan was athletic, tall, certain, decisive; Arthur was not. Should he say he couldn't go, that he was sick and had better stay at school? Should he call his aunt and ask her to pick him up? His face got hot, red; he was embarrassed, he was inferior. He looked ahead and saw another situation where circumstance waited, like the boys from Cutlery, to knock him down.

"Get your bag and laundry. My mom will do our laundry for us while we're home."

Arthur got off his bed in a fog. Events were in control; all he could do was tread water and see where the flow took him. He grabbed his suitcase while Dan reached under his bed to find his laundry bag. Dan turned to leave and Arthur followed out of the dorm, down the hill, to the courtyard where Dan led the way to a black Buick station wagon. The car was new and shiny clean with THE GABLES, GOOSE ISLAND in small gold letters printed just below the passenger side window. Mrs. Clement stood beside it waiting.

"Hi, Arthur," she said with a big smile. "Aren't we lucky you'll be able to come home with us this weekend."

"Hi, Mrs. Clement."

"I talked to your aunt in Boston. She said it was fine with her if you came with us. If you waited for another train you wouldn't get to Boston until early tomorrow morning, so we agreed it would better if you came to Greenwich." She approached Arthur with her hand out to shake his. She wore a camel hair colored cashmere sweater under a houndstooth tweed jacket, pearls over the sweater, gray wool slacks perfectly pressed and shiny black leather shoes with low heels. Her hair looked as if she had just combed it; maybe she had. Arthur would have liked to see her comb her hair.

A black man about fifty years old in a black jacket, white shirt, black bow tie, and a black chauffeur's hat got out of the driver's door, went to Dan and took the laundry bag, then he approached Arthur and took Arthur's suitcase which he placed in the back of the car.

"Arthur, say hello to George; he's our driver."

"Hello, Arthur," said George looking Arthur in the eye with a small smile of recognition.

"Hi," said Arthur.

"Is that it; do you have everything?" Mrs. Clement asked.

Dan was anxious to get on the road, "Yeah, that's it; let's get out of here."

Mrs. Clement sat up front with George. Arthur got in behind George, who put the car in gear, and they headed down the school drive toward town. They drove through town and turned south on Route Seven. Mrs. Clement talked to Dan about who was going to be home for vacation, what parties were planned, who, where, when. Arthur listened. They talked about his brother, Tom, who was already home from Yale, which was closer than Bridge. He wondered what effect this would have on him, would he go to the parties with Dan or stay at the Clements'. Mrs. Clement had the vacation pretty well planned and she and Dan talked as if Arthur and George weren't there, which was fine with Arthur. He rode along, listening to the names of people he didn't know. He looked out the window at bare cornfields with stubble and tire tracks carved in the mud disappearing under the rain; the sky was low and gray, the road was wet and the inside of the car was hot and damp. He wondered if he was inside himself or outside watching things happen, watching the road unravel in front of them, watching Dan and Mrs. Clement as if he were a spy and they couldn't see him. The car headed south to Greenwich with all of them on board, all of them in the same car and each on a different path, to a different place; the paths meeting now and again, bumping into one another, wrapping around getting involved, then separating and bouncing off circumstance, and then separating altogether. Arthur's path bounced along touching the Clements' briefly, then they veered off in a direction he could not follow, and he went his own way, the path leading him without protest.

Dan turned to Arthur. "Did you hear that?"

"What?"

"Tell Arthur, mom; he won't believe it."

Mrs. Clement turned in her seat so she faced George; she could see Arthur and he could see her face.

"It seems the shirts weren't stolen. A friend of my son, Tom, a prefect, Stu, who I think you know, called this afternoon and told me they found the shirts in a cook's bedroom. While Mr. Webster was holding the inquisition, the sixth form searched all the rooms in the school, every bureau, every closet, everywhere they thought the shirts might be. The last place they thought to look when they couldn't find anything in the students' rooms was to search the rest of the school which included the cooks' rooms. And there they were, under one of the cooks' bureaus. When they asked him about it, he admitted it. He said he was angry with some of the students because a few boys stole his cigarettes and beer. It turns out he sold it to them and they were supposed to pay him for it, but they didn't."

"How about that?" said Dan.

"When the school called early this morning to say vacation had been delayed until a problem with the students had been cleared up, I wanted to know what was going on. But Mr. Smith, he's the master who called, the fellow with chalk everywhere, couldn't tell me; he simply said the headmaster had delayed the vacation and might cancel it altogether. I called Mr. Webster right away, but he wasn't available, so I called his wife and she told me what was going on. I told her I was on my way, and here we are."

She said the last "and here we are" in a playful way, with a smile as she raised her hands in a questioning motion. She was happy with herself

"I like Mr. Webster. I think he does a great job with the school or I wouldn't have sent Tom or Dan. But I think he gets carried away. He's a big fish in a very small pond and he looses perspective. Some of the things he does are not in proportion to the reality of the outside world, and I think this is one of them" as she turned to the front.

Arthur looked at Dan, "I bet I know who took the cigarettes and beer."

"Did you know about it?" asked Dan

"No. I didn't know, but it makes sense. I wonder if they'll be back after Thanksgiving?"

"This shirt thing might help you out. With them gone, Mr. Webster might not be so interested in asking who's been doing what this semester and with the shirts not really a problem then he might back off from making another scene."

A RICOCHET FROM CIRCUMSTANCE

Mrs. Clement heard their conversation and said, "Yes, I imagine this is going to have a little backfire effect. I don't think I'm the only parent whose Thanksgiving plans have been upset over a false alarm."

George drove. Arthur thought about how much of this George heard, how much he thought about it, what his reaction was, did he have kids, were they in school? He didn't appear to have any reaction.

They made some turns and after an hour or so they were in Greenwich going through the middle of the town. They went through a shopping area that looked like an adGrettaisement for a Vermont Country Town overdosed on too much cash. There were policemen standing in the middle of each intersection directing traffic and lots of folks crossing the street paying the police no attention. Lots of kids in tow and towheaded. It was crowded with money.

George drove down the main street, made a right turn, then a left out of the business district, passed under a railroad bridge and glided about three hundred yards further to a little shack in the middle of the street where he slowed down. A gray haired man with a fat, glittery, gold colored, too big badge that nearly pulled the left pocket off his white shirt sat in the shack looking at the car. George waved at him and the guy smiled; George must have known him. There was a speed bump in the road, Arthur guessed it was there to make sure folks drove slow enough so the old guy in the shack could wave at his friends.

Around some more turns with the houses in the neighborhood going from big, to real big, to enormous, so you couldn't see the whole thing without turning your head or backing up maybe a quarter of a mile. They continued downhill and the street became a lane without houses through some trees and then the trees opened up on a hay field and beyond that a big lake or the ocean, Arthur couldn't see the other side but it was getting dark and misty so it was difficult to make out things in the distance. They passed through the hay field and then onto a causeway to an island that had a fortress on it. The fort was made of brick and stone and was five stories tall if you counted the boathouse at the base. There were patios and turrets and windows and wings and curves and roofs over roofs and more chimneys than Brooklyn. They drove over a bridge, between stone pillars into a courtyard; they were on the island and inside the fort.

The courtyard was stone. The paving was stone and the walls which surrounded it were stone on four sides except for the gate which was wide enough for a big truck. The gate was black iron and it was anchored to stone pillars which sat at the ends of the wings of the fort. Both ends of the gate were swung back, open, parallel and alongside the wings. There were a lot of different sized windows set deep in the walls, the windows looked black from the outside except those where lights had been on inside and those were yellow. Arthur got the impression he was in the pit of a stone quarry.

In addition to a lot of windows, there were two double paneled, arched, blonde wood doors with black iron hardware; one on either side of the courtyard facing each other and ninety degrees to the gate. The doors were set about four feet into the front walls so there was an arched brick entry in front of each. George brought the car around in a left hand circle and stopped in front of the second door, which was open above three stone steps that made a small patio in front of the entrance. Two large trees lived in pots on either side of the entry; these weren't little shrubs like you might see in front of a florist shop in Grape, things that might be rolled in at night and thrown away when the weather got cold in the fall. These were trees a child would be proud to climb or trees that could be felled in front of the entry to discourage a mob.

When the car stopped, a little, round, brown woman who must have been sixty years old and who wore a black dress with white apron rolled out and toddled toward the car. She moved as if she were on wheels. You couldn't see her legs move inside her skirt or her feet under it, all you saw was a little round dress with a head perched on top move toward the car. Dan was out before the car stopped; he met the woman and they hugged.

She said in an accent different from Grape's. "Dannyale, you're back. I worried you wouldn't come back. Your mother said they might not let you come home." Arthur only knew one accent and it was Grape.

"Hi Carmen, I'm here. Did'ya miss me?" Dan said holding her at arms length, looking down with a laugh on his face.

"Yes. I miss you, gone too long." she said pushing his hands down and looking at him in a scold. "Why do you make fun?"

He laughed and then holding his hands out wide still looking at her, "Because it's funny. I've only been gone a few months and I am back. So, here I am."

Arthur got out of the car. Maybe this wasn't a fort. Could this be their house? It was bigger than the courthouse in Grape. There must be a hundred windows facing in on the courtyard and it was big enough to play a reasonable full court basketball game with room for seats and cheerleaders.

"I am glad you are back." Carmen turned to Mrs. Clement "Mrs. Clement, it went OK?"

"Yes, Carmen, they aren't running a prison up there in the woods, even though they have a jailer." Mrs. Clement made the introductions. "Carmen, this is Dan's friend from school, Arthur; he's staying for the weekend."

"Hello, Arthur; we are glad you could escape with Dannyale," Carmen said looking straight at Arthur with what seemed to Arthur a commanding presence. While she was small, less than five feet tall, she was not small in more important ways. Arthur got the feeling she was an important member of the family from the deference paid to her by Dan and his mother.

Carmen turned toward the front door and went up the steps through the entry into the building; Mrs. Clement followed with Dan at her side. Arthur waited. He didn't know what to do about his bags of dirty clothes, too-short pants and gray laundry; he turned to get them but George revved up the car and went out the gate. So Arthur, at some delay, followed Dan inside.

The ground floor of the house was another courtyard. The entry hall went to the center of the building. There were living rooms, music rooms and a library on either side of this and the hall which was about twenty feet wide and twenty feet high ended at an indoor garden with no more ceiling than a glass roof five floors above. The house was built around a central shaft, a five-floor greenhouse. Greenhouse may not have been the right word but that's what it looked like to Arthur. Each floor had a walkway that circled the column of greenhouse. The garden at the center looked like no one would be allowed in. It had a fountain on the facing wall and terraces of blooming flowers and a small marble path from the entrance across a little strip of green grass to the fountain. Arthur was clear he wasn't supposed to go in there. He'd be afraid he'd have dog poop on his shoes and leave it on the marble steps or create great black divots in the little grass around where the marble steps had been planted. He wondered if the flowers were real.

Arthur followed the voices; they went left around the garden. The hall floors were covered with large tiles, maybe eighteen-inch by eighteen-inch, dark red, not quite brown. Arthur took the left turn, went around the garden and beyond it through another door and into a living room sixty feet long by forty feet wide, lit yellow by candle light and shaded lamps. One wall was nearly covered by windows, black in the night looking out onto the void of what tomorrow would become Long Island Sound in the light. On the wall opposite the windows there was a fireplace big enough to camp in. Carl would have appreciated this fireplace, and Arthur could have pitched a tent in it. It must have taken two men to carry the logs they were burning. He caught up with Dan and Mrs. Clement.

The house made Arthur tired. There was too much. It reminded him of a time when his grandmother had asked him to go to the Woolworth's in Grape to get her some knitting needles. He was in second grade. He'd walked ten blocks to get there and by the time he arrived he'd almost forgotten his mission, but, while heading for the knitting needle department he walked by a glass case filled with bins of candy. Bins of licorice and lemon drops and chocolate kisses rolled in aluminum foil and M&M's. He'd almost forgotten why he was there when he went in the door, but he entirely forgot when he got to the M&M's. He asked the girl behind the counter how much they cost and she said forty-five cents a pound. He had fifty cents so he asked her for a pound of them. She scooped them into a metal dish on a scale behind the counter. She squinted at the needle on top of the scale as it swung back and forth in a little pie-shaped glass house in front of a card with lines printed with weights and amounts of money at each weight depending on the per pound cost. The numbers were too small for Arthur to see since he could barely see over the counter and into the glass bins. He didn't really care about the scale, his imagination was working up an excitement about the M&M's.

She shook a few more M&M's out of her scoop into the dish and squinted and shook till she figured she had about the right amount of candy in there or you were tired of watching her, whichever occurred first. She picked up the little tray and the needle bounced around for a second, then shot to zero and rested there waiting for the next kid who was stealing his grandmother's knitting needle money. She took a white paper bag from a stack, shook it open with a flick of her wrist, which Arthur later found was a harder trick than it looked, and poured the M&M's into it. She rolled the top over; she's done the whole job in about five seconds.

As she handed the bag to Arthur, she said, "That's forty-seven cents if you eat them in the store, forty-five if you take them out."

Arthur didn't understand the different prices or the Oklahoma tax code either; there were a lot of people in Oklahoma in that predicament. All he cared about was the M&M's. He gave her the fifty-cent piece his grandmother had given him. She pushed down on some keys on a cash register and it responded with a ring, a chunk, and some numbers jumped up in a window on the top.

She handed him a nickel. He went out of the store and walked home. About halfway there he finished the candy; the last few handfuls didn't taste as good as the first and by the bottom of the bag he was finished with M&M's for a long time. When he got home he opened the front door and vomited on the hall rug.

Sometimes there was just too much; this house was having the same effect; he didn't think he'd vomit but he was worn out by the size and complexity of all the things to look at and wonder about and find yourself around in. A strange house was bad enough, a strange fort was too much.

He went to the windows. It was too dark to see outside so he stood as far on the margin of things as he could and tried to disappear. He waited for the next circumstance. He had no idea what was next: the driver, George, had taken off with his clothes, he was in a greenhouse fort, the fireplace was cavernous, the window looked out over a void and he was a stranger.

Arthur heard a noise in the hall as someone was coming toward the living room. Was Arthur invisible, he tried hugging the draperies, maybe they wouldn't notice he had disappeared. A boy, a young man, about six feet four, blond wavy longish hair, blue shirt open at the collar, gray flannel pants, and requisite polished brown loafers came smiling his way into the room.

"Hi, Mom," with a nod in her direction, "Hey, Dan, when did you get here?" He walked toward Dan who walked toward him. "Little brother, what's happening?" said Tom.

Dan interrupted them, "Hey, Arthur, this is my big brother, Tom, the only big thing about him is talk."

Tom walked in Arthur's direction while Arthur tried, with moderate success, to disengage himself from the safety of the draperies. He wanted to wrap them around him and stick his hand out of one of the folds in greeting but his legs brought him a few paces into the room and to a handshake with Dan's older brother, Tom.

"Hi, Arthur, how was the trip? I hear Unkey Lou nearly had you guys locked up for the rest of the year?" He took Arthur's hand and looked to Dan for response.

Dan stepped into the conversation saving Arthur, "Can you believe that?"

"Yeah, I can. I was a prefect you know." Tom said turning back to Arthur, including him in their conversation. "I had to eat dinner sitting next to him at the head table for a year. I have a pretty good appreciation of OZ." He asked his mother "Hey, Mom, what's the plan for supper? Do we have time to play a little tennis?" Tom looked at Dan then Arthur. "You guys want to play before dinner?"

"Yeah let's go," said Dan.

"Dinner is at seven-thirty." said Mrs Clement. "Be back by six thirty so we can have a chat with your father before we eat."

Tennis. Who played tennis on Thanksgiving in the dark and rain? Arthur didn't have any shoes or tennis gear or clothes for tennis. He had taken lessons years ago but they didn't stick very well, so he quit.

"Come on, let's get changed," Dan said to Arthur, dragging Arthur out of the room to another door. Arthur went with Dan to another hall and a stairway. They went up a long curve of carved stone stairs to a landing and through a door into another hallway one side open to the garden below. A little farther down the hall then Dan opened a door to his bedroom, it was smaller than the living room but had a fireplace and huge windows looking out onto Long Island sound.

"Dan, I don't have any tennis clothes."

"No sweat, we have everything you need. Go in my closet," Dan pointed to a door, "and look around in there for a pair of tennies that might fit. I'll get you shorts, shirt and socks." He went to his bureau and threw things from the drawers onto his bed.

Arthur went to the door and opened it; it was another room, big enough for a bedroom only it didn't have a fireplace or a window. Instead it had stacks of rods along the walls with suits and shirts hanging from them. On the floor were little bleachers with shoes of every description in rows: black, brown, lace up, tasseled, high, low, golf, hunting, boating, skiing, walking around, lying down … it didn't matter, he had a shoe for it and not just one but two or three pairs of each. Luckily they were organized so Arthur found a pair or tennis shoes that looked like they might fit and sure enough, no more Pa Brown fitting salon specials, they were just right.

He came out of the closet and found Dan standing in the door already dressed in white tennis shorts and white shirt covered by a sleeveless cream colored wool v-neck sweater. "Here, get dressed," Dan pointed to the uniform on the bed.

Arthur put on clothes the same as Dan's except he didn't have a sweater, a windbreaker instead. It all fit fine. He didn't look like Arthur when he saw himself in the mirror on the closet door. If he'd had a hat to cover his haircut, a mask to hide the spots and some high heels for a few more inches, he might have passed for a resident.

131

"Hey, Dan, you know George took off with our suitcases; we forgot to get them out of the car."

"He didn't take off with them; he drove them down to the basement and Clara or someone brought them up. They're unpacked in your dresser, except what needs to be washed and dry cleaned, and that'll be done tomorrow or Friday." Dan moved to the door and Arthur followed. They went around the garden, down two flights of stairs to a basement, through some doors to a garage with three cars in it. One was the station wagon that had picked them up, one was a Jaguar XK120 conGrettaible and the other was a Cadillac sedan. Tom sat behind the wheel of the sedan, Dan jumped in the passenger side, and Arthur got in back. They drove through some neighborhoods to a country club where Dan and Tom knew everyone. They signed in at a desk, went to a locker and got racquets; they found their court behind a canvas curtain that hid a huge room with four indoor tennis courts.

Tom took one side of the court while Arthur and Dan stood on the other. It was warm up time, so Tom shot a ball to Dan who hit it back directly to Tom's forehand, then Tom returned the ball to Arthur. Arthur swung but the ball squirted by so without a word Dan hit another ball to Tom's backhand and Tom eased up a bit and hit it back to Arthur but it squirted just out of range either too low or too high, Arthur couldn't tell. He was so nervous he couldn't see the balls, his legs and arms felt like wood sticks.

Arthur turned to Dan. "Dan, I think I'll wait for you guys outside."

"OK. See you in a couple of minutes." Dan turned to his brother and the pace picked up. The ball went back and forth over the net. The pop of balls on tight strings gave a clean sound like sucking your mouth open real quick. Pop pop pop.

Arthur left and went to the car. He didn't want to be there; he felt like he was interrupting a family vacation; he was a stranger from the other side of the moon. He sat in the car as time dragged; the seats were cold and it was quiet with the windows up and motor off. Condensation formed on the inside of the windows and gave the outside lights haloes. Dan and Tom came out of the building and when they got to the car, Dan badgered Tom to let him drive home.

"No, you're not old enough."

"I can drive. I drive the tractors; why can't I drive the car."

"Because, if you have an accident then it's my fault."

"I won't have an accident."

"What if someone hits you, it's your fault cause you don't have a license."

"Come on?"

"No can do, man. Mom would kill me."

"She lets me drive."

"Then she can let you drive. I won't let you. That's it, end of discussion." Tom got in the driver's seat and Dan mockingly slouched to the passenger side.

They went back to the island and Arthur followed Dan to his room.

"Hey, let me show you where your room is," Dan said walking out his door and down the hall to another door. He opened it and went in; Arthur followed. It was just like Dan's; there were two twin beds, dressers, mirrors, chairs, a desk and a couch. "Your clothes are in the closet or in the bureau if they aren't there, then they're being cleaned. The bathroom is here." He opened a door next to the closet and stepped in. It was lined in white tile like an infirmary, the curtains and towels were white; there was a tub and a separate shower, a glass enclosure with three shower heads and ten valves. Arthur was stunned by the variety of the plumbing.

Dan pointed to the shower and said, "All the valves work, the hot and cold and fresh and sea water combinations. If you want a saltwater shower first, you use the bottom set of handles; the top set are for fresh water. Try them out; they're fun." Dan turned around and left the bathroom, "Dinner's at seven thirty downstairs. My dad wants to talk to Tom and me before dinner, so why don't you take a shower, clean up and hold on here till I come get you. It will be about an hour, there are magazines and books over on the desk," he pointed to a desk against the wall by the windows. "After dinner there's a party down the street; do you want to go?"

"OK," Arthur said, "I'll wait for you here."

He didn't want to go to a party where he would be the strange guy with the funny hair and the too-short pants. He wanted to go home or back to school; he felt like he had a huge wart on his nose and everyone was looking away, too embarrassed to look at it. The wart was more important than the boy.

He took off his clothes and went into the shower where he ran the water for awhile experimenting with the different selections. There was soap and shampoo and creams and conditioners, shaving cream and oils and liniments. He showered in fresh water, dried in a towel the size of pup tent and inspected his hair in the mirror. It stood straight out of his head and he looked a little like a porcupine might if it had spots on its face. He glanced away then went with his towel to the bedroom where he lay on the bed and thought about nothing. He lay in a cocoon of remorse. He let it wrap itself around him and swallow him up.

Dan knocked at the door and came in. "You hungry?"

"Yeah, did you talk to your dad?"

"Yeah. Come on, put on your clothes, they're waiting for us." Dan had on a jacket, a tie and twill pants.

Arthur went into his closet where his jacket and pants were hanging. He found a shirt from the bureau after looking around for a minute, dressed, then he followed Dan down a flight of stairs by the greenhouse garden into a dining room that could have seated the UN General Assembly. The table in the middle was twenty feet long and it was covered with linen, candles, silver and crystal, all of it reflecting off the windows that looked out onto Long Island Sound.

Mrs. Clement came to him and instead of shaking his hand this time, she gave him a little hug. "Arthur is everything all right? Did you find everything you need?" She smelled of soap and sherry. She was soft and warm and kept her arm around him.

A man came into Arthur's view from the other end of the room; he approached with his hand extended. He was as tall as Dan but he was rounded where Dan was angular, a series of rounds stacked on each other. His head was round, bald on top with a fringe. His head sat on his chest without too much neck to speak of. His chest was round and it sat on a larger roundness of abdomen and hip. Arthur couldn't see his legs in the dark. His features were blurred, it was a face without a smile, his mouth was small, he had gray eyes under thin brows, the eyes were trained directly on Arthur's and through him, judging, evaluating, about to test, "Hello Arthur, I'm Harold Clement, welcome to Goose Island."

His hand was smaller than Arthur expected. It was soft and trapped Arthur's at the fingers; he held onto Arthur longer than he needed to, and pulled a little as if he were going to pull Arthur to him, but as Arthur was about to fall forward, he let go. His eyes were on Arthur's face throughout.

"Hello, Mr. Clement, it's nice to meet you." It was all Arthur had in him. Arthur looked at his shoes; they needed a shine.

Mrs. Clement interrupted the silence. "Arthur, you sit here next to me." She pointed to a seat and Arthur stood behind it.

Tom and Dan took their places on the other side of the table and Mr. Clement held Mrs. Clement's chair. When she was seated, they took their places.

She said as she took her napkin and spread it on her lap, "We only eat in here when we're having a party or on the night before

Thanksgiving. It's too big to manage without some of the folks who help us with the house and they're off on Thanksgiving and the rest of the weekend, so we have the big dinner on Wednesday evening. We eat in the smaller dining room, buffet style, for the rest of the weekend," she said this without looking at Arthur, but her words seemed directed at him as the rest of them would have known. "Dan, would you say grace, please?"

Dan said the blessing; the same one they said at school.

Carmen came through a swinging door with a glass pitcher of wine; she poured everyone a glass and set the pitcher on a sideboard. Then a tall man whom Arthur hadn't seen before came in; he wore a black suit, white shirt, and black tie, and he served Mr. and Mrs. Clement, then Carmen returned with plates for Dan, Tom, and Arthur.

"What is it tonight, Carmen?" asked Mr. Clement.

"The first course is fresh herring. After, we will have filet mignon, potato Anna and spinach soufflé," Carmen said without looking at Mr. Clement. Neither was he looking at her, but seemed to ask the question as a routine rather than genuine interest.

Mr. Clement asked the boys about school. Dan related the story about the missing shirts' imprisonment. Tom talked about his first semester at college where everything he had been assigned to read he had already read at Bridge. Mr. Clement listened but, again, out of routine rather than interest. He didn't get involved in the conversation; he held it at a distance until it looked like it might get close enough to fall on him, then he let go of it. He performed in a play he was tired of.

"So, Arthur , where are you from?" asked Mr. Clement. He looked Arthur between the eyes.

Mrs. Clement answered for Arthur. "Arthur is from Oklahoma, Grape, Oklahoma, isn't that right Arthur?"

"Yes ma'am; Grape," said Arthur. He was confused; was he supposed to answer Mr. Clement or Mrs? He chose Mrs. He didn't know what to do with the half a raw fish on his plate so he let it sit there; maybe Carmen would come get it.

"What does your family do there in Grape?" asked Mr. Clement.

Arthur looked at Dan, across the table, there was no help there. Confusion again, the question, its literality battling its implication in a fourteen year old head. Darkness cloaked conflict in boiler room confusion. Where is the light?

"Arthur's father is a physician," said Mrs. Clement.

"Really, what kind of physician would that be?" lilting. Mr. Clement challenging Mrs. Clement, not Arthur.

"Dr. May is a cardiologist. He is a partner in the invention of the electrocardiograph, which you seem to have used recently."

"Isn't that interesting. Are you in the "Register?" he asked.

Mrs. Clement knew more about Arthur's father than Arthur did. How was this possible?

"Yes, it is interesting," said Mrs. Clement. "I talked to his aunt in Boston this morning on the telephone. He is a direct descendent of John Winthrop, first governor of the Massachusetts Bay Colony. A member of his family has been an officer in the British or American military for every generation since 1600. I think the 'Register' would be flattered."

She continued, "Curiously, Arthur's great grandfathers, on his father's side, was Baron Marian von Tolkacz, who was commander of the Prussian Army and later finance minister to the Prussian court. And should he choose, would have us introduce him as Baron."

"Charming," said Mr. Clement, now more interested in his fish than Arthur.

Arthur couldn't believe it. How did Mrs. Clement know this? Arthur heard stories at home, but no claims as concrete as Mrs. Clement's. His aunt Barbara in Boston must have told her on the phone this morning as they talked about plans for the vacation. The revelation was interesting to Arthur but not impressive. He did not know this fellow John Winthrop or Baron von Tolkacz. He never met them, so how could they be important? The electrocardiograph was not a toaster so he wasn't impressed, he knew toast; he didn't know cardios. Arthur sat intrigued, brought in from the cold of his anonymity.

There seemed a contest. Who would set the tone for the dining room, Mr. or Mrs. Clement? Mrs. Clement won, not by force, but by superior preparation. Mr. Clement had relied on a lazy intimidation while Mrs. Clement relied on history and principle and she had survived in grace. She survived equally in blond and Chanel and cashmere in the scent of sherry and Ivory soap. There was no contest.

Mr. Clement knew and resented it.

Dan interrupted Mr. Clement's downhill slide. "Hey Arthur, tell the story about your tie, the one at Steve Black's table."

While Arthur's ancestry may have been remarkable to the others at the table, it had no effect on him as it didn't change him. He was still Arthur. No magician appeared to erase the spots from his face, no barber threw a bib about him and trimmed his porcupine impersonation, no seamstress put him on a stand and hemmed his too-short pants.

He said, "Dan, you tell it if you want. You tell stories better than I do."

Dan told the story of Arthur's experience at the dining room table when Steve Black asked whether Sears sold farm implements and whether Arthur had got his zits there too. Mrs. Clement listened without moving, Tom chuckled at Dan's rendering.

"How is this possible?" asked Mrs. Clement. "How can anyone be so mean? How can you allow this?" She looked at Tom.

"Hey, mom, I didn't do it, I'm at Yale, remember?" said Tom smiling.

"Well then, how can you laugh; this isn't funny. A child comes to the school and they persecute him."

"Hold on. Take a look at Arthur, does he look like he's been persecuted. He doesn't play tennis worth a damn, but he's not persecuted. It happens to everyone but Golden Boy there," pointing to Dan. "It happened to me, they picked on me and I survived. Arthur is surviving and probably doesn't even remember it that well. He's in great shape, look at him, I'm calling him 'Baron' from now on." He burst out laughing.

"It's not right. You're in college, you're to old to remember what it was like. They made fun of his clothes, his family, his condition. That's not right."

"His condition?" Tom burst out laughing again. "Jesus mom, it's zits, we all had zits, I still have them and I'm in college. It's not a condition, it's a part of growing up, we all have to put up with it except maybe you and Golden Boy. How about it Golden Boy, have you had a zit yet?" Tom looked at Dan still chuckling.

Dan laughed, "Mom and I are too high on the evolutionary scale to have zits." He raised his hands to his face and started squeezing imaginary zits. Arthur would have done the same but they would not have been imaginary and the distinction wasn't lost on Mrs. Clement.

"I don't like it. Enough of that. Maybe growing up has some spots on the face but it doesn't have to include clothes from Sears." She looked at Arthur. "What is your phone number?"

"My phone number in Grape?"

"Yes, in Grape, how would I get your father on the phone?"

"It's Grape 46669."

Mr. Clement was roused from his fish. "Christ. They don't even have regional codes, what are you thinking about?"

"I'm going to call Carl May. I intend to find out if he has a charge account at Brooks Brothers, and if he does I am going to take Arthur to town on Friday and get him some clothes. Do any of you have an objection?"

When there was no reply, she said, "Carmen would you bring the telephone?"

Carmen must have been standing just outside the dining room on the other side of the swinging door, listening, anticipating. She appeared with a black telephone in about thirty seconds. She walked it in, cord trailing, and set it on the table next to Mrs. Clement; she turned and left but it looked like she would have dialed the right number if Mrs. Clement needed it. Nothing would have needed saying, Carmen read the household currents and had a special appreciation for Mrs. Clement.

"Arthur, would you tell me that number again?"

"Yes ma'am. It's Grape, Oklahoma 46669."

Mrs. Clement dialed "0" The operator must have come on. "Long distance please," pause "Grape, Oklahoma," pause "46669. Dr. Carl May", pause, "No; anyone in the household. I think it's called station to station."

What station would that be Arthur wondered? Pony express, gas, social, of the Cross, what could it be with a telephone; how many telephone stations were there?

"Is this Carl May, Arthur's father?"

All questions, Arthur wondered when the accusations would flow.

"Hello, I am Clara Clement. Arthur is staying with my family in Greenwich this weekend because of some problems at the school."

"Yes, I know, he was going to Boston, but he missed his train; he's staying with us in Greenwich Connecticut."

"He's fine."

"Carl, is it alright if I call you Carl?"

"Carl, Arthur needs some new clothes. I will take him to New York City on Friday, if it's all right with you, to get him some new clothes."

"That's nice of you, thank you; we're happy to have him; he's a nice young man."

"Do you mind if I take him with my son to New York City Friday to get some clothes?"

"Good. Fine. Do you have a charge account at Brooks Brothers?"

"That's fine. Good then you can expect a bill from New York, Brooks Brothers on your next statement for Arthur. Would you like to speak to him?"

Mrs. Clement handed Arthur the phone. He wanted to take it to the pantry with Carmen.

"Hi, dad."

"Hello Arthur, is everything all right?"

"Yes, everything's fine"

"I thought you were going to aunt Bar's for Thanksgiving, what happened?"

"There was a problem at school and we left late so I missed the train to New York and would have missed the train to Boston so the Clements were nice enough to invite me to stay here for the weekend."

"Do you need anything?"

"No, I'm fine. I have everything I need and I'll be going back to school on Monday."

"OK. Well, give me a call if you need anything, and be sure to get Mrs. Clement's address so you can send her a thank you note. Take care and I'll see you over Christmas."

"OK, Bye dad."

"Bye."

Arthur handed the phone back to Mrs. Clement who hung it up. Carmen took it from the table as if it didn't belong there.

"Pretty short conversation." Mr. Clement offered from his plate.

Mrs. Clement didn't pay any attention to Mr. Clement's comment. "OK. We're set, George will drive us into town on Friday. Dan, you need to go."

She turned, "Tom, do you want to come with us?"

"No, mom. I can't, I have things to take care of at the club. I've got to get the children's tennis program set up for the summer; I won't be back here till June."

Dinner returned to normal chatter about who had come home for vacation, who had gone south and who north. More courses served, Dan and Tom reestablished connections, testing status, was Dan still a little boy? Mr. and Mrs. Clements did not talk.

When dinner was finished they rose in unison as Mrs. Clement got up. Mr. Clement went to the living room while Dan and

Tom stood talking; Arthur tried to resume his position inside the draperies.

"Arthur, there's that party down the street, one of the guys I went to school with, do you want to go?"

"OK"

Dan led the way upstairs, "Before we go, let's clean up a little."

Arthur followed Dan to his room where Dan went to his closet and got a white shirt, trousers and a blue cashmere sweater and put them on the bed. As he lay them down he said, "If we're going over there, then you're going to need to brighten up a bit. How about trying on those clothes on the bed? They're too small for me but they will probably fit you OK."

Arthur went to the bed and picked up the shirt. It was cotton but it was soft and smooth and felt like liquid. He draped it over his fingers and it conformed to the shape of his hand. The pants were gray and pressed neatly, not like the ones he had on from school which hadn't been cleaned or pressed in weeks. Arthur took off his shoes and shirt then his pants and let them fall to the floor. He put on the new pants and they fit; there was no gap at the ankle; they were a little long but they would do fine.

When he had a belt in the pants but before he had the shirt on, Dan called him form the bathroom. "Hey, try some of this." He stood in the doorway holding a tube in his hand.

"What is it?"

"It's some stuff that keeps my hair from flying away. It might work on yours, keep it from looking like a shoe brush." He said it in a joking way with a big smile that Arthur didn't mind. He was trying to help, and Arthur realized he needed the help. His hair didn't matter at school but it didn't fit in here. Arthur took the tube and looked it over not sure what he was supposed to do.

Dan demonstrated. "Squirt a little in your hands, rub them together to spread it out and then rub it in your hair."

Arthur did what he was told. The stuff was greasy in his hands but when he spread it around on his hair it didn't look greasy just shiny and his hair didn't stick straight out from his head but lay down a little.

"Here." Dan offered a brush. "Brush it to the side and you'll look civilized. The girls at the party like their men civilized." Dan was still kidding, but Arthur took the brush and pushed his hair to the side. It didn't look like Dan's, but it was an improvement.

Then he put on the shirt and sweater. They were looser than his clothes but they felt fine, as if they were supposed to comfort rather than itch. He looked in the mirror and didn't recognize himself.

"Go on over to your room and brush your teeth." Dan said, "These girls won't kiss you if you smell like herring." He was still guiding in a friendly way.

Arthur never considered the possibility of being kissed or smelling like herring. He went and did as he was told; he brushed and looked at himself again and was surprised at what he saw and how little it resembled his impression of himself.

They went down to the living room where Mrs. Clement was reading. They entered and Dan went to her.

"Hey mom, we're going to Sheila's for her party; we'll be back early."

"That's fine. Tell her to drop by before she goes back to school."

"OK. See you later."

They were about to leave when Mrs. Clement looked up and regarded Arthur. She looked at him for a minute. "Arthur, what have you done to your self, your hair, your clothes, what is it?" She rose to her feet and came to him; she put her arms around him and gave him a kiss on the cheek. She was smiling "You've changed."

"Yeah, mom, I told him to brush his hair, big deal." said Dan.

Arthur stood frozen. He didn't want to move, didn't need to go anywhere; he was happy right there.

"Let's go, Romeo," Dan said and they left for the party.

They walked out the front doors, through the gate, across the bridge and up the lane through the field. After passing through a small woodlot they came to the street, and two houses later they were in front of a Tudor mansion. Every light was on and music pulsed and groaned from every window. Elvis Presley, they had that in Grape.

They went to the front door, it was open and they went in. There were about thirty people there, standing around talking in the front hall and living room and dining room combined, and they all knew Dan and said "Hi" or "Hello" in turn. Dan introduced Arthur; their greeting he received was polite, perfunctory.

After half an hour following Dan around being introduced and listening to conversations he couldn't contribute to, Arthur excused himself and sat on a sofa in the living room; there were more than a few. This one had been pushed against the wall to make room for dancing. The lights were lower than they needed to be, and the music was too loud; other than that it was just fine sitting in a living room being ignored by a lot of people he didn't know. Dan was dancing. He had introduced Arthur and then drifted away, into the crowd, to dance and talk to old friends without the weight of Arthur's inconvenience. Arthur sat waiting to go home, waiting to follow Dan back to the fort. He didn't think he could make it himself. While he sat, a little girl, maybe twelve or fourteen, came into the room and sat next to him.

"Hi, I'm Sheila," she said and sat looking at him. She was weightless, small, blond, thin, translucent, bony with a big open smile riding out front.

"Hi, Sheila, I'm Arthur."

"Arthur, you're Dan's friend aren't you?"

"Yeah."

"Are you staying on Goose Island?"

"Yup, I think so. I don't know where I am."

"Isn't Dan neat?" she asked looking over the crowd.

"Yes, he's neat."

"I mean, isn't he nice. I've watched him for years with his brother and mother. They live right over there. They're always nice to me," throwing her hair in a direction that might have been toward Goose Island.

"Do you live here?"

"Yeah, it's my little brother's party. He's big on parties when my parents are away."

"Your little brother, how old is he?"

"He's fifteen."

"How old are you?"

"I'm sixteen. I go to Miss Hall's right up the road from you and Dan. My brother goes to Brunswick here in Greenwich."

"Oh," looking at the crowd.

"Do you want to dance?" she asked without reservation or hesitation.

Arthur was tired, more like strung out. He didn't want to dance because he didn't know how. He didn't want to get into another dilemma where he floated along with the current waiting patiently to go over Niagara Falls and then drowning after surviving the fall.

"Come on?" She jumped up and stood in front of him offering her hand, palm up, she bent back at the waist, indicating the direction they had to go if they were going to dance.

Arthur couldn't resist, he rose and she grabbed his hand and pulled him to the middle of the room. Patsy Kline was singing something about not loving him enough, the lights were down, couples were snuggled up moving together.

Arthur didn't know what to do. Sheila had his left hand in her right, facing him, waiting. He leaned toward her. "I don't know how to dance. I've never done it before."

She leaned toward him, "That's OK. No boy knows how to dance. Only girls know how to dance. I'll show you if you want."

"OK."

She held his left hand in her right; she held it high, then she took his right in her left and she put it behind her and said, "Put your right hand on my back, not my butt, guys always end up sliding their hands down to your butt, yeah there and keep it there."

She put her left hand on his neck and by the time they had that arranged they were close, right up against each other.

"OK, now just move with me. Don't try to lead, I'll lead; you just try to glide along out of my way but in my happiness zone, close but not humping me."

Arthur felt like the man made of sticks and string again. Gangly, dangling, pushing, leaning. She was weightless, a kite he could not fly. He thought of Steve Smith's broom and Steve's advice, don't try too hard, it will tell you when it likes the rhythm. He tried to relax and when he relaxed it was better, he felt her next to him, felt her move, but when he forgot to relax she seemed to get away and he couldn't follow.

"Relax, just let it happen," she said in his ear too close to be an accident; he felt the warmth of her breath. He felt her warmth on his front, felt the warmth of her hand in his. She got closer, he relaxed. It started to work.

"Hey, time to go." Dan was at his side, "Hi Sheila; I see you met Arthur."

"Hi, Danny. Yes, I met Arthur and he's too nice to go to your school."

"Well, mom wants him home early because he's fragile, so we have to leave."

They stopped dancing but they held hands neither wanted to drop.

"I'll walk you home," she said.

Dan said, "You're home, so we'll walk you home. Arthur I'll meet you out front in five. Bye, Sheila." Then he disappeared.

Sheila asked Arthur, "Do you know what that means; I'll walk you home?"

"I guess it means you'll walk me home."

"No. It's an excuse to get outside the house with your date."

"Why do you want to get outside with your date?"

"To make out," she said as if in an academic discussion. She had his hand in hers and led him to the porch. She stood looking at Arthur, his left hand in her right. They were close. Arthur didn't know what to do.

"Are you going to kiss me?"

"No."

"Don't tell me; you don't know how. Do I have to show you everything?" She reached behind Arthur's neck with her free hand and drew him to her.

He leaned over and she put her mouth on his and stayed there for minute. He stood still, sticks and strings.

"You're sweet but you need a lot of practice." She turned and left him watching her.

Dan came out and grabbed him by the arm, "She's cute and she's a handful. Little Miss Boss. Did you have fun?"

"Great time." Arthur was in a fog unanticipated. He wandered from fog to fog, direction didn't belong to him; breathing and going along were his. All he had to do was make sure he didn't drown. He went where the river took him, he trod water and when he expected Niagara Falls, he met Sheila, when he expected dinner, he got a genealogy lesson. When he expected to sit and hide, he danced. He liked the dancing, no talking, no football, no tennis, no dinner with Torquemada, he wanted her arm around him, her hand in his. He didn't want to leave but there was no choice.

Dan and Arthur walked to the island, got some chocolate in the kitchen, drank milk from the bottle and went to their rooms.

15

REVELATIONS

Arthur woke in bright sunlight; it came through the windows straight on and it reflected off the water so the combined effect made the room one eye, squinty bright. He got up, went to the bathroom, came back and looked out the window. What he couldn't see in the dark last night was clear. His room was above the water, high enough so he wouldn't have jumped, maybe three floors above. His view didn't look directly across the Sound but looked across a little harbor at one or two other islands with houses on them; fancy houses with important looking architecture. There was a yacht club at the tip of land on the other side of the harbor, Indian something from a sign he couldn't quite make out on one of the buildings, and the harbor wasn't more than two hundred yards wide. The water was flat and looked black with silver glints of reflection from the sun. When he looked to the right he saw the Sound; it was bright, flat, silver and the reflection made his room light.

He took a shower and put on the shirt and gray flannels he had worn to the party the night before. He made sure to put some grease on his hair and combed it flat. Then he went out of his room, down the hall in the direction he had come from last night, down the stairs and found the living room. No one was up, no noise, but he smelled coffee so he nosed around and found the small dining room and the kitchen. These rooms were large, not huge like the rest of the house, they were arranged as if there was an apartment inside the fort, and most of the time was spent in a few rooms in the apartment. He wondered what the rest of the place was used for.

The kitchen was big by anyone's standards. It had white tile from floor to halfway up the walls. The stove was a large commercial size thing, black with six burners, a grill on the right side and two ovens you could cook a whole cow in. A copper hood with a painting of a Canada Goose in flight hung over the stove. Goose Island he supposed. Next to the gas stove was an electric range with coffee in a Pyrex, hourglass shaped coffeemaker with a wood girdle for a handle; the filter and grounds had been removed but the coffee was hot. He looked for a refrigerator and didn't find one till he discovered it, nearly walk-in size with double doors, white like the rest of the kitchen built into the wall. He opened one side and found milk, then he remembered it from last night when he and Dan had come to get some dessert.

A counter dominated the middle of the room between cupboards lining the walls on one side and the stove on the other. Pans hung from steel racks attached to the wall next to the stove. There was only one chair at a desk in an alcove among the cupboards so there wasn't anywhere to sit around and drink coffee and read the paper. The room was designed for work, not for entertaining.

Mrs. Clement came through the swinging door to the pantry. "Good morning Arthur, happy Thanksgiving," She wore Levis and a light blue cashmere sweater over a white turtleneck shirt. She was perfection; her hair in place, clothes clean and they fit, even her Levis were creased. She wore slip-on loafers with no socks; the loafers were shiny. Arthur was learning slowly; one message that repeated was shiny shoes. Not cheap shiny but saddle leather shiny, slightly worn, neat and tidy, good leather well cared for. Good leather, cashmere, tweed in undertones, soft cotton shirts and suits that were half a size too big, loose but not baggy seemed to be codes or signals the wearers sent to each other about where they had been, where they were and where they expected to stay, signals that people who hadn't been exposed could neither receive nor understand in casual acquaintance. They were inoffensive, subtle signals that got so refined Dan could tell where you bought your shirt by the size of the buttons and where they were placed on the cuff. He could tell the model, thread count and fabric weight of your suit by the way the sleeves were attached at the shoulders. He knew custom-made from off-the-rack by the way the lapel folded away from the chest and the way the jacket fit across the back of the shoulders, how the trousers rode when sitting and standing. These were subtle things that Arthur didn't know existed. Arthur had been wasting his time hanging out in Tiny's back seat.

"Hi, Mrs. Clement," Arthur smiled and his voice showed it.

"Do you want juice or coffee?" she asked as she went to a cupboard and got out two cups and saucers. She went to another and got two glasses. "Juice and coffee, that's a better idea," she continued her hunt. She brought out a tray and china coffeepot, went to the sink, rinsed the cups and pot with hot water, got cream and sugar and juice in a pitcher, put it all on a tray and said, "Let's go," as she pushed her way backwards through the swinging door to the pantry and then through another to the dining room. She put the tray on a sideboard, put the cups and glasses on the table, and sat. Arthur sat where she had set his cup, next to her.

"You're up early," she said, "did you sleep well?"

"Yes, I slept fine, thank you, I think the sun woke me up."

"That's right, your room gets the morning sun. There are drapes in there; you can pull them tonight so the sun won't wake you tomorrow."

"That's OK. I like getting up early; it's the quietest part of the day."

"Yes, it is; I like it too. Don't expect to see Dan or Tom much before ten. They would stay in bed all day if I let them. What do you think of Goose Island? Most people who visit are put off by it but I grew up here so I feel at home. Dan and Tom grew up here so they're comfortable but Mr. Clement finds it trying. It's as if the house is bigger than he is which I guess it is."

"I've never seen anything like it. I don't know what to think of it yet, my first impression is big, but that's not the right word."

"Some people let it intimidate them; they think in comparatives. 'It's bigger than my house' so that has to mean something, but that's not the way I think about it at all. I'm happy to live here; it's been in my family for three generations. My grandfather saw a palace in Venice. He had part of it copied, some was made there and brought over here; some was made here by Italian craftsmen who were brought here to do the work, and many of them never went back to Italy. He collected art and furniture and filled the place so it's become a museum. Everything here will last past me and Dan and Tom, so we look at it as if we are caretakers of our grandfather's dream. It's not as if we own it, we do legally, but it belongs to those who come next. Mr. Clement has thought about donating it to the Museum of Fine Arts as an off-site campus or a college campus for fine arts or music. That's not possible because of the restrictions on the neighborhood and also because it is not his to donate. So our view is we are privileged caretakers and that relieves our guests of some of their anxiety. We're not showing it off; we take care it."

"How old is it?"

"It was finished it 1914, but it has had some additions and renovations. The boathouse was added in the thirties; the bridge has been rebuilt several times. A cement truck caved it in once, it was weeks before we could get here other than by boat and that is no fun if you're trying to manage a place this big. Eventually my father hired a barge that made four runs a day to the landing in town. The barge would pull up on the island on a ramp that was made for it. We drove onto the barge on the island, then it would pull off and go to town, where we drove off it. We never had to get out of the car; it only took about fifteen minutes. Delivery people and workers used the barge. It was fun for a while. Those were the days when my father bought a used PT boat to get from here to his office in town, New York, in the summer. The boat picked him up at the dock right out there," pointing out the window, "in the morning and went to the tip of Manhattan. Then picked him up and brought him back in the evening, That was fun too if you wanted to go to work with him in the mornings. It was beautiful going by LaGuardia airport through Hell's Gate and down the East River in the morning as the sun came up."

She sipped her coffee. "Enough about this place. I love it, but I am tired of talking about it. One of the problems with being a caretaker is answering the same questions all the time and looking as if you're interested or it's the first time the question has been asked. If my motive is to make sure the person who is asking the question feels good about asking and about the answer, then the job is easier, but then I'm not always thinking that way as much as I wish I were. Let's talk about you. You have a curious habit of answering in one syllable if possible, two if pushed and three at most. Are you shy?"

"I don't know?"

"Must have been hard, that one, three syllables." She smiled. "Dan says you're shy, I don't think so, I think you're thoughtful."

Silence.

"What about your mother? Your aunt says she's been sick, in the hospital."

"I don't live with my mother; I haven't for a few years; my parents are divorced." Arthur was on slippery ground. He didn't get along with his mother for reasons he couldn't articulate. She disappointed him, she was more a dependant than a parent and this embarrassed and confused Arthur.

"Has she recovered; is she out of the hospital? I noticed you didn't call her yesterday. Mothers notice these things."

A bitter stone like a peach pit saturated with bile grew in Arthur's throat, it clawed its way up from the back, trying to get hold of his windpipe. It would make him cry if he let it get too far. He sat losing the battle with the stone that resided there just below the surface, always ready to take advantage of Arthur's forgetfulness, of his failure to protect himself.

"I'm sorry Arthur, I don't mean to bring up sad thoughts." She rose and came around the table to stand behind him with her hands on his shoulders so she wouldn't have to watch the tears run down his cheeks. She didn't want to embarrass him.

The stone won. Tears came down his cheeks; he tried to keep them in his eyes but they were too many, a squad, a platoon, a company of tears and that's too many to hold back, so they overran their embankment and charged down his cheeks to the corners of his mouth, they ran to his chin and carelessly off onto his shirt.

He sat looking at his hands; she stood behind him, her hands on his shoulders, not heavy but with enough weight that Arthur knew they were there on purpose. The great void swallowed him, hopelessness won, there was nothing to do but give up and wait till circumstance caught up with the conditions and pushed him over Niagara again and he got close to drowning. Time was lost. He wiped his face with a napkin but his eyes leaked anyway.

Mrs. Clement went back to her seat. "We don't have to talk about that. I'm sorry, Arthur. I'm sorry I might have hurt you."

"You didn't hurt me. I don't know why this thing creeps up on me and I can't stop it. It makes me sad but I don't know why," he said. "My mother is sick. She's in and out of hospitals; they don't know exactly what's wrong with her. Sometimes she can't get out of bed. She'll stay in bed for more than a week, crying and then screaming at people. Then she'll sleep for days and go through the cycle again. If she stays in the cycle too long then she goes to the hospital for a while and comes home helpless. She can't make a decision; she sits around not talking, just sits and looks out the window."

"Has it always been like this?"

"I don't think so; it's getting worse."

"You have sisters; don't you," she said as clarification, trying to keep the thoughts moving.

"Yeah. They live with my mother, they try to take care of her, but I don't think they can do much. They don't like my father."

"You live with your father?"

"Yes."

"You get along all right?"

"Yes, OK."

"Arthur, I'm very sorry to hear about your mother. I'm sorry it hurts you so much. But I'm glad you told me; it helps me to get to know you a little better. Do you want more juice?"

Arthur wiped his face again, his eyes felt puffy, his throat was raw from trying to hold the stone down. She poured juice and they sat looking out the window at the Sound.

"Do you want to take a walk? I can show you around outside; it's a pretty day and not too chilly. Go get your coat and we'll walk." Arthur didn't have a choice. If he refused she would feel bad that she had upset him or she would think he was pouting. Neither was the case so he would walk.

"OK," he said and went out to get his jacket.

He came back to the kitchen and she had a jacket on, brown herringbone tweed. With each new outfit he got more curious about her clothes, about the fabrics, the style and cut of the jacket, the colors. It intrigued him.

She looked sad, and he felt guilty for making her sad. It was sad company, each taking the blame for the tangled emotions. She led the way out of the kitchen and down a set of stone steps. He had no idea where they headed, going down to another part of the house. She opened a wood door whose panels were held together with black iron straps, and they entered a workshop. It had a cement floor and brick walls. One of the walls had windows that looked out under the bridge to the shore. There were workbenches in the middle with power tools spread about on moveable stands. It smelled of turpentine and linseed oil.

"This is where the craftsmen made the woodwork and cabinets for the house. When the masonry was finished in one section, the masons moved out and the carpenters moved tools into that section and completed it. They moved along section by section. Many of the tools they used are still here and we still use them to make repairs. We added power tools to make it faster." She went across the room and out a door to a path at the base of the foundation where it joined the granite rock of the island about fifteen feet above the water.

"The tide here is about nine feet; looks like we're about half tide now. Sometimes in a hurricane the tide comes over this patch and into the basement but not too deep, so we know how to move things to higher elevations, things that would be damaged by salt water."

She took him around a corner of the foundation to a ramp that led down to a floating dock. The dock was moored by chain and cable to the granite block foundation.

She talked to Arthur over her shoulder as she moved along, as if she were guiding a tour at the Statue of Liberty. "This foundation is made of granite blocks from an island in Maine. The blocks were shipped down to New York City to make the big buildings there in the early part of this century. Blocks that broke in handling or failed inspection were then cut up and used for foundations. Some of this block is from Vinalhaven and was supposed to be a column for the front of the New York Public Library. But, when it got there they found it had a fault, so it was cut up and shipped from New York up here to Greenwich. And there it is. Even granite has a history."

Arthur imagined this might be an example of what she had referred to earlier when she got bored giving the same information all the time. A silent walk would have been fine with Arthur, but this was OK. It was interesting but his mind wasn't on it; he was still floating in the river, dog paddling in the dark.

They went down the ramp; it had raised treads to help with traction; it must have been a problem in the rain. And at the bottom they came to the dock itself. It was free to rise and fall with the tide. When the dock rose the ramp, with wheels on its end, rolled farther out on the dock making the angle less steep. However, at low tide the angle must have been about forty degrees. From the end of the dock they could see inside a covered boathouse. It was part of the foundation and had three separate bays with open garage doors. Arthur saw three power boats in slings suspended from the ceiling about fifteen feet above the water, suspended by belts, pulleys and cables that went from the slings to electric motors; they must have raised and lowered the boats because the boats were too big to be raised by hand. The boats were made of varnished wood with stainless steel, chrome and brass fittings. One of them looked like it was at least thirty feet long and had a tiny cockpit in the front and one in the back. Arthur looked for the PT boat but he didn't see it.

They went back up the ramp while Mrs. Clement described the engineering marvels that supported and maintained the place. They went to the bridge by way of the perimeter path and across the bridge to the field at the edge of the water. A large barn stood at one end of the field. It was made of tile and rock with lots of windows and two silos attached at the end; there was nothing like it in Oklahoma. The tile was brown, glazed and rounded so when they were stacked they made a circle for the silo shape. Mrs. Clement walked a little ahead of Arthur; she didn't say anything, the time was right for walking. The barn was built into the side of a hill so if you walked in the hillside door and out the other side you'd fall about twelve feet.

Arthur thought about driving a car down the hill, in the front door and out the back airborne. He wondered if it had been done. On the downhill side were twelve garage doors; each door was green painted wood with black iron hardware, and each had a cement apron connected to the drive. Mrs. Clement went to one of the doors and opened it. Inside, facing out in greeting was a red Ferrari with a black number painted on a yellow circle. She went in and Arthur followed. Behind each door was a magic car, a green Aston Martin, a yellow 1923 Rolls Royce conGrettaible, a cobalt blue Duesenberg, a brown Hispano Suisa, part was wood or looked it, Masseratti, Packard, Bughatti, too many to remember, all shiny, all in perfect condition.

"This is Mr. Clement's hobby; he collects cars."

"Does he drive them?"

"No. They are never driven; when they come or go they're on a truck. But they all run perfectly." She delivered this news in rote performance, colorless, as if looking at something most people would find fascinating and she found infantile.

They left the barn; she walked next to Arthur as they went back across the bridge to the courtyard and in the front door. When they got inside she said, "I'll show you some of the house." She went left around the garden, up a flight of stairs, and into a gallery. Pictures and rugs covered the walls, antique furniture was arranged around the perimeter. Everything was old. It looked like the inside of a castle.

"Most of these things are from the fourteenth century. My Grandfather bought them at monasteries and castles in Europe over years of collecting, He had a room for each century from the thirteenth through the eighteenth He also had rooms for Middle Eastern art, Indian, Japanese and Chinese. Some of these tapestries are from what is now Belgium but when they were made they were Spanish."

Arthur was overcome by the amount of detail. There were thousands of things and each was a mountain of detail in its own right. It was a museum.

They went back to the kitchen and found Mr. Clement standing at a counter making toast.

"Good morning, Harold," said Mrs. Clement.

"Good morning," he said without looking up from his buttering.

Arthur went to the dining room and was going to go to his room but Mrs. Clement came in following him.

"Don't you want some breakfast?" she asked.

"No; it's OK. I'll wait for Dan."

"It may be a while, but that's fine. Our talk this morning, what you told me, I'll keep it between us," she said with a crooked smile. "It's our secret."

Mr. Clement asked while he entered through the swinging door, "What's your secret?" .

"Just something Arthur and I were talking about this morning. If I told you, then it wouldn't be a secret, would it?" She returned to the kitchen.

Arthur went to his room and lay on the bed looking at the ceiling. What a confusing place. It was too big and there was obviously some tension between Mr. Clement and the rest of the family; even Carmen reacted to it. After about ten minutes on the bed Arthur was bored and got up and went to the windows. He looked out over the harbor and saw there was activity at the yacht club; some folks with shotguns stood on the point and took turns shooting at clay pigeons. He could see a group standing in a clot, then one of the group moved to the end of the point maybe five yards in front of the others. The point person raised his gun and shot, then another person took his turn. It looked like they were shooting a variation of trap and skeet without the regulation houses and launching pattern. He couldn't see where the launchers were. The gun reports were hollow sounding and soft around the edges from the distance and the humidity.

Dan came in. "Hey, you're up early,'" he said. He was in his pajamas and his hair was fluffed on one side.

"Yeah. I've been up for a while. Your mom took me for a walk around the island and to the barn."

"Did she give you the tour guide speech?" he asked lying on his side on the bed next to Arthur's, one hand under his ear supporting his head.

"I don't know; she told me about some rocks from Maine and showed me the cars in the barn." Arthur thought about Mrs. Clement telling him she would keep their talk a secret, and he wanted to keep it that way too, so he gave short answers.

"Yeah, the cars, my dad's hobby," said Dan in disinterest.

"The boathouse and workshops are neat," said Arthur in honest interest.

"In the summer it's great. We could go out in the boats if it was summer but it's too cold to keep everything set up, so they get put away about halfway through October, after the leaves are gone. Mom likes to go out in the boats in the fall when the leaves are changing, when there isn't a lot of traffic on the Sound, and look at the trees along the shore from the boat."

"What are those people doing over there?" said Arthur pointing to the club across the harbor.

Dan rolled off the bed, stood, and came to the window in bare feet. "They're shooting skeet; that's what they call it, but it's not really skeet, it's a local variation, there's not enough room over there to shoot real skeet."

"Do you shoot?" asked Arthur.

"Yeah, sometimes. I don't like it much, but it's fun; why? Do you want to shoot, we can today if you want. Dad's the shooter."

"Where do you shoot?" asked Arthur.

"We can shoot right here on the patio off the dining room if you want, or we can go to the club where there's regulation skeet and trap; have you shot?"

"Yeah, I've shot some in Oklahoma."

"Hey, let's do it. There's nothing else scheduled today. We could go after lunch; Mom likes to shoot and Tom probably has something to do at the club anyway." Dan walked to the door.

"It's almost time for lunch now. Are you going to have breakfast; your mom's in the dining room waiting for you."

"Yeah, I think I'll wander down there and have a little of both."

Dan left and Arthur lay back down on the bed. He didn't know whether Dan was going to come back and get him or head to the dining room by himself. He didn't really care. If Mr. Cement was there then Arthur would rather stay in his room looking at the ceiling and thinking about whatever popped into his head.

He had shot some in Oklahoma; everybody did. Their country club didn't have indoor tennis but it had skeet and trap which were busy all year long. Arthur had hung out there in summers and shot quite a bit so he was a respectable shooter for his age, better than most of the weekend shooters. At one point he had a job as a "trapper," sending the clay birds out the window of the shack, in the low house on the skeet range. The skeet range had two little houses about fifty yards apart. The shooters stood between the two houses and back some from a line connecting them on things called stations, three by three cement pads placed to mark where the shooter was supposed to stand. There were eight stations in an arc, a half circle with the flat side being an imaginary line between the two houses. The shooters moved from station to station along the arc shooting at the clay pigeons that came flying out of little windows in the houses.

Sometimes two birds would come out at the same time, one from each window.

Arthur's job was to throw the clay pigeon out the window and down an imaginary line connecting the two houses at about twenty feet off the ground. The shooter's job was to break the clay pigeon as it crossed in front of him and before it got away.

When one of the skeet shooters stood on his mark and called "Pull.," Arthur released a clay pigeon.

The clay pigeon was supposed to fly out of a window in the house- not really a house but a shack with a door on one side and a window about the size of a page from a notebook on the other- and across the field in front of the shooter. And the shooter was supposed to shoot it, on the fly, before it went out of range or hit the ground. The clay pigeon was thrown out of the window by a big throwing contraption which had an electric motor attached to a spring and arm mechanism. After the bird was thrown out of the window at about a hundred miles an hour, the electric motor would cock the arm by pulling the spring tight. When it was cocked, Arthur would place another bird in the tray on the end of the arm and wait for someone to call "pull," then he would push the release switch and the arm would fly in a circle ejecting the bird out the window. If you screwed up the sequence or had your hand on the release while you put a bird in the tray, it would take the tips and maybe a little more of your fingers right out the window with the clay bird and them somebody would blow them to smithereens with a twelve gauge shotgun so there usually wasn't much to sew back on.

The idea was, Arthur was supposed to release the clay pigeon exactly one half a second after the call. "Pull"- …just like that. That was the idea. Sometimes things didn't go like the idea. It was hard to sit there for hours paying attention to "Pull" and Arthur's fuzzy head would wander off on something else and there would be "Pull" —- release or maybe Pull --------------release, really late, followed by; "Hey you little asshole, what are you doing in there; stop beating off and pay attention."

Some of the shooters got excited if the bird didn't come out exactly when they wanted. It made their timing bad and they'd miss. If there was money bet on the score, then people got real picky about the quality of the pulling and they'd ask for older boys to trap for them and they'd give the trapper tips for a good job. The trappers knew who the big tippers were, so if there was money on the line, the big tipper would get really good pulling while the cheap tippers got some delays and broken birds and empty pulls. If you gave someone an empty pull on the seventh or eighth station, which were doubles, two birds coming at a hundred miles an hour from different directions at the same time, they'd shoot one and look for the other and, on not seeing the second bird, would think they'd missed it, when really they hadn't, it was a bad pull, there was no second bird. So they'd get all pissed off to find they had to shoot again but glad they hadn't missed the first time and they'd be thinking the trapper had screwed them and they should have done something else and by this time their concentration was all gone and they'd miss the second shot which was the point of putting an empty in the line and getting a bigger tip from the big tipper.

Unless the shooter had been a trapper at some point in his life, in which case the story took a different turn. On getting an empty or broken bird on the seventh or eighth station, the experienced shooter would empty his gun, set on the rack and come around to the door of the shack where he would open the door, grab you by the collar, drag you out and kick you in the ass.

Arthur had quit trapping the day one of the trappers had got his shirtsleeve caught in the thrower; it tried to send him out a little window about half the size necessary to accommodate a comfortable ride. While it had failed in its primary job, it had managed to rotate his arm 360 degrees and remove some fingers. When the shooters saw blood and parts come out the window about the same time they heard a scream and the thump of his body hitting the side of the shack, they thought there might be a problem. So they ambled around to the door, found him, and separated him from his tormentor. A doctor, who was in the shooting squad, covered the wet parts with towels, backed his car up to the shack and they loaded the trapper in the back seat and drove him to the hospital, They thought it would be quicker than calling the ambulance.

The next day the rules at the club were changed. No member or family of members could work as trappers. Those jobs were reserved for unknowns. Arthur couldn't recall that any thought had been given to changing the machines or procedures.

Dan came back into the room still in PJ's. "OK. It's all set; we'll shoot after lunch."

They chatted for a while about nothing Arthur could remember; it was more mutual noise than information.

"What did you think of Sheila?" Dan said, lying on his side on one of the beds, one hand propping his head up.

"I like her."

"I noticed," he said. "Did she kiss you?"

Arthur didn't want to answer; there was no good answer so he didn't say anything.

"She's sixteen, did she tell you? She looks about twelve."

"Have you known her for along time?" asked Arthur.

"Sure, she grew up here; we went to the same grade school, she was always ahead of me. She comes over here a lot. She likes Tom but he's not crazy about her. He thinks she's too young, she doesn't think so. She likes my mom too, and her parents aren't home much so she used to spend a lot of time over here after school following my mom around."

Arthur didn't want to talk about Sheila, but there wasn't much of a way around it, Dan wanted to talk about her. It made Arthur uncomfortable, as if he were telling secrets or listening to someone else's phone conversation.

Dan started again, "There's a party on Sunday night before we go back. We have to be at school at four thirty Monday, so George is going to drive us up. Mom can't go and my Dad will be in New York. Do you want to go to the party? Sheila will be there; she called Mom this morning and asked if we were going."

"Sure, I'd like to go."

"Good, I already told Mom we would, so she RSVP'd for us."

"What'd she do?" asked Arthur

"RSVP'd, an RSVP is an answer to an invitation; we were invited so mom told them we were coming?"

"We were invited. How did they know I was here?" asked Arthur.

"They didn't really. It's kind of an assumption; if you're invited to a party and you have house guests, the guests are invited along, just so you tell the hostess ahead of time so she can make arrangements, get enough food or places at the table or that kind of thing. It's pretty normal. I'm going to shower and get dressed, then we can head down for lunch. Hold on here for a minute; then we'll go down together." Dan got up from the bed and left the room before Arthur could answer.

16

TURN THE OTHER CHEEK

Dan came back in fifteen minutes and they went to the dining room where Tom stood at a sideboard putting turkey on a plate. Mr. Clement sat at the head of the table reading a paper and Mrs. Clement poured water into glasses. The table was set except for plates which were stacked on the sideboard next to platters of turkey, ham, mashed potatoes, sweet potatoes, brussels sprouts, gravy, salad, everything anyone might want for Thanksgiving and of course more.

Mr. Clement looked at Arthur from the head of the table. "Dan tells me you are a shooter."

Tom jumped in before Arthur could answer, "I hope you shoot better than you play tennis." He was smiling at Arthur.

"I didn't say that, I said he'd like to try it," Dan tried to get things back in perspective.

"Have you shot before?" asked Mr. Clement.

"Yes sir, in Oklahoma, I shot some," said Arthur trying to look at Mr. Clement as he talked to him but he failed and looked at the plate in front of him instead.

"What did you shoot?"

"I've shot skeet and trap and backyard stuff."

Mr. Clement looked at Mrs. Clement. "That's good. We're shooting this afternoon. Clara, who's coming?"

"Dan and Arthur for sure. Tom," she said looking at Tom, "are you coming with us?"

"No, Mom I can't; I have other plans," Tom responded while taking a divot out of the mashed potatoes then licking the spoon while he thought his mother wasn't watching. She saw him but didn't say anything.

Arthur waited till everyone had served himself; he stood as far in the corner as he could then Mrs. Clement said, "Arthur get a plate and serve yourself."

Arthur did as he was told but he wasn't hungry.   His nervousness at being in their house and not at his own home was difficult all by itself and would have been enough to make him choose school over this. But the hostility he felt from Mr. Clement was like a vice around his chest. He wasn't hungry, and he was nervous about not having the right things to say, didn't know what was coming next. He had in some way angered the man and the situation made Arthur sick to his stomach.

They ate lunch and after lunch they went to change for shooting. Arthur didn't have shooting clothes so he wondered what this was about. When he and Dan got upstairs he asked Dan what he was supposed to wear. Dan said he was fine, to wear a sweater and he'd get Arthur a jacket. Arthur went into his room and sat on the bed. Waiting again, for what, waiting, being uncomfortable, being apprehensive, not liking it in the house. He liked Dan but he didn't like the unknown, the feeling of insecurity. He got a sweater out of the bureau; it wasn't his but it looked like it would fit so he put it on.

Dan came in wearing a green canvas coat and carrying another one just like it over his arm. It looked like canvas with some sort of oil or wax on it. It was long and loose fitting with a zipper and button flap covering the zipper. It had a corduroy collar and corduroy lined the cuffs, the inside was lined with green plaid   The pockets were large and expandable and it had a little pouch in the back where you might put your lunch if you wanted, but you'd have to be careful not to squash it if you sat down. Arthur thought it was more complicated than it had to be. Arthur imagined it was some sort of shooting uniform.

They went downstairs to the hall and Mrs. Clement was there in a tweed jacket with suede patches at the collar, elbows and right shoulder. She had changed her shoes to high top leather.   Mr. Clement made his appearance in a tweed jacket like Mrs. Clement's, but his pants were short, like long shorts, just below the knee tucked into high socks, which were in turn tucked into brown lace-up shoes, shined more than might be necessary on the range in Grape. If he showed up at the club in Grape dressed like this the folks might think he was about to play both parts in "The King and The Duke" scene from *Huckleberry Finn*.

Dan and Tom disappeared and came back through the front door where the black Buick was waiting in the courtyard. They got in,

Dan Tom and Arthur in the back, Mr. Clement driving, Mrs. Clement riding shotgun. They got to the club and stopped the car under a portico where a man took it and drove it off somewhere while they went inside to more greetings and introductions. They continued out the other side, down a crushed stone path toward the sound of shotguns.

They came to an opening in the woods where there was a field with four skeet courses and three trap fields. At the edge of the field there was a half-timbered, half-stone log cabin sort of building, but it was too big for a log cabin. It had an entry hall and on the right of the hall there was a reception area. On the left there was a dining room where folks were at lunch and to the rear a bar, clubhouse, card room and locker rooms. The Clements signed in, talked to the man behind the desk and went to the rear where Mr. Clement and Dan went to the locker room. There were lockers for what Arthur couldn't guess, fancy wood paneling, recessed lighting, benches, leather couches and chairs, newspaper racks, two card tables and folks waiting to take care of you. They went to lockers and got shooting glasses, hats, gloves, ear plugs some of which Dan shared with Arthur. They left the locker room with all their equipment and went to the reception area where they met Mrs. Clement; there must have been a ladies locker room too. They walked to one of the skeet courses; it looked just like the ones in Grape minus blood stains on the low house which the Grape folks refused to remove from around the window, thinking it was quite a macho decoration.

When they got to the high house, there was a fellow dressed in something like Mr. Clement was wearing, waiting for them. Four shotguns held down a stand next to him.

Mr. Clement made the introductions as if he were instructing a kindergarten class on how to arrange the rugs on the floor at nap time. "Bob will be our trapper and marker today, Bob this is Arthur, he's visiting from Dan's school."

"Hello, Arthur." No hand was extended and he made no eye contact. This was an introduction of names only, requiring no further commitment.

Mrs. Clement got things going. "Mr. Clement and Dan prefer to shoot twelve gauge, Mr. Clement because it hits more birds and Dan because it makes more noise. I prefer a twenty gauge; we brought out a twenty-eight for you because I think it will fit you better than the others. They may be a little long for you, but you are welcome to use any of the guns you like, Arthur."

"I do not prefer the twelve because it hits more, I prefer it because it fits me better. I always shoot twelve," said Mr. Clement, more to the trapper than to his family. Arthur thought he would like to crawl into the house with the trapper. Dan handed Arthur the gun, which Arthur opened and looked at. It was a twenty-eight gauge, over and under with a lot of engraving, it was light, a field gun not a skeet gun, but it would do fine. He didn't recognize the make, Holland and Holland. The trapper started a standard safety briefing which Arthur listened to and understood.

Dan said. "Club rules require that the trapper give a safety briefing to any new shooter on the course so there are no accidents." Mr. Clement looked as if he were being held up by the briefing.

Arthur nodded, kept the gun open, then returned it to the rack.

"What order would you like to shoot?" asked Bob looking at a small clip board.

Dan said to his father, "Let's make this fun, Mom and I will take on you and Arthur,"

Mrs. Clement joined in, "That sounds fair. Harold is the best shot, Arthur is new, so maybe we even it out with Dan's poor shooting."

Dan jumped in, "Come on, Dad, paper scissors rock, who shoots first, winner's choice."

If Mr. Clement thought he was going to run this show, he had missed the bus, it was already out of his control. Mrs. Clement and Dan had a relationship that was so close they read each other's minds and Mr. Clement was never going to catch up. He must have understood it and should have resigned his self-appointed commission as captain of this boat.

"Ready, dad," said Dan with his right hand extended "One, two, three." They shook their hands toward one another. On three they chose their weapons, Dan paper, Mr. Clement scissors.

"All right," said Mr. Clement, as if happy to have won this first encounter, "you shoot first. Arthur, you shoot after Dan, then Mrs. Clement, and I'll shoot last."

Trapper Bob wrote down the order of shooting. He had an electrical switch box on a long extension chord in his left hand. "Dan, you're up."

Dan took his spot at the first station under the high house, fiddled with his hat, then his glasses, then his gloves, looked down the tube of his gun, got two shells from a pocket of his coat, loaded them, looked at the sun, licked his finger and held it up in the wind, knocked imaginary dirt from his shoes as a batter might in baseball, looked down and removed imaginary grass from the concrete, as if he were lining up a putt, fiddled with his hat again.

"All right, goddammit, that's enough!" Mr. Clement roared.

Dan took a shooter's stance and called, "Pull,"

Bob pushed a button, a bird flew out of the house and away from Dan, "Boom", the bird escaped.

Bob said "No bird."

"Pull." Another bird came from the low house toward Dan.

Boom, the bird fell to the lawn in a couple of large pieces.

"Bird," said Bob.

Dan opened his gun. Two spent shells ejected to the grass; he put two more in, raised his gun, "Pull."

Bob pushed his button, two birds flew, one toward Dan, one away.

Boom boom.

"Bird, no bird," said Bob. "Arthur you're next."

Arthur moved to station one when Dan was clear. He was nervous; he was always nervous or numb. There was too much to think about, maybe he should be an idiot, just wander around noticing nothing at all, listen to no one, feel only the wind on his face or the ground under his feet and stop trying to figure out what was going on around him. Take up his favorite position as a leaf floating on a river carried along by both wind and current. Maybe he should ask them to take him to the railroad station and he could get a train for school. He had developed his habit to high art, he went along hoping to be saved at the next turn in the river.

He put two shells in the gun, closed it, raised it to the ready, "Pull."

A bird flew out of the house away from Arthur, he waited what he thought was too long, put the bird about a finger above the barrel and pulled the trigger.

Boom.

"Bird," said Bob

Dan was laughing. "Lucky shot," he said

"Pull."

Boom.

"Bird."

"Luckier shot," said Dan.

Arthur opened his gun and the two empty shells ejected automatically; he pulled two new shells out of his pocket and put them in the gun. He stood ready then raised the gun. "Pull."

Boom boom.

"Bird and bird."

"Great shooting," said Mrs. Clement, "you've obviously shot before."

"Thank you, yes ma'am," said Arthur nervous at acknowledging her compliment. He was sweating; little streams ran down his chest under his arms, they were cold and didn't make it to his belt, must have gotten grabbed up by his shirt in passing toward his underwear, which felt funny. Everything he thought about acquired the importance of a life raft to a drowning man. He would see something inconsequential but instead of letting go of it, he would seize it and it would squeeze everything else out. So the sweat under his arms seemed like the most important thing in the world until the dirt on his shoes captured his attention and for a moment blocked out every other thought. He was frozen looking at his shoes for a moment until the sound of the gun closing pushed his shoes out of the scene. He bounced from image to image, none complete in view or appreciation, each seeming a life raft till it was abandoned to ignominy when the next one came along. Arthur swam in circles, never getting on one raft but changing his focus every time a new twig or sound or the feeling of sweat rolling down his chest to be consumed by his shirt snatched him on a new course, a course with as much logic and importance as the course of a blind man on a wobbly bicycle bouncing off trees in a forest, the tree he just hit wiping out the memory of all the previous collisions.. He tried to act normal.

"Mrs. Clement, you're up," Bob said, looking at his card.

Mrs. Clement took her place and hit three of the four at station one.

"Hey Mom, you're going to have to do better than that if you're going to keep up with Arthur. I'll take care of Dad."

"Mr. Clement, your turn," said Bob.

Mr. Clement went to the pad under the high house and fiddled with his equipment for a while, got ready, "Pull."

Boom.

"Bird," said Bob.

"Pull." Loud, like coxswain at a crew race.

Boom.

"Bird," said Bob.

"Pull."

Boom boom.

"Bird and bird," said Bob without expression.

Dan went first at station two and hit two out of a possible four.

Bob looked at Arthur. "Arthur, you're on station."

Arthur negotiated with his perception, he was on a high wire, the difficulty of each step erasing the triumph of the last, he remembered being told it was the one you fell from that was important and you always fell from the one you were on, not the one you came from. Sweat ran down his chest under his shirt, and it was still cold. He took his position and raised his gun.

"Arthur," Dan spoke up. "You better put some ammo in that thing or you're going to have to chase the bird and swat it with the stock of the gun. He shoots good when he's got bullets." Dan was laughing again, having more fun with the commentary then with the shooting.

Arthur opened the gun and looked in at the empty tubes; sure enough, he'd forgotten to load it. His vision had narrowed to the vanishing point; he was sliding down a little hole in the pavement, becoming so small he could slide through the cracks. He wanted to quit. Why was everyone watching? Bob wasn't, he was looking at his clipboard. Maybe you had to tip him more to get him to look up at you. Mr. Clement was watching him. Mrs. Clement was watching. Dan was, but he was smiling. The Clements had rented a bad movie and were about to turn it off. Why didn't he just shoot in the air four or five times and be done with it. He opened the gun, put two shells in and snapped it back closed, stood on the pad and thought about what he was supposed to do. Watch the bird for a second, bring the gun to it like you want to capture it, it's a butterfly net, let the bird fly into it, keep the bird in the net then pull the trigger. That's it, that's all you have to do, simple.

"Pull."

Boom.

"No bird."

Arthur hadn't seen it; he wasn't looking, maybe his eyes were closed, he couldn't remember. Get it over with. "Pull." Arthur saw it, put the gun on it and instinctively pulled as the barrel came up under the black spec flying at him.

"Bird," said Bob without emotion as if marking refrigerators on an assembly line. Did he know what was at stake here? He couldn't. Arthur didn't. A ritual was playing out, a contest, Arthur was in the middle but he didn't know the rules or the stakes.

Arthur reloaded. "Pull."

Boom boom.

"Bird and bird," said Bob.

Mrs. Clement shot two of four.

Mr. Clement got to the line He was serious, studied.

Dan spoke up in an imitation announcer's voice. "OK Dad, the pressure's on. The little boy from Oklahoma who hasn't shot anything bigger than a BB gun may have the lead if you screw this up."

"Pull."

Boom.

"Bird."

"Pull."

Boom.

"Bird."

"Pull."

Boom boom.

"Bird and bird"

Mr. Clement had eight, Arthur seven, Mrs. Clement five and Dan four.

"Station three, two birds," said Bob. "Dan, your shot."

Dan took his position and got one of two. Arthur two of two, Mrs. Clement one of two and Mr. Clement two.

Mr. Clement and Arthur were within one bird of each other at station seven. "Dan, your shot," said Bob.

Dan took his place, fiddled with his hat and gloves and shoes, tested the wind. He kicked at mud and was about to move imaginary grass when his father said, "Stop the horseshit and get on with it." He said it seriously in a harsh whisper, he wasn't kidding around.

Dan stood still for a moment, turned and smiled at his mother then called, "Pull."

Boom.

"Bird."

"Pull."

Boom.

"Bird" said Bob. Everyone knew it was a bird, Dan had smoked it, nothing left but a puff of dust.

"Pull."

Boom. Dan shot the moment the coming bird appeared in the far window. He shot so fast the bird pulp bounced off the high house. He shot the coming bird first, then shot the going away bird which was a nearly impossible shot except by a very good shooter with a twelve gauge.

Boom.

"Bird and bird" said Bob, no expression although it was clear he had seen and appreciated what Dan had done. Normally you would shoot the going away bird first so it didn't get too far away, then shoot the coming bird which would be in range of catcher's mitt when you hit it. The way Dan had shot, both birds were hard to hit; the coming bird had to be taken early or the going bird was impossible.

"So, Dad you're going to have to be steady here; the Baron's got his gun and obviously he knows how to use it even though he has only about half the gun you do."

Mr. Clement said in a tired voice, "Dan. Shut up."

"Harold don't use that word," said Mrs. Clement.

"Goddamit, Dan is trying to irritate me, take my mind off the shot. You know what he's doing. He knows. I know. He's trying to irritate me, and guess what, he's succeeding."

He turned to Arthur, "Would you like to use my gun for this shot?" asked Mr. Clement.

"No sir, this gun is fine and it's the right length. You were right about a gun that's too long, it makes you lock your arm or pull in too hard on the stock, so you can't see the target." Arthur tried to vent a dangerous situation, he wasn't drifting now; he was paddling out from between Dan and Mr. Clement. He had to get out of the way and he wasn't sure how to do it. He didn't want a showdown on station eight, the next station after this one, with Mr. Clement. The easy choice was to try to duplicate Dan's shot. If he missed, which he would, that would give him an excuse and Mr. Clement would remain safely in the lead. If he hit, it was obviously a lucky shot, he'd be hotdogging, and that wouldn't count anyway.

"Arthur, your shot," said Bob.

Arthur took his spot, loaded, snapped the gun together, lifted it and called "Pull"

Boom.

"Bird."

"Pull."

Boom.

"Bird."

Easy shots. Arthur wouldn't miss these unless he were throwing the match and that would be insultingly obvious.

Arthur reloaded. He decided to try Dan's shot, he would probably miss both and then the pressure would be off.

"Pull"

He shot the instant the far bird was out of the window thirty yards away and got it before it cleared the porch. The second bird was hard to find, it was just in view, put the gun on it, stroke it once, then pull, about two fingers under the bird to have a chance. By the time he pulled the trigger the second bird was nearly on the ground and past the high house.

Boom pause boom.

"Bird and bird" said Bob without expression, looking at the score card.

"Great shot, Baron," said Dan. He didn't believe it himself. He thought maybe Arthur hadn't seen what he had done on his shot but now there was no question.

Bob looked at Mrs. Clement "Mrs. Clement, you're up."

Mrs. Clement took her spot beside the low house and said. "Well, I guess that's the way this station is shot, so I'll have to try it myself."

She shot the first two normally and hit two out of two. She missed both on the double waiting too long to take the coming bird. "Well, that was fun," she said waving to the bird that got away by her on the left.

"Mr. Clement, you're on station," said Bob.

"OK, ladies and gentlemen," Dan resumed in his announcer's provocation, "this is the world final shoot off. On your right is Harold Clement who is about to shoot his penultimate round. In order to stay in the race he needs at least three of the four birds. However, to keep his dignity he has to shoot the shot reverse as the Baron demonstrated with a 28 gauge gun."

"Dan, enough," said Mrs. Clement.

If Dan thought he was funny, Mr. and Mrs. didn't. But Arthur didn't think Dan was being funny; there was an edge in the situation that exposed itself in Mr. Clement's reaction.

"OK, Dad, show 'em how it's done." Dan was pushing too hard.

Mr. Clement had stopped talking, he was stiff as if near a breaking point, his modulus of elasticity decaying, stress turning to strain. He took his position and called, "Pull."

Boom.

"Bird."

"Pull."

Boom.

"Bird."

He reloaded and had to make the choice. He didn't have to go for the long shot, and he didn't. He wasn't a hot dog.

"Pull."

Boom boom.

"Bird and bird."

They went to the last station. Two overhead shots, easy most of the time unless there was pressure, then not so easy as they looked. You had to be loose.

Dan got two.

Arthur went to the pad, loaded, and said, "Pull."

There was a hesitation, just long enough to be a timing problem. The bird came overhead, Arthur lifted his gun but didn't pull the trigger. He lowered the gun and said. "How stupid, I forgot the safety." He'd learned this in Grape; if you got a bad pull, don't shoot it. Act like there was an equipment malfunction and then everyone is off the hook. The shooter gets a second shot, the trapper has done his job for the big tipper and can't possibly be late again without giving the game away, and the big tipper has given it a try.

Arthur looked at the safety, fiddled with it, then lined up again and said, "Pull."

Boom.

"No bird." said Bob. Arthur figured Bob understood what he had done. Arthur was telling Bob and Mr. Clement he wasn't playing.

You win, your club, your rules, no enemies.

Arthur hadn't been in a situation like this before. He remembered sitting around the clubhouse in Grape between shoots, listening to some of the old farts who hung around telling stories of things that happened to them over the years. One of the cardinal rules was; "Never confront a man who has a gun." Even if you have one yourself, the odds were not in your favor; the odds were, both of you would get hurt. "Confront the guy when you have a gun and he doesn't." "Ha, ha, ha," they'd laugh and tell stories about how people tried to screw their opponent with tricks or too much talk. They'd buy or make special birds out of tire rubber and put them in the stack for the trapper to send out against their opponents. It didn't matter if you stood three feet away and shot the thing dead center; it wouldn't break, just bounce around a little and keep flying. They'd reload shells with just enough powder for the shot to roll out of the end of the barrel and dribble to the ground, Then they would sneak the reloads in their opponent's kit. "No bird."…"Ha, ha, ha." They told stories about giving the opponent five broken birds in a row to get their timing off. They had strategies on broken equipment and how to use it in your favor. If the opponent was getting upset or a client was shooting badly, use the broken equipment rule, make one up. Their second rule was: "Never make an enemy on the range." The theory being, enemies were too easy to make off the range and no reason to "screw up a good day shooting with the gun pointed at you, Ha, ha, ha." Arthur listened to all their stuff.

One of the old guys whom Arthur liked told a story about going to someone else's club and being in a tie with his host to the last station. The trapper pulled the late bird trick, and the guest, Arthur's friend, says to himself, never shoot a bad pull, so he lets it fly by and claims his safety was on. No one argues a safety. So he lines up for the second pull and misses both, on purpose. Never make an enemy on the range he thinks. His old friend said he didn't think the opponent put the trapper up to the bad pull, the trapper was just protecting his tip. Don't confront a guy with a gun. All the rules right there in one story, and there they were again for Arthur. They worked fine.

Mrs. Clement shot, then Mr. Clement; he hit both and won the shoot by three. The trapper got his tip and Mr. Clement had a little more respect for Arthur. Arthur didn't suspect Mr. Clement put the trapper up to his questionable pull; Arthur figured the trapper was protecting cash flow without instruction, just like his friend and the trapper years ago, he knew who paid the bills and he hadn't seen Arthur's name on any Christmas checks.

Dan looked at Arthur with a smile. "Well, Baron, you're not as bad with a gun as you are with the tennis racket," They left their guns in the rack, the guns would be cleaned, cased and returned to the car by the trappers.

Some of the nervousness was gone. Arthur felt not so much like a leaf floating on the river as a guy who has managed to grab a life raft and now has a chance to survey that situation. He was still a foreigner and the tension between Mr. Clement and Dan was still obvious but it was less likely he would drown as a result of it.

Someone brought the car around; the guns were in the back and they went to the island.

Dan asked Arthur if he wanted to shoot some hockey pucks. Arthur said OK, so they walked off the island to the side of the barn where Dan had painted an outline the size of a hockey goal. Dan went in a side door and brought out a piece of board about four feet long and a foot wide He put it on the ground about twenty feet in front of the goal, then went back in the barn and came out with a hockey stick, a bar of soap and a bag of hockey pucks. Arthur hadn't seen a puck before, it was a hard black rubber disk about the size of a flat paperweight and weighed about the same.

There were four holes in the board and Dan proceeded to drive tent stakes through the holes level with the surface of the board and into the ground with the back of a shovel. "The stakes keep the board from moving."

He emptied the bag of pucks next to the board, then got down on his hands and knees and rubbed soap on the middle. He got up and flipped one of the pucks onto the board with the flat end of the stick. He took the stick in both hands, his right hand a little above the curve where the stick flared into a blade and his left at the top where a knot of tape was wrapped around the end. He twisted, brought the blade end up behind his head, then released, uncoiling with the blade slashing down at the puck on the board. As the blade hit the board the stick bent as a leaf spring would under pressure then the blade met the puck and as it cleared the board the stick recoiled with the twisting of Dan's body and Dan followed the stroke through toward the barn wall. There was a slapping noise as the puck took off and a crash almost as loud as a shotgun report as the puck hit the barn in the middle of where the imaginary net was drawn.

Whack, bang, whack, bang whack bang, three more in the imaginary net.

"You want to try it?" asked Dan.

"Sure." Arthur took the stick and approached the board. He tried to flip a puck onto the board using the blade as Dan had but the puck must have run out of juice because all it did was squirt around sidestepping as Arthur was flipping. He tried a few more times then leaned over and picked up one of the ones that hadn't got too far away in his groping and placed it where he wanted it. He tried Dan's grip but the stick was too long so he could either hold onto one end and the middle or the other end and the middle or the middle and the middle, but both ends at once was beyond him. He took the blade end and the middle then tried to imitate Dan's stance but rather than looking like a mad Samurai about to remove a head, he looked like a man who got tangled up with a stick and the stick was winning.

He coiled up like he imagined Dan had and then uncoiled in a great flurry of arms and hands and stick, which was still winning, and whack. The blade hit the end of the board and stopped dead, about ten inches from the puck as if it had got tired of screwing around with Arthur. It sat there, the puck sat there, nothing was moving except Arthur who was still uncoiling a little more than he wanted to right into the ground. He ended up twisted around the stick on his knees.

Dan looked down. "The first half's a little stronger than the finish." He reached down and took the stick from Arthur. Dan was

171

pretty glib with the terminal, smart-ass remarks. He wasn't this way at school and Arthur wondered what the difference was.

"Try this." He demonstrated not so much windup and more follow through. "Try it without the puck." He handed the stick to Arthur.

Arthur took it and did as Dan instructed but the stick hardly went past the middle of the board.

"OK, through the board and out the other side," Dan said.

Arthur tried again and not much improvement so they put a puck down and it managed to slide off the board, more out of embarrassment than being hit. One of his tries actually made it to the barn on the run, rolling on its edge.

Arthur was tired of it and preferred to watch Dan, so he stood on the sidelines as Dan whacked away sending bullets against the barn. After a while Dan asked, "Want to play goalie?"

"How?" Arthur asked?"

"I got a glove in the barn, you stand in front of the barn and try to catch the pucks I shoot; try to keep them from getting through to the outline on the barn wall."

"Are you kidding me, a glove?"

"Really, it's a goalie glove made to catch pucks; it looks like a first baseman's mitt only a little bigger." Dan put the stick down and went to the barn door and came back with a big leather glove that looked like a giant lobster claw. "It's not that hard; Tom and I do it all the time, try to shoot past each other," he said. He threw the glove to Arthur picked up the stick. "Put it on and stand down there," pointing in front of the cage drawn on the barn door. "I'll send you some soft ones."

Arthur backed up to the barn and put on the glove. It was way too big and floppy; and was hard to open and close.

"You ready?" Dan asked.

"OK."

"Open the glove and stick it out front, get down in a crouch and lean forward," said Dan.

Dan looked down at the puck on the board, put the blade behind it and lifted it off the board and toward Arthur in a soft arc. It fell short; Arthur reached out but missed. Dan tried again and this time the puck got to Arthur and he managed to catch it but it rolled out of the glove.

"That's it, glove open, stop the puck, put it on the ground."

They hit and caught for a while with Dan picking up the tempo as Arthur got the hang of it. It was easier to catch a puck hit hard than one hit easy because the puck had a straighter flight and seemed to stick in the glove better. It didn't take Dan long before he was banging away pretty hard and Arthur felt the tug on the glove when he caught the puck, both of them enjoyed the rhythm of the shoot and catch. About ten minutes into it, one of the pucks glanced off the top of the glove and hit Arthur in the side of the head. It didn't look like it was going very fast but it knocked him down and made a terrible burning feeling in his ear and he saw stars for a minute. He got up and put his hand to the side of his head and it was slick and warm. The puck had hit the top of his ear and mashed it against his head, in effect splitting the top of Arthur's ear open and his scalp behind it for about an inch and it was bleeding pretty hard.

By the time Arthur stood up, Dan was in front of him. "Jesus, what happened?"

Arthur looked at his bloody hand, then put it back to his head, feeling around for the problem.

"Does it hurt?" Dan asked, hoping the scene into reverse; it didn't accommodate him.

"I think it cut my ear," said Arthur. His ear was still bleeding and the blood ran off his chin and down the front of his jacket.

"That doesn't look too good. I'll go get my mom; you stay here."

"I can walk OK, I'll come with you."

Arthur could walk OK, but he was dizzy and nauseated. When they got to the house, Dan ran up the stairs calling for his mother and Arthur stood in the hall feeling sick holding his head but not touching his ear while the blood ran down his neck and chin.

Mrs. Clement came out of the hall to the kitchen followed by Dan and Mr. Clement.

Mr. Clement approached Arthur. "You dumb asses, playing goalie with no equipment; are you retarded?" He said it before he saw the damage. Mr. Clement had been interrupted by Dan and thought maybe there was a nick or a bruise, but when he got close to Arthur he changed his tone. "My God, what did you do?" as if asking Arthur what he had done to himself, maybe he'd taken a hammer and beaten himself in the head.

Mrs. Clement came to the rescue. She said in a calm voice, "Harold, go get the car; we'll meet you out front. Arthur sit here on the floor, just sit down, right now, I'll be right back." Mr. and Mrs. Clement disappeared.

"Man, you should see your ear." said Dan, "It looks like two flaps of steak pumping blood.".

Arthur sat in a fog again, familiar territory. He was lightheaded and sitting on the floor sounded like a great idea. Mrs. Clement returned with towels and put them on Arthur's ear, not rubbing or scrubbing just covering the thing up, then she put a little pressure on, "Can you stand?"

Arthur thought he could stand, no problem, but when he started up he was going up sideways and Mrs. Clement caught him and helped him up while holding a towel on the side of his head. They walked to the front door, Arthur in mixed emotions between feeling like he could go on his own and a desire to sit down and shut his eyes for minute.

Mr. Clement had the car at the front door. Dan got in the front; Mrs. Clement pushed Arthur into the back and climbed in right after him. "Can you hold this towel on your head?" she asked.

"Umhm," said Arthur, reaching up and holding the towel. This was a mess, he thought. Then myopia grabbed him; he felt sick and didn't care about the mess.

They pulled up at the emergency room of the hospital. Mrs. Clement got out, then Arthur stumbled and followed her into the emergency room holding the towel but it slipped down around his neck and shoulder. By the time they were inside the doors, folks in white coats had Arthur by the arms. They nearly carried him to a table and hefted him on it. He lay on the table looking at the lights above him.

Someone took the towel off and was searching around in his split ear, looking for what Arthur couldn't imagine. Someone else was trying to raise him enough to get his coat off, then his shirt. Mrs. Clement talked in the background; Dan said something, Arthur was sprayed with a hose and it dripped and ran all over him, spray in his mouth, the cot was cold, he was watching a movie again where he was an actor, but he watched from a distance.

A face appeared above him. "Can you hear me?"

Arthur didn't feel much like talking, he wanted to go to sleep; he nodded.

"What's your name?"

Arthur nodded. It seemed like the easiest thing to do, nod. He closed is eyes.

"Son, try not to go to sleep. I need to ask you some questions, if you can't talk then nod or shake your head or squeeze my fingers." He held one of Arthur's hands but Arthur didn't know which one.

Arthur nodded with his eyes closed.

"Can you open your eyes?"

Arthur nodded and opened them. The fellow asking the questions pointed a light in Arthur's eye, "Can you follow the light?"

Arthur nodded but didn't follow; he didn't care.

"Do you feel sleepy?"

Arthur nodded.

"Keep your eyes open for just a minute, try to follow the light with your eyes as I move it around." He moved it around, left, right, up, down; Arthur followed sloppily, but got it about right.

"OK, that's great. Can you squeeze my fingers?" Arthur squeezed; they went through a lot of little tests, squeeze this, follow that, lift, does this tickle, can you feel that, sharp or dull ... Arthur got most of the answers right.

"If you feel sick, just lean over. There's a pan right next to you."

A nurse stayed with him as the guy asking the questions talked to Mrs. Clement. Arthur couldn't hear the words just the mumbles of conversation, short questions, short answers. Arthur had his eyes closed but the light came through his lids in pink and red. He liked holding the nurse's hand and wondered if she liked it too. The place was cold, the table was cold even the nurse's hand was cold. After a while they rolled him into a room and rolled him on his side, bad ear up. They put pillows under his head and moved the cart and moved a thing that hung down from the ceiling. When they had run out of interior design ideas and done all the rearrangement they could think of, they left the room to consult and then the thing hanging from the ceiling whirred and clicked. They came back and moved him some more, and came and went and whirred and clicked, then they wheeled him out of the room and parked him in a hallway, as if they didn't need him anymore.

He lay thinking a nap might be nice except he had a headache where his head was split open and his ear was on fire, other than that, a nap would be good. Someone grabbed the cart and pushed it down a hallway, then onto an elevator that smelled like a chemical factory: ether, alcohol, Merthiolate, acetone, anti-bacterial soap, cigarettes and bad perfume. He'd had better olfactory experiences. Off the elevator, down a dark hall, he expected to be put on the loading dock for the dumpster pickup but they had stopped at a nurses' station for a small chat about someone's daughter's school play that Arthur didn't care much about. They stopped, they were in a hospital room or a strange hotel, two beds both empty, lots of pipes and wires hanging from the wall above the beds and a little curtain not enough to discourage a mosquito dangling between them.

The guy pushing the cart said to Arthur, "We need to get your pants off, can you lift your butt high enough so I can slide them off. Then I'll give you a hospital top to put on." He talked to Arthur as if Arthur was at the other end of a twenty-foot drainage pipe, slow and deliberate, Arthur was right there, no need for treating him like he didn't speak English.

Arthur put his weight on his feet and his shoulders and pushed his hips in the air while he slid his trousers down, someone had already undone his belt and zipper; he wondered if it was the nurse who held his hand. His shoes were gone, maybe they were thinking on divvying up his belongings before they put him in the dumpster. The guy pushing the cart and doing the wardrobe work handed Arthur something only Pa Brown would have understood. It was a rag with two worn out strings on it. It was only big enough to cover what he didn't mind showing, and it was so thin that what it wanted to cover would have to be colorless, shapeless and close to invisible to have any effect at all. It would have been better as mosquito netting except it was too small even for the mosquitoes to have paid it any attention and it had a few holes in it..

The guy pushing took Arthur's pants and put them in a closet in the corner of the room, then he took his socks and put them in with his shoes which had already got in there, they must have been on the cart with him. He kind of wished they'd lost his shoes as they had embarrassed him since his first day at school and he didn't look forward to wearing them out. Maybe he'd just scrape them on a rock till they had holes and make his father get him different ones now that he knew what kind of shoes he was looking for.

A nurse came in and they pushed the cart up against his bed. The two of them slid their hands under him, all four hands, flat, palms up, one each under his head, shoulders, hips and knees, and slid him onto the bed without missing or putting him in the crack between the cart and the bed. He wondered if they ever missed. He could see some old lady in a crumpled up pile between the bed and cart and the nurse saying aviation and medicine's most un-favorite word: "Oops."

Mrs. Clement came in. "How do you feel?" Silly question, but he was happy to see her.

Arthur didn't know what to say so he said, "I have a headache." He didn't know which was sillier, the question or the answer.

"I called your father; he's talking to the doctor now." she said. She stood next to the bed and he could smell her perfume.

Arthur turned to her, "I'm sorry; I didn't mean to mess up your Thanksgiving," It leaked out of him; he hadn't planned on saying it, it was the sum of his embarrassment. Every time he saw her he was doing something stupid, sitting on an unmade bed, telling her about his mother, wearing bad clothes, irritating Mr. Clement, now the hospital. And every time he saw her she was picking up after him, making his bed, holding his hand, bringing him home for vacation, sticking up for him in front of Mr. Clement, making him feel good, and now driving him to the hospital. This was a pretty lop-sided relationship. He felt like crying again, blind and helpless, feeling around for a door in a wall whose dimensions he could not appreciate.

"You didn't mess anything up, everyone is fine, this will be over before you know it." She stood near the bed looking at him and then looking out the window.

The doctor came in. "The x-rays seem OK, no fracture, maybe a concussion so we want you to spend the night here so we can keep an eye on things, then, if no more problems, you can go home tomorrow." He turned to Mrs. Clement. "I talked to Dr. May; he's got a good read on the situation, no emergency. He asked if you might give him a call later this evening." Then back to Arthur, "A plastic surgeon will come later tonight to sew up your ear so we're not going to do anything to it now except put ice on it to keep the swelling down. He'll stitch it up in the emergency room where he has the equipment he needs. Any questions?" looking at Arthur, then Mrs. Clement.

She asked, "What time do you think he'll be able to leave tomorrow?"

"I want to take another look tomorrow and get some more pictures, so I think about nine in the morning," he said. "I'll be here when the plastic surgeon comes in later, so I'll see you then."

He left.

Mrs. Clement sat in the chair next to the window, a chair designed for waiting and sleeping.

Arthur didn't think she should wait here with him. "Mrs. Clement you don't have to wait here, I'm OK,"

"That's all right, Arthur. I'll stay until the plastic surgeon comes. Let's see how that goes and then we'll decide if I need to stay. I'd get you some aspirin for your headache but the surgeon doesn't want you to have any medication before he gets here."

Arthur had a loose bandage around his head over his bad ear and an ice pack next to it, so he lay looking at the ceiling; he really wanted to lie on his side with the bad ear up but the bandage and ice pack wouldn't line up right except when he lay on his back.

He was talked out. He had nothing left to say. His visit to the island had drained him emotionally and the puck to the head had taken the rest of juice out of him. He didn't want to move or talk or think about anything. He was happy Mrs. Clement was there, he liked her and he was more confident with her in the room than if she had gone home with Dan and Mr. Clement, but he didn't want to ruin her vacation with Tom and Dan. Mixed up, all of it, wanting and guessing at what other people wanted. He closed his eyes and let the whirr of the ventilation system take over.

He woke up when a fellow came into the room with a wheelchair and pushed it next to the bed. Mrs. Clement rose from her chair. Arthur felt fuzzy-headed.

The man with the chair said, "We're going to take you down to Emergency to get your ear sewn up. Can you stand up or do you need help getting in the chair?"

Arthur swung his legs over the side of the bed and remembered he had the silly bib tied around his neck. It was supposed to be a gown or PJ's or something but it was a loose, thin bib with holes in it. He seemed to be the only one concerned about it. The guy held the wheelchair as Arthur slid in, then Mrs. Clement grabbed one of the blankets off the bed, folded it and put it over Arthur's lap. It was the only thing in the hospital that was warm.

"You fell asleep," she said, walking beside him.

"Yeah, was I out long?" It was dark outside; the halls in the hospital were quiet.

She looked ahead, swimming in her own thoughts. "No, about half an hour,"

He wondered what she was thinking. She should be at Goose Island with the boys and Mr. Clement and instead she was hanging around hospital with a wrecked weekend guest. She put her hand on his shoulder.

When they reached the emergency room, the plastic surgeon and a nurse were already there chatting. The surgeon was only about five feet tall; maybe he was a child prodigy or a midget who worked on small things. They helped Arthur get onto a table and told him to lie on his side. The nurse and surgeon chatted with an occasional question or instruction to Arthur but it was clear that as far as they were concerned he was an ear on a table that needed sewing. They gave him some shots around his ear and chin and scalp; the shots

178

didn't hurt, only stung a little, burned a little, then went away. They sprayed and picked and shaved, wasting time.

"Can you feel this?" the surgeon said while he tried to remove Arthur's ear with a pair of pliers. Seemed Arthur didn't have to answer when the tears shot out of his eyes. The surgeon and nurse looked at each other as if to say, maybe a little longer, then they tried the pliers trick again and on the third time he couldn't really feel it, all he could feel was someone trying to tug at his head; it was numb.

The surgeon mumbled through his mask, "OK, Arthur, tell us if it hurts too much. We gave you a shot to help you relax and some Novocain for the ear but if it hurts too much let us know." He had a headlight suspended from a black band around his head, a blue paper cap, glasses, paper overalls and rubber gloves. He could have been Frosty the Snowman.

The surgeon started to sew and talked to the nurse about his Thanksgiving; the high point was sewing Arthur's ear. They chatted on, muffled by their masks, as if Arthur wasn't there. They could have been shopping for broccoli. They quit sewing and bandaged.

"Arthur, you hang on here for a while; we'll send you upstairs in a minute." Arthur wasn't going anywhere. Mrs. Clement had watched the whole thing from the corner of the room. The surgeon took off his disguise and went to Mrs. Clement. He didn't stand real close to save her from leaning over too far. They talked and he left. Mrs. Clement came to the side of the table.

"That wasn't so bad, was it?" she said. It wasn't really a question; it was propaganda meant to alter the truth.

"Only the part where he tried to take my ear off with the pliers." Arthur tried to laugh but the emotions were confused and it came out with tears attached. "Mrs. Clement, you don't have to stay; I'm all right. It didn't hurt too much and it feels fine now."

She stood next to him, looking at him as if he were a lost then found puppy, "I'll go up to your room and make sure you're tucked in, then I'll go home. How's that?"

He was glad she was staying and he wasn't glad, everything was mixed up, nothing had cleared except his feelings for her. The last person to make sure he was tucked in was his mother and that was a long time ago, it was a hazy, wishful recollection of the way he wanted to remember the past rather than an accurate memory. He felt it again at the prospect that Mrs. Clement cared about him.

They went upstairs, Arthur on the cart, Mrs. Clement walking beside. He got off by himself and discovered the size of the bandage; it was as large as half a grapefruit taped to the side of his head completely covering his ear and some of his head The bandage went around his head and was there only to hold the grapefruit in place. Arthur got in bed and lay on his back waiting. Mrs. Clement tucked him in, gave him a kiss on the cheek, and said good night. When she left she turned out the light. Her scent, her warmth, the feel of her weight on the bed where she'd put her hand down when she leaned over to give him a kiss, and the smell of her lipstick lingered.

Arthur lay for a while. He thought about the skeet range, where he had figured out what he ought to do about the bad pull. It was a good plan and it rescued him from being a leaf blown about by the breeze. He had taken charge and managed the situation and it worked out just about the way he figured it would. He'd changed his course on the river, he hadn't had much effect on the river itself, it flowed the same, but he was different. When he had gone to shoot pucks with Dan the confidence he got from shooting skeet carried over, he was still in charge of small things, and as the pucks came faster he felt more in command, more relaxed. And then one hit him in the head and all the confidence leaked out between his fingers. He was back to foreigner status, confused, alienated. No happy thoughts crossed his horizon as he drifted, and then he fell asleep.

A cart arrived at five-thirty with breakfast on trays. It was a blonde breakfast, plain, steamy, except where it had gotten cold waiting in the elevator. It smelled like the elevator. Arthur wasn't hungry; he lay in bed and waited for the nurse or doctor to come and tell him he could go, but no one read his mind. He got out of bed and walked to the nurse's station; what remained of the bib, which stayed tied around his throat and with which he had wrestled and lost all night, flapped in the breeze of his passage. The two little strings meant to hold it in place had got pulled into an impossibly small, tight knot around his neck and were near extrangulating him from the front. Beyond that, the flapping behind and extrangulating in front, the bib served no useful purpose. Arthur supposed they made you wear them to humiliate you so you wouldn't complain about Dr. Mengele and his pliers on your ear or about the blonde breakfast. They seemed to have figured it out pretty well because as he approached the nurses' station, one of them, one of the wardens, gave him a look that sent him back to his room without answers to questions unasked.

About eight-thirty the doctor came in and did some of the tests he'd done the day before: pull this, feel that, follow the light up, down, left, right, cross your eyes, sharp or dull.... Arthur passed; he was bright awake and had a terrific headache, but that was it, no serious injury.

"OK, Arthur, you can go home, no running or horsing around till the stitches come out in a week. I mean it; if the stitches come out then we'll have to sew it again without Novocain, ha, ha, ha. The nurse at your school can pull the stitches and change the bandage if she has too. No showers, no washing hair, no brushing or combing. Understand?"

Arthur nodded.

"Mrs. Clement sent someone to pick you up, so you can get dressed and wait for them downstairs." The doctor left.

Arthur changed. He had blood on his pants and shirt, his jacket was gone. He went downstairs to the reception area and waited. The station wagon pulled around the drive and stopped in front. Arthur went to meet it.

Dan got out, "Hey, what are you growing on the side of your head?"

"Does it look weird?" asked Arthur putting his hand up again to assess the size of the bandage.

"Yeah, it's weird; have you seen it?"

"Not yet"

"Jump in, we'll go back home."

Dan got in the front, Arthur got in back and they went through town to the island. Mrs. Clement was in the kitchen with Carmen when they arrived, when Carmen saw Arthur she screamed and put her hands over her eyes.

"What they do to you, Arthur?" she asked.

"Good morning Arthur."

"Hi, Mrs. Clement."

"Do you want breakfast or a bath, maybe both, which first?" she asked.

"I'd like to clean up if it's OK?" he said wanting to get out of the clothes that felt gooey and must have looked used up.

"Go on up; we'll be here when you finish. Bath, remember, no showers and no brushing hair."

Arthur turned to go to his room; Dan followed. They went up to Arthur's room where Arthur took off his clothes and threw them in a pile on the floor. Dan sat on a bed.

"Does it hurt?" asked Dan.

"Not now, but it did last night."

"Mom said they had to sew up your ear and the side of your head; she said she watched the whole thing."

"Yeah, they did that last night. The worst part was a little gown they make you wear."

"How long do you have to wear your bandage?"

"A week then Miss what's-her-name, the nurse at school, can take it off." Arthur went to the bureau and got clean underwear and socks and threw them on the bed. He walked to the bathroom and Dan followed him in.

"My dad was pissed."

"Yeah, I could tell yesterday when we came in. He yelled at us."

"He didn't finish yelling till last night. Tom and I have done the hockey thing for years; Tom taught me. My dad told us not to do it or someone would get hurt, but we did it anyway. I got hit in the stomach once, not hard; that was the worst till you. I guess we'll have to give up slap shots for a while."

"Why was he mad at me?" asked Arthur turning on the tub water.

"He's always mad at someone. He was mad because you got hurt and you should know better. You got hurt at his house and inconvenienced him. He claims Tom and I are always bringing people home from school, people who need help, lost puppies, and interrupting his routine. He's mostly mad because Mom pays attention to us, to Tom and me and now you. He thinks things should revolve around him."

"Should I go back to school?" Arthur asked. He didn't know how he'd get back, maybe he should go, he would be more comfortable and Mr. Clement would like it better if he weren't there. No one wants a mummy walking around his house.

"No, don't worry about it. All you have to do is be quiet for a while and he'll forget it.

Dan left. Arthur took a bath, put on clean clothes, and returned to the kitchen where Carmen was making something on the stove. She brought him a glass of juice. He walked to the living room where Mrs. Clement and Dan were talking. They stopped when he came in.

"Arthur, do you feel like a ride into the city?" Mrs. Clement looked at him.

"OK, fine."

"Dan, do you want to go?"

"Sure."

"Let's go. Get a coat. George is ready; I'll meet you at the car," said Mrs. Clement as she got up from a sofa.

George drove, Dan and Arthur sat in the back. When they got into mid-town the buildings towered over canyons of honking cars. There were people and cars and buildings in every square inch, the sky was just little thin strips of pale blue, like ribbon on a package if you were inside looking out. They pulled over to a curb where Mrs. Clement got out, Dan followed, then Arthur figured he should get out too. They went into a huge store whose first impression was yellow, a pale yellow alcove in a canyon of dark brick, dirty cement and wet black streets. An alcove of yellow walls, mahogany cabinets with glass tops covered with bright silk. Arthur almost fell onto a counter with thousands of ties loosely arranged on its glass top. To the right another counter with shirts in glass cases, suits and jackets and pants on hangers inside mahogany cases, shoes on shelves, luggage, all of it clean and shiny. And in the background pale yellow framed in mahogany and the smell of Bay Rum mixed with saddle soap.

Mrs. Clement led the way to the elevators at the back of the store. They got in. The elevator was made of polished wood on the inside and it had an operator who wore a clean uniform and asked what floor they wanted. The elevator's floor had carpet in spotless maroon so thick Arthur wanted to stand on it barefoot.

In Grape there was one building with an elevator and the guy who ran it wasn't too interested where you wanted to go because he was an amateur statistician. There were only three floors in the building and you were on one of them. He figured most of the time people wanted to go to the third floor or they would have walked up the stairs to the second rather than put up with his wheezing cigarette smoke to get there. And he was right, most of the time. Sometimes people walked to the third but he didn't worry the probabilities on them. So he didn't ask. He half stood, half sat on a little black circular wood seat that folded out of the wall and he looked at the floor to make sure your foot wasn't outside when he closed the door. He had a switch that stuck out of a panel on the wall. He pushed or pulled the switch to make the thing go up and down. He didn't ask what floor, he just took you right up to three and if he was wrong and you didn't get off, then he'd drop you at the second floor on his way down. He was right most of the time and nobody complained because they couldn't remember it being any different.

The floor of the thing was made of squares of linoleum meant to look like checkerboard, black and white marble, but the effort was in vain because the linoleum was cheap and hadn't ever fooled anyone in the beginning. Later it had worn through under the operator's feet and at the entrance, so some wood showed where you were hoping to find marble. At the entry to the cage there was a brass strip on the floor with grooves in it. The grooves were always filthy, filled with gum, shiny gum wrapper tidbits, and sand.

The doors opened and a man stood waiting for them. "Good morning, Mrs. Clement."

"Good morning, Mr. Downs. You remember my son Dan?"

"Yes. Good morning, Dan."

"And this is his friend from school, Arthur May."

"It's a pleasure to meet you Arthur," he said to Arthur, then he turned to Mrs. Clement. "How can I help you?"

No one shook hands; this was not a meeting of peers.

"Arthur needs some clothes for school," said Mrs. Clement, "suits, jackets and trousers."

"Good," he said knowing that when Mrs. Clement said some she meant lots. "Would you want those readymade or tailored?" he asked.

"Off the rack, there won't be time to have them made," said Mrs. Clement.

"What size are you Arthur?" he asked.

Arthur looked at Mrs. Clement. Would she know; who would know? "I don't know," he said to her rather than to the man.

He approached Arthur. "Well, then, let's have a look. Why don't you take off your jacket?"

Arthur took off his jacket. The man took it, held it at a distance, never having seen a Sears jacket before, and put it on the top of a wood cabinet that held racks of suits. He took a measuring tape from his shoulder and placed it across Arthur's back at the shoulders and stretched it out to his fingertip. Then he reached around Arthur's waist nearly giving him a hug, and then he goosed Arthur with one end while letting the other end drop to Arthur's heel.

"That should get us started; what are you thinking about in suits?" he asked Mrs. Clement.

Arthur was again an ear on the operating table or a guest at the dinner table, he was an object attached to Mrs. Clement and he was therefore important because of that attachment.

"Three suits, one gray flannel, one brown herringbone, subdued, and one blue pinstripe," she said. "All of them will need vests. We also need four pairs of flannel trousers and four jackets, three tweed and one a blue blazer."

Mr. Downs led the way to an alcove with a mirror, a leather-covered chair, a window onto the street and a view into the building across the street where people sat at desks under bluish fluorescent lights. He asked them to wait for a moment while he fetched suits.

He came back with six in a pile on hangers. He took one jacket off its hanger and held it for Arthur to try on, then another, then more. After the jackets he handed Arthur a pair of trousers and showed him to a little room that was barely big enough to turn around in. It had two sides lined with hooks, a bench along the back wall and a mirror hung on the door. He put on the pants Mr. Downs had rolled up, but they were still a yard too long, and went back to the alcove where Mr. Downs told him to stand on a little platform. Then more pants. Mrs. Clement chose three suits and Mr. Downs took the rejects away. He returned with more jackets and pants and finally they were finished trying on.

Mr. Downs left again and returned with a little fellow who must have been ninety years old. He had white hair, walked with a limp, and was hunched with age and arthritis, his legs weren't straight. He wore a vest over a white shirt and a tie. His pants were baggy and a tape measure dangled over his shoulder.

"Good morning, Clara," he said as he came to her to shake her hand. He had an accent, not a lot but Arthur noticed it. He had a big smile, genuine, as if he really liked her.

Mrs. Clement took his hand and held it, not in a shake but in an embrace as if she wanted to hold hands rather than greet. "Good morning Peter."

"And you, Danielle, you're back from school?"

"Hi, Mr. Fierro," said Dan with the Clement just-between-us' smile.

"Peter, this is Dan's friend, Arthur. He's with us for the weekend and needs some school clothes.

Mr. Fierro looked at Arthur, smiled and included him in his party. Mr. Downs stood quietly on the sidelines.

"Arthur, you look funny on the pedestal with your head in a sling and your pants trailing behind you, maybe we can fix you up a little. You want a break in the cuff, yes?" Mr. Fierro said, still smiling. He reached in a pocket of his vest and pulled out a flat sliver of soap about the size they give you in cheap motels. It was sharp on the edges. He bent over and marked the pants with slashes and muttered numbers while Mr. Downs took notes.

"OK, next trousers,'" said Mr. Fierro.

Mr. Downs handed Arthur the next pair of trousers and Arthur put them on in the dressing room and then jackets, Mr. Fierro slashing with the soap and Mr. Downs taking notes on tickets and putting the tickets on pants or jackets with little pieces of string wrapped around buttons.

"That's it?" Mr. Fierro asked.

"Yes that's all," said Mr. Downs.

"Thank you," said Mrs. Clement, "We'll see you over the holidays."

"Good day, Clara," said Mr. Fierro, and he left waddling on crooked legs for the back room.

Mr. Downs said the suits and jackets and trousers would be altered and mailed to Arthur at school; he could bring them back for a second fitting over Christmas. He walked them to the elevator where he waited until they were on and the doors were closed before he turned. They went to the first floor where they bought shirts and ties by the armload and two pairs of shoes. The shirts, ties and shoes were boxed up and someone ran them out and put them in the car at the curb in front. George got out and opened the back deck for the fellow with the boxes.

As they walked out of the store Mrs. Clement said, "Next stop, lunch." They got in the car and drove around for a while between huge buildings that looked like they were going to fall into the street, down avenues with trees planted in the middle, around a park, and finally stopped in front of a hotel where the car doors were opened for them just as the car stopped. They got out and went up marble steps to the lobby, went left to a dining room lined with dark wood on three sides and a window that looked out onto the park across the street on the fourth. The ceilings in the room were at least twenty five-feet high. A man dressed in a black suit greeted them at the door and showed them to a table by the window. No one seemed to notice Arthur's head band. They looked by him and followed Mrs. Clement's lead; Arthur could have been an Afghan hound.

Lunch and too many details, a menu, ordering, what did he want, a burger, great choice, no soup, no salad, just a burger and catsup and, OK, mayo on the side, Coke. Arthur looked around the room, it was too big, too much, too many people, he couldn't concentrate, the pattern on the carpet would take a day's reckoning, the silver on the table another, the glasses where did they come from, who washed them, why so many, did they break in the kitchen, where was the kitchen? Arthur ate too much, his pants were tight, his head ached. They went home.

"Hey, there's a party tonight, you want to go?" asked Dan as they went up the stairs to Arthur's room with shirts and ties.

"No thanks, my head hurts. It's my head or my ear; I can't figure it out."

"You want me to tell my mom? Maybe she has some medicine."

"No. Don't bother her. I don't want to go to the party unless it's costume. I'd go as a mummy," said Arthur wondering if he should lie down for a while. "Do you mind if I lie down for a while?"

"Go ahead. I'm going up the street to see some friends; I'll see you at dinner." Dan left Arthur's room.

Arthur put the packages on the floor by the bed, took off his shoes and socks, pants and shirt and got in. He lay on his back thinking about the boxes, too many boxes.

"Arthur?" It was Mrs. Clement standing by the bed. "Do you feel alright? I'm sorry to wake you but I was worried, you didn't come down for dinner. Dan checked and said you were asleep; we didn't want to wake you. Do you need anything?"

The room was dim, lit by one lamp on the bureau, the shades were drawn. Arthur pushed his way through the fog and things came into focus.

"It's nine o'clock. There's some dinner saved if you're hungry."

"I'm OK. I'm not hungry; I must have fallen asleep."

"Yes, you did. Dan went up the street to a party; he said you didn't want to go."

Arthur felt as if he should get out of bed and stand up to talk to Mrs. Clement. He swung his legs over the side.

"Stay there, don't get up, if you're not hungry just stay in bed," she said putting a hand on his shoulder.

He sat on the edge of the bed in his undies not thinking about them, not thinking about anything, trying to wrestle with the sequence of events passed, not looking at the future, disoriented.

"I'm going to bed but I read for an hour or so before I go to sleep, if you need anything just let me know. Does your head hurt?"

Yes, it did hurt. As she mentioned it, he realized what hurt. His head and ear felt hot. Even his jaw was stiff. "No I'm fine, just waking up when you came in; I don't need anything." He lay back down.

"Call me if you need anything."

"OK."

"Good night."

"Good night."

The door clicked as it closed. He shut his eyes.

17

COVET

George drove Dan and Arthur back to school on Tuesday afternoon. Mrs. Clement was busy and Mr. Clement was at work in New York. Arthur and Dan didn't talk much on the way. They had talked enough over the weekend and neither was looking forward to going back. They got their stuff out of the car where George parked behind their dorm and carried bags and boxes to their bunks. The dorm was dirty from packaging and trash; it smelled closed up and old. It was wet and gray outside at the bottom of the year and the damp and the drab had seeped inside their moods; boys unpacked without enthusiasm.

The next morning the gloom continued. Arthur thought they should erase school for the three weeks between return from Thanksgiving and release at Christmas. No one wanted to be there, not even the masters, who were bored. Morning assembly started as usual. The prefects gave admonitions on the evils of dust rolls, the penalty for tardiness, their displeasure at sloppy dress. Arthur's clothes had not arrived; his old clothes were acceptable but in the lower third and just over propriety's bar.

Mr. Webster stood in his customary way. He moved around the desk at the front of the room, stood before it partially sitting on it, both hands wrapped around its edge behind him, supporting him. He looked out the window for a moment then started. Arthur had a flashback of the inquisition, hours sitting, waiting for someone to admit something they hadn't done.

"Gentlemen, I owe you an apology. It is as simple as that; I was wrong. I was wrong in at least two ways. First, I was wrong to suspect you, the student body, when you had in effect said you had not taken the shirts. Second, I was wrong in the methods I chose to get at the problem. Group punishment was inappropriate in that instance. Group punishment may work if all those punished are conspirators

189

and know of the risk they run in their enterprise. It does not work if those who are punished are innocent and unknowing. To you and to your families, my sincere apology. I have written a letter to each of your parents. I am humbled by this experience."

No one said anything; no one moved. He didn't move; he half sat on the front of the desk looking at the students directly in front of him, and they did not return his glance. He was not finished.

"As you may remember, before we went home for Thanksgiving we talked about the rules by which we wished to live and the rules we wished other people would live by. We conducted a poll, and the results of the poll led us through consensus to a set of rules which closely resembled the Ten Commandments. I propose that we, as a matter of custom and clarity, adopt the Ten Commandments as our operating rules, our laws for a good society.

"We have consensus. The rules are clear; each of us has a fundamental understanding of them. Now, I will ask a question which you need to consider before you answer; it is only necessary to answer to yourself. You do not need to answer to me or to anyone else; simply answer to yourself. Did you abide by these rules over the vacation? Did you treat your neighbor as yourself?

"This is a hard question. I don't suspect many of you had a problem with murder, but what about coveting, what about stealing, what about bearing false witness, what about honoring your parents? Did you obey these rules, did you only break them a little or a lot? Does it matter, the difference between a little and a lot?

"These are questions for you to think about today; tomorrow, I will want to talk not about how much or how little but about why and why not." He left the room, and when he was gone desktops slammed shut, feet scuffled, a voice shouted for someone to "wait for me."

Arthur opened his desk, retrieved his books, and headed upstairs with Scratch. Everyone sat where he sat before vacation; there were no changes except for Arthur's ear which was the topic of small conversations between classes. Next period in English Mr. Smith talked about adverbs and drew lines on the blackboard, lines over, under, and around words, so when he was finished Arthur had no idea how to get the adverb out of jail. That's what it looked like to Arthur, horizontal words, Grettaical words, words on a slant, some underlined, some with arrows, words in jail.

At the end of the day Arthur sat with Scratch at a table in the center of the dorm. They were nearly alone; a few other boys came and went without paying attention. They talked about vacation.

Arthur told Scratch about the hockey experiment and the hospital and how nice Mrs. Clement was. Scratch talked about going to his grandmother's house on Cape Cod. They had gone sailing on Thanksgiving Day; it was a tradition. Scratch and his father spent the rest of the weekend hauling in the sailboat and getting it ready for winter storage.

Scratch asked Arthur, "Have you used that notebook planner thing I gave you yet?"

Arthur had forgotten it; it lay in the bottom of his desk. "No, not yet."

"Are you going to?" pestered Scratch.

"Yeah, I guess so," Arthur said to make time; he had no plan.

"Where is it?"

"Downstairs in my desk," answered Arthur not really sure if it was still there; he hadn't seen it in a while.

"Hey, go get it and we can compare assignments. There's nothing else to do."

"OK." Arthur got up from the table and wandered to the stairway not interested in going downstairs or in the book, but going along with Scratch's idea because there was nothing else to do. It was a good thing there were no organized sports this time of year. He would not have been allowed to play because of his ear. He came back with the book and laid it on the table, then sat across from Scratch.

"Here's how I do it," said Scratch. He opened the book and wrote in the days and dates in the squares at the top of the page; then he wrote in the class hours along the left column. "Here's a week's schedule, each class has a square. Like today, here's English and here's what Mr. Smith assigned." Scratch opened his planner and showed Arthur what he'd written.

Arthur had written it somewhere but wasn't sure where.

"Here, I'll write in the assignments for today; then all you have to do tonight in study hall is look at the assignment do it and then check it off. Then you'll be ready for tomorrow." Scratch wrote all of tomorrow's assignments on the page. Arthur watched, not really interested.

"What about Mr. Webster's apology?" asked Arthur "Do you think he's sorry?"

"My dad talked to him on the phone over vacation. Dad said he was really pissed-off."

"I bet he was; Mrs. Clement had a talk with him when she came up to pick up Dan and me. I wouldn't want to be on the other end of a confrontation with her," Arthur said.

"She's not the only one; a lot of parents were mad and told Mr. Webster. I think he feels pretty bad. Dad didn't think it was a good idea."

Scratch got a book from a pile he had next to him on the table and started to read. It was the English grammar book.

"Do you understand that stuff?" asked Arthur. "It seems stupid to me drawing lines around words."

"I'm getting the idea. It's the same with Latin; you have to know what the word is so you can make it work in the sentence, especially in Latin because of the endings. You have to know if the word is the subject or object to get the ending right. Mr. Smith is trying to show us by drawing lines to show which words work with the other words in the sentence." Scratch said thinking out loud.

"It's stupid," said Arthur, getting up from the bench.

"Why do you say things are stupid? It's not stupid; Mr. Grand and Mr. Smith aren't stupid. The people around here who are stupid are Mike and Doug. They're stupid; they don't do their work and they try to screw other people. That's stupid. You better figure out what side of the fence you're on. If you don't like it, why don't you leave?" Scratch returned to his book.

Arthur thought Scratch took things too seriously. Scratch took it personally almost as if Arthur had insulted him. Arthur didn't mean stupid, he meant he didn't like it, didn't think it was important. So in a way he had said Scratch was stupid for taking it so seriously and that insulted him. Arthur hadn't given any thought to leaving. Did he want to leave? No, he didn't, but he didn't like it either. He felt the sting of disgrace, the coppery taste of defeat when he thought about getting thrown out. It wasn't clear to him; he didn't like it, he'd rather be riding around in Tiny's car with Martha on his lap, but he didn't want to leave either.

Arthur picked up the notebook Scratch had written in and took it to study hall where he put it in his desk. He sat and looked at his English grammar book and thought about what Scratch had said. Stupid, not stupid, Latin and English, all confused. He looked at the English book some more. Then it was time for jobs so he closed his desk and left. That evening he did what Scratch suggested. He did the assignments in the book and checked them off as he completed them. When study hall was over he felt relieved as if a load of stones had been taken out of his pockets.

The next morning at assembly Mr. Webster took his position in front of the desk, leaned back and with both hands wrapped around the edge. He started.

"Yesterday I asked you to think about our rules, our Ten Commandments, I asked you to evaluate your own performance against them over vacation. I am going to assume, for the purposes of this talk, that none of us performed perfectly. Right now I am not going to address which rules were broken or the gravity of our misdeed, a little or a lot. What I want to do is talk a little about why. Why do we break what appear to be very clear rules that we ourselves have committed to follow?

"Let us take for instance the rule we should not covet. It is a good rule; we have agreed. And then we walk out of study hall and see someone who has a better suit than we have, and we want it; we envy the person who has it. We envy the person with the fancier car or larger house or better job or bigger bank account. We want the things they have. This is a natural reaction; you do not have to practice long hours to become a coveter, it will develop without much attention at all. Let me suggest we have within us a power which is as strong or stronger at times than the power of good rules. We have within us an influence which will turn us against our own rules. Further, I suggest that if we do not recognize that power, if we are not prepared to deal with its difficult influence, if we are blind to its consequence, and if we do not strengthen ourselves against it, we will lose battles we could have won, we will make choices that will led us down paths we do not want to follow.

"We are, in many cases, led to want things we do not have. We are led to believe that happiness accompanies those things. And we are led to do things we know to be wrong in order to acquire what we do not have. The question here is: Who is leading us?"

He stopped, pushed himself forward off the edge of the desk and walked out. The more Arthur thought about him, the more Mr. Webster reminded Arthur of Abraham Lincoln. He was tall and angular with big hands, and his face looked like a postcard Arthur had seen of the Old Man in the Mountain. He walked in long strides, and had his mind ahead of his feet. The difference was his hair; Mr. Webster's was short, wiry gray, cut close. In Arthur's recollection, Mr. Lincoln's hair always seemed long and shaggy.

Arthur went to class and for the first time felt good about being there; he wasn't ashamed of being half prepared or not prepared at all; it was a simple thing being prepared. He was involved; he was a partner; he raised his hand and asked a question whose answer clarified a difficulty he had with last night's assignment. He didn't feel the need to hide to duck or avoid. The same feeling held through math and Latin; he became a member rather than a visitor, a participant rather

193

than guest. He wrote his assignments in the book Scratch had given him, and in the afternoon after classes Scratch asked whether he wanted to go over the assignments; they did. That evening he did the assignments as he crossed them off the list in Scratch's book.

The next morning Mr. Webster continued. "Who is it who leads us to betray ourselves?

"It might be easiest if we take a specific example. Think back to the last time you lied, this relates to bearing false witness. Pick a time when you clearly broke the rule, not a time when there was a maybe or it was questionable. Pick a time when there was no doubt about what happened. Those of you who have never lied just bear with the rest of us for a minute."

Some of the older boys laughed; Arthur didn't get it.

"When you lied, it was probably clear to you that you were doing 'wrong'; that is, you were working against what you believed was right. When you did it, when you lied or coveted, who was it who caused you to lie or covet? Was there someone else to blame, did someone force you to do this thing or did you do it for a perceived advantage?

"Only you can answer these questions. But I would guess if you are like most of us, you made the decision for your advantage, an advantage in material things, in power or approbation. Most of us betray ourselves in an attempt to acquire what we do not have. Most of us lie so that we appear to be who we are not, and we believe who we will appear to be after the betrayal is better than who we are.

"I suggest to you: if we believe we are better after a lie than before, we have a lot to learn and more to practice. We have more to practice because we already know the lesson; it is practicing the lesson that is the difficult part."

He pushed away from the front of his perch launching himself down the center aisle and left without a look back or to the sides as if he had been speaking to himself in an empty room, as if he were practicing for a bigger day.

Arthur didn't get it; he couldn't hold the train of thought. When Mr. Webster asked about the last lie he had told, Arthur's first instinct was to deny he told any lies at all. It wasn't long before the absurdity of this position breached his unfinished ethical standards, so he retreated and adopted a more flexible stance in which he prevaricated to himself, who was always his first but not always his last customer in this pursuit, about those lies which were clearly infractions but about which he might be able to talk himself into a more forgiving final judgment. He attempted to separate the marginal candidates from those that were serious beyond prevarication's remedy, and from one ragged rationalization to the next he was stumbling downhill because there were so many candidates. He got tied up in his excuses and reasons and justifications, trying to argue with himself about the marginal cases while the guilt associated with the truly big ones outran his ability to dodge and left his conscience bruised inside a burlap bag of confusion. He was still sorting out the big ones from the little ones when Mr. Webster walked out of the corner of his eye.

The three weeks between Thanksgiving and Christmas slid along without bumps, without upsets. Arthur got the hang of classes and enjoyed some of what was making its way into his collection of ideas. He noticed that preparation transformed new ideas into friendly discovery. The concepts he tried to grasp while catching up on neglected assignments were elusive enemies which had already escaped him and which had to be subdued, unwillingly, to stay in his head long after their capture. He relied on Scratch's book and Scratch's good wishes.

Ten days after Arthur's return to school he got a three by five card in his mail box announcing he had packages to pick up at the mail counter. He presented his card to the mailman and four large flat brown boxes, almost too big to be put through the window, were pushed at him. Huge, flat, brown boxes neatly wrapped. Scratch helped him carry them to the dorm where they laid them in a stack on a bench of the picnic table. He chose the top one, slid it onto the table, and cut the packing tape with a penknife. The boxes were stuffed with layers of white tissue paper begging to be saved, separating pillows of folded wool trousers and jackets, suits and vests. When he lifted their lids, lime and Bay Rum enveloped him. He sat on the bench of the picnic table with a box in front of him and lifted the lid about half way, just enough so he could put his head inside to obscure the dormitory bleak. He put his hands in and buried them in the fabrics and he was transported by the textures and colors and the scents to the store that smelled so good. Each suit and trousers had a wood hanger with the store logo printed at the apex. He did not imagine wearing these things. Looking at them, feeling them, possessing them was enough. One of his new words "impeccable" flashed into his head. Owning them was enough.

18

FEW ARE CHOSEN

The day before Christmas vacation Mr. Webster came to assembly and sat through the ritualistic ablutions and prefect admonition. He stood before the desk and said, "I would like anyone who has smoked this year to stand up, please."

Arthur was not paying attention, he was looking at something carved in the corner of his desk; he had forgotten his fear. Each morning since he smoked had been a nightmare and a release. Each morning he sat at his desk in anticipation, and when Mr. Webster stood Arthur fell from a great breathless height into the darkness waiting to be smashed at the bottom. And each morning he had been saved from the destruction by Mr. Webster's opening on another topic. The anxiety of anticipation, the fear of discovery and the relief at having been spared each morning, for so many mornings, had diminished with each escape, so this morning his anxiety, which lurked in the background as a dull pressure sharp only when consciously recalled, was overcome by boredom and the hieroglyphs on his desktop. Mr. Webster's words came as a gunshot from the back of the room. Unconsciously he heard the words and it took a moment for them to register. When they did, he was overcome by the shock, like breaking the sound barrier, the meaning took a moment to catch up to the hearing. Someone had plugged his chair into a light socket. He was alone surrounded encased in a high pressure bubble. He looked up, his face caught on fire, he was not in control. The bullet was coming, he saw it in slow motion and he was powerless; it had already struck.

He looked around and saw no one. He rose, he didn't know why, there was no other choice. Why was meaningless.

"I would like to see those boys who have smoked in my study after this assembly." Mr. Webster left looking straight ahead.

Arthur sat and again he saw no one; he didn't know how many others had stood with him. The pressure in his head mounted, his vision was limited to a small circle on his desk, nothing registered as if watching a movie running too fast, each scene spit into forgotten haze, trying to catch up to the scene on the screen. Desks crashed shut from a distance, feet scraped the floor from rooms away, people and voices on the periphery.

Scratch appeared at Arthur's desk. "I thought you might make it through to Christmas vacation."

Arthur didn't hear him, Arthur was escaping down a rabbit hole.

Arthur got up from his desk and paused for air. The room was empty; there were a few boys in the hall. He turned and went out of the study hall following his feet down the path to the main building through the green door and up the stairs. He was about to knock on the door to the headmaster's office but saw someone else was in there talking to Mr. Webster. Arthur waited, then walked to the end of the hall and looked out at the fire escape not wanting to see the other boy or to be seen.

Mr. Webster's door opened and shut, steps disappeared down the stairs. Arthur approached the door, he didn't know what to do so he knocked lightly hoping in self prevarication not to be heard.

Mr. Webster said, "Come in."

Arthur pulled the door open and went in. He stopped two steps in and waited.

"Arthur, come in," Mr. Webster said, without smile or frown, "I'm surprised. Do they start smoking early in Oklahoma."

"No sir."

"Were you a smoker before you came to Bridge?"

"No sir." It felt good to let Mr. Webster do the talking; Arthur did not want to talk. Good was maybe too strong a word; it felt better.

"Did you smoke with other boys?"

"Yes sir."

"Were they older than you?"

"Yes sir."

"Did they have the cigarettes?"

"Yes sir."

"And you knew about the rule, about not smoking?"

"Yes sir."

"Why did you smoke?"

"I don't know, it seemed like something to do, risky I guess."

"I think I know about this incident already. I am not going to ask you to identify the other boys, they will be dealt with separately on a different matter. If I am right, you did not smoke at the school, is that right?"

"Yes sir."

"Were you signed out with a parent or relative off school grounds?"

"Yes sir."

"Arthur, these are serious issues we are dealing with. Smoking in itself is not a serious matter. Breaking rules is; it is a betrayal of the trust we have in the school community. When we come here we agree to abide by a set of rules. Other people in the community depend on us to obey those rules, other people depend on our trust and we depend on theirs."

Arthur wanted to move, to shake his hands, jump up and down, run out the door, to run away; he thought of the boy in the football shed, he was frozen in front of Mr. Webster and had a sense of falling which seemed to him his usual reaction to stress.

"Under normal conditions we expel those boys who break serious rules."

"Yes sir."

"I think in your case we have a situation which is not so clear; it requires further examination. You were a guest at someone's house while you were signed out with a relative or parent of one of the boys. Technically you were not on school property and you were not in the custody of the school, known as 'in loco parentis'. Have you gotten that far in Latin yet? It means the school is serving as the parent while you are at the school. But you were not at the school, so I suppose you were not bound by the school rules at the time. I think you were bound by the spirit of the rules while you were at a parent's house. But, I realize a lawyer or someone else might make quite a good argument on the other side, so I am willing to let that influence my judgment. That is a technicality but it has a bearing on how we might look at the problem.

"Secondly, you did not have the cigarettes; you were offered cigarettes in a tempting situation under considerable pressure from older fellows. Right?"

"Yes sir but they didn't push me or threaten me."

"I understand. However, they were older and exerted an influence because of their status. There is a clear moral distinction between sharing immoral gratification among peers and offering it to minors, it is a theory called corruption, and quite a serious thing.

"Additionally, your teachers and prefects say that you have made good progress in the past few months and as far as I know you have had no other discipline problems other than some minor disagreement with Mr. Grand.

"Arthur, because of these circumstances, your situation, I am inclined to allow you to stay at the school under some conditions which you must agree to. The first of these is: you will not break the honor code again. If you do, then I will ask you to leave without discussion. You are, as we say, on probation; is that agreeable?"

"Yes sir" Circumstance was rushing out of the weeds this time, along this rough path, not to trip Arthur but to mark the narrow way and to save him from ignominy. Circumstance had many disguises.

"The second condition is that you take your work here seriously, that you join with the rest of us at the school to do the best you can in academics, sports, and jobs. For this condition I have no test, but if you know now that you cannot agree to this commitment, then you should say so."

Arthur stood paralyzed; the impact of the decision was not penetrating the pressure in his head.

"Will you do your best?"

"Yes sir."

"All right then, good day."

Arthur stood unsure of what to do.

"You may leave my office, Arthur, but you are welcome here at the school."

"Yes sir." Arthur turned and left He walked to the stairs, down into the parking lot, up the path to his dorm and sat on his bed, head not working, things going too fast, a runaway movie projector, he couldn't focus on any idea as every other one crowded its way into his head without any order. Class bell rang. He went to study hall, to his desk, got his books and went to Latin where everyone stared at him for a moment but said nothing.

"I thought you might be late, but I knew you'd make it," said Mr. Grand.

Arthur went through the rest of the day in a fog. He wasn't happy about the reprieve, he didn't feel as if he had beaten the odds or been rewarded in any way; he was tired, worn out by the turmoil of his shock, despair, anxiety, and finally relief. He wasn't in love with the school, he was frightened of rejection; he didn't want to be there necessarily, he just couldn't think of where he should be; he didn't mind failing, he minded his father's reaction. His position wasn't great until he considered the alternatives and the alternatives were unfathomable, too deep a river to plumb, there was no string in his pocket let alone one long enough to follow back home, that string had been cut. He defined himself now by his association with the school, and now attached, he would measure himself by his success there.

After class Arthur went to the dorm with Dan and Scratch. Scratch wanted to know how it had gone. What had Mr. Webster said? Arthur didn't want to talk about it; he told them he was on probation. He didn't know for how long. Scratch said Mike and Doug did not stand up when asked and he didn't hear anything about what happened to them if anything had. Only one other boy had stood and they didn't know him; he was a fourth former and lived in a different building, played on a different team, went to different classes. He wasn't coming back because he didn't show up for classes later in the morning. Dan didn't say anything, he listened to Scratch and Arthur but kept a distance.

Getting ready for vacation, Arthur packed his father's B-4 bag with new suits, ties and shirts. He wasn't excited about them and wasn't excited about going home, he threw things in his bag without plan or care just to get it over with, to get today behind him.

The next morning breakfast and jobs were on a normal schedule. At morning assembly, Mr. Webster took his position in front of the desk, hands behind him.

"The last time we talked, in our ongoing discussion about the purpose of the school, we talked about the reasons we break rules. I suggested that we break rules to obtain an advantage, in material things, in gratification of an appetite, in power or in appearance. We break the rules in order to appear who we are not and we believe we will appear better, feel better, be more powerful after we break the rules than before.

"The desire to transform oneself into a better person is admirable. To transform oneself through murder, adultery, lying, stealing or coveting is simply counterproductive.

"I urge you to consider these ideas while you are at home. Think about what you want and whether what you want will make you a better person.

"Merry Christmas; I'll see you next year." He launched himself down the center aisle with a smile.

Desks slammed and a collective response rose from the assembly, "Same to you, Unkey Lou."

Arthur went to the dorm and got his coat and hat. He would take the train back to Grape, so he had left his bag in the central courtyard earlier in the morning. The school truck had loaded it and all the other bags of the boys who were taking the train to New York onto the platform at the train station in town. He went to the courtyard on his way to the station and saw Dan and Mrs. Clement. He said hello to her and wished her a Merry Christmas and was in a strange way pulled to her, wanting to go to Goose Island rather than get on the train. She waved, then returned her attention to Dan who was saying something. He walked down the hill with the other boys into town onto the train platform surrounded and by himself.

19

THE THIRD RAIL

The five boarding schools on the rail line that linked Bridge, Connecticut with New York City had the same vacation schedule, so on first morning of Christmas vacation the train to New York was crowded with boys on their way home. On vacation mornings the railroad added five cars to the train to Stamford. Each school had an assigned car with the school's name posted in the window. The train stopped at each of the five schools, lining up the school's car with the platform. The cars were connected, so by the time they were half way to Stamford, some boys had changed cars to find friends or brothers or cousins.

Arthur stood on the Bridge platform with other boys, milk cans, and baggage crates. There was light rain and mist and the view north along the tracks was obscured by damp. Arthur heard the whistle as the train cleared a crossing out of view. Everyone on the platform bent forward, turned his head and leaned into the moment, anticipating, anticipating in a way as effective as anticipating Christmas morning, it didn't come any faster for the wanting. A red and gray Cyclops parted the mist; it had teeth in its lower jaw and it blew smoke and fire from the top of its head. It rolled the mist aside as if parting a carpet and it bellowed an announcement of its importance as it gnawed its way down the line devouring rails and ties in its advance toward the platform.

It stopped with a crash of loose joints as worn couplings contracting like a Slinky coming to rest, coiled. A man in a conductor's uniform opened a door inward, pushed a metal plate across the gap between car and platform and announced, "Stamford! All aboard for Stamford!"

Arthur followed other boys and found a backward facing seat; he put his bag in an overhead rack and sat by himself.

The cars smelled of diesel exhaust, wet cigarettes, and urine. The engine pulling the train was a steam locomotive; the generators and auxiliary equipment were diesel. The windows were dirty with gray streaks where the rain had guttered the accumulated soot; the seats were covered in a worn, shiny, stained, gray fabric and the floors in tortured beige linoleum.

The conductor closed the door to the outside then closed the door from the car to the vestibule connecting the car to the rest of the train. "All aboard." Not a question, a confirmation. The platform outside was empty; having celebrated its fifteen minutes of service, it returned to useless.

The train lurched to a roll, the Slinky uncoiled and the cars bucked and jolted on decayed roadbed leaning precariously around inadequately banked curves. The rails floated on a spoiled raft of creosote ties, the raft trod water in oil stained, gray-black stone ballast. The train whistled at each crossing, and each whistle encouraged small wood barriers to descend in blinking red curtsy. The barriers were accompanied by a carillon cacophony and protected the crossing from passenger cars which were lined up, foggy windowed, their passengers peering at the boys who were peering at the cars stopped on the wet black road.

Arthur couldn't remember being on a train before. He knew he'd been on several because his mother told him stories of their going from Grape to Boston and back after the War, but he had no picture of it. The plan was for Arthur to take the train from school to New York City with a change in Stamford, Connecticut. He would reach the City by noon and catch the Ohio State Limited for Cincinnati that afternoon and arrive there the next morning where he would get a train for Saint Louis and then Oklahoma City, arriving the next day. There were about a hundred boys on the train to New York, from there a few would go on to the Ohio State Limited but no one else from Cincinnati to Oklahoma. Carl had gotten the tickets and mailed them to Arthur and he was surprised they had arrived on time because, based on his experience waiting at the mail room each noon, he didn't think the mail route from Grape to Connecticut was connected yet.

As the train left the rural part of the state and got into the more populated areas and the curves got tighter and the crossings only several blocks apart and the houses within stick distance of the tracks, the train picked up speed as if tantalizing physics or tempting the insurance company, as if daring the wheels to stay on the tracks. Most of them did. The cars lurched and slammed against their couplings, testing nineteen-twenties' technology with nineteen-thirties' maintenance. As the cars swayed wildly, nearly tipping over on one side to fall slouching back through equilibrium to test fate at the other side of balance, the engineer put on more speed. The crossing warning bells became frantic; their alarms urgent as the locomotive's whistle confounded Doppler and appeared to get louder and higher in pitch the closer the buildings got to the track. The train roared through intersections, jumping madly from rail to rail at junctions, attempting to climb the confines of the track on the turns until the engineer changed his mind and applied to the brakes all the grace he had applied to the throttle. It came to a screeching halt in the middle of a rail yard where thousands of grimy gray lines and wires converged and separated and reemerged from underneath and over each other, its designer having this convolution as his death wish granted for rural commuters.

When the train stopped, Arthur expected a company of state police to surround it, weapons drawn, and to arrest the engineer and anyone else in authority in order to liberate the victims of this kidnap. Instead, a small man in a shiny, worn, blue serge suit, conductor's hat, and black scuffed shoes, carrying what appeared to be a huge lunch box or tool crate, threw himself and his box into an open doorway and up the stairs of the car next to Arthur's. The train started again and accelerated dangerously through the tangle of joints and junctions and convergings of rails and overhead wires. Finally, selecting one set of rails to test, it rocketed out of the rail yard.

The little man who had just thrown himself onto the train appeared in the door to Arthur's car. He put his box on the front seat, opened the lid, took off some cellophane and announced, in an acned voice that he had snacks, candy, crackers, sandwiches and drinks. His delivery was rote, uninterested, singsong; his snacks rubber and acrylic. His drinks colored water. He couldn't have been less attached to what he was doing. He was small, smaller than Arthur, made of blobs of skin, rounded, with tiny hands and pixy fingers. Arthur wondered how he carried the box, his fingers couldn't have reached around the handle which was rope; that was the answer.

No one bought anything, conversations continued, and the man moved to the center of the car where he repeated his sales routine. No one bought.

Someone yelled, "Hey, it's Last Chance Charlie. How'a ya doin', there, Last Chance." in a fake and derisive accent.

Arthur didn't know the boy and didn't recognize him, so he was probably from another school.

"Hey, Last Chance. How long ya been doin this?" Too loud and not funny, coming up on bullying real fast.

The man ignored him, but the bully would not be ignored. He got out of his seat and went toward Charlie; when he was close, he grabbed some candy bars out of Charlie's box and threw them at other boys in the car.

Arthur didn't see it coming and neither did the bully. One of Bridge's seniors, a large boy Arthur recognized but did not know, walked up behind the bully, grabbed the bully's jacket collar in his left hand and the tail of the jacket in his right and jerked the jacket almost over the bully's head so his arms pointed straight up in the air and he had to stand on tiptoes to avoid being jerked off the floor. It was sudden, violent and effective, the bully was surprised and he was late, by the time he figured out what was happening the Bridge senior had spun the bully around, pointed him at the rear door of the car and marched, rushed him toward the door so fast the bully would not have remained standing if the Bridge senior hadn't been holding him up. They crashed through the rear door and the Bridge boy let go of bully who fell to his knees in the vestibule between the cars.

"You don't belong in this car," said the Bridge senior; he returned to his seat.

Charlie disappeared in the opposite direction; he knew no good would come of this for him.

Arthur sat by himself facing backwards and watched out the window as black trees and wet roads and back yards disappeared without the benefit of having grown into view, they were suddenly present, next to him and receding before he had a chance to register them. The car was overheated, grimy, it swayed and bounced off uneven track, slowed at small towns then sped up in emptiness. Other Bridge boys sat in ones and twos and appeared unaffected by Charlie's adventure, their thoughts already transferred home, but Arthur was undone by what had just happened. In one minute the Charlie guy was selling junk from a box, no problem, then from nowhere a boy picked on Charley for no reason other than meanness, and then, just as suddenly, the Bridge senior threw the bully out of the car and the train ride returned to normal as if nothing had happened. Arthur wasn't troubled by the bully, he had seen that kind of thing before in Grape, what was surprising was the senior's immediate reaction. He didn't negotiate with the bully, he didn't warn him, didn't appear to loose his temper; he simply did what he thought was right without equivocation. No stumbling and stalling, no fits and jerks of conscience or afterthought.

The train stopped at a station and the conductor came through shouting, "Stamford. Everyone off at Stamford. Get the connecting train to New York City on track three." He pinned the door open and proceeded out of the car and into the next.

Arthur got his bag from the overhead rack, pulled it out, and let it fall, bounce off the seat and then fall to the floor. It was too wide to carry at his side along the aisle so he carried it in front, bouncing it off his knees while other boys lined up at the door waiting to get off. They went out the door onto a steel plate that separated the cars and across the plate to a concrete pier. Some of the boys would meet parents at the station, some would go on to New York, while others would take another train to Boston; everyone except Arthur seemed to know his destination.

Arthur didn't know where track three was; that was the track to New York. There were several tracks in a ditch between the concrete platforms; what if track three was on the other side of the ditch? He looked around and then saw a sign hanging from the roof above the platform across the ditch; the sign announced track three was on the other side. A train came into the station on the track on the other side. Arthur panicked, how was he supposed to get from where he was to the other side, was he supposed to jump into the ditch and cross there in front of the train. Would he miss his train, how much time did he have before his train left? He looked right and left, everyone had left the platform except the senior who had thrown the bully out of the car. He stood in front of Arthur looking over his shoulder at someone who was getting off another car.

Arthur approached him in a panic. "Do you know how to get on the train to New York? Is that the track over there?"

"Yes, that's the track, and the train to New York is coming in. Don't worry we have lots of time."

"Are you going to New York?" asked Arthur.

'Yes, I'm going; we have time." He looked back searching for someone. Then he turned to face Arthur. "Hang on a minute and I'll walk over with you."

Arthur waited unsure of whether the senior was right. If he was wrong then what would Arthur do? He wanted to jump in the ditch and run over to the other side before the New York train cut them off. If it got too far down the track, then they couldn't cross and Arthur would miss all of his trains to Oklahoma. Arthur went to the edge of the platform, put his bag down and sat on the edge with his legs over the side, one hand on his bag, ready to jump.

The senior came to Arthur and put a hand on his shoulder. "What are you doing?"

"I don't want to miss my train."

"You can't go that way; that's a good way to get killed. Get up here," he pulled Arthur to his feet.

Hanging onto Arthur's jacket, the senior asked, "Were you going to cross the tracks right here?".

"Yeah. The train to New York is over there."

"You don't cross here, you have to go down the stairs then back up on the other side. If you crossed here you'd be run over by the train or electrocuted by the third rail."

Arthur turned and looked. No wonder no one else was clambering across the tracks, they'd all known to go under the tracks and up on the other side.

"Just hold on here for a minute and I'll take you over." The senior turned for one more look than said "OK Let's go."

The senior picked up his bag and walked toward a broad set of stairs with a hand rail in the middle; the stairs were covered by a porch roof. They went down, Arthur following closely, turned right, went across a hallway, then up an identical set of stairs on the other side of the hall. The stairs on either side of the tracks appeared to be identical to most people; to Arthur they were confusing, one side went up while the ones on the other side went down.

When they were on the platform with track three in front of them and the New York train parked within easy reach, the senior asked, "Do you have your ticket?"

Ticket. Arthur didn't have a ticket; he didn't think he did, not for New York; he had one from New York to Oklahoma City but not from Stamford to New York. Panic again.

"Where do I get a ticket?"

"We can get one on the train. Don't worry you're not going to miss your train. Do you have your ticket from school?"

"Yeah."

"Let me see it" he said, sticking his hand out toward Arthur.

Arthur reached in his pockets and found his ticket from school; he handed it to the senior.

"This will work; it's from school all the way to New York. No problem." He handed the ticket back to Arthur. "Where are you going in New York?"

"I have a train this afternoon from New York to Cincinnati, then to Oklahoma City."

"Big trip. OK, let's get on, no point in standing here."

He let Arthur go first. Arthur got on; the platform was even with the vestibule but he didn't know which car to get in so he waited for the senior.

"Take the one to the right."

Arthur turned right, opened the door, went into the car. It was half full. He went down the aisle a way and picked an empty seat, hefted his bag over his head, and put it on the overhead luggage rack where it barely fit. The senior came behind Arthur and put his bag on the rack on the opposite side. Arthur sat in the window seat and the senior took the place next to him.

"You're Arthur May, aren't you?" he said facing Arthur. He stuck out his hand. "I'm Chris Lyttle."

Arthur took his hand and shook it. Chris was big, over six feet tall, with sloping shoulders and a powerful neck. His hand was big in Arthur's. He had short hair, blue eyes, thin arched eyebrows and a smile for Arthur.

"Yeah. I'm Arthur May; how'd you know?"

"Seniors have to know the new boys' names. We're supposed to look out for you, make sure you don't get into trouble, like running in front of trains or electrocuting yourself while we watch. Were you really going to go across the tracks to the other platform?"

"I guess so. I didn't know how to go and I could see the train I was supposed to be on."

"I'm glad I was there; it'll make a great story when we get back to school."

"When you threw that kid out of our car did you know him?"

"No. I knew he wasn't from Bridge and he was sitting with Duncan whatever his name is. Anyway, I knew he was bad news."

"Why did you throw him out?"

"Because he was a bully?"

"I know. I mean how did you decide to throw him out. Were you going to warn him or anything?"

"Warning bullies is a waste of time. It draws you into their scene, that's what they want. The minute you start talking with them then they know that's all you're going to do, so they mouth off and get a big charge out of the confrontation. You're ultimately stuck with the same alternatives, action or no action."

"Could you have told him to leave the car?"

"I suppose so and then he would have bullied someone else or given me a ration of his lip."

"Do you think he learned a lesson?"

"I don't know; bullies are a character type. I don't know if they learn lessons or blame someone else. For me, the important thing is other people may have learned a lesson. The people who saw what happened learned that you can confront things you think are wrong and you can take action to correct them. It is OK to throw a bully out of the car."

"Do you listen to the things Mr. Webster says in the morning?"

"Most of the time."

The train pulled out of the station headed for New York. A conductor came along and collected the tickets; he punched them five or ten times in different corners and on the sides and then a few more times to make sure they were dead before he put them in a little clip on the seatback in front of Arthur and Chris. The tracks were in better repair than the ones from school so the train clicked along without the rolling, bucking, and jumping. Arthur could see the Long Island Sound once in a while, and when another train came in the opposite direction there was a great whooshing sound and a vacuum that almost pulled the two trains into each other and the lights and faces in the windows of the other train would scream past so fast no details were visible. Then the other train would be gone as quickly as it had come and the rocking and clicking would start up again as if nothing important had happened.

Chris asked, "Aren't you one of the guys who stood up when Mr. Webster asked who had been smoking?"

"Yeah."

"What happened, did you go to his office?"

"I went and there was someone else in there so I had to wait in the hall. Then I went in and he talked for a while. I can't remember what he said; I was so scared I couldn't hear him. Then he said I would be on probation and I could stay at the school."

"You're lucky. Normally he asks people to leave. I think his problem with Thanksgiving may have given you an advantage. He was in a forgiving mood and hoped everyone else was too."

They talked about the school and college, where he wanted to go, and home. Then Chris took out a book and started to read; Arthur looked out the window. After an hour or so the train came to a city and the tracks were elevated as they crossed highways and a river. After the river it stopped at a station that looked like what Arthur imagined a bombed-out city in Germany looked like after the War. There were apartments on either side of the tracks, buildings empty, roofs gone, trash in the street, a real shock after Goose Island. No one got on or off. The train continued for a few blocks then went from elevated to underground through tunnels black with blinking lights or an occasional lonely bare bulb hanging from a cord on a tunnel wall. The smells changed, more diesel fumes, more urine, more steam. They slowed and rattled back and forth as if jumping from one track to the next then crept the final five minutes to land at an underground platform in a sloping tunnel.

Chris stood up and grabbed his bag from the overhead rack across the aisle; Arthur got his, and they went to the door, Chris leading, out onto the platform which was in a cave, a cavern with trains parked along cement piers, everyone who got off the train scurried up the sloping cement walkway to doors about fifty yards away. It was hot in the cavern, crowded with fuel vapors, steam and the smell of ozone from shorted wires.   Arthur thought maybe someone had decided to take a shortcut, one platform to the next, and had hit the third rail.

They got into the stream of people and it took them through the doors and into a huge vault of a room. It was a hundred feet high and three football fields long with tunnels going off it in every direction and an octagonal brass doll house in the middle where people sat inside and talked through bronze ventilators to people on the outside who asked for information. The night sky was painted in blue-black on the dome ceiling with lights shining where the stars would be. There were banks of dozens of ticket windows along one wall and above them a sign board with the schedule of arriving and departing trains; it showed the destination, time, and track.   Every minute or two the sign board would clatter and the letters seemed to rotate and disappear then reappear as different letters until the whole list, the schedule, was moved up one place on the board, the topmost entry disappearing altogether as if the train had taken it when it left, making space for the second to become the top, and a new entry was inserted at the bottom.

At one end of the hall there were marble stairs fifty feet wide leading to an upper level. Along the opposite end was a movie theater, a telephone exchange, and bank. And in the middle of this gargantuan architecture were ten thousand people each one rushing in a different direction. There were exceptions, people who walked slowly, nowhere to go, they were obvious by their failure to fit into the rhythm of the place. And there were people sleeping on benches in a waiting room off to one side behind the ticket windows. But most people were in a rush to leave, carrying things, boxes, bags, coats, hats, children, briefcases; most people carried something.

Arthur and Chris fit the pattern; they carried bags and coats and were going somewhere. Chris was going somewhere, Arthur was following somewhere, like an imprinted gosling he followed the gander.

Chris stopped by the information booth and turned to Arthur. "OK, here we are. Your train will be listed on that board over there." pointing to the big black scheduling board above the ticket windows. "All you have to do is find the listing for your train, read the time and the track number and then go to the track before the time on the board. The train leaves at the time listed, so don't show up at that time or you'll watch it pull out without you. Come on over, I'll show you." Chris lead Arthur closer to the board, he looked up and found Ohio State Limited, Cincinnati, track 12, 3:40, on time. He pointed to it. "Got it?"

"Yes, I see it."

"OK, you go over there," pointing in the other direction to the wall of track doors, "to track twelve at about 3:20, no later, walk down a ramp like the one we just came up and your train will be parked there. Show a conductor your ticket and he'll show you where to go. Got it?"

"I understand. Where are you going?"

"I'm going up to Columbia to see some friends, then home tomorrow."

Arthur didn't want him to leave, he had four hours until his train left and he didn't want to be alone in the building with a thousand strangers.

Arthur asked, "What did you mean about the third rail, before, when you said I could be killed by the third rail?"

"Some of the trains that come in here are electric. They get the juice from a rail on the ground next to the regular rails the train travels on. It's called the third rail and it has almost a thousand volts of electricity so if you step on it, or get too close, it electrocutes you. They say if you fall on it, you burn up like a twig and all that's left after the smell is gone is some cinders and your teeth."

"Are you going to Columbia now?" asked Arthur.

"Yeah, I can take the subway from here."

Arthur didn't know what to say so he didn't.

Chris stuck out his hand, "Arthur, have a good trip. I'll see you next year."

Arthur took Chris' hand, "You too, thanks for the help. I don't want to burn up."

Chris smiled, hefted his bag, turned half right, and walked into the crowd.

20

THE BOWELS OF THE EARTH

Arthur stood in the middle of the room, his bag at his side. He was drained again; the newness of the train and having to change tracks had overloaded his emotions. He had four hours till his train left for Cincinnati. Chris had pointed to a movie theater but it was closed. He looked around, there was nothing to hang onto, everything was granite or marble or in a cage or moving to get somewhere else. He picked up his bag just to be doing something, to give himself the impression of purpose, but he didn't know where to go. He spotted the waiting area behind the ticket booths so he decided to go in that direction. As he walked, he looked mostly at the ceiling, trying to avoid looking into peoples' faces, and when he accidentally looked someone in the eye it was like bumping into them, rude and hostile, no smiles, no welcome. There were too many faces so there wasn't enough space or time in his registry to arrange the images before they disappeared.

He got to the waiting area; it was another huge granite and marble room with fifty foot ceilings and it had twenty-five-foot long wooden benches, they could have been pews, arranged in rows facing the schedule board. There were at least fifty of them in two banks and there were people waiting, sitting and sleeping on them who looked different from the folks on the move in the main bay of the building. These people looked as if they were not in a hurry; they lacked the purposeful appearance of expectation, apprehension and fatigue that travelers have; they looked more like residents taking naps.

Arthur found a half empty bench; there was a man sleeping at one end on the other side of a wooden arm rest barrier halfway down the bench; Arthur's side was empty. He put his bag down and sat leaning forward, looking, on overload, nothing sticking, like the same movie, one that had run out of control, he saw it when there was too much.

215

A man appeared in front of Arthur. He walked by, stopped, turned and looked Arthur in the eye.

"Where are you going kid?" he said without accent, smiling in unearned friendship through bad teeth. His hair was black and long, swept to the side of his face, his coat, black wool herringbone, that had been nice once but had been slept in since. His pants were black, rumpled, baggy, nearly covering filthy shoes. His shirt was open at the collar. He had Grettaical creases in the skin of his cheeks as if he had slept with his face pressed into the pavement, creases that needed washing and shaving and ironing. His nose was long and thin, dripping over a lipless mouth, his eyes black in browned out hollows, thin brows that looked frazzled from too much pulling. He slouched, he bent over toward Arthur, as if telling secrets, looking at Arthur then looking to his side, telling a confidence he did not feel, in danger of being overheard or apprehended.

"Cincinnati" said Arthur, not encouraging him but answering.

"That your bag?" he said indicating with his head Arthur's bag which sat on the floor beside them.

"Yes."

"You have some time then, don't you?" he said, nearly a whisper. He was building a conspiracy, trading on an intimacy that didn't exist. He leaned forward but looked to his side as if expecting trouble from his flanks.

"I guess so."

"Why don't you put your bag in the baggage room, then you can take a look around, I can show you around. I can show you the city." Looking at Arthur, imploring, inviting, implying adventure.

"Where's the baggage room?" asked Arthur.

"Just down there, around the corner in that tunnel," he said. "Not far, I'll help you carry it."

"No thanks, I can carry it myself." Arthur got up and looked in the direction the man had pointed.

The man walked crablike sideways a few steps keeping Arthur in his view and indicated with his head and hand that Arthur should follow him, "Come on; I'll show you where it is."

Arthur was hesitant He didn't like the fellow but he wanted to get rid of his bag so he would be more mobile, he could walk around without lugging it and without worrying or watching it all the time. He grabbed the handle of the bag and went in the direction the man indicated, following but trying not to associate.

The man walked ahead almost sideways leading the way but half turned to Arthur to make sure he didn't lose him. He went around a corner and down a ramp toward a poorly lit tunnel. There were no people scurrying in the area they were heading for; it was dark and empty except for abandoned construction material.

Arthur stopped and looked back up the ramp. "I don't think the baggage room is here, there's no one down here."

"No. That's right. I was going to save you some money; you can leave your bag with my buddy down here. He'd watch it for free. Then I can show you the city. You don't want to waste your money do you?" he stopped, evaluating Arthur.

"Is there a baggage room?" asked Arthur.

"Yeah. You want to waste your money, yeah, I'll show you the baggage room."

The man reversed and went back up the ramp and into the main gallery. Arthur followed; they went around a corner behind the marble steps to a smaller gallery that had food shops and newsstands embedded in the wall along one side. On the other side was a long brass countertop with a sign above. Baggage Room. Arthur watched as a traveler put his bag on the brass counter, told the attendant the time he would pick it up, took a ticket and left. Arthur did the same. The man from the waiting room loitered nearly out of sight on the other side of the corridor.

When Arthur had his ticket and as he walked away from the baggage room the man reappeared at Arthur's side.

"You want to see the city. Come'on, I'll show ya."

"I don't know, I don't think I have enough time."

"Yeah ya do, you have four hours; that's plenty of time." he said. "How much money ya got?" leaning close watching his flank for intruders, saving Arthur for himself.

Arthur didn't like the guy, he was pushy, dirty, he tried too hard.

"I don't think I should tell you," said Arthur.

"Yeah, you can tell me. I'm Jimmy, Grand Central Jimmy, everybody knows me. You tell me. When I know how much money you got, then I can figure out what you can see. You want girls? I can get you girls if you got the money."

Arthur thought about it. Girls, what kind of girls? "What kind of girls can you get?"

"Any kind, young, old, pretty, fat, thin, you name it. You got fifty dollars, I can show you a hotel where you can meet girls," he said smiling through rotten teeth.

"Is it near here?" asked Arthur just curious.

"Yeah, we can walk, right down the street."

"How much money would it cost?"

"How much you got, they cost different depending what you want." Jimmy was getting interested. "Anywhere from fifty bucks to a hundred and fifty."

Arthur had a hundred and fifty dollars in his wallet. It was supposed to last for the trip. He didn't want girls, but he was intrigued by the possibilities of seeing what the place was like, what the girls were like. Maybe he'd just go to the hotel with Jimmy and take a look. That's all, just a look.

"I've got enough," said Arthur.

"Let's see it. I don't want to get over there and then you say you don't have the money." Jimmy said getting a sterner voice.

Arthur pulled out his wallet and showed Jimmy three twenty dollar bills; it was obvious there were more bills in there and Jimmy could see them. It was lucky Arthur hadn't held his wallet out any longer or farther in front of him than he did or the folks on a passing train could have grabbed it; he almost handed it to Jimmy so he could count it for himself. Arthur closed the wallet and put it back in his pocket.

Jimmy looked disappointed, "OK, you need to give me some up front money, twenty bucks, so I know you're for real and not going to chicken out at the last minute."

Jimmy was right, that was Arthur's plan. But if Arthur gave Jimmy money now, he was pretty sure Jimmy wasn't into refunds. Maybe this wasn't a good idea, maybe just forget it. Arthur didn't want girls and he didn't like Jimmy and he didn't want to lose his money, he was bored and he was playing with fire under the barn. He'd done it once a few years ago in Oklahoma, before he had moved in with his father. He'd played with fire under the neighbor's barn, and later that night, all night long, he'd stayed up wondering if he got all the fire put out. And he looked out his bedroom window expecting to see a fireball where the barn had been. He'd gotten away with it that time. Not real smart, but exciting and this reminded him of the hollow thrill of disobeying his better judgment, which was a pretty weak customer to begin with.

"No. Forget it. I don't want to give you money now, then you take off," said Arthur figuring he could get out of the transaction and save face.

Jimmy had no face. "OK, just so you got the money, let's go."

Jimmy led the way out of a tunnel with lots of people coming and going. The tunnel ended on the sidewalk of a major street. Jimmy

218

did his crab walk, half leading and half keeping an eye on Arthur who was lagging, not wanting to be there in the first place. He was trying to think of a good way out of the predicament he had got himself into. They were halfway down the block when two men stood in Jimmy's way. Jimmy was looking at Arthur when they moved in front of him so he almost ran into them. When he saw them he looked around for a place to run but one of the men took him by the coat collar. The other moved to Arthur as if to corral him. The one in front of Arthur pulled a black leather wallet from his hip pocket, flipped it open, and showed Arthur a badge. The one holding Jimmy didn't bother with the badge flipping business as he and Jimmy appeared to know each other already.

The man in front of Arthur said, "Son, I'm with the Police, I need to ask you some questions."

Arthur looked around; he didn't know what was going on; he didn't say anything.

"Do you know this guy?" the policeman asked, indicating Jimmy.

"No sir."

"What are you doing with him?" he asked.

"He was going to show me the city," Arthur said, looking at the people who had stopped to look at them.

"I need you to come with me and my partner and Jimmy here to the station house so you can answer some questions. Will you do that?"

"I don't think I can; I have to catch a train."

"When is your train?"

"At three forty."

"We'll have you back here in an hour, latest."

Arthur wasn't sure what to do; he didn't know what he was getting into or what he was already in.

The policeman holding Jimmy interrupted, "Shit, Fred, charge his ass and bring him in. You going to stand around all day negotiating with some snot nose kid?"

The one talking to Arthur ignored his partner. "Look, son, I can either charge you with something and make you come and then you'll be there all day till your parents can come get you or you can come in on your own and leave when we're through. One hour max. What'll it be?"

"OK, I'll come." Arthur said falling into the void, drifting on the river, out of control.

The four of them walked to the end of the block and got in a car that was parked illegally around the corner. They put Jimmy in handcuffs, pushed him into the back seat, and the guy who was holding on got in next to him. Arthur got in the front with the policeman who had asked him to come along. Jimmy didn't say anything and the guy holding him didn't say anything either; the fellow driving drove. It was a short ride, about ten blocks. They parked in front of a big limestone building, twenty stories, set back from the street. Police came and went; no one noticed Jimmy was in handcuffs. They went down some steps and in a side door that was below street level.

The man holding Jimmy took him to a door with a window in it, showed his badge, a buzzer sounded letting them in a hallway; the door closed. The man who asked Arthur to come to the station took Arthur through another door that wasn't locked, down a messy linoleum corridor that was lit by fluorescent bulbs and had doors on either side but no windows. It smelled of cigarettes and cheap disinfectant. He opened a door for Arthur and indicated with a tilt of his head that Arthur should go in. Arthur entered a small office with two desks facing each other, a green metal waste can, a gray metal filing cabinet with barn doors, one of which was bent so they couldn't shut all the way. Hissing fluorescent lights hung in a broken metal bracket from the ceiling. The desks were covered with newspapers and drowning ashtrays.

"Have a seat."

Arthur looked; there was one straight back wooden chair in a corner under a coat and sweater. The policeman followed Arthur's glance to the chair, moved to it, removed the coat and sweater and put them on one of the desks.

Arthur sat.

The policeman shut the door, looked at Arthur "What's your name?"

"Arthur May." Arthur said knowing he had to answer.

"How old are you?"

"Fourteen."

"Arthur, do you know that guy Jimmy?"

"No sir."

"How did you run into him?"

"I was waiting for my train in the station and he came to me and asked if I wanted to see the city."

"Did he ask you for money?"

"Yes sir."

"How much?"

"He wanted twenty dollars and then more depending on what we did."

"Did he offer to find girls?"

"Yes sir."

"Did you give him any money?"

"No sir."

"Arthur, that's probably the first smart thing you've done today." He wasn't mean; he was businesslike, treating Arthur as an adult. "OK Arthur, here's what we're going to do, if it's OK with you. First, we're going to call your parents and tell them where you are, that you witnessed a crime and we have you here as a witness and would they mind if we ask you some questions. If it's OK with them, we're going to take a statement on exactly what happened from the moment you entered the station till right now. Is that OK with you?" He said it in a soft voice, matter of fact, as if he had done it too many times before. But he wasn't disinterested or bored, more that he was tired of having to do it again after he thought he'd solved this problem yesterday.

"That's fine with me," said Arthur, going with the flow of the river.

"Would you write down your name address and phone number for me on this piece of paper?"

Arthur took the paper and printed the information. When he finished, he handed it to the policeman who took it, put it on the desk and picked up the phone. He dialed and waited a while, then hung up the phone.

"No one home, do you know where your mother or father is?"

Arthur gave him his mother's number which he dialed. His mother answered and the policeman said, "This is Detective Sparks with the New York City Police Department; we have your son ... He said exactly what he said he would. Arthur's mother agreed to the request and Detective Sparks hung up.

"So far, so good. Now, we need a statement. A lady stenographer is going to come in a minute and take your statement. I want you to tell her exactly what happened from the minute you walked into the station till you met us on the street. I'll be here to prompt you if you get off track. She'll type the statement, then you'll sign it, and last, we need you to identify Jimmy in a lineup. Then you can go back to Grand Central."

The lady came and sat at the other desk and transcribed Arthur's account of what happened. It only took about fifteen minutes and then she was gone.

"Now, let's go look for Jimmy," Detective Sparks said, standing by the door "Follow me."

Arthur followed Detective Sparks through corridors, up a flight of stairs, and into a room with bright lights at one end. They waited a while not saying anything, then some fellows entered and the detective asked Arthur to point out Jimmy. Arthur did and they went back to the detective's office.

"We'll have to wait a little while for the typed statement," he said. "What were you doing in Grand Central this morning. Did you catch a train from school?"

"Yes."

"One of those schools in the Housatonic Valley? Pretty fancy schools."

"Yes sir, I go to Bridge."

"Do you know what would have happened to you today if you had gone with Jimmy to his hotel?"

"No sir."

"This Jimmy fellow, your new friend, has a record. He's been in prison and in mental hospitals for fifteen years. He was just released based on a new law that frees mental patients if they promise to take their medication and go to counseling. He doesn't do either. The last time I ran into him about three years ago he had picked up a kid about your age at Grand Central station. Took him to a hotel where he said he would get the kid some girls. Instead, he beat the kid almost to death, raped him, took his money and clothes. The kid was on his way home for vacation, from one of those boarding schools up your way. The kid's parents wouldn't let him testify, so Jimmy got away with it. He was sent up over a year ago for armed robbery, but since he has a mental illness he was on a special program, released till he could really hurt someone. You were almost the one. I'm glad you weren't." He paused. "Don't they teach you anything up there?"

"How do you mean?"

"All you kids who go there are rich or you couldn't go. The tuition is more than I make in a year. There you are learning stuff at the best schools in the country and you don't have any more brains than to follow Jimmy around the streets of New York looking for girls. What kind of girls do you think Jimmy would find for you?"

"I don't know. I didn't really want girls. I was bored and he didn't seem dangerous. I wasn't going to go in anywhere with him; I was just curious."

"That's interesting; that's what everyone says. I was just looking and then one step leads to the next and pretty soon you're in over your head, which you almost were."

"How did you know Jimmy was going to take me somewhere?" Arthur asked

"We were watching Jimmy. We saw him take you to the baggage room, so we followed to see if was up to his old tricks; he is."

The woman with the statement came in; Arthur read it and signed where they asked him to.

"That's it. I'll drive you back to Grand Central." Detective Sparks rose and opened the door to let Arthur out first. Arthur left and they went to the car parked at he curb, got in, and started for the station.

Detective sparks turned toward Arthur, "Did you learn anything today?"

"Yes."

"I hope you remember it; there are bad people out there and they will hurt you if they can. And if you think because you are sheltered up there at that school nothing can happen to you, you are dead wrong. You came close today. Everyone isn't like you and everyone doesn't like you and a few hate you for what you have. They will kill you and take what they can if they think they can get away with it. Read about Stalin some day when you are bored and want to flirt with disaster. And talking isn't going to make them go away. You talk, they take. Got it?"

"Yes sir."

"Here you are, good luck, stay out of trouble."

"Thank you, I guess you guys saved my bacon, thanks." Arthur shut the car door and went into the building. It was three o'clock and time to retrieve his bag and head for the train. He found the baggage room, looked for Jimmy, he wasn't there. He took his bag to track twelve and down the ramp to a cavern of smoke and heat and fumes, into the bowels of the earth.

21

THE OHIO STATE LIMITED

The platform was just like the one he had come up a few hours before; it was a concrete ramp which descended into a tunnel; the ramp leveled out and became a pier about fifteen yards wide and a hundred yards long banked on either side by rail cars under soot stained ceilings twenty feet above. Two trains were parked along the pier, one on either side, their engines out of view hidden in the length of the tunnel extension. Everything in the tunnel was hot and filthy and smelled of diesel fumes and high voltage gone wrong, except the train that was parked on the right-hand side of the pier. It was sleek, shining, stainless steel and tinted glass; each car had a name plate and a black conductor in spotless white jacket, neat black pants, and shined black shoes standing at the door.

Arthur wasn't sure what to do. He went down the ramp to a spot where it leveled out with the train and looked around. He'd looked at his ticket earlier but didn't know how to read it. It had a car assignment, a compartment number, and a destination, but he didn't know how to locate any of the numbers. He was early, only a few other passengers came down the ramp with him so he had time.

A conductor was nearby and figured Arthur was lost. "Can I help you sir?" he said.

Arthur looked around and went to the conductor. "Is this the train to Cincinnati?"

""Yessir, this is the Ohio State Limited to Cincinnati, Ohio, three-forty, track twelve," in a singsong. "Are you going to Cincinnati?"

"Yes sir," reversing the titles, "I'm going on to Oklahoma from there. Should I get on here?"

"May I see your ticket? It will tell us what car you're in."

Arthur put his bag down and fumbled around for a his ticket which he thought was in his jacket pocket but it wasn't there, he had looked at it so many times in nervousness that he'd put it in a different place. He found it in his pants pocket and handed it to the conductor.

"Yessir, this is your train and this is your car and I'm your conductor. Let me take your bag and follow me if you will." He picked up Arthur's bag, entered the vestibule, and turned left into a small hallway which was barely wide enough for two people to pass; it had windows about chest height on one side and a series of doors that opened onto little sitting rooms on the other. The conductor chose one of the rooms, entered, put the bag on a seat and turned to Arthur.

"My name is Ransom, I'm your conductor. Have you been on a train before?"

"Once today from school and when I was little." said Arthur looking around at the compartment. It was about eight feet by nine feet with one corner taken by an alcove. There were two double seats facing each other by the window, a mirror, a luggage rack, and the walls were light gray and the seats were royal blue fabric. There was gray tile on the floor and it was spotless, clean.

Ransom was spotless. His shoes were shined, pants creased, hair cut very short, his jacket precise. He was about six feet tall, broad but not loose, heavy by design. His face was wide with prominent full features and he had small ears tacked to the sides of his head, dark brown skin drawn tight over his broad nose and forehead; he was symmetrical, handsome. He stood straight and walked with purpose as if he knew exactly what he was about, exactly where he was going. He wore white gloves.

Ransom opened a narrow door to the alcove which turned out to be a small bathroom with sink and commode. "There are towels and wash things in there," he pointed to a towel rack by the sink which was about as big as a goldfish bowl. "When you're ready for bed I'll come in and turn down your bed," he pointed to an overhead bunk bed that was folded up against the wall. "Will you join us for dinner in the dining car this evening?"

"Yes, I think so," said Arthur not having thought about dinner.

"I'll make a reservation for you; what time would you like to eat?"

"Six-thirty, is that OK?"

"Yessir, Mr. May that's fine. I'll come get you at six thirty. If you need anything you just push that button by the window and I'll come soon as I see it. Is there anything else I can do for you?"

"No. This is great, thank you."

Mr. Ransom left and closed the door. Arthur didn't know whether Ransom was his first name or last. Arthur looked around again; there wasn't much to see. There was a foldout table under the window where he could put a book or papers; the seat resembled a seat on any rail car. He was intrigued by the fold out bed hiding in a lump on the side of the wall; it was about the size of a bunk bed with a handle at the bottom. Outside the window a dark commuter rail car was parked along side. It was gray and dingy, empty, dark and only two feet from his well-lit cabin. There was a shade that pulled down from a roll up contraption. Arthur tried it and found he had to squeeze two small handles together to get it to move up or down and when it was down it covered the window completely in opaque, gray plastic. He put his bag on the floor, sat on one of the seats and looked out the window. There were comings and goings in the hallway, more people getting settled. There was a train schedule in a folder beside the table. Arthur took out the schedule and looked at it for a minute then put it back. He was bored. He didn't have anything to read and nothing to look at or investigate. He fidgeted, got up, opened the bathroom door, checked the towels and the sink, they were still there. He sat down. This was the first time he had been alone since he left Grape three months earlier. It was a strange sensation; he didn't have to be anywhere or talk to anyone for the next thirty hours. He could hide in his cabin until he got to Cincinnati.

He sat for a while looking at the commuter car parked next to his. It was grimy like the station, it was dead without lights. The activity in the hallway stopped and Arthur heard metal plates banging together and doors closing, then the car started to move, jerking its way through the switching yard of the station, black tunnel walls with bare bulbs hanging from sooty cords passed the window; they were making progress. They picked up speed, then came out of the tunnel and immediately climbed to an overhead track headed north for the Harlem River crossing. It was nearly dark outside, lights were bright in buildings but there was enough light to see outside without turning on headlights.. They clattered over the Harlem then went through the extended city, Yonkers and the suburbs where the houses, apartments, and businesses crowded the tracks. Before long it was dark outside and Arthur looked in the windows of houses trying to figure out from his brief glance what was going on inside. Occasionally there were people in the frames that passed, mostly it was snapshots of empty rooms, lit signs, or cars stopped at crossings. Images flashed by, none committed to memory, simply the impression of distance and isolation remaining after a brief view into someone else's world. It was as if each snapshot made a dimple in the smooth curve of his experience, a dimple that should have been filled with details: name, address, school, likes, dislikes, loved or not, and then the snapshot was gone and none of the details, none of the flesh, was there to fill the dimple and all the dimples, arranged like rough spots on a vegetable grating, tool became unpleasant. He stopped looking out the window and looked around the cabin again, unsettled.

Arthur got up from his seat and went to the door. He opened it without thinking what he was going to do, maybe look around the car see what else was on the train. He walked back to the door he had come in, no one was there, the car swayed with the motion of the train so it was like walking on one of those amusement park fun houses where the floor moves, but not the walls or railing, not exactly but the same impression. He turned around and went forward along the narrow passageway. Some of the doors of the cabins were open, some shut. In the open ones there were mostly adults sitting looking forward, reading at the fold-down table. They didn't look up as he passed. He went to the end and opened the door to the connecting car and continued for several cars until he came to the dining car. When he opened the door he was flooded with moist smells of roast beef and potatoes. People were already seated at small tables for four, about twenty of them in all, ten along each side with a central aisle. It was well lit; each table had a window and a light. The tables were covered in white linen, knives and forks and several glasses per place. It looked like a good restaurant. Waiters in white coats served from a kitchen at the other end of the car. Arthur turned to go back to his car as people came in behind him; he went around them and back for several cars but was not sure which was his; they were all the same. He tried to remember how many sets of doors he had opened to get where he was, but he wasn't sure. He kept going till he got to the baggage car he hadn't seen before and turned around. He went back toward the dining car and saw a conductor in the hall.

"Hi, can I ask you a question?"

"Sure you can, what can I do for you," the conductor replied.

"I think I'm lost, I forget what car I'm supposed to be in and what compartment."

"That can happen, they're all the same. I know this isn't your car because I didn't get you settled. Can you tell me who your conductor is?"

"Yes sir, it's Mr. Ransom," Arthur replied, lucky to have remembered his name; it was only because of his wondering whether it was a first or last name that helped it stick in his memory.

"Ransom's car is the next one forward. If you go to the next car and knock on the first compartment door, Ransom will be glad to show you to your compartment," the fellow said with a smile and what appeared to be a genuine interest.

"Thank you."

Arthur turned and went one more car and knocked on the first door. It opened and Mr. Ransom was there in a smaller compartment that appeared to be a pantry. When he saw Arthur he smiled.

"Yessir, what can I do for you, Mr. May?"

"I forgot what compartment I'm in; I took a walk around and then couldn't find my way back."

He continued to smile. "That's happened lots of times. You're in the third door on the right; this door is number one," he said.

"Do you have anything to read?" asked Arthur.

"Yessir I do. I have magazines and newspapers. If you'll go to your compartment, I'll be right there with some things to read."

"OK. Thanks."

Arthur turned and walked to his door. He went in and it was as he left it, spotless. He left the door open. In a moment Mr. Ransom came in with magazines and newspapers in a satchel. He put it on the table.

"Take a look in there and see if you want something, I'll come back in a while and get the satchel."

"OK, Thanks."

Arthur looked through the magazines and didn't see anything he wanted but took *Life* and another. He wasn't interested in newspapers. He sat down and leafed through the magazine looking at pictures of President Eisenhower trout fishing in Arkansas, Marilyn Monroe smiling at no one, a black Labrador retriever driving a truck in New Hampshire. He read the stories but they weren't interesting. He didn't really want to read; he wanted to be home and have the trip over. He thought about what he would do while he was at home. He hadn't heard from his friends Fred and Tom since he left in September; he supposed they were doing what they had done last year, riding the bus to school, looking at girls, smoking cigars by the railroad tracks, telling stupid stories, wasting time, waiting for whatever happened next. He wondered if they had changed or if the town had changed since he had gone.

Mr. Ransom knocked on the door, "It's six thirty, Mr. May; the dining car is three cars up front."

"Thank you," Arthur said.

He stood up swaying with the train. It was going pretty fast, Arthur guessed it was about sixty miles an hour. He went in the direction of the dining car and when he got there two other people, a couple, were waiting to be seated. He stood behind them. A waiter came and asked if the three of them were together and the fellow in front of him said they weren't, so the waiter asked if they minded sitting together. They agreed and asked Arthur if it was OK; he agreed and they were shown to a table on the left side. The couple took the seats next to the window facing each other and Arthur took the forward-facing aisle seat next to the man. There was a menu but Arthur wanted the roast beef he'd smelled when he visited earlier. The couple didn't introduce themselves; they appeared to be about thirty years old, younger than his parents.

The man next to him was tall, lanky, stooped, with a droopy sad face, his eyes sloped down away from the center of his forehead as if the inside corners were held up by string tied to a point between his tangled eyebrows, the outside corners free to droop away at different angles. He had a lantern jaw with a fringe of mean in his lips. His clothes were not pressed, his shoes were scuffed colorless. The woman was about Arthur's height, dumpy with hair dyed reddish purple and combed into some sort of doughnut on top of her head. She wore so much makeup you couldn't tell what color her skin was. She had small blue eyes that seemed to poke out of her head as if there was too much pressure behind them and she played at her false teeth with her tongue when she thought no one was looking.

They didn't pay any attention to Arthur but talked to one another leaning close over the table. Arthur couldn't help but overhear some of their conversation. They talked about who would know and if it was a secret and when they were supposed to be back what story they would tell. It didn't make any sense to Arthur. He ordered roast beef, mashed potatoes and string beans; they ordered chicken. The meal came and was served and Arthur noticed the fellow next to him nearly stuck his face in his plate to eat. He leaned forward with both arms on the table surrounding his plate and put his head about two inches above the chicken, then he used his fork as a shovel pushing wads of food into his mouth rather than lifting it to his face. He forced one wad on top of the previous without swallowing so that at times he looked like his cheeks would explode. He didn't talk while he ate; he was focused on the job at hand, getting to the bottom of the plate before anyone could take it away.

The man's manners struck Arthur as grotesque, out of place, hostile and he wondered if other people looked at him and his manners and thought he was grotesque.

The man finished the food on his plate, then drank his glass of water in one swig. He put the glass on the table, reached in his pocket and pulled out a small flat bottle with brown liquid in it. He put half of it in his glass and poured the rest in the woman's glass. She didn't appear to care. He took a drink, put his glass down, and turned to Arthur.

"Where ya goin, kid?"

"Oklahoma." Arthur responded looking at the liquid on the man's lips.

"You from Oklahoma?"

"Yes sir."

"What are you doin out here when you live in Oklahoma?"

"I go to school in Connecticut; I'm going home for Christmas vacation."

"You ain't old enough to be in college are ya?"

"No. I'm in high school."

"What kinda school is that where you gotta come all the way from Oklahoma, a reform school?" He seemed serious.

"It's just a school where you live at the school rather than go to one at home." Arthur tried to explain.

"Ain't the one at home good enough?" he asked.

"I don't know; my parents wanted me to go to this school in Connecticut." Arthur wanted to get out of the conversation; the man was belligerent in his questions and not satisfied with the answers.

His partner interrupted, "Honey, it's one of them boarding schools, you know, private school where they stay over; rich kids go there."

"You a rich kid?" asked the man looking straight at Arthur more in accusation than question.

"No sir."

"What's your daddy do?" he asked.

"He's a doctor." Arthur said trying to back out of the way of the man's accusation.

"Yeah, you're a rich kid. You got one of them cabinets?" he asked.

"What?"

"Not cabinets, honey, compartments; you got a compartment?" she asked turning from her partner to Arthur.

"I don't think so," Arthur replied. There was nowhere to go; he hadn't finished his dinner or paid but he wanted to leave and so he stuck with his custom of doing nothing and letting circumstance take him down the river.

"What d'ya mean, ya don't know? You got one or not?"

"I have a little room thing, I don't know what it's called."

"We got two of us here an we gotta sit up all night on them rough seats and you, a kid, all by yourself, you got a compartment with a big bed and some niggers to wait on you. Wha'd'ya think about that, Charlene? How come he gets a compartment and we gotta sit up all night."

"Don't worry about it, Stan, that's the way it is; they've always had stuff that we don't, we aren't gonna change it."

Stan took another swallow and finished his glass.

"Goddamn rich bastards sticking it to us all the time, robbing us. You little punk, you probably think you deserve to be in that compartment while poor people sleep in the coach section don't ya." he said. This wasn't a question, it was a statement of Stan's truth. "I worked all my life, hard, an I can't ride in a bed, an you, what have you done but had everything handed to you?"

"Stan, settle down; people are looking at us." Charlene said and she was right; people were looking.

"I don't give a damn if people look; let 'em look I'm tired of bein robbed by rich people," he said but not so loud. He took a swig of Charlene's drink. "I wanna see that compartment," he said. "When we're finished here, I want you to show me that compartment." Looking at Arthur. "I'm telling you when we finish with this mess, all the rich people will be finished just like Russia, all the rich people got poor or got dead and that's what we're going to do here."

Arthur didn't respond; he ate the beef; it had become tasteless, finished his potato and tried to get the waiter to bring his check. The waiter brought both checks at the same time. Arthur put money on the table and stood to leave. Stan stood and put some money next to his check.

"Come on, Charlene, we're going to see his compartment."

Charlene looked around the dining car surveying peoples' reactions. "I don't think we better do this; it could cause some problems."

His belligerence rose with Charlene's hesitation. "Charlene, I said come on; let's go." He grabbed her arm and she rose from her seat.

Arthur didn't know what to do so he walked out; Charlene followed him and was followed by Stan. They walked through the cars not talking because they were in single file. Arthur didn't hold the doors open for Charlene because he wanted to act like they weren't with him. He wondered what he should do to get rid of them; he could run down the aisle and then lock his door when he got to the compartment. He could ask a conductor for help; he could let them come and see what they wanted. Maybe they only wanted a look. He did nothing but walk to his compartment and they came with him. As Arthur opened the door, Ransom stuck his head out of the pantry.

"Just give me a buzz when you want that bed turned down, Mr. May," he said looking at Arthur with a question in his expression.

Arthur went in and Stan and Charlene followed.

Stan didn't hesitate. "So how do you like that: 'Just give me a buzz when you want your bed turned down,' isn't that something," "So it's Mr. May is it. You're fifteen and it's Mr. May. Who the hell do you think you are?"

"OK, Stan, we've seen enough, let's don't start trouble, this boy hasn't done anything." Charlene was imploring Stan, standing at the door trying to leave,

"What the hell do you mean 'Don't start anything.' It's been going on for years, this little snot nose rich kid and his compartment and we're gonna sit up all night. I don't think so. I think we're gonna trade right here. How about you give us your compartment and we'll give you our seat, Mr. May?"

"Stan?" Charlene started to say something.

"Shut up," he snapped.

Stan took Arthur's bag and started to hand it to Arthur. "Here, here's your bag. You just tote that up to second class and see how you like it"

Ransom appeared in the hall just outside the door. "Can I help you?"

Stan looked at him. "Who asked you?"

Ransom looked at Arthur. "Mr. May, are these people your guests?"

"No, they're not; they followed me back here," said Arthur.

Ransom looked at Charlene. "Excuse me, ma'am would you mind stepping into the hall."

She backed out and Ransom entered. He was as tall as Stan, but more substantial, heavier and he stood straight, almost as erect as Carl. And while he may have been a little older than Stan, he looked like he was in better shape. His demeanor gave the impression he was completely confident in what he was doing. It was as if he had been through this drill a hundred times and knew exactly the outcome.

Ransom stood directly in front of Stan, looked him in the eye and said evenly, "We can do this the hard way or the easy way, which would you prefer?"

"No rich man's nigger's going to tell me what to do," Stan spat.

"I have asked you to leave and I have witnesses," replied Ransom as he took Stan's left arm and left shoulder and spun him toward the door.

Stan tried to resist but Ransom had him under control. By this time two other conductors appeared in the hall to make sure the outcome was unchallenged.

"Harold, would you see that these two get to their car," Ransom said as he released Stan in the hall.

Arthur stood watching, not knowing what to do.

Ransom returned to Arthur, "They won't bother you anymore; we'll put them off in Utica."

"How did you know there was a problem?" asked Arthur.

"The waiters in the dining car heard the whole thing; they couldn't stop it there because they're too busy, too many people around, so they called back here and told me to be on the lookout."

Arthur asked in confusion, "They'll be put off the train in Utica?"

"Yes. We have a regular stop there; they'll call the police when they get in and offer to let the people go or swear out a complaint if the man wants trouble."

"How often does this happen?"

"Not very often, once in a while, and it usually involves alcohol." Ranson turned toward the door ready to leave. "Do you need anything?"

"No. Thanks for the help."

"Buzz me when you're ready for me to put the bed down," he said and left shutting the door behind him.

Arthur put his bag on the rear-facing seat and sat on the other looking out the window at passing lights. Occasionally he heard a frenzied clanging whiz by as the train went through a crossing. The train bisected small towns with a road and a whistle and passed other trains going in the opposite direction while Arthur sat in his cabin as if it were a space capsule watching the passing scene out the window, detached from everything around him. He didn't understand what was going on, how he seemed to be a ricochet from circumstance, bouncing from event to event without any control over what was going on. He had become used to going along with whatever was happening, letting the river take him where it wanted. There were small events like preparing for class or shooting with the Clements when he was able to look ahead and see what was coming and act in a controlled way, but most of the time he was where he was because some unrelated minor circumstances led him in a direction and he followed. He wondered if this was true for most people, or was he unique. It seemed the people he admired, Mrs. Clement, Ransom, the prefects at school, Mr. Webster, didn't let circumstance dominate their lives; they seemed to plan ahead of it and let it chase them. Arthur stood and out of boredom buzzed Ransom to get him to put the bed down. Ransom knocked on the door and Arthur let him in. He entered and went straight to the wall where the bed was hiding, turned the latch with one hand, and with the other he eased the bed to horizontal. It was already made with white sheets that looked like they had been starched and a blue wool blanket. He went in the alcove and brought out two pillows and put them on the bed, then he turned down the covers. He didn't say anything and neither did Arthur.

When he finished he turned toward Arthur. "Do you need anything?"

"No, I guess that's it."

"I'll wake you at seven so you have time for breakfast before we get into Cincinnati."

"Thanks for the help," said Arthur.

"Good night, Mr. May." Ransom left, closing the door behind him.

22

THE FORTUNES OF WAR

When Ransom had gone, Arthur climbed onto the bunk with his clothes on and left the shade open. He lay on his stomach looking out the window where it had started to snow. White puffs flashed horizontally across the window. There were lights in the distance and crossing bells and the constant background rhythm of click-click as the train wheels crossed joints in the track. There was also the rumble of wind and creaking of tired joints between cars and a rocking motion. Arthur lay for a while unable to sleep, still confused over the two incidents of the day, one with Grand Central Jimmy and the other with Stan. He was confused over should. Should he have avoided Jimmy? Yes, he had a feeling while he was with Jimmy that it wasn't the right thing to do or the smart thing, but there was adventure in it. Yes, he should have known better, just like the cigarettes. With Stan it was different; he should have asked for help rather than letting circumstance pull him along. He should have said something to make it clear he didn't want Stan in his compartment. All this was clear in reflection but it wasn't clear at the time it was happening. There must have been some ingredient he was missing, something that was there in the doing and missing from the reflection. Because, in the reflection both situations were clear, but in the doing both were confused and he had reached the wrong conclusion. It was almost as if he were acting against his best interest, tempting fate, trying to lose before the contest was started.

He slid off the bunk and went into the hall. It was late; no one was up, the train racketed through the night while people on and off slept through its passing. He went to the end of the car where the pantry was. The door was open, the light was on and Ransom sat on a stool reading a newspaper; he wore glasses and his jacket was off with his shirt sleeves rolled up. Without moving his head much, he looked over the top of his glasses.

"Yesssir, what can I do for you?" he said just loud enough to be heard.

"Nothing, I can't sleep and wanted to walk around a little." Arthur replied.

"I can make you some cocoa if you want."

It sounded great to Arthur, but he didn't want Ransom to go to any more trouble.

"I was just going to make some for myself when you came along, so now I have an excuse." Ransom stood, folded the paper and put it on a shelf. He reached for his jacket and put it on, then he got milk from a small refrigerator and started making cocoa.

Arthur watched. "Don't you get to sleep?"

"We can take little naps now and then but we're supposed to be here and ready to help if we're needed, so it's hard to sleep. We get a day off between runs so it works out fine," said Ransom as he put a pan on a hot plate.

"How long have you been doing this?" asked Arthur.

"I've been working with the railroad for two years, before that I was in the Marines. I was in the Marines for twelve years."

"Were you in Korea?"

"Yessir, I was."

"That must have been pretty scary."

"It was. I was in World War Two in the Pacific and in Korea; Korea was scarier."

"How did you decide to go in the Marines?"

"It was December 1942 and there wasn't a lot of deciding, everybody went, I was seventeen, I told them I was eighteen, not too much older than you are now I guess, you must be fifteen aren't you?"

"No, I'm fourteen, but I'll be fifteen in a few months."

"And you're going home for vacation. Where are you from?"

"Oklahoma. Grape Oklahoma."

"You go to one of the prep schools around New York; we get a lot of boys and sometimes some girls going home for vacation from New York to Cincinnati, Cleveland, and Saint Louis."

"Yeah, I go to one of the schools in Connecticut; it's my first year." Arthur paused. "What should I have done with that guy Stan, the one who came to my room tonight? I didn't know what to do with him. I didn't invite him but I don't think I was very good at letting him know I didn't want him hanging around."

"Not much you could have done with him. He was older and bigger. You could have tried, NO, but that doesn't always work, not with drunks when they see they have the advantage. You were out-gunned."

"It seems I just let it happen. I didn't have a plan or anything; I just let it roll along till something new interrupted what was going on. I was lucky the new thing was you. What if it had been more Stans, more bad luck instead of good?" Arthur asked following the train of thought he'd been working on while he was looking out the window.

"Sometimes you need luck and it's nice when it obliges you. But the older you get, the more you find you have to plan on some bad luck coming around. You have to put some things in reserve, save for the times when the bad luck is on a roll, and it does get on a roll," Ransom said, not looking at Arthur, looking at the pot on the hot plate; it was more comfortable for both of them.

"Have you ever been in a situation when you thought you didn't have enough reserve, you didn't plan enough?"

"Sure, plenty of times, sometimes you can't plan enough; fate has you in a place where you're in trouble and you need some luck, but that doesn't mean stop planning because I've found most situations, when they're bad, can still get worse and will unless you do something about it."

"How did you know how to handle Stan, it's like you'd done it before?"

"The Stans of the world are easy, they're mostly mouth, bullies, they only pick on people they can scare easily. But just in case, I called on my friends as backup; we didn't need it but sometimes drunks make bigger mistakes than they planned to, they misread the situation, which is what drunk is all about, and then they can be a problem. Stan is not a problem. Don't ever try to reason with a drunk, get out of their way if you can or put them away. The minute you start to reason with them you're in their game."

"Did you ever run out of luck?"

"Yes, that's happened a few times."

"Can you tell me about one of them?"

"Yes, I suppose I can. I don't like to talk about it much because it's not very pleasant. But if you can learn something from it then maybe it's worth telling. I wish someone had told me about it before it happened, then it wouldn't have. I was in the Marines in Korea. I was a platoon sergeant; you know what that is?"

"Yeah, I think so; you were in charge of the platoon."

"Sort of, an officer is in charge but the sergeant is right there with the officer. I was a platoon sergeant and we were in North Korea pretty close to the Chinese border; we thought we had won the war because we had run the North Korean Army almost out of the country. Our planning maybe wasn't as good as it should have been or we had stopped planning because we had won, almost.

"Our unit was sitting about ten miles from the Chinese border and we had pretty much defeated the North Koreans so we were sitting there waiting to go home or back south. We weren't waiting for the Chinese to roll two hundred thousand troops across the border at us. That's what they did. In the early winter, actually it was the end of November 1950; it seemed like winter because it was so cold. Anyway, they came across the border and rolled right over us. We weren't ready; we didn't have enough men or ammunition to hold them off; they just kept coming. We got orders to pull out; what was left of our unit, so our platoon was heading down a road into a valley. It must have been about ten below zero; we didn't have any trucks, half the unit was wounded or dead, we hadn't slept in two days and the Chinese were right on top of us the whole time. Luckily they didn't have trucks and were running out of ammunition and sleep too or we'd have been done in.

"We came to a lake where we were supposed to go on the east side with some other units and the rest of the division was going around the west. I don't know exactly what the plan was, but we got cut off from the division at Changjin, and we were surrounded by the Chinese there. That should have been the end of us. We were surrounded and out-manned and no one was coming to pull us out of the mess. So we had a choice, we could fight our way back to the rest of the division or we could give up. It was only a couple of miles but it was day and night, live or die. Some folks wanted to surrender or talked about the possibility, but when we thought about it, it didn't seem like the right thing to do, you're in the Marines; you don't give up. We also knew how the Chinese and North Koreans treated prisoners, they executed them after a torture program, except those few they wanted to keep as trophies for later peace negotiations. Talk of surrender never went very far.

"We fought for two days and inched our way back to the division. It was like no fighting I had seen before. Normally in a battle the fight only takes a little while, maybe twenty minutes for the main engagement. That's because a man can't fight any longer than that. It tires you out, you're carrying forty or fifty pounds of gear, you're running and shooting and crawling and then running again.

The noise is like nothing you can imagine and the dirt is everywhere. Dirt and smoke and people yelling; it's just pandemonium and a man can't do that very long. So, after a while, there's a lull in the action while everyone takes a breather, counts up what he's got left, and decides if he wants to go for round two. Most folks choose to wrap it up after round one, one side quits looking for some distance and the other side is happy to let 'em go. It's a little like a dog fight, it's over pretty quick with the loser deciding it's better to move on down the road.

"That's not the way it was at Changjin. We didn't have anywhere to get away to because they were all around us, and the Chinese didn't want us to get away, so the battle was ragtag for two days, constant moves and constant contact, neither side satisfied with the outcome. But we made it, some of us did. We finally linked up with the rest of the division and made it to a little port, Huang Nam, where we were evacuated.

"We didn't have the right plan, but luck was partly on our side. The Chinese were poorly outfitted; they didn't have winter gear so their guys were freezing to death. They didn't have the ammunition or training we did, so they couldn't take advantage of their numbers.

"So sometimes luck is with you and sometimes against and sometimes the planning isn't enough, but there's one thing that always works, and that's do what's right. Most of the time we know what that is, and that's what pulled us through Changjin, doing what's right by our brothers, not giving up. If it can be done in Changjin, the rest is easy.

"Guys like Stan, they don't do what's right. You know it and they know it. In their case you have to let them know you will do what's right even if you have to cross them, even if there is some danger in it. Sitting and watching and talking won't do it. You'll find a lot of people want to sit and talk and negotiate and use words to confuse issues, and they don't do what's right, they do something else, and then in the end someone else has to solve the problem or the problem solves them. When you see something that isn't right, do right."

Ransom stopped for a moment, "OK. So, how about some cocoa."

Arthur wanted to ask Ransom if he'd been wounded or killed anyone, but he didn't think he should so he didn't. After the story about Korea, Ransom acted like he was finished for the day. They drank cocoa, shuffled their feet, and then Arthur went back to his cabin and looked out the window and thought some more about how calm Ransom was, how straight he seemed, unconfused, clear. He wasn't simple; he was sure. He wasn't looking for adventure; he was working his way around it. He wouldn't have given Grand Central Jimmy one second of his time. He made it clear to Stan how things were going to be in less than a minute. He wasn't excited, boastful, full of himself, he was sure. There was nothing new in his confrontation with Stan, nothing surprising, because he did what he always did, he did the right thing.

It seemed simple to Arthur, he had a pretty good idea of what the right thing was; doing it was the problem.

23

HOME

Ransom woke Arthur the next morning as a friend rather than a child in his custody. They chatted for a moment; then Ransom had things to do and Arthur went to breakfast. He got a table next to the window and ordered cream of wheat and grapefruit. He looked out the window and was surprised at the friendliness of the view. The train and the houses and barns and trees and everything in the window frame was sandwiched between the smooth gray blanket of sky and dark flat earth, and there was a thin, straight line where the sky met the ground at the horizon. The fence lines were straight in the envelope between land and sky, and the fields, a hundred acres or more each, were laid out in patterns, in squares of different colors, gray from the bean trash remaining after combining, brown with corn stalk stubble and green where some winter wheat was coming up. They were on the edge of the Midwest, on a train track, straight as an arrow, rocketing from Columbus to Cincinnati. These were the beginnings of the Great Plains.

They got to Cincinnati on time and Arthur got off and said good-bye to Ransom hoping he would see him again. Arthur was another school kid on the way home for vacation, another child Ransom looked after, Arthur was not memorable. Ransom on the other hand was a hero of many tests. They were on different paths0.

The Cincinnati station was nearly empty. It was built as half of a clam shell with a one-hundred-yard-long, three-story-high curved wall meeting a straight wall at either end. The insides of the shell were covered with huge tile mosaics, pictures of men working in steel mills and butchering hogs and making soap. Otherwise it was boring and run-down, with a little shop made of wood, like a portable closet with a window folded down, perched in a corner and out of place in the concrete, mosaic, and marble hall. A woman with gray hair gone to yellow-white, deeply creased skin, and squinty, watery-blue eyes stood

243

inside the thing with her head tilted to the side trying to avoid the smoke rising from a cigarette loosely purchased in partly closed lips while she unwrapped a bundle of magazines. She sold newspapers, candy, cigarettes, paperback books, small bottles of aspirin and Cincinnati memorabilia. He didn't want anything, but he was bored so he went and scratched around examining without interest; he didn't want to read, he wanted to be home.

Arthur caught his train to Saint Louis without difficulty; he read the track, car and compartment information correctly. The conductor was pleasant but Ransom had ruined the role for whoever followed. The conductor showed him to his car and gave the introduction to the bathroom and towels and left. Arthur sat, his mind adrift, he didn't want to think, to wrestle with should and why, so he forced himself to imagine what it would be like at home, who would be there, would he have changed, had they changed? Carl was going to pick him up in Oklahoma City and then they would drive the hundred miles to Grape. Beyond that, there was no plan.

He knew he would see his sisters and mother sometime and more than once but he didn't look forward to it. His mother was difficult and blamed him for some of her problems; she said Arthur was like Carl but Arthur didn't understand the similarity. Whenever Arthur was with his mother there was a great tension of unexplained expectation, of guilt and remorse and confused emotion at fantasies that had failed to materialize. It would start off OK, with false smiles, formality and pleasantry and news of inconsequential things, but before too long his mother would find a fault in him and his father and then she would start to accuse Arthur of things he had never done. She accused him of setting their summer house on fire, stealing her money, wrecking the car, drinking her Scotch. The things she accused him of were bizarre, unreal to Arthur but real to his mother; he couldn't understand the gulf between their differing views of common events. The last year he lived with her she spent most of her time in bed either reading mystery novels or looking at the ceiling. She had a complete bed wardrobe, different sets of nightgowns, slippers, and robes. She liked the leopard skin patterns most, and when she wasn't in bed she cruised silently around the house padding here and there in soft slippers, a leopard skin robe and horn rimmed bifocals, seeking the cause of her confusion in closets, basements, cupboards or in Arthur. She left the girls alone, let them do whatever they wanted, not concerned about their absence or intentions.

Last year, Gretta, Arthur's younger sister, went missing for two days before Roz noticed she wasn't around. If it had been winter, the school probably would have called to ask about her absence, but it was summer and no one was watching. Gretta had stayed at a friend's house for the weekend and Roz had forgotten. When it finally struck her that her daughter was missing, she adopted a television induced imitation of hysteria, she screamed from her bed for Gretta, throwing herself into improbable and dramatic poses, putting her hand to her head in despair as if waiting for a photographer from one of the detective magazines she read to appear and snap a shot of her heroism. She did nothing to find Gretta, that was up to Susan, Arthur's older sister, whom Arthur called Lulu.

Lulu and Arthur phoned Gretta's friends and asked for Gretta without admitting she'd been gone, unnoticed, for at least two days. On the third call they found her safe, and Gretta relayed that the mother of the girl she was staying with had talked to Roz before she left. When Susan told Roz that Gretta was found and safe, Roz was disappointed because she thought her chance to meet J. Edgar Hoover had been ruined. She was fascinated by the police, hospitals, murder and kidnapping.

Once, shortly after Gretta went missing, Roz called the police and said there were strangers in the house and then hung up on them. After she hung up she left the house and drove down the street leaving Arthur at home alone without telling him what she had done. The cops responded to the call to make sure that everything was OK at the May house, so they sent a squad car with a twenty-five year old midget girl cop and her forty-five year old male partner to check things out. Roz had previously told them that Arthur was mentally ill and about to abuse her, so they were ready. The two cops, Mary Jane and Jeff, came and knocked and Arthur answered the door not knowing why they were there. They explained that they needed to search the house to look for bodies. When they said Roz had called, Arthur knew almost anything was possible so he let them in. Mary Jane appeared to be in charge, taking things very seriously. The barrel of her .38 S&W police special nearly dragged on the carpet because she was so short and the pistol so large. The combination of the pistol belt and body armor (all built for a six-foot man) made her look more like a mound of equipment than a safety officer.

Mary Jane must have been reading Roz's discarded *True Detective* magazines because she shared Roz's ambitions relative to a visit from J. Edgar Hoover. As a result, she assumed there was a body stashed under a bed. Jeff, the older guy, rolled his eyes and tried to smile at Arthur as if to say he didn't have anything to do with looking under beds or in closets.

A RICOCHET FROM CIRCUMSTANCE

Meanwhile, Roz had gone to the police station and said there was a shooting at the house. The next thing Arthur knew there were four cop cars with lights winking, one pulled up in the driveway and the others stopped at crazy angles in the street. Police jumped out of the cars and drew their weapons. While the police cars were pulling up outside, Mary Jane got stuck under one of the beds when her body armor was hung up on a renegade bed spring. Her only way out was to call for help which the police outside heard.

Arthur, not knowing that Mary Jane was stuck, watched the police line up outside. He went out to ask them what the problem was and was about to say something when they told him to raise his hands. He didn't think they could be talking to him so he turned around to look for Jeff who was behind him. Jeff came around the corner and got hung up in a rose bush so he raised his hands.

The lead cop out front yelled at him, "Not you, Jeff, the little guy there, raise your hands."

Since Arthur had no idea who was supposed to raise his hands, he didn't do anything and he let Jeff straighten it out with his supervisor. Jeff talked to his boss and everybody relaxed, got back in their cars and left. Jeff had been around long enough to know about Roz and her visions. Mary Jane found her way out of the bed spring problem and they were soon gone. Roz came back about half an hour later and acted as if everything was as normal as it got at the May house.

One of the few things Roz was truly concerned about was animals. She had a cat and a dog. The cat, Mr. Horace-Whigg, was almost normal except he spent about as much time in bed as Roz did because Roz scratched him and talked to him and the cat couldn't understand what she was saying. The dog wasn't normal. It was a toy poodle which apparently could understand Roz and worse than that, believed her. It followed her everywhere and when Roz spent days in her leopard-skin robe in bed, the dog did not get walked, so it frequently had accidents, little dried up sausages left in a heap in the middle of the carpet. It only liked to relieve itself on oriental rugs. The dog, Whitey-Joe Roz called him, all her animals had hyphenated names, was neurotic or psychotic or both. Whatever its psychosis, it was a mad dog. It slept with Roz and the cat, and if Arthur got too close to the bed it snarled and bared its teeth, little yellow-brown knives dancing behind curled lips. It wasn't into bluffing much because if Arthur didn't back up quickly, Whitey-Joe would launch himself in a fit of rage, ears back, mouth open, and bite whatever he could get. He was surprisingly quick and vicious and always had pink eye and knotted hair. Maybe it was all the knotted hair that made him mean. Arthur thought if his own hair was that knotted he'd probably be mean too.

Roz loved hospitals. She would go to one at any opportunity and occasionally try to get herself admitted. The hospital in Grape knew her and treated her nicely, they let her sit with her suitcase in the waiting room until she got tired and went home. The year before Arthur moved in with Carl, Arthur came home from school one day and found Roz sitting at the kitchen table with her suitcase at her feet.

She demanded, "Take me to the hospital."

"What's wrong, Mom?"

"I'm going blind. Can't you see?" she replied.

Arthur didn't understand her response, how was he supposed to see that she was going blind, but he let it pass.

Theatrical urgency pushing her voice into an imaginary packed house. "I have to go to the hospital right now," she said.

"Have you called Dr. Grossman?" Arthur asked. Dr. Grossman was her doctor and generally had a good way of handling Roz.

"Yes, he wasn't in. Quick, take me to the hospital." She was irritated at the delay.

"Mom, I can't drive, how do you want me to take you?"

"Call a taxi."

"OK." Arthur called a taxi and waited with Roz for it to arrive. They didn't talk as the oncoming blindness had also affected her speech. The taxi came and honked in front of the house.

Roz got up. She was completely dressed, she had on a hounds-tooth tweed coat, black pumps, and a little hat that sat on top of her head; she looked like she going to church. She also had a cane and made a great point of tapping it around the kitchen as she supposed a blind person might navigate the street. She turned toward the front of the house and as she was about to leave the kitchen she said, "Bring my bag. I'll need my bag."

With that she navigated quite well to the front door, looking normal and not tapping so much until she got to the front porch where she stumbled and knocked into the railing and got herself turned around backwards for the taxi driver, so he'd know she was going blind too. She found her way to the taxi and let herself in after waiting a few unsuccessful moments for the driver to open the door for her.

Arthur followed with her bag which was a three "suiter" suitcase, nearly a trunk. It was huge, and it was heavy. Arthur could hardly carry it. When the taxi driver, who had remained sitting at the wheel of his car, saw the bag, he turned almost completely around in his seat as if to look out the back window, reached back and grabbed a coat hanger that was sticking out between the backseat and the left door. He gave it a good yank, and the trunk popped open.

"Put her in there," he said to Arthur, not intending to move from his perch.

Arthur hefted the bag into the trunk and slammed the lid. He was about to say good bye and good luck when his mother said. "Arthur, you're coming with me aren't you?"

"OK," he said and got in next to her.

"Where to?" asked the driver.

"Mercy Hospital, quickly, I'm going blind," said Roz, trolling for sympathy.

The driver pulled away from the curb and headed for the hospital; it was only about a mile away. They arrived and Roz told the driver to pull into the emergency entrance. Arthur didn't object; he was along for the ride and didn't want to get between Roz and her destiny.

Roz turned to Arthur. "Go in and tell them I'm here," she said. She expected doctors and orderlies and crash carts as her reception but no one had come out to greet them.

The driver, getting a little suspicious, interrupted the scene, "Before you get too far away, why don't you pay me."

Arthur paid the driver and went into the emergency room where people were busy sorting, checking, reading and doing medical things but not paying attention to Arthur. He found a nurse who didn't look too busy and asked her what to do with Roz who was still in the taxi. The nurse told him to check with admitting, so he went to admitting and waited a while before the woman behind the cashier's window would see him. When he got to the window he asked the admitting person what he should do.

"Is Mrs. May your mother?" she asked.

"Yes."

"Why don't you bring her in and put her in a chair here in admitting. I'll call Dr. Grossman." she said.

"I thought she already called Dr. Grossman," Arthur said.

"No. She usually says she's talked to him, but most of the time she hasn't."

"Has she been here before?"

"Yes. She comes in once in a while and wants to be admitted, but she isn't sick and only a doctor can admit here, so when she comes in we call Dr. Grossman, and we ask her to sit in a chair for a while until the doctor can see her. He calls back in a while and asks to talk to her, so we let her talk to him on the phone, then someone comes to pick her up and takes her home," she said in a friendly way as if she understood Arthur's dilemma.

Arthur went back outside to the emergency entrance. The taxi was gone and Roz was standing in the drive next to her suitcase; she looked mad as if she was ready to scold someone for dereliction of duty, but no one was around.

"Well?" she said when Arthur came out the door.

"Mom, come on in. They want you to wait in admitting while they talk to Dr. Grossman."

"I don't want to talk to Dr. Grossman. I should be admitted immediately. I'm going blind; if I go blind I can sue them. Go in and get a wheel chair; I can't stand out here all day," she said, as if Arthur were an orderly.

Arthur went into the emergency room again and asked the nurse for a wheel chair. There was an empty one next to the door but Arthur didn't know if he should take it so he asked. The nurse looked at him, then out to the driveway, and recognized the situation. She said Arthur could have it. He took it out the door to Roz and she got in and put her cane across her lap.

"Don't forget my suitcase," she said.

Arthur pushed her through the automatic door and down a hallway to admitting.

"Mom, they want you to stay here till Dr. Grossman calls; why don't you sit in a chair so I can take the wheelchair back?"

"I will sit right here in this wheelchair. They'll need it to take me to surgery any minute. I can't see; I'm going to be blind if they don't operate right away," she said, confirming a matter of well established fact. "Go get my suitcase before someone steals it."

Arthur went back to the driveway and lugged the suitcase to the admitting room. When he got there he lifted it to put it on a chair so he could open it to see what was inside. When he tried to lift it onto the chair, it tipped sideways, slipped off, hit the floor on its side and spilled its contents of at least fifty books and a hundred True Detective magazines.

He looked at the mess. "Mom I thought you were going blind?"

She didn't miss a beat, "I am. But when they fix me, I'll be in here for a long time and I'll need something to read."

Arthur didn't expect a rational explanation. He asked, "Should I stay here?"

"No, it's fine if you leave your mother in the hospital, alone, waiting for surgery. It's just like you to think of yourself at a time like this. Go home. I don't want you here." She invoked her adopted English accent which was so popular in Grape, Oklahoma, theater circles, placing her hand on her forehead, looking at the ceiling and waiting for audience applause which did not come.

Arthur left the hospital and walked home thinking about what was wrong   He didn't know what the problems were, but he knew his mother was not like his friends' mothers.

24

MARTHA

The ride from Cincinnati to Oklahoma City was boring and uncomfortable because it was full of introspection. Arthur spent a lot of the time pondering the imponderable. He knew he had changed a lot since leaving Grape; the school had changed him and he had seen a lot of new things in New York, in Greenwich, and on the train. He wondered if everyone had changed or if everyone else would be the same as when he left. He had new clothes and shoes, he had let his hair grow out of its butch and he parted it on the left. He had grown an inch or more and he'd listened to Mr. Webster and to Ransom.

Carl met Arthur at the Oklahoma City train station. He was happy to see Arthur and Arthur was happy to see him. Carl treated him differently, as if Arthur were an adult. Arthur had achieved a stature in Carl's eyes, Arthur had survived a torture of Carl's imagining and therefore deserved respect. Carl didn't say it, but it was clear in his deference to Arthur's tales of school life. On the ride home Carl said he had some news, he was going to marry Liz the next summer and how did Arthur feel about it. Arthur had no immediate reaction. He didn't know what it meant. He didn't know enough to ask if it would change their relationship; he didn't ask why. He liked Liz, so his first reaction was positive and he left it there; he didn't consider it farther because he didn't think it involved him.

Carl was dressed as thoughtfully as ever but his clothes no longer seemed extraordinary to Arthur. They were better than most of the boys' at school, but Dan dressed as well. Carl's Chrysler convertible was new and big but so were most of the cars that arrived to pick up boys for vacation, and some had drivers and names of exotic places on their doors. Carl did not seem quite so imposing and mysterious as he had when he dropped Arthur at Bridge and said Amen.

A RICOCHET FROM CIRCUMSTANCE

They had dinner at a restaurant on the way and got home late in the evening, so it was too late to call Fred or Peter. He wanted to check in with a few friends to let them know he was around and to find out what had happened since he left. Liz was at Carl's when they arrived. She made him feel like a returning hero, asking about classes, sports, masters, his room in the dorm, and she listened with interest. He told her about the incident with the cigarettes. When he told her about the Clements and Goose Island she acted slightly offended and later he figured out that he told the story about Thanksgiving with too much reverence for Dan, Mrs. Clement, and the island, he was too impressed by them and that had offended Liz. Carl was strangely quiet throughout his descriptions.

Arthur thanked Liz for the boots. Carl asked about the boots, what boots, and Liz said it was something between Arthur and her. She was happy he remembered and gave him a conspiratorial smile which left Carl out of the story and irritated him to the point of his asking again, but Liz wouldn't relent, she was building allies before she entered a new household. She hadn't been married before and Arthur thought maybe she wasn't one hundred percent sure she wanted to live with Carl. She had known him long enough to have seen his more difficult personality characteristics at close range, some of them occasionally pointed at her, and so she wanted to make sure that she had at least a neutral party and, if possible, an ally in Arthur.

After a few stories and a winding down, Arthur went to his room and unpacked his B4 bag of mostly dirty laundry and a few of his new clothes from Brooks Brothers. Liz stayed later talking to Carl; Arthur heard their subdued conversation about the details of the wedding and social arrangements. He went to bed.

When he got up the next morning Carl had already gone to work so Arthur was alone in the house. It was the Friday before public school Christmas vacation so Peter and Fred were in school and wouldn't be available until the weekend, and Susan and Gretta were in school till the afternoon, so there was no one to see and nowhere to go until later in the day. This was the first taste Arthur got of his being different; he sensed his connection to Grape was less than he left with.

Later in the afternoon he called his mother's house and Lulu answered. Arthur got along fine with her but they weren't close. They had grown apart by his living with Carl, and school separated them by one more degree, but the major difference was she was a sixteen year old girl and she had no interest in fourteen year old brothers. They had no common ground. She was pretty, a good athlete, and popular with her friends. Her social program was complete without him and

252

would have been ruptured if she had included him in her schedule. They chatted for a minute, she asked about school, but she wasn't interested and Arthur had no way to make his experience relevant and no energy to develop a story she might listen to, so the conversation was short. He told her he was going to visit Roz that evening after dinner and Lulu said that was OK but he couldn't stay too long because she was having a slumber party and the girls were arriving at nine.

In the afternoon Arthur took a walk around the neighborhood and nothing had changed. He had a mild expectation that the trees and houses would look different, that things would have rearranged themselves while he was gone, but nothing had happened. He felt a distance he had not previously experienced. It was as if he were a visitor rather than at home. He was a stranger.

Carl came home at five and Liz came by at six. They cooked steaks on a frying pan, Carl said all the good restaurants in New York cooked steak on a hot cast iron pan, not on a grill, and he demonstrated his technique which was not catching on in Grape, as Oklahoma considered grilling a lifestyle. Carl had given up on grills after his and Mr. Stuart's earlier experience with the volcano and gasoline project. His visit to New York with Liz in the fall had given him an excuse to change his approach. Liz made baked potato and salad; they ate at the dining room table. Carl drank beer and Arthur and Liz drank water. Arthur avoided talking about Goose Island and the Clements. They talked more about school and the train ride. Arthur told them about Ransom, and Carl asked if Arthur had tipped Ransom when he got off in Cincinnati. Arthur said, "No". He didn't know he was supposed to. Liz suggested they call the railroad on Monday and get Ransom's address so they could send him a check.

Liz and Carl were going to a friend's house to play bridge after dinner, so Arthur asked them to drop him at Roz's on the way. He would get Lulu to drive him home later, and that's what they did

Arthur got to Roz's about eight. Roz was in bed with a headache so Arthur went upstairs to her room and they talked for a minute but it was obvious Roz was not interested in Arthur or his school so he went back downstairs. Lulu was there and when Arthur asked for a ride home she said he would have to wait because her guests were about to arrive for the slumber party. She was preoccupied with making arrangements and dismissed Arthur with a huff. Arthur didn't know what a slumber party was; she explained. She was going to invite her friends over to spend the night; they would stay up late, play music, and talk. She made it clear he was not invited to hang around;

he went upstairs to his old bedroom and it was unchanged from the day he left to live with Carl. He went through his bookcase and looked at some of the books his grandmother had read to him. He found his Erector set and got it out, thinking about the cranes and trucks he had built, cranes with electric motors and gears, pulleys, levers, cranks, turntables, screws and boxes of nuts and bolts. He found his chemistry set, opened it, and the familiar sulfur smell grabbed at the back of his throat. Lots of things, forgotten, which were part of his growing up and now no longer useful except as fishhooks to memories of simpler times.

He had the feeling he was floating again, disengaged, an observer connected only by the slender threads of spun recollection, an observer on the tangent of his experience no longer directly connected but still able to see flashes and glimpses of himself in a different life.

He put his toys away; it was late; he'd been going through his things for more than an hour. He went downstairs to find Lulu to see if she would give him a ride home. She wasn't in the living room but Arthur noticed some of the girls were there chatting and laughing. One of them was Martha Schummaker, the girl from the back seat of Tiny's car. The recollection took Arthur's breath away, his lips got numb. He didn't understand the numb thing and he wondered if everyone went numb from time to time. If they did that sure would explain a lot of what didn't happen and was supposed to. He wanted to talk to her but he was embarrassed so he went back upstairs and sat on the landing and watched.

The party was in the living room. The girls sat around in a circle on the floor, in chairs and on the couch; they chatted and played music, drank Coke and ate potato chips. Once in a while when a popular song came on they danced with each other laughing, giggling, and when it was over they threw themselves back into their circle taking up the conversation where they'd left it. Arthur stayed on the second floor landing and occasionally peeked down into the living room to see what was going on. Roz had gone to bed for the evening so she was well out of the picture by the time the party started. About eleven o'clock Lulu opened the front door and her boyfriend and a few other fellows from her class came in. Not "B" street fellows and not Grape's 'Who's Who' either. They came in, hung around for a while, they talked, and they danced with some of the girls, and then things got quiet as the lights went out and the girls and guys paired up and started making out. Arthur could see them on the couch and on the floor. Some of the girls didn't have boyfriends; they sat together and talked quietly.

Arthur wanted to go home and needed a ride from Lulu. He went down the stairs to the living room to ask her for a ride, but she wasn't in the group. He looked around and then asked them where she was and Martha answered him "Susan's busy; what do you want?" just loud enough for him to hear.

"I need a ride home," he said.

"Can it wait?"

"I guess so," he said. "Where is she?"

"She's in the library with Paul, you don't need to bother them."

She'd been sitting on the couch when he came to ask about Lulu, but she stood up to talk to him. She acted concerned, like she didn't want him to make trouble for Susan. Maybe she wanted to distract him "Do you want to dance?" she asked.

He remembered dancing in Greenwich and how much fun it had been, but he really didn't know how to dance. He could shuffle around but not really dance. He was thinking about what to say, he wanted to dance with her but he wasn't sure if he would embarrass himself. His hesitation was too long.

"You can dance, can't you?" she asked.

"Not really, I tried once, but that's all."

"Come on, I'll show you," she said. She took his hand and led him to a table where the record player was. She lifted a stack of 45s and reset them, then she turned to him. She had on pajamas, black and white sheep on a blue background with white clouds. The sheep were grazing crazily, some on their heads, some upside down, some right side up. The pajama top was loose over the bottom and she had socks on.

"Take off your shoes," she said with a slight giggle, "so if you step on my toes you don't break them."

Arthur leaned over and took off his shoes. She was only a little shorter than he was, the top of her head about even with his eyebrow. She took his left hand in her right and came to him; he remembered to put his right arm around her but that's all he could remember. She started to move and he tried to move too but was confused. Why do all the girls know how to dance he wondered; maybe it's always that way, the girls teach the boys how to dance.

"Relax," she said, "you're too stiff, just rock side to side with me. You can feel me move to one side, just rock to that side and then back again in time with the music."

255

He loosened a bit and rocked one side to the next.

"That's it, leave your feet on the floor, just rock, when you feel me move, just move with me."

The lights were nearly out; he saw her profile and features dimly. He remembered her scent, shampoo and flowers. He felt her warmth against him, her breast touched his chest where his right arm was around her.

They rocked back and forth for a while and he got use to it so he relaxed. She moved more, moving her feet forward and back and he felt the lead and he followed, missing sometimes when his attention strayed to the heat, to her hand in his, to his hand on her back where he could feel the muscles along her spine move before she did.

After a little while she came closer to him so that her arm was around his neck and she was leaning against him, her head on his shoulder. Her hair was in his face and it tickled but he didn't want to move it, afraid he would interrupt. He wanted to lean over her, put his lips against her neck, smell her hair, but was afraid of shocking her.

They moved together. She sang part of a song in his ear, barely audible. Then she was quiet and they moved in a tiny circle on the floor.

She got closer to him and held his hand next to her chest, her left hand on the back of his neck. She caressed his neck with her fingers. Lightly, with her fingertips, then she moved her fingers to his ear and traced the outlines and the circles inside. It was as if she had an electric sponge that left a tingling numbness in its wake. She stopped, put her hand on his neck and drew his head toward her and kissed his ear. A small kiss, he felt it and heard its slight inhale. He had stopped moving he could hardly stand, he couldn't think about his feet and his ear at the same time.

She stopped and looked up, "Are you going to kiss me?"

He didn't have a chance to answer, she pulled his head toward her and put her lips on his. He stood still and didn't know what to do. He liked it but didn't know what he was supposed to do or if he was supposed to do anything. After a moment she drew away.

"You haven't spent a lot of time kissing, have you?" she asked with a little laugh.

"No, only once," he said.

"That's good," she said. "You need to learn how to do it right; you can't teach yourself."

They held each other.

She let go of him and backed up. "Here's what I want you to do; stand there,"

He stayed where he was.

"Now, put your arms at your sides." She took his arms and put them at his sides and held them there. "OK, stand still and don't move your head. I'm going to put my lips on yours; all you have to do is relax and try to figure out what I'm thinking by reading my lips. Try to listen to me through my lips. You can only do it if your lips are soft and relaxed; if you make them stiff or pushed out or if you try too hard you can't feel mine. The point is to feel mine, read what I'm feeling by the way my lips react to yours."

She moved closer. "OK, relax." She stood in front of Arthur and let him try to relax for a moment. Then she reached with her lips and put them on Arthur's and just barely touched, just a whisper of a touch then she drew away. "Here, I'll touch your lips with my finger; all you have to do is relax so you can feel my finger. Pucker up real hard make your lips hard . OK, keep them that way." She ran a finger over his lips "Can you feel my finger? Now relax and we'll do it again." She drew her finger across his lips again and he felt the difference.

"Don't try to push me anywhere with your lips; your job is to find out where I am with your lips and that means soft and listen."

"OK," said Arthur, standing thrilled and frightened that it would stop.

She reached up, put her hands on his cheeks, held him still and put her lips on his. He relaxed, he felt her lips and the firmness of her teeth behind them, he felt the center of them and the edges, he felt her open her mouth slightly; her lips were warm and soft, wet, full, hungry; they tasted of lipstick. She pulled away for a moment then tilted her head sideways and put her lips on his again and he focused on her; he relaxed and listened to her breathe. She tasted of almonds. He smelled the crease where her nose met her cheek, it smelled soft and sweet like a baby's head. He heard her breath shorten and then her exhale.

She pulled away. "That's nice, just remember to listen and not to push. Most boys try to push you with a kiss; girls don't want to be pushed, they want to fall." She hesitated, "The next step is the tongue. Use your tongue to taste, to caress, to tease; you can't eat a meal with your tongue so don't try, don't force it; keep it soft and slow. Stand there, relax, are you relaxed? OK. I'm going to kiss you, just part your lips, a little, not a lot, just barely open your mouth."

Arthur stood with his hands at his side and opened his mouth a little, he didn't know what kind of face to make and couldn't imagine what he looked like. He closed his eyes instinctively and waited for her. His feelings were confused. At one level she was an instructor and he was following instructions but at another much deeper level he was becoming attached, the intimacy couldn't be blocked out, and it was obvious to Arthur that Martha wasn't simply going through her instructional task as a chore, she was involved in the heat and she enjoyed the play.

She put her lips on his and stayed still for a moment reading his lips then she opened her mouth and let her tongue trace his lips on the outside and then she traced the inside and then the tip of his tongue.

Arthur wanted to laugh, it tickled and seemed strange to have her tongue moving around on his, like they were sharing a live goldfish. They were standing face to face, not touching except at the lips and she moved closer so that she pressed against him at the hips.

"I could do that all night," she said as she pulled away. "This time use your tongue a little, explore with it, listen with it, see if you can tell what I'm thinking, what I want, then try to give it to me. Remember, keep it soft; a hard tongue doesn't feel very good and it can't listen to me."

Arthur leaned forward, not waiting for her to initiate. He tilted his head and closed his eyes as they met. She had her lips parted, they didn't move, then Arthur traced her lips and found different tastes as he slid his tongue over hers, then around it, exploring, as she did the same. She moved closer making contact at hips and breasts. He wanted to put his arms around her and engulf her, possess her, bury her, but he didn't, he stood and nearly drowned in her lips.

"I think you have it pretty good," she said. "Now to the next step. Every boy wants to grab a girl, wants to grab her breast or butt whatever he can get his hands on. They go about it as if they're shoplifting, snatch and run. They don't have to do that. Everyone wants to be caressed. No one wants to be grabbed. So, if you take your time and listen and look for the signs, a girl will tell you when it's time to put your hands somewhere new. If you're kissing and a girl sighs when you run your hand down her back, then move a little closer to the front and listen, and if the sigh gets louder then she's telling you something. If she pushes your hand away, then stay away till she moves it to where she wants it. If you listen, you won't miss a thing but if you push too hard then you're likely to turn her off; she's not ready.

"OK, stay where you are, hands at your sides. I'm going to run my hands up and down your chest and your back and sides, softly, as if I'm trying to find out if you've hidden a postage stamp under your shirt. I'm exploring and listening to you. You stand and tell me without words what feels good."

Arthur stood looking at her; she looked directly at him, her face was pink, and her neck and the little part of her chest he could see was flushed red as if she had been slapped. She put her hands on his shoulders, then moved them down his front, her hands flat against his chest not pushing, more like slowly skimming the surface, hard enough so she could feel him under his shirt. She paused, moved her hands to his sides, then down a little more and tickled him. It was a shock; he instinctively grabbed her hands and brought them together in front of him. She laughed a big smile, looking at his eyes. She turned her hands over so she was holding his and drew them to her chest. She put his hands on her breasts while she looked him in the eye, unblinking, she kept her hands on his. He didn't move, he couldn't feel anything but the roundness and weight of them pushed up a little where her hands pressed his.

"Nice and slow, I'm not going anywhere, see if you can get an idea of what they look like by feeling them." She moved her hands over Arthur's so he traced the outlines of her breast, felt how they fit in his hands, how they had weight of their own.

"It's hard to get a sense of what they're like through my clothes." She took his hands and put them on the top button of her pajamas. "Go ahead, undo it."

Arthur was shaking so badly he couldn't get the button undone. He fumbled around for a minute, then her fingers joined his, she was calm and sure and she had it undone in about a second. Then she moved his hands to the next one. "Try this one by yourself."

Arthur was still shaking but he got it undone and moved to the next without her guiding him. There were five of them and he could see her, she wasn't wearing a bra. When they were undone he looked up at her with his hands on the last button.

"OK, put your hands flat on my chest , high, above my breasts." She placed his hands flat on her clavicles, "Now slide them over my shoulders so my top slides off, backwards, then ease it down my arms and off. I want to be undressed, I want to be appreciated, I want you to look at me and I want you to want me."

Arthur took the shoulders of the pajama top and slid it down while she put her arms behind her and let it slip off onto the floor. She stood in front of him, her breasts pointing away from her chest hanging slightly, her areolae dark and puckered, nipples erect like raisins on pears. She kept her arms at her sides, her head cocked a little and watched him as he studied her and waited for him to react. He brought his hands up along her abdomen and cupped her breasts, felt her nipples, looked at her neck and then into her eyes. She returned his look without blinking and sighed. She brought her hands up to his head and pulled him to her, pulling his head down as she whispered, "You can kiss them, remember a soft tongue, explore them and see what they tell you."

Arthur leaned forward and kissed her neck; he moved down to her chest above her right breast and took her breast in his mouth and played with her nipple with his tongue. He heard her breathe, she arched into him and moved his mouth to her other breast. He repeated, kissing his way across her chest, lingering on her nipples holding one in his hand while he had the other in his mouth. She put her head back and sighed. Then she put her hands on the buttons of his shirt and undid them one at a time in no hurry, she reached over his shoulders and pulled his shirt back and down his arms and he let it fall one sleeve at a time. She put her arms behind his head and pulled him toward her and they kissed and he felt her breasts on his chest, he felt her hips pushing against his. This wasn't practice.

"I'm not sure how far we ought to go," she said, leaning back away from the kiss. "Do you want to keep at it or is this enough for tonight?"

"I don't want to stop," he said in a whisper, keeping his arms around her so he could feel her skin against his.

"OK, but you can't tell anyone, especially your sister. Deal?"

"Yes" he said. She was leaning away from him although he still had his arms around her.

"Let go for a minute." She backed up and covered her chest with crossed arms. "So far this has been fun, but now it gets a little more serious. Remember, girls do the choosing. Boys run around and grab and poke, but girls give the signals. They can tell a boy to stop or start, whether they're interested or not, with little signals. You have to read the signals. You'll see guys at parties running around in circles chasing girls, following them, trying too hard and at the end of the night they're not getting anywhere. Other guys will sit in a corner or on a couch, minding their business and pretty soon a girl will sit by them and start talking and they end up dancing or making out. The guy didn't have to chase the girl, all he has to do is be there and stay awake. The girl will find a way to indicate she's interested. So don't be one of those sniffers; guys who run around all night trying to find anyone who might be willing.

"Girls don't like to be with sniffers because sniffers will take anyone; they're just in it for themselves; they don't care who they're with. Girls want to be adored, caressed, devoured by someone who wants them, not by someone who wants anyone. Sniffers never read the signals and usually they can't dance and can't kiss. And beyond that no one cares cause it never goes beyond that."

"How do you mean sniffer? Who's a sniffer?" Arthur asked, he didn't quite get the picture.

"You know that guy, Steve Lenobba, he's a friend of your sister's, he's a sniffer; always cruising around looking for someone to grab or poke or impress. He tries too hard; he's too obvious."

"No, I don't know him." Arthur didn't know him and wasn't really interested.

"Here's what you have to remember. Don't chase. Relax. That's all you need to know. If something good is going to happen the girl will let you know. If nothing is going to happen, chasing won't help."

She made sense. Arthur remembered the party in Greenwich where the girl sat next to him and then asked him to dance. She said he needed practice. And tonight had been Martha's idea, not Arthur's. Martha seemed to know what she was talking about. How did she know all this stuff; someone must have taught her?

Arthur wanted to put his arms around her and feel her skin against his. It seemed like she had cooled off and wasn't in the mood anymore; she was covering herself with her arms so he couldn't see her breasts. He leaned over and tried to put his arm around her, to draw her in. She backed up.

"That's a signal," she said "When a girl crosses her arms over her chest, she's giving a signal that she doesn't want to be touched. So when you see it, just wait a while for it to go away because you're not getting anywhere till it does." She said looking at Arthur tilting her head playfully with a little scowl. "I'll let you know when you can kiss me. Or maybe I'll kiss you when it's time. Come over and sit on the floor with me."

She took his hand and led him to a place where she had put a blanket for the slumber party, there were two blankets and a pillow in a pile on the floor, almost under the piano, out of the way and out of view if someone came in the room. She sat down on the blanket and he followed, sitting in front of her. She leaned toward him and put her hand on his neck and drew him toward her, eyes shut, mouth slightly open. He followed willingly and they kissed a soft experiment to test whether the interest was still there. It was; he felt the heat rise in him.

She put her hands on his chest and pushed him over backwards; she followed, lying on top of him laughing. He lay still not knowing what to do next, if there was a next. She rolled off onto her side next to him and stroked his chest and abdomen. She drew circles on his skin with her fingernails and on one of her circles her hand slid under his pants and stopped just below his navel. She played with his hair, pulling it gently, teasing it; then she sat up and with both hands unfastened his belt and undid the button on his pants then pulled his zipper down. She tried to pull his pants down but they wouldn't come so he arched his back, lifted his butt off the floor and pushed them down around his socks and she took them from there. She took his underpants and did the same with them, sliding them down and taking them off his feet one at a time. She lay down next to him on her back, arched and slid her pajama bottoms and undies off in one push, raised her legs off the floor and kicked them off the rest of the way.

Martha pulled one of the blankets over them and rolled toward Arthur. She took his hand and guided it down her flank and across her belly to the thicket of hair below her navel.

The lights went on. Roz stood in the hall and shrieked, "Susan, who are these people?" She looked around and not seeing Susan shrieked again, "Where are you?" She wore a leopard-skin bathrobe and pink slippers and was menacing a boy and a girl who had been making out in a chair with a flyswatter, threatening them with the jabs and thrusts she had seen in a pirate movie.

Martha screamed, reached for her pajamas and panties, and pulled them on. Not a loud scream, but enough of a scream when combined with Roz's that Arthur got the signal and it wasn't good. He knew no matter how long he sat around being calm the night was over. He pulled on his pants but his shirt was in the library and so was Martha's top. He crawled under the piano through the hall and into the library where he found their shirts; he put his on without tucking it in and took Martha's to her under the piano.

Susan appeared from the sunroom and grabbed Roz by the flyswatter. "Mother, it's all right, these are my friends," she said pulling Roz toward the kitchen. Roz had come down the back stairs to the kitchen so no one had seen her and no one was listening for her pink slippers.

"Why are all the lights off?" Roz demanded in honest inquiry.

"We were watching TV and it's better if the lights are off." Susan said.

"My God, its twelve thirty, its too late for TV, you should be in bed. Who are these boys?"

"They're just friends who came over for a while. Come on, mother, it's time for you to be in bed."

When Susan tried to steer Roz into the dining room, Roz protested and Whitey-Joe got a signal which he interpreted to mean "bite Susan", which he did with the vengeance of a deranged midget. He got her by the cuff of the pajamas and shook her pant leg as if he had a rat. She tried to kick him off and guide Roz at the same time but it appeared that neither Roz nor Whitey-Joe was finished with the theatrical elements of the scene.

Roz stood her ground. "Tell these people to go home; this isn't a bordello," she said in public speaking delivery, happy at having an audience which was shocked to attention and embarrassed into silence, not willing to let them get away before she finished her melodrama.

"Who are you?" she approached the girl in the chair, threatening with the flyswatter.

The intended victim jumped from the chair and ran across the room in her PJ's. The fellow she had been sitting with followed as soon as she was off his lap. Their clothes were in disarray, mostly on and not entirely buttoned up.

"Call the police, we have been invaded by hooligans!" Roz shouted to the stunned audience, some of whom were looking for shirts and pants, socks and shoes. The boys took off in a flight of five, together they bolted for the door, and leaving the girls to Roz, they saved themselves. Arthur went to Susan's aid and took Roz by the arm guiding her to the dining room, headed for the kitchen and the back stairs to the second floor. That was the plan, and Susan was happy to see him as he could handle Roz while Susan herself beat off Whitey-Joe. Susan stood on the foot Whitey-Joe was attached to, balanced herself, leaning on the dining room table, and with the other foot wound up and delivered a terrible kick to Whitey's head. If she'd had her shoes on, it would have killed him. As it was, she knocked a few of his teeth out and he left whining at Roz's side as she departed the scene in Arthur's care, waving at her devoted fans while demanding to know who all the people were.

When Arthur came back to the living room after tucking Roz in for the night, most of the people were gone. Arthur looked for Martha but she wasn't there. He asked Susan and all she knew was that Martha had gone home with one of the other girls. Susan and the two remaining guests gave Arthur a ride to Carl's.

25

LAYING ON OF HANDS

Arthur went home. The house was dark and Carl had already gone to bed; there were remnants of dinner in the refrigerator and an empty wine bottle in the trash. Arthur grazed for a while, not hungry, not interested in bed. He was recreating the time with Martha in pieces, flashes of recollection not tied together in series or in context, flashes of a smile, the way she cocked her head and looked out from under her brow as if asking a question, her fingers on shirt buttons. There was nothing to do but let the reverie intrude on his wandering. The change seemed impossible. To have been with her thirty minutes ago and to be alone now, as if nothing had happened, was the difference between the deck of a crowded swimming pool and the pool's interior on a hot afternoon. The chatter of voices around the pool, children's shouts, the sun hot on the pavement, bare feet on wet cement, the smell of chlorine, all the details crystal clear, outlined in high-noon relief and then under the water in a second. Cool, quiet, disconnected, sights, water blurry, blue halos, half bodies attached to the floor, bodies cut in half at the interface, no arms, no heads, just legs and belly. He felt like he had dived into the pool and could no longer see the sun or its warmth, he couldn't remember accurately the scene on the pool deck although he had just been there; he was out of air and there was no way to the surface.

He went to bed and lay awake with an ache in his gut. He was confused, he was thirsty for her, for something, but he wasn't sure what it was, hungry for her, but what about her, what did he want: to be with her, to continue their lesson, he didn't know what he wanted, all he could do was feel the want pulling at him at the back of his throat, at his chest, at his gut as if he'd been caught on fishhooks.

He tossed and turned and between moves he tried to recreate her face, but he couldn't. He would remember it when he saw it again but he had no clear picture. He tried to remember what she looked like with her shirt off and again he had no clear outline, only vague forms. Her scent and taste, the feel of her fingers on his abdomen were abstractions, the truth was far away, not lost but out of reach. He wished he had a picture, some of her perfume, her taste in a bottle. He rolled and tossed and turned and the fishhooks would not let go.

He got up early and ran into Carl in the kitchen.

"What happened to you last night?" asked Carl while putting some things in the sink.

"I stayed at Mom's later than I thought, Susan gave me a ride home."

"What time did you get in?"

"About one."

"What was going on over there that kept you so late?"

"Susan had a party and I stayed up talking to some of her friends."

"Did you have a good time?"

"Yeah, until mom broke things up with a flyswatter."

"Pretty late; it was time to come home anyway," he said. "Do you want to come with me this morning? I'm going to the hospital for rounds, then to the office for a while. We'll be home about noon."

Arthur didn't have a plan so he said he'd go with Carl to the hospital. Carl made coffee while Arthur poured himself a glass of milk; they both had toast and ate it standing over the kitchen table. They didn't say much, and when they finished they went to the garage, got in the car and drove through town. Nothing had changed. The same cracks were in the pavement, the same telephone poles, the drugstore on the corner of Main and D still had the same signs hanging in the window advertising Pet milk. Arthur assumed everything would change in his absence. It seemed to him he'd been gone half a lifetime, but Grape hadn't noticed his absence.

Carl was in his emerald green Chrysler convertible, down in the seat so only his head showed out the side window. Arthur could see over the dash but not by much; the car was huge, a tub with a moving roof. The upholstery smelled like it had been rained on. The windshield was split in the middle with a center post that the top hitched to when it was up.

"You've changed," said Carl, not looking at Arthur, watching the road.

"How?" asked Arthur, thinking he'd changed but not knowing whether Carl would see the things that Arthur thought were different.

"First, you're bigger, not just taller, you're more defined. Second, you're more confident, you don't act like you're trying to hide all the time."

"Did I used to hide?" asked Arthur.

"No, you didn't hide but you were shy and not very inquisitive. You let things go by without paying attention to them, you're more engaged now."

"How can you tell?"

"Just by the way you talk, the way you meet people, like Liz last night. You're more confident. Are you getting along all right at school?"

"Yeah, I told you about the cigarette problem. That could have been the end. Other than that everything is fine."

"Your friends the Clements sure know how to spend money; you should have seen the bill from Brooks Brothers. Do you like your clothes?"

"They're OK. Some of the boys at school made fun of the stuff I took with me. I still have it and wear it mixed with the new stuff. They don't bother me anymore."

"Are you learning anything?"

"Yeah, stuff I wouldn't learn here, French and Latin. I guess math is the same everywhere. The difference is most of the boys at school take the studying part seriously. You can't hide in class because there are only eight or ten boys in the room and the masters know everybody pretty well."

"That's what I mean about your changing. Before you went, you wouldn't have answered the question, you'd have mumbled a three-word answer and then avoided the subject. Now you're giving it full sentences and thoughtful analysis. Big change. I'm glad to see it and don't think it would have happened here. Do you like the school?"

"Yes. It sure is different from Grape. I think I like it because I'm part of it. I didn't like it at first because I wasn't part of it, I was an outsider; now I feel like I'm part of the school."

They pulled into the physicians' parking lot near the emergency room, got out of the car and went in. Carl's friend Jim Scott was there with a cup of coffee. The nurses all said "Hi", and Carl introduced Arthur to everyone. There weren't any patients so everyone was standing around chatting.

While they were chatting Arthur asked, "Hey dad, do you remember that guy we saw at the train station when we sent my trunk to school, the guy with the sores on his hands and face? What happened to him?"

"Yes, I remember him, Jedd Buehl. Jim and I saw him the morning after you sent your trunk. Jim took a look at him and made a diagnosis. He has a degeneration of the soft tissues; it's the result of some chemistry we don't understand very well. The sores you saw are the result of the disease, but their cause is in the immune system or allergic reaction; it's not quite clear how it gets started. He came in and we saw him and told him what he had and offered to call his wife, but he said he'd rather she didn't know; that it would upset the family and if there wasn't anything we could do for him then there wasn't any point in getting everybody upset early. We gave him medicine to make him more comfortable and directions on how to treat the sores, but there isn't much we can do for his liver and kidneys; that's where the serious problems are."

"Is he still around?" asked Arthur.

"Yes. Jim sees him once in a while. He can't work anymore, but he's at home."

"Should we go see him?"

"We could. We could take him some medicine." Carl went to Jim to get the address and information on the medicines.

After talking to Dr. Scott, Carl left the emergency room and went to the different wards of the hospital to see patients. Arthur stayed in emergency and the nurses offered juice or tea. He said no thanks, he couldn't slip out from under the memory of Martha and he wasn't hungry; he still had a fishhook in his gut.

Carl finished on the wards and met Arthur in the hall outside emergency. They went to the car and then to a drugstore where Carl bought some medicine, then back in the car and headed for the Buehls'. Their house was in a part of town Arthur hadn't seen before, between the railroad tracks and the river, and the houses looked like they were built on stilts. They had stairs leading to a front door and another set of stairs at the other end. The Buehl's house was an elevated, one-floor rectangle which had been painted white once but was mostly brown wood. Carl stopped the car on a mud path leading to the house; there were broken bicycles, lawn mower parts, a sagging swing set with no seats and a used up car in the yard. Carl went up the steps and knocked. Arthur stayed down a few steps from Carl and couldn't hear exactly what was said. Someone came to the door and opened it a little. Carl spoke then someone else came to the door and in a while the door was opened and Carl was let in. Arthur followed and no one paid any attention to him.

The front room was as wide as the house; it was the living room and had a sofa and some chairs and baby toys scattered around the floor. It was dark; the shades were drawn so it was hard to make out detail. The house smelled stale, closed in, acrid. A chimney stuck through the roof in the back; it oozed yellow-gray smoke

Carl followed a woman whom Arthur couldn't see very well into what looked like a dining room, but there was a bed in it. It was darker than the front room and Arthur didn't follow because there were too many people, too much confusion, the household had been upset by the intrusion and Arthur didn't want to be a part of the upset. Arthur stood by the doorway and listened.

Carl went to the bed and put out his hand, not to shake Jedd's but as a peace offering. He put his hand on Jedd's shoulder, "How are you doing Jedd?" he asked so quietly that Arthur could barely hear.

Jedd mumbled something.

"Can I take a look?" Carl asked. He leaned over, pulled the covers back, took the hem of Jedd's pajama top in both hands and raised it nearly to Jedd's chin, exposing his belly. Then he probed Jedd's abdomen with the bunched fingers of his right hand, pushing them up under Jedd's rib cage, then moving down to where Jed's liver would have been and then to his pancreas. He was gentle but firm at the same time, looking thoughtfully at his fingers and not at Jedd who was also watching Carl's hands. "I brought some medicine that might help with the pain. I'll tell Jim I saw you today and he'll be over sometime soon to check on you. Is there anything I can get for you?" Carl asked in a near whisper, acting as if he and Jedd were the only people in the room.

Jedd said something Arthur couldn't understand.

"All right then, get some sleep." Carl pulled Jedd's top back to where it had been, replaced the covers, rose to full height, and backed away.

The woman came out of the room followed by Carl. Arthur backed to the door. Carl gave the woman the bag of medicine and instructions on how to take care of Jedd. As Arthur watched the exchange, he saw Frankie Buehl in the back room looking at him. Neither said anything, Arthur didn't know what to say and Frankie would not have said anything in any case, so they looked at each other across the dark room where Frankie's father lay dying.

Arthur went out the door and down the step. Carl followed. They got in the car and backed out of the yard and onto the dirt street.

"He looks really sick," Arthur said.

"He is. It's a wonder he's still alive." Carl pulled over to the side of the street. "Do you want to drive?"

"Yeah." Arthur said.

Carl got out and went around to the passenger side while Arthur scooted over to the driver's seat. Carl had never done this with Arthur so it was a shock. When they were settled and Arthur had pulled the seat up, he eased the car into the street.

"Is he going to die?" asked Arthur while his eyes were glued straight ahead, his hands throttling the steering wheel, feet barely on the peddles.

"Yes. I think it will be soon," Carl said from a distance; he was thinking of something else, his attention was not in the car.

Arthur oversteered them home, weaving slightly trying to keep the left side of the car in his lane while keeping the right side from hitting parked cars. Even though he was driving the car, which was about the most exciting thing he got to do, Arthur could not dislodge the fishhooks, he couldn't go for more than a moment or two without the thought of Martha grabbing at his gut, yanking his attention away from whatever the diversion was. Carl seemed lost in thought; Arthur wondered for a moment if he was thinking about Mr. Buehl.

26

RIPPLES

Carl and Arthur arrived at the house at the same time Liz did. She had a black Cadillac conGrettaible with red leather upholstery, automatic transmission, a tan top and electric windows; it was a great car and seemed to go with her red lipstick. They all went into the house together. When they got inside Arthur went to his room out of habit and without a goal. He felt disengaged, lost, confused by the past twenty-four hours' emotional collisions. He couldn't get Martha off his mind; he should have exhausted his recollection of her but the yearning was still there. He had nothing specific left to recall, the memory of last night was nearly worn out with overexposure; it was a general ache of loss and missed opportunity. If he saw her, he had nothing to say, nothing in particular to do, but still he wanted to see her.

The visit with Mr. Buehl had been upsetting too. He was the only person Arthur had seen who was dying. Arthur felt these things he had seen over the past twenty-four hours should make sense; they should organize themselves in his memory and be logical and comfortable. Instead they were a jumble, disorderly, uncomfortable, temporarily resting as unfinished sketches, unfinished assignments that would eventually have to be completed at another time. He wanted to make sense of his feelings, to reconcile what he felt when he saw Mr. Buehl in his bed and Frankie in the darkness and not speaking to him. It was as if he was a witness to great things but had no idea what he was supposed to do about them or about how he should feel after seeing them. It was as if circumstance had put great holes and slices in the fabric of his tent and unwelcome breezes entered without invitation, without his having to open a door or window. The breezes were troubling and he had no idea how to sew up the holes or close the flaps against the wind.

271

His door was open and he heard Liz come up the stairs and cross the hall.

She leaned in his door. "Arthur, are you upset about something?"

"Sort of," he said without thinking about it.

She came in. "Have I done something?" she asked.

"No, it's not you; it's some of the things going on today."

"I thought I might have annoyed you by being here so much; do you think I'm here too much?"

"No, it's fine."

"Some people have said that I caused your father's and mother's divorce. Has anyone told you that?" she asked quietly.

Arthur sat on his bed. "No, no one said it to me."

"I hope you don't mind my being here. You know your father and I will be married while you're at school and then I'll be moving in here with you. Have you thought about that?"

"I haven't really thought about it. Dad said something on the way home from Oklahoma City, that you were getting married."

"Did your mother say anything about it last night?" she asked.

"No. We didn't talk about it."

"She has told some stories which aren't very nice and I suppose I can't blame her, but if something bothers you I hope you'll ask me about them if I'm involved."

"OK. It's not you. We went to see Mr. Buehl today; do you know who he is?"

"Yes, I think so. Your father told me just now."

"It makes me feel sad, I feel like I should do something, but I don't know what."

"I know what you mean, there are a lot of things that can make you sad, but I don't think you can do anything for Mr. Buehl."

"He seems so helpless, as if all the fight is gone, somehow it's leaked out of him and he's waiting to die, and I was standing there next to him thinking I should do something and I didn't know what. It seems unfair, sort of sad, like a stone slipping from the riverbank under the water without any sound or splash, just slipping out of sight and gone without any ripples or signal that things have changed, and in the next moment everything is the same on the riverbank, but it's not for Mr. Buehl or his family. We'll be the same tomorrow but he won't and Frankie won't."

"Yes, I know what you mean." She came closer to the bed. "Things seem to move ahead, out of our control and against what we hoped for or think is fair. There are some things you can influence

272

and some you watch that are out of your reach, but they still have an effect on you. I'm sorry it makes you sad."

"Did you ever wonder why things work out like they do? It seems like we follow a path and Mr. Webster, the headmaster, says each step along the path is a choice and everything that follows will be the result of the choices we make. It seems like some of the biggest things that happen to us are the result of tiny choices we made before. There's luck and choices." Arthur was thinking out loud, happy to have Liz around. Maybe she knew the answer.

"I think everyone wonders about that. Some people believe in fate or preordination, but I think a lot of what happens to us is the result of the little decisions we make. That's why it's important to do the right thing in the big and the little choices."

"I wonder where the dividing line is?" Arthur said. "I mean, a lot of what happens to you depends on where you're born, like Frankie Buehl, he's different because he was born in a different family. But then he has choices that will change his life as much as my choices will change mine. I don't understand it. How is it supposed to work?" Arthur asked more to himself than to Liz not expecting she knew the answer.

"Supposed to is a difficult question. Supposed to assumes there is a fixed set of rules with a score and the plan all set out. The plan isn't all set out; its moving all the time. That's why the supposed to probably relates more to the values we use when we make choices than it does to end points or results. I think the best we can do is make good decisions based on values and then the results will come and we live with them."

Liz continued, not as a lecture but in the same mode thinking out loud like Arthur. "Frankie Buehl is different because he was born into a different family, each of us is different in that way. Those differences are important in some ways and they are unimportant in others. While Frankie is different because of family and place and time, what is important is character, what Frankie does with his starting point, where he takes it from there. Where he was born will not define who he is; it is only his starting point."

"I guess that's what Mr. Webster talks about in assembly," Arthur said. "He talks about values and uses the Ten Commandments as a guide. He says they represent a set of values most people have in common, that most people would agree to. Some people are better at practicing them than others."

Liz thought about it for a minute then responded. "I would agree with that. The Greeks talked about virtue and I think that practicing values is virtue. It seems most people have the same values or feelings about killing and stealing and taking care of your parents."

"I can see that," Arthur said. "But I don't understand where fairness comes into it. I feel guilty about Frankie Buehl, it doesn't seem fair that he lives in that house and his father is dying. I feel like I should do something about it, but I don't know what to do."

"I don't think you can do anything for Frankie. Fair is a difficult thing; I think there should be at least two words for fair. Fair according to fate and fair according to deed. Where you are born is fate and isn't fair or unfair. It might look unfair by comparison, but it's not the same thing as treating someone unfairly. You can't do anything about fate, you have no control over where Frankie is born, you do have control over how you and to some degree others treat Frankie. It comes back to values and practicing them or virtue." Liz was thinking it through for herself while trying to answer Arthur's question.

"There was a guy on the train, the conductor I didn't tip, who said about the same thing. He said you have to do the right thing, knowing the right thing is the easy part of it, doing it seems to be my problem."

Liz agreed that it is in the doing where most people fail; she got up and went out of Arthur's room, across the hall and down the stairs.

THREE MEN IN A TUB

Christmas had lost its appeal several years earlier when Carl moved out. Roz wasn't capable of managing the detritus of failed relationships. Arthur celebrated it with Carl for two years but neither was able to bringing a smile to the occasion, so it became a tourist event where they visited friends and family and tried to sneak under the blankets of other people's celebration. They were successful some of the time and strangers at other events, traveling misfits; they were relieved when it was over.

This year Liz directed the Christmas schedule and focused on Carl's house. She bought decorations and got Arthur to help her put them up; she got a tree and found boxes of lights and ornaments. She stapled Carl's Christmas cards to wide red ribbons and hung them on either side of the arch between the living and dining rooms. Arthur strung lights on the front porch and he easily was caught up in Liz's spirit, which was her plan. Carl took on a new attitude, leaving some of his cynicism behind and smiling at the brightness Liz brought to the house. Before Liz was involved, Arthur and Carl moved through the house room by room turning lights on and off as they entered and departed so the house looked like a partially used office plaza. When Liz was around she turned on as many lights as she could and left them burning day and night whether she was in the room or not and the house looked alive by itself. The house was warm with her attentions and it had a positive effect on Carl and Arthur.

Arthur, Liz, and Carl spent Christmas morning at Carl's house making breakfast and opening presents. Liz was more than generous with Arthur. She bought him a lamb shearling fleece coat from Abercrombie and Fitch. Arthur hadn't seen anything like it before and was surprised. Around noon Susan and Gretta came for a short visit which was tense and formal and they left as soon as they could. In the afternoon Carl and Arthur went to visit Liz's family who all appeared normal and were nice to Arthur; they had small presents for him and inquired politely about his school. He didn't feel he was a stranger and again it was because of Liz's planning that they had a good time.

After Christmas Arthur spent time with Fred and Bill, his friends from public school days, but he had lost track of the thread they were following, no longer taking any joy in smoking cigars behind the garage. He didn't enjoy the aimless wandering around town simply to waste time. He no longer found watching wrestling on TV entertaining. He had grown apart, finding the conversation about girls and cars boring.

He hadn't grown tired of thinking about Martha. On the day after Christmas he called Lulu to find news about Martha. She had none. She said she hadn't seen Martha since the night of the party. Arthur asked for her phone number and Susan wanted to know why Arthur wanted it, so he told her that he had spent some time with Martha at the party and he wanted to see her again. Susan laughed and said Martha wouldn't want to spend time with a pip-squeak like Arthur, but she gave him the number anyway.

Arthur called Martha. He was nervous and it took nearly an hour of sitting by the telephone contemplating what he would say before he finally dialed the number. Martha's mother answered and Arthur asked to speak to her but her mother told Arthur Martha had gone to Georgia to visit cousins for the rest of vacation. He asked if her mother would tell her he called; she took his name and said she would. When he hung up he felt empty, abandoned as if someone had tied a brick to his umbilical chord and it was trying to pull his insides out onto the floor. He had no idea how to feel; he had no expectation; he was driven by blind passion. She did not belong to him; he hardly knew her and yet he felt connected to her in the strangest way, dependent on her, drowning without the promise of seeing her again. And he had no idea what he would do if he saw her again. He was snagged on an abandoned fishing line, fighting against an unmanned pole, unable to dislodge the tug at his gut.

He was tired of vacation, bored with his friends and anxious to return to Bridge. He thought if he could get back to school, then the nagging intrusion of wanting Martha might leave. He wanted a diversion and there was none in Grape.

New Year's Eve was amusing but disjointed; Arthur felt as if he were on the outside looking at events from a distance. His friend Peter, whom Arthur had known for two years and who was considerably older than Arthur, stopped by on New Year's Eve afternoon. Peter was seventeen and while not good friends they occasionally palled around together at odd times, slack times for Peter since he was older and had his driver's license. Arthur usually enjoyed his time with Peter since Peter always seemed to have a plan; he was constantly on the edge of a conspiracy, contemplating a revolt, designing an escape from Grape. He was mysterious; he disappeared from time to time to visit friends or family in New Orleans, Philadelphia or Oregon. When Peter was in town, he worked on a plan to be somewhere else, a plan which could not be shared because of its secrecy. He was elliptical; he told stories of adventure that soared with exotic detail and eventually returned to Grape because Peter was anchored in Grape. It was difficult to tell what parts of Peter's stories were true and what were fabrications; he maintained that each of them was absolutely true and if you didn't believe them then you were an enemy of Peter's World, in addition to being an idiot. Peter's purpose in life was to be the king of Peter's world. It was a relatively easy job for Peter but it put strains on his family, his friends, and his school which he attended sporadically, claiming he got a better education at the public library. He claimed to visit the library frequently but there was no record of his having checked out a book and no one there knew him. "Not that public library, the other one," was his answer. No one but Peter knew which other one. The way he saw it, when you were in his company you were in Peter's World and that meant he was King. It was a simple universe if you followed the constantly changing rules. While being with Peter was exciting for Arthur, Arthur couldn't understand what Peter got out of it.

Peter was nuanced before it was fashionable; he was a master of circular logic, ending where he began with flourish and better for the trip, he was the master of perpetual energy and a confusion to the laws of physics which maintained that something could not be created from nothing. Peter created controversy from vacuum. He sought peoples' weaknesses and played with them to the point of violent reaction at which point he was "surprised and troubled" at his victim's hostility.

As a rule, parents were not happy to see Peter at their door.

When Peter stopped by that afternoon he was driving his older brother's cream yellow Mercury V8 convertible. The car was an excitement to most everyone who saw it and an entertainment to anyone who had a chance to ride in it. Arthur rode in it once when Peter had stopped to visit over the summer and had taken Arthur to Peter's aunt's house. His aunt was not remarkable, but the ride to and from was. Peter believed stoplights were suggestions, voluntary conventions which one might obey in unhurried times but they were not for him in his busy world, and as a result he went through them, red, green or yellow, with equal disregard. When he was occasionally stopped behind someone who appeared to have too much time on his hands or for some reason honored the red light, Peter used the sidewalk to circumnavigate the blockage, weaving around pedestrians, light poles and parking meters on his way through the intersection.

Peter believed that government at every level was invented by legions of bureaucrats for the sole purpose of interfering in his freedom. He believed that government was a conspiracy of idiots who had nothing to do but create problems and encourage crime; corruption being government's major enterprise, consuming in its appetites Peter's taxes. His argument was only marginally discredited when he was reminded that he paid no taxes.

"Hey Arthur, where have you been, off to prep school, did they prep you or perp you?" asked Peter on greeting at Arthur's front door.

"Hi Peter, come in."

Peter came in and asked about school and what had gone on and whether Arthur liked it. Arthur gave generalized answers, never quite sure with Peter if the information would come back later to bite him in parody, so Arthur stayed general and Peter didn't mind since his questions were form rather than substance. After some chat, Peter asked Arthur to come to his house for a party that evening after dinner about seven. Arthur accepted and Peter left in a roar, not bothering to back out of the driveway but turning around in the front yard leaving great divots and black tire tracks carved into the sod in his wake, thumping over the curb when he entered the street from the sidewalk.

That evening Carl gave Arthur a ride to Peter's and dropped him off on his way out for the evening. Arthur would call if he needed a ride home. As Arthur approached the house he noticed there were only two lights on. Maybe he was early. He rang the bell and waited.

After a long wait in which Arthur supposed he might have the wrong day or house or hour or had misunderstood the invitation altogether, Peter opened the door.

"Hey, man, come on in." he said, partially stepping out the door after Arthur entered, twisting right and left as if looking outside for secret police or gate crashers hidden in the shrubbery. "Come on in, not every one is here yet but they will be soon."

Peter led Arthur into the library where he had a fire in the fireplace but no lights on.

278

"You want a drink?" he asked from the doorway, looking behind himself, down the hall for someone or something that wasn't there. "I got oldfashioneds ready to go, or beer; what do you want?"

He wore dungarees, a turtleneck sweater, and a blue navy watch cap pulled down so low his eyebrows were hidden; he had to look out from under the crease where it was rolled up on his forehead. He hadn't shaved in a few days so he had the beginnings of a beard. He was about five feet ten inches tall with black hair and black eyes and very light skin. The girls in town thought he was handsome and exciting, a rebel without a clue, a pool player without a cue; their parents thought he was something less.

"Do you have a Coke?" asked Arthur, he didn't know what an old-fashioned was.

"No Coke, that'll kill ya, you don't know what they put in that, you don't need that stuff, it's a false need created by adGrettaising and the government, you know they want you to drink that stuff. No Coke," Peter said standing in the doorway looking toward the front door

"Nothing, thanks."

"I'll be back in a minute. If someone rings the bell, don't do anything, just stay in here."

Peter left and went somewhere through doors and down stairs. He reappeared fifteen minutes later with a glass of brown liquid, two ice cubes, and a cherry bouncing around on the cubes.

"Some people were going to come over tonight but they couldn't so it's going to be you and me and Fred. My brother was going to lend me his car but then he changed his mind when the cops followed me home this afternoon. They said I ran a red light but they didn't give me a ticket because Jack talked them out if it. Fred should be here in a minute." Peter sat and waited so Arthur sat and watched the fire.

"I invited some girls from school to come over tonight but they said their boyfriends wouldn't let them come. What is this about boyfriends, all the good looking chicks go steady or something. I told them their boyfriends are pukes, pipsqueaks, so they told the boyfriends who then threatened me after school. Punks. I'm not worried about them. Can you believe those guys? They're going to borrow dad's car, pick up their girlfriends and cruise through Frish's all night. That's where all the chicks are going to be, cruising Frish's with their boy friends."

"What's Frish's?" Arthur asked, not knowing what Peter was talking about.

279

"It's down on Route Four," Peter said in animated disdain. "It's a drive-in restaurant. Guys drive in the parking lot, cruise around the building, go back out on the street on the other side of the building, then they go through the parking lot again in a circle, sometimes it blocks traffic; it goes on for hours. People in cars driving through a parking lot looking at each other, it's a circle jerk, really dumb."

The doorbell rang. Peter got up peered around the corner to make sure it wasn't the National Guard, then slipped to the front door and opened it. Fred came in.

"Hey man, come on in." Peter shut the door and they came to the library where Peter offered an old-fashioned and Fred declined.

They sat around talking and Peter explained to Fred about the lack of guests and how the girls at school had turned down his invitation and how the guys had threatened him and how the girls would be cruising Frish's. Fred appeared to know about Frish's, although he had never been, it was one of the things he looked forward to when he got his license, so he didn't share Peter's disdain for it or the boys who drove there as it was something he aspired to. He kept his aspirations to himself and let Peter continue his campaign.

"Hey, here's the plan," Peter said. "I don't have wheels tonight, but I know where we can get some. Old man Petry, the guy who has the exterminating business, lives behind us on Fairfield Road. He has a beat up termite truck he doesn't use anymore parked in back of his barn. It doesn't look real good but it runs. How about we borrow the truck and go to Frish's on our own, check the place out, see if some chicks are there?"

"You mean drive around Frish's in a termite truck?" asked Fred.

"Yeah, we'll just go down there and check the place out."

"You think the chicks are going to want to jump in a termite truck?"

"Naw, we'll just show them how stupid it is, going to a parking lot to cruise around."

"OK," said Fred, only half interested and thinking it wouldn't happen anyway.

"Arthur, you in?" asked Peter looking seriously at Arthur.

"I guess so," Arthur said not giving it any thought.

"OK. We gotta go over to Petry's house real quiet since he's home. I'll drive it through the back yard over here with the lights off and then we'll fix it up for the trip."

Arthur asked Peter. "Are you allowed to use the truck?"

"Yeah.. Yeah all the time, he let's me borrow it; he leaves the keys in it so I can use it when I want but I don't want to wake him up to ask about tonight so we'll just borrow it without waking him up. It's fine, all the time, I'm his best friend; I take care of his garden and look after his sheep and do all kinds of stuff for him." Peter got up and went to the front door, waiting for Arthur and Fred to follow.

Mr. Petry had no sheep.

"You guys should a' dressed different; you don't need a tie for a termite truck."

"I didn't know we were going to borrow a pickup truck tonight," Fred responded not sure how much he liked the plan. "Usually I dress different for rides in Petry's termite truck." Fred was usually skeptical and slow to jump on runaway trains. He did mostly what his mother told him and she had good sense, so while he didn't have a lot of imagination regarding termite trucks he usually got on the right side of things.

"Come on, man, we gotta go," Peter said to his crew.

Peter led the way through the backyard and into Petry's field, then behind his barn, crouching all the way, stopping and listening for police or wayward gangs of marauders. It was so dark they couldn't see their feet so there was some stumbling and complaining as they negotiated a fence and a pile of boards. They got to the barn and Peter went to the truck. It was closed but not locked. He slid a door back and climbed in the driver side.

He whispered pretty loud, "Get in the other side, but don't close the door. Just leave it open till we're at my place."

Fred and Arthur got in the passenger's side; it was more like a van than a truck with its sliding doors. There was only one seat beside the driver's, and it was loosely mounted to a wobbly pedestal so it was easy to fall off of when you forgot to pay attention. Fred took the wobbly seat while Arthur got in the back. Arthur couldn't see right off, but he felt around in the junk on the corrugated metal floor making a lot of noise as he groped; he pushed some stuff aside and made an empty spot where he sat on the floor. After three tries Peter started the truck; he revved it up and made enough noise to wake the neighborhood but once he had it started he didn't hesitate; he was on a mission. He didn't turn on the lights because he didn't want to wake up Mr. Petry. He put the truck in gear and headed for where he guessed the gate was, but he didn't have a real good idea. After some time on false starts and noising up against the bushes and hedges and fences, he found the pass-through and they got to Peter's back yard and then into his garage. When they were inside the garage he turned on the lights and left the truck running while he got out and went to a work bench where he looked around for some tools.

Fred got out with Peter and followed him to the bench. "What are you looking for?" he asked.

"We need a drill and a funnel. I set them out here this morning but they're not here; somebody must have stolen them." He was rummaging around through piles of junk. He went to a cabinet and came back with a hammer and a drill.

Arthur got out and looked at the side of the truck where there was a faded black and yellow sign depicting a huge termite hovering over and about to devour a primitive rendering of the globe. Petry's name and phone number, posted under the apocalyptic artwork.

"I'm going to put a hole in the muffler and one in the truck bed right above it." He got on the garage floor and wiggled under the truck with the hammer and a file; he banged around for a minute and then came out and climbed in the back of the truck and started hammering again. He was hammering on the blunt end of a round file, pushing the sharp tip through the floor of the truck right above where he put the hole in the muffler. He made a hole in about four whacks with the hammer.

Arthur thought most people used a file to scrape things, but Peter had a more primitive approach, using the file like most people would use a nail.

Peter came out of the truck and headed for the workbench. "My brother showed me how to do this."

"Do what?" asked Fred who followed the activity with passing interest.

"Make a fire bomb," said Peter, as if it were an everyday activity for him.

Fred wasn't sure he'd heard Peter right. "What kind of bomb?"

"You put a hole in the muffler and then you put hole in the truck bed right above the hole in the muffler. When you got the holes lined up, you run a tube from the inside of the truck down into the muffler. When the tube's fixed in the muffler you fix a can of gas to the top end of the tube, the one that's sticking up in the back of the truck. Then, while you're driving, someone pours gas in the can and it runs down the tube and into the muffler and it explodes out the back in a big spout of flame, like a flamethrower." Peter continued rummaging on the bench. He came back to the truck with a can with a copper tube coming out the bottom. He got in the truck and fed the end of the tube down through the hole he had made, then got under the truck where there was more banging. Arthur tried to see what was going on but couldn't make out the particulars.

Fred was curious, testing his exit point. "Why do you want a flame thrower?"

"Those guys at school, the ones cruising Frish's tonight, we're going to give them a little New Year's excitement. Hey, Arthur, would you hold this can while I put a wire on the exhaust pipe? The wire will hold the tube in place."

Arthur got in the truck and held the can. It was an empty, rectangular, metal, paint thinner can about a gallon big with the top cut out and copper tube sticking out the bottom. Peter got back under the truck and banged around again, then he came out.

"OK we're ready," he said. "Get in."

"Is this going to be dangerous?" asked Fred.

"No, nothing to it, just a little flame out the back of the truck then we'll be gone and they'll all think they've been hit by the termite extermination," he laughed.

Fred got in and then Peter jumped out, ran to a corner of the garage and got a can of gasoline that was there for the lawn mower. He put it in back with Arthur, climbed in the driver's seat, and they backed out of the garage and into the street.

Peter wasn't a very good driver; he didn't stay on his side of the road much and seemed to lose his concentration, looking out the side windows for extended periods, correcting the truck only when absolutely necessary. When he swerved hard, making one of his infrequent corrections, gas spilled out from where the missing cap should have been on the gas can. It made a puddle on the floor and saturated the air with the powerful stink of gasoline. Arthur tried to keep it from spilling but Peter's jerky driving overcame Arthur's efforts.

Peter turned all the way around in his seat to brief them on the plan. "We'll be there in about ten minutes. When we're there I'm going to pull in the driveway and then when I tell you, pour some gas from the lawn mover can into the can with the copper tube." He turned back just in time to save the truck from going off the road, clipping a mailbox. He wasn't concerned.

"How much gas do I put in it?" asked Arthur.

"Probably ought to use all of it; we'll only go through once so we want to give it a good hosing," Peter replied.

Frish's was on a four-lane highway, and as they got closer the traffic got heavier. It was on the other side of the road, so they were going to have to turn left across traffic to get into the parking lot.

Peter got in the left lane ready for the left turn; there were about ten cars lined up in front of the truck waiting to pull in. The parking lot was jammed with cars, some were parked and some were cruising at five miles an hour revving up their motors and honking. Kids were hanging out the windows of the moving cars or standing beside the parked cars; everyone was looking at each other and talking or calling out to friends. Occasionally the line would stop and then start again after boys or girls jumped out of one car and into another.

Peter inched forward as cars in front of him made the left turn. As Peter got within three cars he noticed a cop standing in the middle of the road directing traffic.

"Oh man, see that?" asked Peter.

"Yeah, I see him," answered Fred. "Are we in trouble?"

"No. We're just like everybody else; we're cruising Frish's. They can't do anything to us," asserted Peter.

"It doesn't look like we're everybody else," said Fred "We're the only ones in a termite truck."

"Nothing to worry about, they won't notice us, we'll just sneak right through."

Peter pulled up and was next in line, right in front of the cop who looked at the truck with a curious expression as if it was strange for two boys to drive a termite truck through a restaurant parking lot at nine in the evening. Peter didn't pay any attention him. They got the go ahead from the cop and turned into the parking lot and in line behind a blue Buick sedan. They inched forward, following close behind the Buick and they were followed by a red Ford with four people, two couples, one in front and one in back. When they were about a third of the way around the loop and stopped for a delay while people switched cars, a boy who was standing next to his car near where the truck was stopped pointed at the truck and yelled something to a friend. Then he pointed at the truck and yelled at Peter.

"Hey, nitwit, how's the termite business?" He laughed with friends.

"Hey, termite." came from someone else.

The red car behind the truck honked and the driver yelled something.

Peter yelled back, "Hey, shove it."

"You got bugs, nitwit?" more laughter.

Peter revved up the truck but the result was a low complaint from a wheezing four-cylinder engine. Everyone laughed louder, the line wasn't moving. They sat in the truck while people honked and laughed. Arthur was kneeling in the back looking out the window close to Fred's seat, holding the can and waiting for instructions.

The guy driving the red Ford yelled out the window. "What you got in there some roaches running your engine?" More laughter, "Nice date, bozo." He seemed to be working himself into a comedy routine. "You wanna drag?"

"I'll drag your ass outa there in a minute," Peter yelled out the window.

"Think you're big enough nitwit?"

Peter leaned out his window looking back at the red Ford. "Just hang real close there and I'll show you how hot this truck is."

"A hot termite truck, ha, ha, ha."

"Goddamnit," said Peter, stalled in traffic. "We'll wait till we're almost ready to leave the lot. If we do it now we'll be boxed in and can't make a getaway."

"I don't know if this is such a good idea," Arthur said, not knowing where it was going to end but the beginning didn't seem too good.

"OK then, let Fred do it. Fred, get back there; all you gotta do is pour the gas in the paint can till it leaks out the copper tube" Peter instructed.

Fred jumped in the back and took the contraption from Arthur. By the time they were half way around the loop they had become the night's entertainment with people shouting and pointing. As they got near the exit with only one car in front of them and the red Ford following close on the bumper of the truck, Peter stopped.

"You ready back there?" Peter turned to look back. "OK, give it to 'em."

Fred held the gas can and poured the contents into the contraption with the copper pipe coming out the bottom, holding it in his left hand as he poured with his right. He got about a pint of gas in and nothing happened so he emptied the can which was about half full. The level went down so the gas was getting to the muffler but nothing was happening outside. Like all great and untested experiments, the first trial did not go according to plan. And like all untested theories when it got rolling it continued with some speed to achieve some unanticipated consequences.

When Peter hit the gas a great fireball erupted behind the truck. It must have been ten feet in diameter and burned for a minute, climbing into the air with a roar and a woosh. When the fireball ascended Arthur saw the hood of the red Ford was on fire, nearly consumed in the blast, it was no longer red but black with smoke coming from underneath. The four people inside the car jumped out just before the windshield popped and the dashboard fell off. Arthur couldn't see anything but fire out the back windows of the truck so he leaned out and saw the front tires of the Ford had also caught and burned sooty orange with black smoke. The boy who had been making the remarks, the driver of the Ford, ran in circles around the car yelling, but they couldn't hear him over the screams of the people who had gathered to watch.

The cop directing traffic stood in the middle of the road watching in amazement.

Peter pulled out of the drive into traffic and shouted back to Fred, "Ok that's enough."

Fred had quit pouring a few moments earlier but fire continued so the only thing visible out the back was orange, yellow, and red flame.

Fred turned around to look back, "Hey, I think the truck's on fire."

"No, it's not; that's just a little left over; it'll burn out in a minute." Peter sped up trying to outrace the flames that chased them down the road; in a minute they got a little smaller.

Cars pulled off the road in front of them and behind them as Peter bounced his way toward his house trailing a jet exhaust. The fire eventually went down and out, and as they crossed through town they saw fire engines coming the other way. Peter weaved through neighborhoods, around a cemetery, pulled into his driveway and finally into his garage. Arthur was ready to jump out, but Peter insisted they sit for a minute with the lights off to see if they had been followed. They sat for a while listening, then they got out and checked the back of the truck. It was singed, the paint was peeled off, and rusty gray metal showed in patches.

Peter whispered, marveling at the damage to the rear of the truck, "We better get this thing back to Petry before they come looking for it, you think they know who it was?"

Fred looked at Peter. "How many Petry termite trucks do you think there are spread all over Grape?" he asked.

"I mean, do you think they know who was driving the truck?" asked Peter.

"Well, between the cop and the guys in the Ford I guess they have a pretty good description of a guy in a blue watch cap driving a termite truck," Fred replied. "I don't think they know exactly or they'd be here about now."

"We better put this thing back, before they notice it's gone," said Peter again.

Arthur said he would wait there. Fred and Peter got back in, and Peter started it, backed it out, then followed the path to Petry's barn. They returned in about ten minutes, sneaking through the bushes when the cop car with flashers going arrived at Petry's front door. The three of them lay in the bushes at the back of Peter's garage watching the scene. Two policemen went to the door and waited for Mr. Petry to answer, and when he came they stood around on the front porch talking for a while. They decided something, the boys couldn't hear the words but they saw the goings on clearly as the cop and Mr. Petry came around the back of the barn, flashlights bobbing, and looked at the truck. They talked some more and between the talk the policeman swung the flashlight, scanning the surrounding bushes, but he didn't see the boys huddled under a juniper. Petry and the cop hung around by the truck for a while then they wandered back to the house, the policeman swinging the light looking at the tire tracks leading to Peter's back yard. After a few more minutes of silence the police car pulled out of Petry's. The boys watched from their redoubt, waiting for the police car to come around the corner and onto Peter's street but it didn't come, so after a while they relaxed.

"We better get out of here," Fred said in a whisper to Arthur.

Arthur agreed; he didn't want to be discovered lying in the weeds behind a stolen, burned up, termite truck. They thanked Peter for the great party.

28

BLINDED BY THE LIGHT

A river ran north-south through the middle of Grape and divided the town in half leaving an east side and a west side connected by three bridges. If Arthur wanted to get form the east side of town to the west where he lived, he normally walked across the pedestrian bridge in the middle of town. Sometimes, if he was feeling adventurous, he'd take the short cut across the railroad bridge. It was about three-quarters of a mile long, half of it over the river and the other half about eighty feet above the streets that ran parallel to the river. That night, after they left Peter's house, they had to cross the river to get home, and if they took the railroad bridge it would cut a mile off the trip.

Arthur had crossed the railroad bridge many times in the daylight and so had Fred, but he had only crossed it once at night. And that had an exception when he had been with Tiny and some boys who lived on the streets below. They were used to crossing at night because they played there frequently and knew the schedule. Arthur was with them one night when they crossed. He thought he had to go with them to be part of the gang, but he was frightened the whole time.

While they were walking home, Arthur told Fred about the night he had crossed with Tiny and the B Street gang. He'd done it to be one of the guys but he told Fred it was easy. Fred didn't believe him so Arthur offered to show him it could be done. After some talk and feeling courageous after the jet termite truck, they talked each other into trying it. Both of them knew the danger was in getting caught on the trestle or bridge while a train was coming, because the only way out was to jump before the train ran over you. There were no railings or pedestrian path. If you jumped and hit the river you'd be hurt, maybe drown, but if you jumped and hit the street you'd be dead.

A RICOCHET FROM CIRCUMSTANCE

They altered their route and headed for the train tracks that would take them to the shortcut across the bridge. When they got to the east end of the embankment it was so dark they could only see a little in front of their feet and the ties between the tracks were so dark they stumbled until they got the rhythm of it. The steel structure ahead was black with the soot of a thousand trains. Their plan was to walk into the black tube outlined by shiny rails, black ties and steel structure. They weren't in any danger as long as they were on the embankment and there was dirt between the ties; they could slide down the sides of the embankment if a train came. The danger would come once they were on the steel bridge with bare ties, no sides to slide down, and no handholds or walkway. A train was wider than the rails and stuck out on either side of the ties. If a train came they would have to jump off the bridge or get run over, their escape was death on the street or drowning in river below.

When they got to the bridge, they stopped and thought about whether they should proceed, neither of them wanting to be the one to say they should give up and go to the pedestrian bridge a mile away. So they went ahead, feeling their way from tie to tie, scuffing their shoes on the gaps between when they miscalculated.

Arthur wondered whether the trains ran at night, he didn't think so, but he wasn't sure. He couldn't recall hearing one. They were about halfway across and Arthur heard dogs barking across the river and train whistles off in the distance on the other side of town where the main rail line was. The bridge they were on was an out of the way route used by a few towns to the northwest, so it wasn't very busy. With each whistle or honk of a car horn Arthur looked over his shoulder to see if anything was coming his way, and nothing was. A little over what he guessed to be halfway, he heard another whistle that seemed closer than the others, and he looked over his shoulder at a single, bright light, bobbing up and down on the end of a string, right in the middle of the black tube created by the tracks and the framework of the bridge. It was a train, and the light was bobbing because the train was moving right along. He looked at Fred, who was looking at the light too, and when he looked back at the light it had gotten bigger. Both Arthur and Fred screamed "TRAIN." at the same time.

The light grew into a giant lantern bobbing and swaying like it was on a string. The two rails were silver stripes in the glare and pointed exactly at the middle of the light. There was nowhere to go. Arthur couldn't tell how far away it was because the light was so bright it blinded him. So, they turned from it to run away but they couldn't see and they stumbled on the uneven ties with the spaces between them wider than their shoes. They ran and stumbled and fell and turned to see the light coming and then they heard the engine growling and huffing. Arthur knew it was gaining on them because the light not only got brighter but it also got higher as if it were growing and going to pounce on them from above.

It kept coming. The roar got louder, the drive wheels screeched on the tracks and the beast's great breaths came like chants, whoosh, whoosh, whoosh, a giant tornado. They ran and ran and were getting nowhere, stumbling and Arthur started to cry so hard he couldn't see but continued flailing away. He knew he would have to face the great thing chasing them or dive from the bridge. He had no idea if they were over the street or the river as he looked back one more time and it was upon them. He had to look up at the light it was so close. Arthur was ready to give up, to lie down and cry till it pulverized him but they kept scrambling and jumping and screaming although no one could have heard them as the noise of the engine was deafening.

And there it was, all of a sudden, the bridge was behind them; they were on ground. They ran off the side of the embankment and fell down only ten feet from the tracks. The train continued but at a slower pace than they thought; it was barely crawling, and as it drew next to them a man, standing on the cattle guard with a flashlight, shone it on them and laughed, "You stupid fucking kids."

They didn't talk the rest of the way home, and when they got to Arthur's, Fred called his mother and asked if he could spend the night. They stayed up most of the night waiting for the police to arrive, waiting for the excitement to die down, waiting and retelling the story of the train and the termite truck. While they waited they told stories about school and Fred's stories seemed as distant to Arthur as Arthur's must have seemed to Fred. It was clear Arthur had lost touch with his friends in Grape. Both Arthur and Fred admitted they would be more inclined to believe Peter's stories in the future after the termite truck experience.

The next morning Fred and Arthur went to the kitchen to make breakfast. Carl had already gone to the hospital. The morning paper was on the breakfast table in the kitchen, and on the front page was a picture of a car on fire in the Frish's parking lot with lots of kids and a cop standing around. The caption read: 'Jet-powered Termite Truck Explodes in Frish's Parking Lot. Catches Ford on Fire. No One Hurt in Blast.'

Peter phoned. "Hey, guess what. Old man Petry called this morning; he told my ma he wanted to talk to me. When she told me who it was, I thought it was over, but he only said he had found something of mine, and I should come over and pick it up. So I went over to his house and he had the gas can out of the truck. He said he found it and it must have been stolen from my garage. He didn't say anything about the burnt up paint, tire tracks or the police coming last night. Nice guy, huh?"

"That's lucky. Did your parents say anything?" Arthur asked

"No, they don't know what happened."

"Did you see the paper this morning?"

"No, was it in the paper?"

"Yeah, you better take a look," Arthur said.

"OK. I'll call you back."

Peter called back about an hour later. "Hey man, I think my dad knows. He was out in the yard looking at tire tracks. He came in and talked to my ma and they decided I ought to visit my cousins in Oregon for a while. They don't know about you; they think it was an accident with the muffler."

"I guess we're OK then," said Arthur.

"Guess so, I'm going to Oregon for a while."

"Have a good trip."

"OK Comrade, see you next time. We'll use a bigger truck." Peter hung up.

29

TAKE ME TO THE RIVER

It was time to go back to school. Arthur was amused by Grape but no longer involved. His experiences with Martha, the termite truck, and the train were fun but not satisfying. Carl and Liz were involved with plans for a wedding and her moving into Carl's house, and Arthur was a vestigial appendage whose mass mattered little whether regarded from Bridge or Grape.

Carl drove him to the station in Oklahoma City; they talked some on the way, but Carl didn't have a feel for the school or what was happening to Arthur. Carl was consumed by his world, assuming everyone shared his view. Arthur's relationship with Roz and his sisters was in tatters because of the underlying uncertainty, the confusion of roles and expectations, embarrassment and guilt. It was time to go; he had grown away and was anxious to return to a place he understood.

He got the train in Oklahoma City and rode to Grand Central Station without losing his way or engaging criminally confused Trotskyites in bedroom survey. He looked for Ransom, but he wasn't on the train. On the second morning of the trip the train rode a track that ran along the Hudson River; the sun reflected off new snow and the outlines of the city rose on the horizon. The train from Grand Central to Bridge was subdued; the older boys knew what they faced: not enough daylight, not enough heat, and not enough freedom. The new boys didn't understand what was ahead: the monotony of the cold, uncivilized isolation, darkness or its prospect most of the day. Arthur sat by himself: the fishhooks were nearly gone. When they arrived at school a bus picked them up at the station and dropped them in the central courtyard. Arthur lugged his bag up the hill to his dormitory. His close friends were already there, unpacked, lying on their bunks or sitting at the picnic tables in the middle of the room waiting for evening assembly. Arthur was the last to arrive.

"How was your Christmas?" asked Dan.

"Great, how was yours?" Arthur responded while he unpacked.

"Sheila asked about you on New Year's Eve. She hoped you were coming back because she had some things to teach you," Dan said smiling.

"How's your mom?" asked Arthur

"She's fine; she says 'hello' and wishes you a happy New Year."

"Thanks," said Arthur.

"Hey, Arthur you're back," said Scratch. "Mike and Duncan's beds are gone; I guess they're not going to make it."

Arthur hadn't thought about them since leaving and didn't care one way or the other. It was strange to see their beds gone and to know he would probably never see them again. He unpacked and waited sitting on his bed chatting with Scratch. He wondered whether he should tell Scratch about Martha and decided not to. It would take too much explaining and it didn't seem like the kind of thing he ought to talk about; it was private between Arthur and Martha and he didn't think she would want him to talk about it.

The bell rang and they headed for the schoolroom. Arthur, Scratch and Dan walked together, then split up when they got to their seats. There was no real business to conduct; the meeting was a method of synchronizing watches, getting everyone back into the routine and into the rhythm of the school, which was quite a bit different from whatever the boys were coming from, whether Grape or Greenwich. They went to chapel, then to dinner and an abbreviated study hall as if they hadn't left in December. Arthur was comfortable in his bed that night; he knew exactly where he was supposed to be, what he was supposed to do, and what would happen tomorrow.

The next morning at assembly the prefects recited the litany of what was wrong: why dust rolls hid under beds, how much soot collected in waste cans, which beds were unmade, where the dirty sinks loitered. Arthur wondered how long this tradition had continued, how many generations of boys had sat listening to the lament of the dirty sponge, the tango of the brooms, the fandango of the forgotten fork, taking it all seriously, in a cocoon perched on the side of a hill, snug in the snow, an assembly of high mindedness about order and its enemy, dirt. It was the perfect medium for looking out the window and escaping by imagination, transference, daydreams, palm trees, a fertile earth, a warm bed. If nothing in their world was more serious than the roll call of the dust ball, then all was well.

"I would like to pick up where we left our discussion before you took vacation." Mr. Webster interrupted Arthur's conjugation of the absurd. "You will recall, I'm sure, that we were talking about breaking the rules. I suggested then that we break the rules primarily to appear to be who we are not. I haven't changed my mind in your absence.

"You could make the argument that theft endows the thief with something he would not have without breaking the rules, rather than its giving him an appearance he would not have. And I could respond that most of having something through theft is an attempt to change appearance. As an example, let us take Mr. Cruso, not the tenor. Ownership meant little to Robinson Cruso while he was alone on his island. It was only after finding his neighbor that ownership entered the picture. In other words, when there was no audience, appearance meant nothing. It is only with audience that appearance becomes important.

"Now let us take another view. Stealing food to stay alive or to feed your family is not considered a crime in most societies; stealing a diamond ring to appear wealthy is considered a crime. I am not suggesting that the act of stealing makes one appear wealthy, it makes one appear as a thief. It is having the diamond which confers the appearance of wealth.

"If you follow me so far, I am sure you have thought of exceptions, and I grant there are exceptions but for the purposes of our discussion I submit that we break the rules to change an appearance. We do not break rules to change our character, we do not lie, steal, cheat, covet to develop character. No. It is our character which determines whether we do these things. Our character is determined before that act; the act is the result of character.

"It is in the doing that we find the wrong or the right. This relates to Christ's admonition that we do unto others as we would have them do unto us. And this speaks to character. Doing. Doing good, doing evil, doing nothing, doing the right thing. What we do, combined with our intent is who we are. Appearance is not who we are.

"If you steal a diamond you may appear to be rich; but, you are a thief."

"So here endeth the lesson. Think about this and we'll continue to cogitate on these things which test us day and night."

295

With the ending of the lesson the Bridge School completed its metamorphosis from an empty place to sealed cocoon. They were in orbit, thousands of miles, light years from Grape and Greenwich. Arthur and his friends went to class and to lunch and back to class and after class they went to the field house to get outfitted by Pa for the hockey season.

Arthur had never been on skates. Some of the boys had skated and some had played hockey. Arthur hadn't thought about it, but Dan knew what was coming and had brought a complete uniform from home. He had custom made skates whose leather was reported to be ostrich and whose blades came from a Canadian foundry that made nothing but blades for hockey skates for the pros and Dan and his brother Tom. He had loose pants with thigh pads, shin pads, shoulder pads and a helmet; all of it bought in New York at a store that provided extravagant things to boys who knew, boys from Greenwich and Darien and Westport and Bronxville and Long Island and Boston. Grape had no such store.

Arthur hadn't considered a replay of his football outfitting, and if he had, he wouldn't have come to the field house that afternoon, but he hadn't, so he was there and Pa was pushing used equipment at him. Pants too big, shin pads too small, helmet without definition, a thick rag with strings attached which would confound cold fingers in their trying but which would be no protection from a puck flying at sixty miles an hour; an experience Arthur had and Dan did not. And there was a box of skates the wrong size, two sizes too big, which Pa assured Arthur were "perfectly good". Arthur knew about perfectly good. When Roz had given him anything and preceded the gift with an announcement that it was "perfectly good" he knew she meant perfectly horrible, like spoiled milk or soggy sandwiches or burnt toast. Arthur had a lot of experience with "perfectly good" and didn't want to expand on it.

"You ain't in the pros," Pa said.

The school had a lake at the east end of the property, down the hill about half a mile from the main campus. The lake was half a mile long and a quarter of a mile wide with one of the long sides tucked up against the north side of the hill so it was protected from the winter sun. When the lake froze in the winter the school built two hockey rinks and a general skating area on the south side, twenty feet from the shore under the shadow of the hill and over the deepest part of the lake. The rinks were made out of sections of three-and-a-half-foot high by twelve-foot long wood frames covered in heavy chicken wire that kept the pucks and players from flying out. The frame sections were linked end to end by eyehooks and steel rods that went through the eyes where one section matched up with the next.

When it snowed, the boys took shovels to the rinks and cleared them and pushed the snow away from the sides, making room for spectators. As the winter progressed, the ice got thicker and cracked under the strain of expansion. If the rinks weren't freed from the surrounding ice, then the cracks ran across the surface of the rinks splintering them and ruining them for hockey, so about once a week the rinks were sawed away from the surrounding ice pack with an ice saw.

Arthur hadn't seen an ice saw until he appeared at the rinks for his first hockey lesson. The thing looked like a giant lawnmower tipped on its side. The blade was forty-eight inches in diameter, a steel disk with teeth and completely exposed, whirling Grettaically. It could be raised or lowered and pushed forward into the ice by the operator who stood behind the engine holding two handles attached to the frame. When disengaged, it was simply a huge revolving disk with several hundred, shiny, two inch long teeth chasing each other around a four foot diameter dervish. It was capable of sawing a person in half in a second or quarters in two seconds, your choice. It had a throaty growl when idling and a menacing roar when engaged in its duty. It was dangerous, intimidating, out of control and awe inspiring. Boys spent hours watching it chew through the ice, imagining what it would do to them if it got away from its handler. It could as easily have been employed as a torture apparatus.

The theory behind the ice saw was that the operator, who had better have had his life insurance paid up, would carve a circle around the rinks creating an island within the surrounding ice. The whole island, rinks included, once detached from the rest of the ice on the pond, would then float above its surroundings and be immune from the cracking and splintering. The theory was good, and the practice, as usual, had not enjoyed the full benefit of theory's company. Even with sawing, the rinks cracked and buckled. Whether it worked or not, Arthur thought it was thrilling to watch the ice saw, growling and throwing a fantail of ice chips in its wake, drag its petrified operator around the rinks while chewing great white rents in the shiny black surface.

The ice saw was at work terrorizing its operator and demolishing the surface when they arrived for their first lesson. They had walked to the rinks; Arthur stayed with Scratch because he felt he would see more of him than he would of Dan, who would be on one of the advanced teams. They wore boots over several layers of socks and coats over their uniforms. They had hockey sticks but no helmets because they were encouraged not to hit each other over the head. If they fell into an iron goal post or head first into the rink boards, then Pa would address that problem with Band Aids, after the fact. He carried a few in his pocket to accommodate any annoyance.

Scratch and Arthur sat at the edge of the pond on a log and took off their shoes and tried on their new skates. Arthur didn't know how Scratch's fit but Arthur's felt too big, wobbly, and he couldn't tighten them. When he attempted to stand on them they collapsed beneath him, folding up like a cheap tent, bending his ankles into serious orthopedic problems. He sat down immediately from the pain and lack of balance. He tried tightening but that was no use; the laces were as thin as piano wire but no stronger than spaghetti al dente, and broke, so he was left holding the tag ends of ruined carpet thread while his skates remained undone. He asked some of the other fellows and Hasty had an extra pair his mother had tucked in his jacket pocket, not for Arthur, but Hasty gave them willingly.

Arthur replaced the laces and they tightened a little better. He tried to stand again but his feet were loose on the floors of the skates so they buckled and fell sideways, mangling his feet and ankles. He got on the ice, propped himself up on the hockey stick and hobbled on the sides of the skates to the practice rink where Pa regarded his approach.

"What's the problem there, Arturo, never skated before?" he asked.

"No, I haven't skated but I think the skates are too loose," said Arthur irritated that it was his fault the skates were too big.

"Go over there in my bag," Pa pointed to an army duffle bag on the snow bank. "Get yourself a couple pair a socks then tighten em up real good. You'll grow into em."

Arthur continued his hobble to the bag where he found two pairs of socks that were big enough to fit over the skates. He put them on and it was some better but not much. He joined the rest of the neophytes gathered around one goal and leaned on his stick. One of the new masters was there demonstrating his facility, going back and forth and in small circles, crossing his skates one over the other as he drove forward then pivoted to skate backward, all the while fiddling with a coat-sleeve button, making sure every one knew he was born on or near skates. Arthur didn't care much for his facility since his feet hurt and he couldn't keep them directly on top of the blades. The skates collapsed on their sides encouraging the bones of his ankles to smash against the ice.

Mr. Devens, doing S curves, pointed to Arthur. "You, Arthur, can't you stand up? What's the problem?" he asked scraping circle patterns in the ice, going backwards in a slightly hunched posture, trailing his stick as if he weren't on skates but Fred Astaire on a dance floor with a broom. He didn't bother to wait for a response. "OK guys, those of you who haven't skated before hang around here with me; those who have can go on over to Mr. Rocart."

Arthur stayed put, not able to move. Some boys left for Mr. Rocart's squad; about fifteen boys remained with Mr. Devens, the young master who continued his excellent display. He was bored, and this was beneath him. He should be coaching the second team, he was sure. He stopped his display abruptly in an ice-spraying chatter of biting blades which left him standing in a slight crouch over his stick with his blades perpendicular to each other and his total disinterest evident, as if the skates did it all by themselves.

"Here's the deal; first we're going to work on basic skating, no sticks for the first couple of days, so put your sticks over in a pile outside the boards."

Arthur walked over on the inside of his ankles, dropped his stick in a pile and walked back. The other boys skated or hopped or pushed but made a better show than Arthur.

"Arthur can't you stand up on the skates?" asked Mr. Devens.

"No sir. The skates are too loose."

"Yes, you can; just try. Go on, get up on one ankle, foot over the blade, then the other and push off a little."

Arthur tried but couldn't hold one skate steady enough to get on the other. After some fumbling he fell over.

"That's enough. Why don't you take a seat over on the bench and we'll work on it later." Mr. Devens went back to addressing the group. He told them to skate in a circle and as they went by he made suggestions. Arthur took a seat and waited. Anger grew from somewhere, rising as he sat rejected. It was cold, he wanted to leave, he sat for an hour. When practice was over; Arthur got up to leave with the rest of the boys and Mr. Devens came to the bench.

"Arthur, you give up to easily; you can do this if you try." He left, skating to the edge of the lake to retrieve his shoes.

The rest of the boys had already gotten to the log where their boots were piled and were putting them on. Arthur didn't want to join the group; he didn't want to talk about skates or Mr. Devens; he didn't want to talk. He sat on the bench on the rim of the island where the rinks floated above the rest of the ice and sulked. Why did every endeavor start as a humiliation? Each new thing didn't start new; it started stale, on pretense, till the details were right, then it started for real. It was like a lawn mower in the spring, it didn't start right away, it took some fiddling and cleaning and filling and "farting around", then it would cough and spit and smoke and jerk your arm off till it finally got going. Same here at Bridge, everything he tried got a false start.

Dan came to hockey with the right equipment, the right clothes, and he knew the rules, he knew what to expect. Arthur showed up at the last minute, in the dark, surprised he had to have skates to play hockey. He showed up without having prepared: to class, to jobs, to dinner, to chapel, to assembly; he was constantly surprised by the procedure which everyone else took in stride. He didn't have the right clothes or equipment; he didn't have the right ideas or the right training, so he started at the bottom of every low point in the school. He thought he was over that. He thought this semester would be different; he had learned the jobs and chapel and was doing OK in class; he had learned football and tattoos and smoking.

But he had only learned to look backwards, a step in the right direction from not looking at all, an improvement over his condition in September, but it wasn't enough. He had to look ahead, anticipate, figure out what would happen next. He had to figure the expectations before he joined or jumped in the water. Did he think someone would put great skates on his feet, did he think he'd be 'First Team' on his first day skating, what were his expectations? He didn't have any; he floated down the river and hadn't really changed much. He learned by looking backward, at mistakes; he survived by trying to stay in the middle of the pack, trying to avoid exposure at the edges, but instead of staying in the middle he found himself at the back trying to catch up. And here he was again, at the back of the pack, pathetic, unprepared. He fought with himself in confusion with no end but frustration.

He took his skates off and his feet were nearly frozen because he'd laced them too tight and then he had sat for an hour without moving. He walked to his boots in the socks Pa had lent him, took them off and hid them under the log. He put on his boots and walked back to the dorm late for showers and late for jobs.

On his way back to Bridge from Grape he had looked forward to school; he had built his expectation on a fantasy that things had changed, that he had changed. He hated where he was.

30

IT'S A LONG WAY DOWN

At the next morning's assembly Arthur sat without guilt; his penalty for smoking was paid in installments by his good behavior, his homework was complete, his job done. The prefects perfected nitpicking, all dust rolls were in their place, bureaucracy's long arm reached into the cocoon. Arthur left the drowsy monotony to drift behind his dreams; fishhooks rose from reverie, awakened, splinters were more fun.

"What is in us that drives us from the path we have committed to follow?" Mr. Webster's voice penetrated the fog. "Why do we choose to do things we know are wrong? How do we make those choices?

"As I said at the beginning of the year, we are here to help you prepare for the choices you will make. The academic scene helps you understand what has come before you. History is a recounting of other peoples' dilemma, and from it you may see examples of good and bad choices and those may someday serve as guides in your travail. Language helps clear the fog of misunderstanding. Mathematics gives us a view into the infinite beauty of God's creation, and science gives us hope that the impossible will some day be possible. Athletics let us see how good we can be; it let's us taste the fruits of hard work and fair play. The honor system gives us experience in commitment and sacrifice to community, and Chapel is our door to redemption. Each of these, in its way, contributes to your experience, tests you, provides a reflection upon which you can see the result of your labor. Each of these is positive and assumes a bright future. And each prepares us to 'Do unto others as we would have them do unto us'.

"Are they sufficient? That is where you come in. We, the school community, are here to help you prepare for choices." He paused.

"You are here to prepare.

"Are they sufficient? I don't know. I know they are necessary, and I know they are the best we have to offer. But I do not know their sufficiency. Maybe you will come back to tell us."

He launched himself and walked down the central aisle, head down, purposeful strides, reflective insulation.

The impatient cacophony which resided in the desks and under the benches found its voice; boys called to one another, desks slammed, feet scraped, noise erupted on the prefects departure.

Arthur sat at his desk for a minute and thought about Mr. Webster. Did he really believe what he said? He sounded like he did; he sounded earnest; he looked convincing. The only thing that didn't look right was his saddle shoes, brown shoes with black patches across the arch, from side to side, where the laces were. The soles were an inch thick and stuck out around the edges. Otherwise he looked the part. He wore a gray and blue tweed jacket made from double-ought steel wool, a blue work shirt with flyaway collars, one pointing at the ceiling struggling from under his tie. The tie was hand woven from stray bits of wool that had got away from the welders and riveters when they built his jacket. Charcoal gray flannel pants that had been washed and hung out to dry; they were clean and round, blown out at the knees without the confusion of creases and cuffs. He looked earnest.

Arthur wondered what this was about. Why did Mr. Webster have his morning sermonette? Did people really pay attention; did it change anything? While he didn't understand all of it, what he got was perplexing. He liked Ransom's approach: do the right thing. That was plenty; he hadn't got the doing part perfect yet, but the right thing seemed pretty clear. He dismissed it and went to class.

Mr. Smith came in the room in a cloud of chalk dust, trailing his broken shoelace. He slammed his books on the table and gave the class a beaming smile behind bent glasses; the left corner pointed at the ceiling as Mr. Webster's collars seemed to. Maybe there was a message here, a secret signal; wear something that pointed at the ceiling. Arthur got stuck on the idea of the glasses and Mr. Webster's collar both pointing to the ceiling and laughed to himself.

Mr. Smith was mostly cheerful, except when he was concerned about losing something, and that was a lot of the time. He seemed OK in class, but when Arthur saw him on campus, he appeared to be scurrying around as if looking for something forgotten or lost. He gave the impression of being overcome by a perpetual flurry of misplaced details.

This morning he was smiling, and Arthur was ready for gerunds which he and Scratch had studied the night before. He started his review of previous work when Hasty raised his hand.

"Yes, Hasty, what is it?" Mr. Smith asked.

"Sir, someone lost his pencil," said Hasty earnestly.

"What pencil?"

"Why, right here sir." Hasty held up a stub. It had been a pencil, but it was only a stub now, no longer than the last knuckle on your little finger. Its point was broken off into the wood, and the eraser had worn down into the little metal tube at the top. If you used it, it wouldn't do anything but tear up your paper after leaving a grimy streak you couldn't get off.

Mr. Smith went to Hasty's desk and took the pencil stub which Hasty offered as intriguing evidence. He took it from Hasty and examined it closely for some minutes as if expecting it to reveal its owner. He turned it over and around in his fingers mesmerized by its imagined history: where had it come from, had it been used on exams, to write the Magna Carta, could the owner be looking for it now, how long had it been in the corner… He was lost in the possibilities.

He looked up. "Is anyone missing a pencil?" he asked.

No one answered.

"Does anyone know someone who is missing a pencil?" he asked, looking from face to face, pleading for an owner.

"Yes sir, I think I know who might be missing a pencil or I can find a home for it." Hasty said. Hasty got up and went to the front of the room and Mr. Smith gave the stub back to him.

"Thank you, Hasty." Mr. Smith said.

Mr. Smith continued his review and then proceeded to homework. Class plodded along until the bell rang. The boys got up and left to go to Latin. While they walked down the hall Hasty said. "Wasn't that funny?"

"No." Dan spat at Hasty; he was red with rage. "It wasn't funny; it was mean and a waste of time."

"Come on, Dan, relax. It was a joke," Hasty said in defense. "You thought it was funny, didn't you, Arthur?"

"No. I didn't." said Arthur. "It was mean. Mr. Smith's always been nice to us; he's a little different but what's the point?"

It came out without thinking. Arthur meant it; it was the right thing to do. He didn't feel intimidated by the scene and he wasn't concerned with what Hasty might think of him; it just seemed like the best thing, the right thing to say.

Hasty turned and looked at the other boys in the group searching for support. No one said anything and they continued to class.

On the way to lunch Dan approached Arthur. "That thing Hasty did this morning was out of bounds."

"Yeah, I like Mr. Smith, he's a nice guy," Arthur responded.

"Hasty's not good for the class; he's never serious, it's always a joke but the joke is always on someone else."

"He's not so bad," said Arthur. "He tries to be funny." Arthur changed the subject. "What team are you on?"

"Second."

"That's great. I don't get the skating thing. My skates are too big and I can't stand up. Mr. Devens thinks I'm not trying hard enough. But I think it's the skates; my feet wobble around in them."

"Don't worry about Devens. He was head prefect here about six years ago and thinks he knows how to run the school. He probably heard you got probation for smoking and thinks you should have been thrown out. My brother thinks he's wound a little tight. He didn't do very well in college, thought he should have been prefect there too, but there weren't any prefects in college and no one was impressed with him. He topped out as Tom says, so he came back here where he's safe."

"Let's take a look at the skates after lunch."

They got together in the field house after lunch and Arthur showed Dan his skates. He put them on and Dan felt around the tops and the shoe part.

"Yeah. They're way too big for you, and they aren't any good anyway. The leather's all soft and the blades are bad. Give em back to Pa; maybe he can have them for lunch," Dan said looking at the skates. "I know Hasty has a pair that might fit and they're pretty good skates. He's not allowed to play hockey this term because his shoulder's bad; if he falls on it he'll damage it or something like that. Why don't you see if you can use his?"

After class, Arthur asked Hasty if he could use his skates and Hasty was reluctant because he thought he might use them later in the year but said Arthur could try them on. Arthur tried and they fit. Dan came to the bench where Arthur and Hasty were changing and checked and said they'd be fine. Hasty hesitated, wanting recognition for a good turn after the morning's showdown over Mr. Smith. Dan eased up and said Arthur would give them back whenever Hasty needed them. Hasty gave in, and Arthur, Dan, and Scratch headed for the hockey practice.

A light snow fell as they walked down the road to the lake with their skates tied together by the laces and slung over their shoulders. When they got to the log they split up; Dan went with the better skaters and Scratch to an intramural squad.

Arthur sat on the log and put Hasty's skates on. They felt fine. He tightened them and tried to stand. It didn't solve all his problems but it helped; he could stand but the wobble was still there. He half walked, half skated to his squad's meeting place. Mr. Devens was there doing his demonstration which was supposed to impress everyone, especially the non-skaters. Arthur was impressed, but not in a positive way. He thought Mr. Devens was a little old to be hot-dogging on skates in front of fifteen-year-olds, and he wasn't happy about the way Mr. Devens had treated him at their first practice.

"OK, gents," Mr. Devens started. "Gather round and hear a tale of woe. Arthur here thinks he can't skate because his skates are too big. Poor Arthur."

Arthur stood balanced on skates, leaning on the rink boards to stay upright. "I borrowed a different pair and I think they're better now," he said.

"All right, everybody, skate in circle over there and we'll do some drills."

Arthur got in the conga line of boys waddling around in a circle, some partially skating, some mostly walking on their skates. Mr. Devens had everybody stop and he gave a demonstration of pushing off on one foot while gliding on the other. He had them line up and try; then he demonstrated again and watched. Arthur tried but wasn't getting the glide part right. Mr. Devens picked him out of the group and had him stay off to the side while he worked with the other boys. Arthur didn't understand why he couldn't fumble around with the group, but he stood where he was told. Eventually Mr. Devens came to him and gave a personal lesson and watched Arthur scratch and waddle. They got back in a line and tried again and Arthur started to get the idea, pushing with the side of the blade while pointing with the other skate. He tried to balance over the gliding blade. Mr. Devens had him stand to the side again.

When they finished, Mr. Devens asked Arthur to stay behind and help him put the equipment away. That wasn't an unusual request except Arthur felt as if Mr. Devens had been picking on him all afternoon. Arthur took off his skates and waited while Mr. Devens got his boots on. He asked Arthur to put the shovels in the shack and take two of the rink boards out so he could sweep the rink. While Arthur was putting the shovels away, Mr. Devens went to the log, got a tractor that was parked there, and drove it onto the lake toward the rinks. It was normal to clear the rinks with the broom that was attached to a front loader on the tractor after the ice got thick enough. Arthur hadn't seen it done before, but he assumed Mr. Devens knew what he was doing.

Mr. Devens drove the tractor across the ice toward the rinks; when he got close, he got off to help Arthur move the boards which were too big for Arthur to move by himself; everyone else had already gone back to the main campus. The idea was, he would drive the tractor through the gap they created when they removed two of the boards. He would drive around on the rink and sweep all the snow and ice chips into a pile and then push the pile back out through the gap to a larger pile that was on the edge of the cleared area around the rinks. The cleared area was the island they had made the day before with the ice saw.

He drove onto the rink and started to sweep by putting the bucket of the front loader with a broom attached down on the ice. He managed to push a pile of snow and ice chips together on the rink and herded it toward the gap in the boards. He got through the gap and pushed toward the edge of the cleared area.

The afternoon snow had covered the scar between the rink and the lake ice and the scar wasn't completely healed, so it was weaker than the rink and that was the plan, that was how they stopped the cracks in the lake ice from getting to the rinks; they had to keep the scar from healing.

Mr. Devens either didn't know about the scar or didn't know where it was. He drove toward it and as he got close he turned the tractor parallel with the cut. Arthur watched out of curiosity; he didn't know about the scar either. As the tractor wheel got next to the scar, Arthur heard a groan from the ice, a giant groan. He looked at the tractor to see if the sound had come from it, and as he studied it he saw its right rear wheel slip into the scar. The tractor tipped sideways; one of the big, rear wheels stayed on the ice while the other slipped through. The axle was hung up on the lip of the scar. It was like watching slow motion, no rush, the tire and wheel disappeared as the ice moaned.

Mr. Devens tried to turn away from the cut, but by the time he turned it was too late and the wheel was down to the axle. He appeared to hesitate for a moment figuring out what to do, then he stood up and tried to jump from the machine, but it was tipped so badly toward the break in the ice that he couldn't really stand, he had to hold onto the steering wheel to keep from falling into the hole the wheel had created.

The tractor continued to lean; it stopped its descent for the blink of an eye as if checking its calculations, then continued sliding following the sinking wheel into the hole it was making in the ice. Arthur watched, petrified.

There was a loud crack, the sound of a tree snapping in two, and the piece of ice the tractor was sitting on broke free, rotated and spilled the tractor and Mr. Devens into the water. As the engine slid in, it hissed for a second, steam came from the top, and then it and Mr. Devens were gone. When the tractor disappeared beneath the black surface, the ice rose and filled the hole and there was no evidence anyone or anything had been there five seconds before. That's all it took, five seconds and they went from joyride to gone.

Arthur ran to the hole. It was filled with the chunk of ice the tractor had been on. He looked around, no one was there, no one was on the lake; it was almost dark. He screamed, "help" but no one heard, he ran to the other side of the hole and no one came up.

He stood, he was a tangle of thoughts, he couldn't stand, he ran around the hole and in the running thought about Ransom. What would Ransom do. He'd jump in and get Mr. Devens.

Arthur sat down and yanked off his boots then stood and took off his jacket and sweater. He went to the edge of the hole, leaned over and put his hand in. It wasn't as cold as he thought it would be. He knelt down and tried to push the ice out of the way so he could see in, but he couldn't lean out far enough to budge it. He turned around and sat on the edge and pushed with his feet and cleared a patch about six inches wide.

He pushed too far. His butt came off the edge, and the only thing keeping him out of the hole was his feet on the ice on the other side and his hands on the lip behind him. It was too slippery to hold. He slid in, his back went first, then his shoulders, his head and feet last like going underneath in a bath tub. He squirmed around, turning over, and kept his hand on the lip not wanting to let go of it. He didn't have a good grip, not strong enough to pull him out, but he wasn't under; his head and hands were in the crack between the pieces of floating ice.

Something grabbed his pants, then his shirt, and it climbed its way up to his arms. He held onto the ice lip thinking he would be pulled under, he barely had a grip and it was just enough to keep his head out of the water. It was Mr. Devens; he still had his hat on, his head came up next to Arthur's, his arms were through the gap and on the lip; he was gasping and panting and kicking to stay up. It was so dark Arthur could hardly see him, though it must have been him; no one else was swimming that afternoon. They were pressed together in an eight inch gap, faces turned toward each other, arms up on the lip of the ice panting.

Arthur remembered something his father had said after a car accident when Carl had run into the back of a lady's car on Main Street in Grape. Carl got out of his car and walked toward the woman who had gotten out of her car to survey the damage. Carl said, "We seem to meet in the strangest places." It put a different light on the situation and they both laughed.

Arthur looked at Mr. Devens and said, "We seem to meet in the strangest places."

Mr. Devens did not react; he sputtered and kicked to stay up in the crack, afraid if he quit, he would sink which he might have; he still had his boots and coat on.

"Can you hold on?" he asked, yelling as if they were yards apart.

"Yeah, but just enough to keep my head up," Arthur said beginning to chatter with the cold. He couldn't feel his fingers and hands; they were like claws.

"Can you reach in my coat pocket and find a screw-driver, my left pocket?"

"I'll try," said Arthur. "My hands are numb."

Mr. Devens was still yelling out of excitement, "I tried before but my hands are so numb; I couldn't find my pocket," he said

Arthur let go with his right arm and reached down along Mr. Devens's coat to where the pocket should have been. His mouth was barely out of the water. He felt around for a while and found the pocket, he put his hand in and thought he felt the screwdriver but couldn't be sure. He closed his hand not knowing whether his fingers were closed and pulled it out slowly. When it was out of the pocket he could tell he had it. He held as tight as he could.

"What are you going to do, tune the tractor?" Arthur asked thinking it was better to be a light than someone who was wound too tight.

"Don't be funny, we're not out of this yet," he yelled. "I want you to hold onto the screw driver, put your hand as far over the lip of the ice as you can, and then drive the screwdriver into the ice. Then pull yourself out. I can't do it because my hands are totally numb. We're going to have to do this right away or we'll be too cold or we'll drop the screw driver."

"OK. I'll try. I just barely have it," Arthur responded in a yell. He didn't know why he was yelling, probably because Mr. Devens was.

Arthur brought the screwdriver up out of the water and reached as far away from the lip as he could. He tried to jam the blade into the ice but it didn't go. It slid in his hand and he was left holding onto the shaft with his fist on the ice. Mr. Devens watched. Arthur slid his hand up and tried again; he got a chip but the blade slid out as soon as he pulled on it.

"Try it at an angle so when you pull on it, it doesn't slide out, like a tent peg."

Arthur tried again. He kept his thumb over the top so his hand wouldn't slide down and he hit at an angle. He thought he had it because when he pulled on it a little it stayed put.

"OK, got it?"

"Yeah, I think so."

"OK. I'm going to let go with one hand and try to push you up, you pull on the screwdriver and try to climb up me with your legs.

Mr. Devens let go with the hand closest to Arthur; he went under except for a hand holding on the lip and lifted Arthur's pants. Arthur pulled with his hand on the screw driver and shinnied up Mr. Devens with his legs. He got his head and shoulders out but couldn't get his chest over the lip because he was crowding the screw driver.

Mr. Devens came up for air. He panted for a minute then said. "Pull the screwdriver out and try it again farther away." He waited a minute then went under.

Arthur struck farther out and made it stick; he pulled again and shinnied and his chest came over the lip. He struck one more time and was able to get his hips and a leg over, then the other.

Mr. Devens came up. "Can you get a rink board?"

"Yeah"

"Don't just sit there, go get it," he said.

Arthur stood, but not well. His feet were numb and his socks stuck to the ice. He trotted to where the rink boards lay, grabbed one, dragged it back and put it across the crack.

"Can you come out on the board and help pull me out. My arms work but my fingers don't."

Arthur crawled out on the board and grabbed Mr. Devens coat at the shoulders; he tried to pull him out but couldn't. He sat, grabbed, and fell backwards while holding on and got his shoulders out; he did the same thing again and got him almost to the hips, then one more time and Mr. Devens was able to scramble the rest of the way holding onto the wire netting of the board.

Mr. Devens lay on his stomach for a moment while Arthur lay on his back. "We better get back to school or we'll freeze death right here after all that work," he said. "Take off all your clothes, everything but your socks, can you find your boots?"

"Yeah I see them."

"OK put them on and were going to run up the hill to school, no clothes."

"Why?"

"Because they're soaking wet and will freeze in a minute."

They stripped except for socks, pulled on their boots; Mr. Devens had to take his off to get out of his pants. They tried to run but couldn't so they affected a running shamble up the hill in the dark. Mr. Devens led the way; he ran straight into the infirmary and fell on the floor. He hadn't bothered to open the door; he ran through it knocking the latch off and making a huge racket. Arthur was right behind him.

The nurse came out of her office, found them on the floor and she screamed. She thought it was a prank which she had a good reason to suspect. When she figured it wasn't, she got them into beds, turned up the heat and called the headmaster who came from his study to make sure they were OK. He didn't say much.

Arthur spent the night in the infirmary because it was warmer than the dorm and his feet looked like they might have frostbite. They hurt and felt like they were on fire, but when they thawed they were OK. Same with Mr. Devens, who had no permanent injuries and lots of good stories.

The next morning Arthur was back to normal. The story had spread through the school, most of it exaggerated by the time he got to assembly, except for the part about running into the infirmary naked. At assembly Mr. Webster gave a short sermonette and talked about the difference between talk and doing, the difference between character and pretense. After the sermonette he asked to see Arthur in his study immediately following the assembly.

Arthur was confused again. He hadn't heard of people going to the headmaster's office except for disciplinary hearing, so he was nervous and wondered what he had done wrong. He went to the main building, through the green doors one more time and up the stairs. He knocked on the door.

"Come in."

Arthur went in. Mr. Webster sat at his desk with Mr. Devens in a chair to the side.

"Arthur, come in, have a seat," he said.

There was a seat directly in front of the desk; Arthur sat as he was told.

"Arthur, tell me what happened yesterday afternoon. Mr. Devens tells me the two of you went for a swim."

"Yes sir. We went for a swim."

"You know it's against school rules to swim in the lake, but circumstance may be important in this case. Did you help Mr. Devens out of the water?"

"A little, but I fell in myself and we helped each other." Arthur said it while looking at Mr. Devens for instruction, wondering how much he was supposed to say.

"And did you ask Mr. Devens if it was funny, your meeting this way."

"I guess so," said Arthur

"And did you ask him if he wanted to tune the tractor?"

"I think I did." Arthur was confused; had he done something wrong? "Did I do something wrong?"

"No, Arthur, you did about as well as you could. I think, in light of your activities on behalf of Mr. Devens, you can consider yourself off probation." He turned to Mr. Devens, who was smiling in agreement.

Arthur was relieved. He couldn't imagine he'd done something wrong, but his lack of imagining it hadn't stopped the hockey puck or the tractor or the train, so he'd come to the headmaster's study with foreboding rather than the specific anxiety which preceded his cigarette inspired visit. He wondered what he would have done at the rink yesterday if he hadn't heard Mr. Webster's morning talks; he didn't know. He didn't wonder about Ransom's influence; that was clear, demanding, instantaneous. Do the right thing. Maybe there was something in the morning talks.

Arthur looked at Mr. Webster, "That's good. I thought maybe you were going to ask me to go get the tractor."

Bridge School	SKS
Arthur May	Philip Schuck
Dan Clement	Don Cleveland
Pa Brunt	Ma Brown

Printed in the United States
113706LV00004B/1-9/A